WHEREVER YOU ARE I WILL FIND YOU

Fafiliana January 2016

*To Gwolyn
What a wonderful
surprise seeing you again!*

Peter

By the same author

The Elephant Within Us, Book Guild Publishing, 2011

WHEREVER YOU ARE
I WILL FIND YOU

Peter Peeters

Book Guild Publishing
Sussex, England

First published in Great Britain in 2013 by
The Book Guild Ltd
The Werks
45 Church Road
Hove, BN3 2BE

Copyright © Peter Peeters 2013

The right of Peter Peeters to be identified as the author of
this work has been asserted by him in accordance with the
Copyright, Designs and Patents Act 1988.

All rights reserved. No part of this publication may be reproduced,
transmitted, or stored in a retrieval system, in any form or by any means,
without permission in writing from the publisher, nor be otherwise circulated
in any form of binding or cover other than that in which it is published and
without a similar condition being imposed on the subsequent purchaser.

All characters in this publication are fictitious and any resemblance
to real people, alive or dead, is purely coincidental.

Typesetting in Baskerville by
Ellipsis Digital Limited, Glasgow

Printed and bound in Great Britain by
CPI Group (UK) Ltd, Croydon, CR0 4YY

A catalogue record for this book is available from
The British Library.

ISBN 978 1 84624 950 1

To Claire
This book is so much yours . . .

Prologue

Our words and actions usually affect no more than a small number of people, and not for very long either. We might wish it to be otherwise but that's how it is: our chances to influence the wide world are limited. Yet, very rarely, an occasion will arise to do or say something that may seem inconsequential at the time but will have repercussions far beyond our wildest beliefs.

Momentous events indeed often have inconspicuous, even accidental beginnings. It is said that the beating of a butterfly's wings can add just the tiny quantity of disturbance needed for an atmospheric instability to build up. And once this grows beyond a certain point it may even carry on to attain the size of a hurricane that could unleash its devastating power somewhere on the other side of the world. Scientists call this the 'butterfly effect'. It is highly improbable but it does happen every now and then – in our lives as in the global weather system.

This is a story about such an effect; about accidental beginnings that set off a chain reaction of unintended consequences, disrupting the lives of several people until they end up in a far-away country where they would never have dreamed of going – an African country ruled by a tyrant for a quarter of a century. The soil of that country is rich but its people are poor. Nothing unusual there, you might say; this is the curse of so many African countries today and there seems to be no way of changing it. But then a butterfly beats its wings . . .

But this is also the story of two young people. And here is one of the poems Anton wrote after he met Gael:

You Have Never Been A Stranger

I have followed your footprints
along dusty country roads
leading deep into the plains
where even now silence pervades.

I have heard you a thousand times
lying on the wet sands
of many, many beaches,
listening to
the endless rolling of the waves,
or holding a spiralling shell
against the hollow of my ear.

I have felt your caressing fingers
searching my warm body
in the wind on the tall white cliffs,
and the softness of your skin
was in the rain
that fell on my face.

I have smelled your sweet scent
in a hedge of wild roses
and honeysuckle;
I have tasted you
in the wheat of ripened fields,
and drank you in a mountain spring,
which was like heaven
on a hot thirsty afternoon.

I've seen the brightness of your eyes
in the dazzling light
of many radiant mornings,
and the enchantment of your smile
in the silvery reflection of the moon
over strangely motionless water.

I have found you
in the laughter of my childhood
and the warmth of long-loved memories.
Haven't I always known you?

Part One

1

Anton was sitting on a chair opposite the director's office in the Belgian Geological Institute, immobile, his legs stretched out in front of him and his broad shoulders leaning against the wall. He stared fixedly at the door, outwardly calm, but his clenched fists and white knuckles betrayed his inner tension. After what seemed an eternity the door opened and the secretary called out: 'Dr Felsen. The director is ready to see you now.'

'Come in, come in,' said the director absent-mindedly, vaguely indicating a chair opposite him. Anton got out a 'Pleased to meet you', shook hands with him and sat down, waiting for what was about to come.

In recent months he had sent his curriculum vitae to a number of potential employers and attended several job interviews, only to be met with a 'We are sorry to tell you that we have no use for your services right now but wish you luck elsewhere, etc. etc.' There'd also been a job going at the prestigious Belgian Geological Institute. Anton had applied months ago and presumed his application had been rejected. He had given up hope when suddenly he had been summoned to this interview. This was his last chance. His future depended on what this man was going to tell him. Would it be just another 'no'? Please, please, let it be 'yes', prayed Anton, holding his breath.

'Now, let me see,' said the important man, rummaging among a heap of papers. 'Ah, here we are . . . yes . . .' He rubbed his chin. 'The selection committee studied your application . . . and I have to tell you that they weren't really convinced. Your qualifications are excellent but you didn't study at a top university. They also contacted your previous employer and there seems to be a problem . . . Now, where's that letter from America?' He lifted up some sheets of paper, dropped one and just as he retrieved it the phone rang.

'Will you excuse me,' he said, picking up the receiver. He listened attentively for a minute or two and then began to talk animatedly, apparently forgetting all about the young man sitting in front of him.

Oh no, not again! thought Anton. That damned scholarship in America! Is it going to pursue me forever? He sat there in a kind of daze, waiting for the phone call to finish and for the inevitable 'no'. This could be the end of his career in research. And he was only just thirty.

When the director finally put down the phone he seemed very agitated. 'Would you believe this!' he exclaimed, speaking more to himself than to Anton. 'An American mining company has lured away one of my brightest geologists. They offered him triple the salary he gets here. I'm disgusted with the way Americans boss us about. But what can we do against big money, that's what I'd like to know? If this continues, I'll lose all my best scientists. And where are we going to find qualified geologists to replace them if the government doesn't offer decent salaries?'

Suddenly he looked at Anton: 'What was it you came here for?'

'I came to apply for a job . . .'

'Oh yes, oh yes . . . I'm with you again. You wanted to work in our institute.' He looked straight at Anton. 'But I must tell you that the salary isn't very good.'

'I don't mind.' Anton's voice was hardly audible, but there was a glimmer of hope in his eyes. Somehow he felt that the atmosphere had changed.

'I am of the opinion that they ought to pay our researchers more,' continued the director, 'but you see . . . this institute depends on government handouts and all they talk about nowadays is "trimming budgets". They don't seem to be interested in anything else. When the really important thing in life is research . . .' He sighed deeply and gazed once more at Anton. 'Are you interested in research? Let's see what your CV says.' He began to rummage through the papers again.

'Oh I am,' replied Anton without leaving the man time to dig up the American debacle. 'I live for research. Lately I've been . . .' He hesitated. 'May I tell you what I've been doing for the last few months?'

The director looked at his watch. 'If it doesn't take too long . . .'

'I've been working on a compact mobile unit capable of locating deposits of rare metals. It's going to contain lasers, a radar system, low-frequency emitters, a GPS receiver and pocketsize computers. And as I don't have a job, I've been working in my garage . . .'

'You've been doing this on your own?' interrupted the director. He seemed very impressed.

'Well . . . yes. I thought it out myself and designed the apparatus . . .'

'But that's extraordinary! Does it work?'

'Not yet. There are still a few theoretical and practical problems. It would help hugely if I could collaborate with some first class geologists . . .'

'But you can. You certainly can! There are several bright geologists in this very institute. Look here, Dr . . .' he looked at his papers, 'Dr Felsen, you must come and work here. The selection committee couldn't decide on your application and left everything to my discretion. So I can engage you on the spot. Do you agree?'

Anton felt a surge of emotion go through his body. He smiled and blurted out: 'Thank you. I'll be proud to join the staff of the institute.'

Professor Briant now stood up, came round his desk and shook hands with Anton saying: 'We are very pleased to welcome a new researcher at the Belgian Geological Institute. You can start tomorrow if you like. The documents to be signed will be ready by then.'

As Anton set off on the hour-long drive home he felt euphoric: at last his life had taken a positive turn!

2

He had stayed so long with his parents that he seemed to have taken root in their house. He had studied at a nearby Flemish university driving back every day, and had continued to do so while working on his Ph.D., spending his days at the university surrounded by all kinds of scientific apparatus, and his evenings at home in front of a computer screen. A very sheltered life it had been. Then he had obtained a two-year scholarship at an American research institute and his parents breathed a sigh of relief when he finally left the nest.

He had liked his new environment from the start. He found a room on the nearby campus and when he wanted to relax he just went for a walk over the spacious lawns that surrounded the institute, or set out towards the adjacent woods. His work was interesting and he didn't mind putting in long hours or coming in at weekends.

His life continued happily and uneventfully, until something occurred that he hadn't foreseen. One day he was having lunch in the overcrowded restaurant of the institute when a young woman came to his table asking if the seat next to him was free. That's how he met Vivienne, a member of the technical staff of another department. She was an attractive redhead and soon they began to see more of each other. She was quite different from the other women he'd met so far: she oozed sex, and the things she said shocked him. With a jolt Anton realised that there was more to life than just work and science. Then the hot summer came along. The days were made for picnics and long lazy walks in the woods or round the shores of a nearby small lake. One evening he found himself lying next to Vivienne after swimming in the lake when suddenly she leaned over and began to kiss his forehead, his eyes and then his eager lips . . . and he was lost.

He soon learned that she was married, but she told him she wasn't happy. She was thinking of a divorce. In the meantime she had to be careful. She wouldn't be able to see him very often in the evening and not even during lunch hour. 'My work takes up a lot of my time,' she said. Naturally she wasn't going to tell him that her husband wasn't aware of anything, and that she was unable to see Anton more often because she was also having an affair with one of the administrators of the research institute.

So she was the one who determined when and where they would meet. Anton had to drop whatever he was doing when she phoned; in fact, he had to be completely at her beck and call. But there were compensations: when they met she gave her all, and she was totally uninhibited. Within no time Anton's mind was no longer on his research, and his work output plummeted together with his reputation when his affair became public knowledge.

It was months before he discovered the truth about Vivienne – how she had lied and played about with him – and his second year in America had ended in bitterness. Vivienne had dropped him for another man, and the institute had not offered him the contract they had promised after his first year.

Anton returned to Belgium and moved in again with his parents while going from one job interview to another. After five or six refusals he decided that he might as well do something useful and began to work on his pet project: the design of a mobile metal detector. And so he had spent the summer and part of the autumn in the garage, trying to build a compact detector and installing it inside his old Land-Rover. If he succeeded – and this was a big if – the Land-Rover would become a mobile unit capable of locating metal deposits. He had no definite idea of what he was going to do when everything functioned properly, but he vaguely assumed that he would drive off to the Sahara or somewhere like that to test the equipment. Needless to say, his parents weren't very keen on the idea.

Still, defeat was always on his mind: even if he tried hard not to think about it, the succession of refusals had begun to affect him. Then, out of the blue, he had been offered a research job at the Belgian Geological Institute in Brussels, and his life changed radically.

3

At the beginning he had driven back to his parents after work but the forty-mile drive was tiring, especially in the dark winter nights. He also had to leave early in the morning to arrive at the institute at a decent hour. What with the traffic jams morning and evening, he realised that he would have to find a room in town very soon.

Before long he discovered that finding decent lodgings at an affordable price was much more difficult than he had imagined; even small rooms were extremely pricey. But luck was with him. One day, as he was walking towards where his car was parked, Anton noticed a sign 'To let, furnished room'. He rang the bell, was taken up and had a look at the room. It wasn't very big but it was conveniently situated near the lab and not too expensive. That was all that mattered for the moment and he took it on the spot.

His new room had no more than the bare necessities and was quite ugly really, but he made it as cosy as possible. He decorated it, pinned some photographs on the wall of out-of-the-way places which he dreamed of visiting one day, and stacked the mantelpiece with his favourite books. At last he had a base of his own in Brussels!

He felt totally at home in the laboratory, too. The atmosphere was informal and relaxed, office doors were usually open, technical and scientific staff mixed freely and everyone addressed each other by their first names. And the work was exciting. Anton was profoundly happy to have become part of the team of scientists of the Geological Institute, and was ready to give his time to this stimulating environment.

Most of the staff left around six but every evening a couple of women remained on duty till nine in order to keep two purpose-built scanning tables busy for a few more hours. A member of the research team had to stay with them in case problems arose, but none of the scientists were keen on this. The others were therefore delighted when Anton proposed to take over most of the evening shifts. And so his reputation as a hard worker, at his task from early morning until late evening, was soon established.

4

On a relatively mild Friday evening at the beginning of December Gael Fernley had gone to a convention on medical aid in Africa. The lectures had just ended and now she was standing in the bay window of a large room where drinks were being served to the participants. Lots of people had turned up: young medical doctors and nurses who had just finished their studies and had come to find out if there was a possible future for them in aid. Somehow Gael envied them.

As a young girl she had always admired Mother Teresa. One day, she was sure, she too would leave Europe to take care of the sick and wounded in some poor country, maybe in Africa, but life never seems to turn out the way you expect it to and most of Gael's dreams had turned out to be illusions. There she was, twenty-five now, her studies over, and she was still single, living with her parents and doing a job she didn't fancy! Maybe she should have become a nurse instead of opting for art history?

One of the lecturers had talked enthusiastically about his involvement in medical projects, his life in the bush in Africa, and the immense satisfaction he felt when the day's work was over. It was all so far removed from her own world where nothing much ever seemed to happen. Medical aid was so different from her job in that interior-design shop. She had never experienced anything even vaguely resembling 'immense satisfaction' in her work. How insignificant her life was! Last year she had thought that she couldn't go on like this any longer and had done a first-aid course. Maybe she should join an aid project and leave Brussels and her monotonous life behind?

She looked at some of the lecturers who were talking animatedly to the younger participants, trying to convince them that enlisting for a year as a volunteer in one of the many aid projects would give them invaluable first-hand experience, and that this was just what they needed. Should she go and speak to them too?

A forceful man of maybe thirty-five to forty had been eyeing Gael for some time while talking to a group of participants. She looked so different from the others with her slender figure, her charming face framed by wavy fair hair, and a vague smile lingering on her lips. He suddenly detached himself from the people around him, came over to where she stood and held out his hand, saying: 'I'm Dr Wilbert, organiser of this convention. Are you involved in aid?'

'I'm afraid not.' Gael blushed. 'I . . . I just came because I thought it might be interesting.'

'You don't look the type that goes out to Africa to live in the wilds,' the doctor commented half mockingly, standing back and eyeing her from top to toe.

Gael felt slightly stung. 'Does one have to be a certain type to go to Africa?'

He laughed. 'No, of course not. But the women that do go out there are usually . . . how shall I say . . . more the rough-and-ready type. Rather less refined than you, I mean.'

The smile vanished from Gael's face. 'Appearances aren't everything.'

Dr Wilbert seemed amused and held up a defensive hand. 'No offence meant. Don't think I underestimate your capacities. But it's rare to see a nice young woman like you take an active interest in aid.' Suddenly he bent over towards her, speaking in an earnest voice. 'Africa needs people who are determined to give their lives to the cause. Why don't you enlist in one of our projects? It would be a pleasure to welcome you to our organisation.' Then he looked her straight in the eye, challenging her: 'But maybe you haven't got the courage?'

Gael stuck up her chin. 'If I wanted to,' she said defiantly, 'I could easily do it.'

Just then a woman in a smart suit touched the doctor's arm, drawing his attention to an important-looking man who was waiting to talk to him. He pressed his card into Gael's hand, saying, 'Contact me any time you want to,' excused himself and turned away.

Gael stood there while her eyes followed the impressive figure of Dr Wilbert as he retreated. Yes, she suddenly thought. Maybe I'll do it.

5

The Geological Institute where Anton had been working for a month now was different from other research centres of its kind. For one thing, the director wasn't there most of the time. Professor Briant occupied the chair of geology at one of the Belgian universities and came to the lab only every second or third day, and then often for no more than a couple of hours. And when he was there he was usually too busy sorting out his papers, catching up with his correspondence and dictating letters to his secretary to have time to bother anyone.

The scientists were all too happy to be left in peace. They lived, not for their jobs because most never thought of their work as a job, but for their research. They were able to let their creative minds loose on any idea they could think of, and the results were astounding.

Contrary to what went on in private research institutions, the scientists of the Belgian Geological Institute were used to discussing what they were doing openly. Work advanced through a kind of symbiosis of independent minds, and the laboratory was in actuality an incubator of new ideas. It supplied the geology departments of most Belgian universities with plenty of projects, but the lab's influence went much further than that. It extended well beyond national borders: the scientists had close contacts with French, and other, geological institutions.

One of the most interesting studies the institute had embarked on was the Mineral Earth Scan project. Two large scanning tables had been built for this purpose in the lab's workshop during the previous year. They allowed the detailed projection of satellite pictures of the Earth's surface. The idea was to check whether it was possible to locate rich mineral deposits from their surface characteristics such as colour and relief. For the time being the study was concentrating on scanning well-known surface deposits. If this was successful, it was hoped that particular features could be used to locate rich unknown mineral deposits in far-away deserts.

The problem was that none of the men were keen on doing this kind of work. The study involved many hours of dull scanning through a succession of satellite pictures covering large areas, and the scanners' attention tended to wane after an hour or two. In fact, women turned out to be much better than men at scanning, and the scientists had therefore trained a team of young women, working part time, to do the job. But what they hadn't foreseen was that those young women tended to chat a lot about their personal affairs to take their minds off the dull work they were doing . . .

6

In the scanning room of the Geological Institute Lottie, one of the part-time team of young women, was glancing sideways at her colleague while flipping a switch and pressing a few buttons as she started to prepare her scanning table for the Thursday evening shift. 'I don't understand,' she said. 'What's wrong? You don't look your normal self today.'

'What do you mean by *normal* self?' Pauline's reply sounded somewhat sharp.

'Well . . . you're usually so talkative . . . and today you're like a tomb. You didn't even say "hi" when I arrived. What's the matter? You're not upset with me, are you?'

'Nothing to do with you.' For a while Pauline carried on scanning, clicking a pointer as she moved on to different features of the projected satellite pictures, and then entering her observations into the computer via the adjoining keyboard. When she noticed that Lottie kept staring at her, she sighed: 'All right. All right! If you really want to know . . .'

'Trouble with a man?'

'*Quoi d'autre* – what else would it be?'

Lottie chuckled. 'Now you see what happens if you entice men?'

'Look who's talking now. I've seen you in action here in the lab! You do nothing but that. Giggling when they make risqué comments as you pass them, and nudging them in the ribs instead of ticking them off.'

'But that's all quite innocent! It doesn't mean that I intend to go any further.'

'What's wrong with going further? Nothing beats a nice hot affair.'

'You can't have an affair at work. That's . . . what do they call it? That's unesthetical!'

'You mean unethical?'

'Yes, that's what I said.'

Pauline shrugged her shoulders. 'Unethical or not, I wouldn't mind having an affair with one of the scientists here . . .'

'You're not serious! With whom?'

'The one who's on duty tonight . . . Anton.' Pauline lowered her voice. 'I must confess that I'm quite attracted to him.'

'Don't tell me that you intend to . . .'

Pauline nodded enthusiastically. 'Don't you think he's very good-looking?'

Lottie shrugged her shoulders. 'Drop it. It's no good. He's not at ease with women. I spoke to him not an hour ago, and he didn't even look me in the eye. A shame really . . .' she turned to Pauline, 'because I've got such beautiful green eyes.'

'I think he's just inexperienced. That makes it all the more interesting.' Pauline stared dreamily at her table. 'I would love to make a man out of him. That would be great fun.'

'Forget it! I bet you'd never be able to get him.'

'Pfft . . . He'll be in my arms in less than a month if I turn my charm on him. I know the tricks! So . . . what do you bet?'

'Are you really serious?' Lottie looked at her colleague with questioning eyes, and seeing Pauline nodding enthusiastically she started thinking hard and finally said: 'There's a nice restaurant in the Petite rue des Bouchers where my husband and I went for our first wedding anniversary. How about betting a candlelight supper there? Mind you,' she added almost apologetically, 'you'll lose and it's very expensive.'

'That's a deal!' Pauline looked defiantly at her companion. 'And if it's so expensive, you'd better start saving straightaway because you're going to lose.'

At once Lottie looked much less self-assured than she had a few seconds ago, and as Pauline noticed the expression of doubt clouding her face she began to laugh aloud, a high-pitched, satisfied laugh. All of a sudden they heard steps in the corridor and in synchronised movement they both bent over their scanning tables, pretending they were working hard.

7

Anton found the evening shifts quite all right. Most of them passed uneventfully. When the two women on shift said goodbye at nine he would go down to the canteen to eat some sandwiches. Then he would lock up the laboratory, go to his room around the corner, set his alarm clock, and by ten o'clock he would be fast asleep.

The only evening that caused him trouble was Thursday when those two annoying young women were on duty. Lottie, the pretty fair one, was always giggling and trying to stick an elbow into his side, but the other one, Pauline, was more disturbing. Last week she had called him to ask his opinion on some unusual feature she said she'd noticed while going through her satellite pictures. And when he tried to get to the scanning table to have a closer look she hadn't even moved out of the way! He had to squeeze between her and the wall and as he did so he felt her body rub against his.

Tonight had been worse. He had been called to the scanning room because Pauline claimed that there were problems with the electric wiring underneath her table. He'd had to slide on his back under the table to check the plugs and discovered that one of the wires had got loose. Can't understand how that happened, he thought, attached it again and began to slide out, but when his head re-emerged he found Pauline standing above him. She was wearing a miniskirt and he was looking straight up her legs. He lay there for a few moments with bulging eyes, unable to avert his gaze.

Then she bent down and offered to help him. She grabbed his hand to pull him out and when he had nearly got up she lost her balance and fell on top of him. They both went down and he felt her body wriggling on his while he lay there for seconds, unable to react.

He finally managed to push her aside and get up, and as he turned into the corridor, his face bright red, he heard the two young women giggle behind his back. He spent the rest of the evening in his office, unable to work, and when the women finally finished their evening shift and left the institute he ate a hasty sandwich and went to his room but couldn't sleep. Time and again he saw in his mind's eye Pauline's legs and the strip of her panties between her white thighs, and felt her warm body move on top of his. By two in the morning he'd had enough of it. He firmly shut her image out of his mind and finally managed to go to sleep.

8

One thousand eight hundred miles further east, in a dimly lit office on the fifteenth floor of one of those monumental blocks of the Stalinist era that line the wide avenues running through Moscow, a man in his early sixties was standing at the window looking depressed. It was a winter morning, the low clouds were heavy with snow and there was little light in the sky, but on the other side of the avenue dozens of neon adverts were flashing aggressively, bathing the façades of the blocks opposite in a multi-coloured commercial light. And, below, a wild mass of Western cars were hooting and flashing their headlights while clogging up the ten-lane-wide avenue. The man sighed, shook his head slowly and muttered: 'Capitalism! What have we become?'

He went to his desk, pressed a buzzer and waited. Nothing happened. But the electricity is working, he thought looking at the single light bulb which hung from a wire above his desk. He pressed the buzzer again and again until the door finally opened and two men in shabby grey clothes appeared.

'Did you call, Viktor Ippolitovich?' asked one of them politely.

'I did, Boris Nicolaievich,' replied the old man in a tired voice. 'A quarter of an hour ago.'

'We did hear the buzzer go,' Boris hastened to say. 'Be assured that we reacted immediately, but we couldn't have got here earlier.'

'We couldn't have got here earlier,' repeated Igor Pavlovich, the other man, 'because the lift is out of order this morning.' Then he added, trying to cheer up his boss: 'But at least the heating is working.'

Viktor Ippolitovich Boronov shook his head in despair and began to mutter again to himself, repeating: 'What have we become?'

'We didn't quite catch what you said, Viktor Ippolitovich,' mumbled one of the two subordinates apologetically. 'Is there anything you want us to do?' added the other one obligingly.

'I was just thinking of the good old days,' replied the old man. 'The days when everything functioned properly . . . when we were respected. This was a proud KGB building, remember?'

He got up and for a while paced up and down, his hands behind his back. Then he began to talk, nodding to himself: 'In those days people knew their place . . . and if they didn't like it they were packed off to Siberia. And a very elegant solution to a big problem that was. Siberia needed to be populated and who would have gone there of their own accord, you tell me?'

He turned his back on the two men, went to the window and stared once more out into the cold grey winter morning. Then he continued to speak while his subalterns kept an almost religious silence: 'Everything was so easy then. People didn't have to think; they just had to follow orders. The principles had all been laid down . . . Communist principles,' he added with reverence in his voice. 'So beautiful they were . . . so true . . .' His eyes became misty. 'Those times seem so far away now . . .'

He sat down again, staring with eyes that didn't seem to see anything. Finally he carried on. 'Communism should have lasted forever . . . and then . . .' his voice almost broke, 'capitalism came!' His face became contorted. 'We now have foreign advisers. Here in our sacred Russia! Our enemies are now telling us how to run everything. Americans!' He spat out the word. 'Who miss no occasion to lecture us that Russia would do well to become a democracy. When we've been a democracy since 1917! What have we become?'

He sighed deeply. 'And the camps in Siberia! They have stopped functioning. How can one govern properly without camps, that's what I'd like to know?' He paused for a while, taking a deep breath. Suddenly he looked up. 'Do you know what I've been told? That our camps have become a tourist attraction!' He became very agitated. 'They're now open to the public! Can you imagine tourists visiting our Siberian camps and filming them? Foreigners even!' He sank down in his chair with his hands in front of his face, groaning: 'Capitalism! I'm sick and tired of it.'

After a couple of minutes he stirred into life again and seemed to notice the men. 'Ah, you're there,' he said. 'Now, what did I call you here for . . . ah, yes, yes . . .'

He got up and walked to the wall opposite his desk, which was completely hidden under a big map of Africa. 'In those days I was responsible for Africa . . . Hah! Those were the days!' He began to tap some of the countries on the map with his index finger. 'We were here, and here, and here . . . all these countries were red. Our cause was advancing rapidly. We should never have stopped. I certainly wouldn't have.' He stood back from the wall while the two men were looking on in awe. Then he began to mill his arms over the map. 'I wanted the whole of Africa to be red. All of it! I dreamed of it by day, I dreamed of it by night. And now . . . and now . . . I shall never live that moment. I shall die and Africa will not be red . . .' He was overcome with emotion, his voice failed him and he had to sit down.

After some time he spoke again, a disillusioned old man now. 'Yes,' he said. 'That's how it was . . . that's how it was . . . I was responsible for Africa.' He got up slowly, looking very tired. 'And I'm still responsible for Africa. I've just received orders . . . orders to foment a revolution in one of the countries.' He nodded absent-mindedly. 'Yes . . . we have to stir up a revolution.'

At once the two men came to life. 'A revolution, Viktor Ippolitovich! Did you say a revolution? But that's great news!'

'I don't know,' replied the old man. 'I don't know whether it's correct to use the term "revolution". In the old days we fomented revolutions for a good cause . . . to spread freedom, equality and justice. But now . . . I've been told that we need to help some rebels topple their government because . . . because they seem to have discovered rich platinum deposits in that country. If we don't do anything, the corrupt government that's running the country is sure to sell out to a French or an American mining company. But if we help the rebels to take over, they would sell the deposits to one of our companies. With what we control already, we would then be able to dictate the price of platinum on the world market. That's what I've been given to understand.'

Once again Viktor Ippolitovich looked out of the window. It had begun to snow, the buildings on the other side of the wide avenue had disappeared from view and the little daylight there was had faded. 'Of course, I'm not criticising our leader,' he said, trying to defuse any impression that he was doing so. 'Our leader knows best. But what's the difference between what we're doing and what the Americans are doing? It's capitalist practices for everyone now.'

He went to a cupboard, got out a nearly empty bottle of vodka and put it to his lips. 'Yes,' he said as he saw his subalterns stare at him. 'Vodka! What else is there left for us Russians?'

'Bah!' he exclaimed when he had downed the little that remained in the bottle. 'Cheap disgusting stuff! But what can we do? Our quality vodka is exported to our old enemies. They have the money and can pay for it. Money! That's all that counts nowadays. No more principles!'

He turned to the two men: 'I must get myself another bottle somewhere in town if I can find a store that's open. I'll be back.' And as he went out of the door he murmured: 'I so wanted Africa to be red . . .'

9

He had barely gone when Boris looked at his companion. 'We must do something,' he said as if moved by some strong emotion. 'This is really too tragic for the old man.'

Suddenly Igor, the other man, had a brainwave. 'I know what we can do,' he said, and he started to whisper something into his companion's ear. 'Don't you think that'll be a wonderful surprise for Viktor Ippolitovich when he returns? Shall we?'

'*Da!*' nodded Boris in agreement, and he smiled when he thought of the pleasure they were going to give their boss. They went in search of the equipment and set to work with great gusto.

An hour later, as Viktor Ippolitovich walked back through the snow-swept streets, the collar of his thick overcoat pulled up around his ears, he was in a much better mood. He had been able to obtain a bottle of contraband vodka from a street dealer he had come across near the entrance of an Underground station. The man had recognised him and had immediately knocked a good half off the price. He was pleased. At least, he still inspired respect in some people.

Back in the old KGB building the lift was still out of order, but that didn't deter him. We've overcome so much, he thought, and one day we shall overcome capitalism, too. And then everything will function properly again. He entered the dimly lit staircase and started the long climb to the fifteenth floor, and every time he reached another floor he felt his spirits rise. No good being upset about the inconveniences fate sends along, he mused. One has to find happiness in the little pleasures of life. And he fingered the smooth shape of the bottle of vodka which was safely nestling in one of the deep pockets of his old overcoat. Its weight felt very reassuring.

When he entered his office he found the two men still there. He got the impression that they were pleased with themselves and looked at them with quizzical eyes.

'Viktor Ippolitovich,' said Boris, drawing himself up and saluting in military fashion, 'we've done it.'

'You've done what?' asked the old man, taking his coat off. He was hot from the long climb and felt stifled in his overheated office.

'We've made your dream come true.' Boris smiled happily. 'After all these years!' He stood aside and with a theatrical gesture he pointed at the wall behind him. 'We've made the whole of Africa red.'

When Viktor Ippolitovich Boronov turned towards his map of Africa his eyes nearly popped out of their sockets. He stared at it with horror and disbelief. The different countries, rivers, deserts and forests had all disappeared under a layer of bright red paint. Some of it had leaked into the Atlantic and Indian Oceans like thin tears of blood against the blue of the sea.

'What the hell is this?' he yelled, his breath coming rapidly and irregularly.

'Well, we . . . we've made Africa red. Wasn't that what you wanted?' replied the two men taken aback.

'Comrades!' In his anger the old man forgot that these were no longer the good old days when you called each other comrade. 'How could you do such a thing?'

'But Viktor Ippolitovich, we thought you would be happy,' replied Boris soothingly.

'Boris Nicolaievich!' shouted the old man, nearly choking with rage. 'You are a nitwit! There is less intelligent life in the whole of your brain than . . .' he was trembling so much that he was almost unable to speak 'than in a plate of borscht!'

At once the men realised that they had made a serious mistake. Under no circumstances should they have taken a personal initiative. It was all the fault of this new fashion, of these capitalist instructors. The two men had recently attended one of those meetings where an adviser who had been schooled in America had spoken about the new way of doing things. 'Be an individual,' he'd said. 'Be responsible for yourself. Take personal initiatives.' And they had done so. See where it had got them? They should never have taken any initiative. They should just have followed instructions. They were safe as long as they strictly executed orders from above.

The two men now began to shake with fear. 'We'll find you another map, Viktor Ippolitovich,' they wailed. 'We'll repair the damage.'

'Out of my office,' thundered the old man. 'Out! I can no longer send you to Siberia – the gulag has gone. But I can still send you to Chechnya and I can tell you that you won't like it!'

The two men sank to their knees, holding up their hands in supplication. 'Please, Viktor Ippolitovich,' they pleaded, trembling, 'please, not to Chechnya.'

'I'll send you to Africa then,' barked the old man. And as the two grey men left precipitously, shutting the door behind them, he hissed: 'And may you perish in the revolution.'

10

'Are you free next Friday?' asked Pauline. 'Because, if you are, you must come to my birthday party.' She sat there, looking very pleased with herself. 'Twenty-nine and feeling fine,' she began to sing, waving her arms in the air. Then she added, in case Lottie hadn't understood: 'That's me! I'm going to be twenty-nine.'

'Who will be there?' inquired Lottie, ignoring Pauline's obvious self-satisfaction.

'Oh! My husband, of course. I can't leave him out, can I? And my sister is going to come with her husband. You've never met them, but they're OK. My sister is a bit of a cat, but Daniel, my brother-in-law, is quite the goods. And another couple – friends of mine. You'll see. And you know who I've managed to invite?' She looked at Lottie with a mysterious flicker in her eyes.

'How would I know?'

'Anton!' She nodded vigorously when she saw Lottie's mouth fall open. 'Yes, Anton. I talked him into it. He objected, saying it was Friday evening and he had to drive back to his parents, but I insisted that my husband wanted to meet him and pestered him so long that he finally gave in. So if you come we'll be eight,' summarised Pauline. 'Four men and four women. Just right for the table and for dancing afterwards.'

Lottie was good at scanning, but otherwise she wasn't mother's brightest. A deep frown now appeared on her forehead as she began to count on her fingers. 'No, you're wrong,' she finally said. 'We'll be nine. There's me and my husband, you and . . .'

'Hey, but I didn't count your husband in!' objected Pauline. 'Can't you leave him at home? If he comes, that would make an odd number. One man too many!'

'I won't come without my Eddy!' Lottie turned away, bent over her table and began to scan.

When Pauline gazed at her from the corner of her eye and saw the stubborn expression on her colleague's face, she knew it was no good. 'All right,' she agreed reluctantly. 'Bring him if you want.'

Lottie took some time to reply and when she did, her voice sounded slightly cold. 'Fine then. We'll come. That's all settled then.' Suddenly her eyes sparkled. 'I'm sure you'll like my Eddy. He is very . . . very nice. Shall I tell him to bring his guitar so he can sing?'

Pauline stopped her at once. 'I don't think that's a good idea.' When she saw Lottie's face cloud over she hastened to explain: 'You don't know my husband. He wouldn't approve. He's strictly limited to opera, the old fusspot.'

Pauline sat there for a while, pondering about the problem of her party. Then she brightened up. 'I know what I'll do. I'll find a way to send my husband to his room after supper. Then we'll be able to put on dance music and have fun.' And she smiled at the prospect of what she intended to do that evening.

11

Pauline's birthday party was in full swing. The supper had been a great success, Pauline had cut the layered chocolate birthday cake with twenty-nine written on it, they had eaten the last crumb, toasted her with sparkling wine and were now lounging contentedly in their chairs and chatting.

Anton felt a bit bored. The wine was going to his head and his thinking processes had slowed down visibly. He was catching only snatches of the quick conversation, and found it difficult to follow the subtleties of the French language.

The wine didn't appear to slow down the power of repartee of the others. If anything, it seemed to stimulate them to embark upon more risqué subjects.

'I've recently watched a very interesting documentary,' said Lottie, trying to sound intellectual. 'About elephants. And would you believe it? Every time the females coli . . . copi . . . colipate, they do it with a different male.'

'You mean "copulate"?' corrected Pauline with a sardonic smile on her lips.

'Yes, that's what I said: with a different male every time. They keep changing!' Lottie looked at her husband. 'So unlike us.'

'I don't agree!' intervened Daniel, Pauline's brother-in-law. 'Take women now . . . they do nothing but change. They buy themselves new clothes all the time. You should see this one's wardrobe here,' he said, pointing a thumb at his wife. 'It's simply bulging.' He paused a few seconds while his wife looked as if she were ready to murder him. 'Or else women waste their money at the hairdresser's. And all that for what? Just to change their appearance. I think that women are not so different from elephants!'

'Oh but we are different!' objected Lottie. 'Elephants don't live in couples like us!' She gazed around with her big green eyes to emphasise how shocked she was. 'Had I not seen it with my own eyes in the documentary I would never have believed it: the females live all together away from the males.'

'Fancy that!' exclaimed Pauline. 'I can't see humans doing that. The men wouldn't stand for it. They'd go crazy with frustration! What do male elephants do, then?'

'They live in separate groups,' replied Lottie's husband, who seemed to have watched the documentary together with his wife.

'That's not so different from humans,' observed Anton. 'Men like being in groups among themselves. Look at the clubs they have in England. So much quieter for the men, too,' he added.

'Listen to that!' came Pauline's mocking voice. 'You're not one for men, are you?' From where she was sitting opposite Anton, she looked straight at him with a beguiling smile while he felt her shoeless toes touch his leg under the table and wander up his trousers. He blushed, tried to draw his leg away and was at a loss as to what to reply.

Pauline's elder sister turned the attention away from Anton's embarrassed silence, remarking acidly: 'If you ask me, men are just like male elephants. They always want to be the biggest, the strongest . . . and they can't stop running after females . . .' She looked sideways at Daniel, her husband.

'People are not like elephants,' repeated Lottie stubbornly.

'But men are!' came Pauline's voice. 'They would never be able to leave us alone, even if we decided to live with other women. We may be peaceful, quiet creatures but men aren't like us. They aren't ruled by feelings of empathy. Nor even by their heads . . .' She paused and her eyes scanned around the table as if to underline the importance of what she was about to say. 'They are ruled by their testosterone levels. They've got only one thing on their minds.' She leaned over to Anton, her eyes sparkling with glee as she spoke almost into his face: 'Your kind is simply obsessed with sex!' Then she turned around to the rest of the table: 'I think men ought to be given injections to reduce their testosterone levels. It would make life so much easier for us.'

'You seem to be under an illusion!' retorted Anton gruffly. 'You wouldn't be able to substantiate your claim with proper statistics. Men don't just have women on their minds. They are busy with all sorts of thoughts. You believe yourself to be much more important to men than you really are.'

Lottie who was sitting next to Anton suddenly burst out: 'Maybe Anton's test-toast . . . toaster-on levels are so low already that he doesn't need an injection!' She emitted a shrill, high-pitched giggle and poked her elbow into his side a couple of times while everyone howled with laughter.

As dumb as they make them, thought Anton shooting a thunderous look at Lottie. A pretty creature with the brains of a hen! He kept silent, his face glowing red, his lips tightly pressed together. Was nothing sacred for these people?

The quick repartee, going back and forth like fencers crossing their rapiers, the superficial jest and badinage, were too French for him. He was not used to ridiculing the most serious subjects. He glanced at Raymond, Pauline's husband, so much older, so quiet and serious. So devoid of anything that could hold a lively woman such as Pauline in check. He had said little all evening. What was he thinking? Suddenly Anton had an inspiration and turned towards him, smiling: 'You wouldn't sing us something? I love opera.'

Raymond's face brightened up as if an internal light had been switched on. 'Do you? That's really nice. I wouldn't mind. Let's see. How about: "O mio babbino caro"? Would you like that?'

'Oh yes! My father often played it on the record-player when I was a child. I would love to hear it again.'

Pauline's husband now got up, pushed his chair back and began to draw breath when Pauline interrupted him sharply: 'Raymond!' She looked as if she were about to lose her temper. 'We don't want any problems, do we? You don't want the upstairs neighbours to knock on their floor, do you?' She shot a disapproving glance at Anton. 'This is a fun party. My birthday party. Let's not spoil it!'

'Of course not . . . of course not, dear,' her husband hastened to reply. 'It was just that . . . I thought that it would please Anton here . . .' He stepped back and hesitantly began to withdraw towards his bedroom. 'I'm . . . I'm going to read for a while,' he mumbled. Then he turned to Pauline. 'You continue your party . . . don't bother about me.'

Her husband had only just gone when Pauline's bad temper disappeared, and she said in a light-hearted voice: 'I'll put on some soft music. Come on, we're going to dance.'

12

President Gwemboka was striding impatiently up and down on the rear terrace of the presidential palace in Bobodiou. He had called a meeting with his Minister of Home Affairs and Internal Security for three o'clock and it was already ten minutes past. This was unheard of! He should have been here well before time, waiting deferentially! Instead he, the President, was having to wait for a subordinate. This was a personal insult!

Gwemboka wasn't one to forgive easily and with every passing minute he was devising more devilish schemes to exact his revenge. He had just come to the point where he had the man thrown to the crocodiles after having cut off his ears and other protruding parts, which were to be fed to the dogs, when he remembered with displeasure that there were no longer any crocodiles in the river. It had become too polluted. A shame, a real shame that was. It had been so nice feeding his enemies to the crocodiles. It was one of the pastimes he had most enjoyed over the years. He sighed. There was nothing to do about it now, with all the mining industry upstream. A polluted river was the price one had to pay for progress, and one shouldn't stop progress. It brought in money. He thought with pleasure of the payment he had just received from the Red Dragon Mining Company for the privilege of an exclusive right to exploit some rich deposits further along the river. Ten million dollars in his pocket! No, one shouldn't stop progress.

The President smiled. And that cheque was merely the beginning. The Chinese had promised to build new infrastructure: they were going to lay down a good road! My country could do with a good road, he reflected. He was getting fed up with all those potholes when he went on inspection tours around the country. A pity, though, that this new road would only run from the mining area to the border and out of the country. But that was all mining companies were willing to do nowadays. They just wanted to get the commodities out.

Not so very different from colonial times, he mused. Maybe even a bit worse. None of these companies seemed to feel any responsibility towards the Africans. Still, that didn't concern him. He thought again with satisfaction about the ten million dollars that were going to be paid into one of his overseas bank accounts. And the country would at least have one new road – which would come for free. No, mining companies were good. Shame though about the crocodiles.

The President looked again at his watch. 'What!' he exclaimed. 'Fifteen minutes late!' Then he heard a sound of rapidly moving feet and his minister appeared, totally out of breath. Throwing himself down on the ground in front of the President's feet, he stammered: 'Forgive me, Mr President, forgive me.'

The President ignored the man crawling in the dust at his feet and pretended to be looking out towards the gardens. A minute passed, and the man in the dust became more frantic, wailing: 'Forgive me, Mr President. It wasn't my fault.'

Finally the President deigned to speak. 'You weren't here on time!' he yelled. 'What lies are you going to tell me this time?' Then his anger intensified as he noticed the minister's dishevelled state. 'You ought to be properly dressed when you visit me!' And he spat on the ground next to the Minister, who writhed, abasing himself as much as possible.

'A bomb attack in town, Mr President. The blast made a deep hole in the street and a house collapsed and fell on my car. The chauffeur was killed but I survived, and I had to run all the way to get here . . .' The Minister was still panting.

'It should have killed you, too,' jeered the President. 'Would have served you right! What's the good of having you as Minister of Internal Security if you are incapable of stopping bombs going off all over the place? Think of my security!' Gwemboka drew himself up haughtily. Then he asked sternly: 'Who did it? Have you caught the perpetrators yet?'

'I shall, Mr President,' wailed the man who lay there trembling. 'It's probably those new rebels but I shall catch them. Rest assured. You will be properly protected.' Then the Minister's extreme sense of survival got the better of him and he managed to say in a honeyed voice: 'What is it you wanted me for, Mr President?'

The question deflected the President's attention. 'Ah!' he said. 'Now, what did I want you here for? Yes . . .' he looked at the prostrate man. 'Get up and listen to me.' He went to sit down in a huge, solid chair that had been specially designed to withstand his bulk. 'I've been thinking.'

'Yes, Mr President . . . that's wonderful, Mr President.'

The President made a quick movement with his fat hand. 'Shut up and listen. At the end of next year I shall have been twenty-five years in power.' He closed his eyes repeating, 'Twenty-five years,' while an almost religious expression spread over his face. 'That's an occasion for rejoicing. Think of that: I shall have ruled for twenty-five years! And I want a huge celebration. Something very special.' Then he added in a commanding voice: 'Give me some ideas!'

The Minister thought for a short while. 'Shall we organise an election which you win with 99.9 per cent of the votes?' he suggested. He looked expectantly at the President.

'What's special about that?' The President's face clouded over. 'It will not do for such a unique occasion!' He spoke with scorn in his voice. 'And you don't seem to understand the risk. Have you forgotten? I won the last election with 99.9 per cent of the votes and how did the international press react? They commented on the remaining 0.1 per cent! Said it was proof that I wasn't popular.' He snorted. 'When I'm so popular that no one wanted to stand against me! I was the only candidate.' The president sat there for a while, thinking deep thoughts. Then he burst out: 'Who were those 0.1 per cent who didn't vote for me anyway? Saboteurs and international spies they must have been. You, as Chief of Internal Security, should have found out who refused to vote for me last time. It mustn't happen again. They must be punished!' The President made a gesture with his right hand as if he cut off a head.

'We shall find out, Mr President, and punish them,' the Minister hastened to reassure him.

'So what do you suggest for this unique occasion?' insisted the President.

'The whole country shall come and pay you homage. Bring gifts . . .' He looked up with anticipation: 'Bring young maidens?'

The President sighed and his shoulders sagged. 'I would have liked that twenty years ago . . . Yes, even ten years ago. But the country has done nothing but pay me homage for so long . . . Wherever I go people always bend down in the dust and dozens of young maidens come forward to offer themselves.' He smiled for a while as pleasant memories stirred within. 'No, I want something really special.'

'A party, Mr President? A huge party! With foreign dignitaries from all over the world coming to pay homage to you?'

'Now, that's an idea . . . Let me see . . . yes, ask the French President to come. I want him!'

'The French President?' The Minister's mouth fell open.

'Why not? I want the French President! You must make sure that he comes, or else . . .'

The Minister swallowed hard when he saw the President make a rapid cutting gesture with his hand in front of his throat.

'Oh . . . and yes . . . I also want General de Lattignie. He's retired now but I want him to come and pay me homage. You see,' explained the President, lowering his voice, 'when I was a young sergeant I served under him in the colonial army. He was a lieutenant then. It would greatly please me to have him come here . . . I have a little idea, yes . . .' his thick fingers moved excitedly, 'a nice little idea. So . . .' he turned again to the Minister, 'you'd better make absolutely sure that he comes too. Or else . . .' And he repeated the cutting gesture with a satisfied smirk on his fat face.

13

Black thoughts went through Minister Mamboulou's head after he had withdrawn. I wish I'd killed that bastard and taken power myself twenty-five years ago, he thought. There were occasions. I could have done it easily. He remembered that night when they had been alone in the bush, just the two of them hiding from a search party. And then he saw a soldier appear from behind a tree ready to shoot Gwemboka, but he had been quicker and had shot first. He had regretted it so often afterwards.

He mumbled discontentedly as he went into one of the big offices inside the palace. He had survived these twenty-five years by exhibiting total servility, but now he was at his wits' end. The first years of Gwemboka's reign hadn't been so bad. Everyone had been pleased when he overthrew the hated regime that was oppressing the people, and foreign investors and mining companies had rushed in. The honeymoon had lasted ten, no maybe eight, years. Then came that disputed election. The President's opponents had lost and cried foul. That's when it had really begun: the intimidation of opponents, the disappearances, the silencing of those who dared to speak up, of those who disagreed. Even the ones in the President's inner circle were no longer safe. He had become suspicious and would kill for a whim. One after the other, all his comrades in arms had been eliminated as they had drawn Gwemboka's wrath, or as he'd got tired of them. And now he, Mamboulou, was the only one who remained.

But how many more years would he be able to stick it out? Humiliate himself, crawl in the dust, eat Gwemboka's shit? He was no longer a human being. He was a puppet without a mind of his own, a puppet whose strings were pulled by that bastard. And the bastard enjoyed it! Enjoyed instilling fear in him, making him tremble.

There were days when Mamboulou hated himself so much for doing what he did that he just wanted to put a gun to his head and end it all.

But he hated Gwemboka even more. Infinitely more. He loathed his round sweaty pig face; his thick hands with which he always made threatening gestures, the fingers like small sausages covered in golden rings; his huge fat body which only wide flowing robes could cover; his sneering voice, his vicious eyes. He loathed everything about him intensely.

But what could he, Mamboulou, do? Stage a coup d'état? That wouldn't work. Gwemboka was very shrewd. He had divided the different ethnic groups of his country and set them up against each other. Even those who protected his regime were divided. The Internal Security, the armed forces, the police, the Special Presidential Guard, were each run by people who didn't trust each other and reported directly to the President himself. No one could summon up a majority against him. Or even begin to organise any opposition.

Everyone lived in fear. Everyone spied on everyone else. And all those threads of information ended in the centre of the spider's web where the big fat spider was lying in wait ready to pounce. And when one of those threads vibrated, the big spider struck and devoured his unsuspecting victim. Yes, the country was well organised, at least from that point of view.

Year after year Gwemboka had been getting worse. He was becoming like a spoiled child. His every little whim was to be fulfilled immediately, or else . . . He was not to be opposed. No one dared provoke him.

Where will all this end? Mamboulou wondered. He sighed deeply. He could do nothing – nothing but crawl before the dictator. He had such a lot to lose: a big mansion, a gleaming Mercedes, four wives, at least ten mistresses and he didn't know how many children. If Gwemboka turned against him, he would destroy them all without mercy.

There was no way out. He would have to carry on and hope for the best. Not stick his neck out; never do anything that would displease Gwemboka. He sighed again. And now that tyrant wanted the French President and a general! He'd better start contacting the French diplomatic service straight away and work the connections he had in the French mining companies.

14

Almost two months had passed since Anton had arrived at the lab in Brussels. His work was going well and he should have been relaxed and happy. But he wasn't. Instead, he felt unfocused, agitated even. Problems had begun in earnest after Pauline's birthday party. When her husband had left, she had put on slow music, dimmed the lights and then invited him to dance.

He tried to hold her at a safe distance but to no avail. She put her arms around his neck and snuggled up to him, whispering in his ear: 'Don't be so stiff.' Then she got hold of his arms and pulled them down her body, saying: 'Put your hands here,' and he was left holding her shapely buttocks while she pressed her belly against him and thrust a leg between his every time they took a step.

She was wearing a silky dress and he felt the lower edge of her panties through the flimsy material. The muscles of her bum were moving under his fingers as they danced and soon Anton became hot and sweaty. It should have been exciting. Instead, he found it very uncomfortable, knowing that her husband was sitting in his bedroom, probably deeply unhappy. Anton was pleased when a break in the music allowed him to free himself. When he told Pauline that he had to leave she was very upset. 'But it's only midnight!' she objected. He apologised profusely, saying that he still had a long way to drive to his parents, and before she was able to hold him back he opened the door and left quickly.

He had done his best to avoid her since then, but several times during the following week she managed to walk up to him in the lab when he least expected it, trying to stir up his feelings. And now it was Thursday evening. He was on duty and she was there!

An hour had passed without incident and he began to feel relieved, when suddenly there was a knock on his door and Pauline came in. She wanted some technical information – at least that's what he made out from her incoherent words – and as she spoke she plonked herself down on his desk, her hazel eyes sparkling and a sensuous smile on her red lips. But he hardly noticed her face. She wore a very short miniskirt, and as she sat just in front of him, the drawn-up skirt revealed a lot of her long, slim legs.

He swallowed hard a couple of times and managed to say no more than 'Euh . . .' His lack of response seemed to worry Pauline and she asked anxiously: 'Are you all right?', leaning slightly forward while doing so. To steady herself, she lifted up one leg and put her foot on the side of his chair. In a flash Anton perceived her fine, transparent panties, which clearly revealed the dark shape of the pubic hair. Suddenly his chair wheeled back under the pressure of her foot and she tumbled forward and fell straight on him. Trying to steady her, his hands seized the back of her legs and as she slid down, Anton's hands moved up her thighs, slipped under her miniskirt and clutched the full shape of her buttocks.

She held on to him, her arms clasped around his neck, and then she began to kiss him passionately as if driven by some irresistible power. Anton was unable to move. His mind had switched off. Then, as suddenly as it had all begun, she wriggled free, straightened her skirt, mumbled an apology and disappeared from his office.

15

'How did it go?' asked Lottie who had been waiting eagerly for her to return to the scanning tables.

'Oh, all right. All went according to plan.' Pauline had a self-congratulatory smile on her lips. Then she chuckled. 'You should have seen him! Big bulging eyes when I showed him my lingerie.'

'How on earth did you do that? You didn't walk into his office and pull up your skirt, did you? You can't do that sort of thing!'

'Don't be stupid! *Bien sûr que non*. There are much more subtle ways. But the result is the same. You show them what stimulates them and they can no longer think. When I fell on him afterwards . . .'

'You fell on him . . .' repeated Lottie, her mouth half open.

'Yes, I slid somewhat helplessly on top of him in his chair and you know how men react under the circumstances. Their natural courtesy prevents them from letting a woman – I'm talking about a pretty young woman like me, of course – slide down to the floor. So he caught my legs and his hands ended up under my skirt. I felt his fingers squeeze my bottom. It was all very exciting.' She laughed at the recollection.

'He squeezed your bottom! What did he do after that?'

'My dear girl! He didn't do anything. It's a golden rule that one must never leave men time to think. Keep the initiative, that's the advice. So I kissed him.'

'*C'est pas vrai!*'

'Yes! Passionately! He was like putty in my hands.' She laughed triumphantly. 'And this is just the beginning.' And she began to press the buttons on her scanning table with great gusto.

16

After Pauline left, Anton sat there, shaken to the core. A world of emotions was whirling inside his head. He felt again the silken touch of her soft panties, the warmth of her flesh underneath, her mouth upon his, the sensuous movements of her body as she lay in his arms. He tried to get up but his legs felt like jelly and he had to stay seated.

He was unable to do any serious work for the rest of the evening and when the two young women knocked on his door at nine and stuck their heads inside his office to say goodbye, he just kept his face in his papers, mumbling a vague goodnight in return.

I must get rid of those evening shifts, he thought as he sat chewing his last sandwich in the downstairs canteen before going to his room for what promised to be a sleepless night.

17

Scientists were allowed a lengthy break for their lunch as long as they put in enough hours per week. This was no problem for Anton who usually worked much more than eight hours a day. Once or twice a week therefore, when he felt really hungry and was fed up with eating sandwiches, he gave himself a treat and went to Chez Dani, a small restaurant conveniently situated a few streets away from the lab, where they served decent lunches at reasonable prices.

Today he was not alone. Michel Legros, one of his colleagues, was sitting opposite him, but at this very moment he wasn't paying the slightest attention to Anton's presence. Michel was overweight and always hungry. He had just been served a heaped-up plate of pasta with bolognese sauce, the item on the menu with the highest quantity-to-price ratio, and was now concentrating on wolfing it down with an expression of intense pleasure on his face.

When there was nothing left on his plate, Michel undid his belt and leaned back in his chair with a sigh of contentment. After a while he began to fiddle with his empty wineglass, blushed slightly and said in a confidential tone: 'Can I ask you something?'

'Go ahead,' answered Anton who was still busy cutting up a *chicon au gratin* into small pieces and savouring every little morsel that went into his mouth.

Michel hesitated a second and then blurted out: 'How do you do it?' looking at Anton as if he expected him to reveal a deep secret.

'How do I do what?'

'Well, you know . . . girls and all that.'

Anton stared at Michel with total incomprehension. 'Girls and all what?'

'Well, you seem to be a great hit. Take Pauline for example . . . she seems to be after you.'

'But . . . but . . .' protested Anton.

'Come on, don't try to put one over on me,' said Michel. 'You try to hide your game but don't think that I haven't got eyes in my head! I've seen her rubbing herself against you when you pass her in a dark corner. A hot chick she is! You're really lucky. Tell me, have you already . . . ahem, you know . . .'

Anton's fork fell on his plate with a clatter. 'Would you mind your own business!' he exclaimed, going red in the face and looking very upset.

'Oh, if you take it like that! Sorry. No offence meant. I just wanted your advice.'

'That didn't sound like asking for advice,' retorted Anton.

'Well, no . . . it was more an introduction to the subject . . .'

'And what is the subject?' inquired Anton sharply.

'I'm not so sure now that I want to talk about it. I thought we were friends and that I could trust you.' He looked a bit dejected.

'All right. I shouldn't have jumped on my high horse. If you want to know, there's nothing going on between Pauline and me.'

'Well, if you say so.' He looked at Anton with doubt in his eyes. 'But there's no denying that you're a success with the girls. Of course, you're handsome and all that: tall, square shoulders, not an ounce of fat on you and a face like a film star. While I . . .'

Anton looked at Michel. No one could call him handsome by any stretch of the imagination. He was chubby; his paunch was hanging out over his belt; he had round sloping shoulders, a double chin, a face that seemed to have been used as a punch bag by a boxer, and two ears that stood out like the handles of a mug. Yet he had a sunny character and didn't take offence when the girls made remarks about his appearance. 'All right,' said Anton. 'What's on your mind?'

'I'm madly in love . . .' Michel blushed.

'Nothing wrong with that. If you court the girl assiduously and keep giving her flowers and other little presents, maybe she'll discover that there's a really nice person living inside your unprepossessing bulk.'

'But you don't seem to realise . . .' Michel sounded hesitant.

'How can I realise anything when I don't even know her?'

'Yes you do. It's . . . it's Lottie.' He stared dreamily at a point somewhere far away over Anton's shoulder. 'Have you seen those curves? And her eyes? They're green. Green mystifying eyes as deep as the ocean. And the way she laughs? Like a silver bell! I'm turned on, man. I'm in love.'

'What! Don't tell me you've fallen for that chatterbox? She's just a pretty body with an empty head on top – all right as long as she doesn't open her mouth.'

'You're speaking about the woman I love!' retorted Michel, offended. 'She's a goddess. I worship the ground she walks on.'

'OK, OK! She's got a perfect body, I'll give you that. And she walks like one of those models. But don't you know that she's married?'

'That's no obstacle for me. I . . . I just want her . . .'

'Oh!' replied Anton, somewhat taken aback. 'Believe me, I do understand you,' he said after a while, trying not to upset Michel's feelings any further. 'But remember that physical attraction is not everything. Won't you get utterly bored with someone like her when the first infatuation has worn off? You're an intelligent man. What would you be able to talk about with her, say, after a year or two?'

'I'm not thinking of what might happen in a few years' time,' retorted Michel. 'I'm thinking of now. I want her now!'

Anton shook his head in pity. 'You wanted my advice, didn't you? My advice to you is: forget it.' He stared sternly at his colleague. 'You'll never get her.'

'But there is hope! A few days ago I raked up enough courage to approach her. And you know what? She said that she had given me a number and put it in her lottery machine. "One day my number might come up," she said, "and then, bingo!" And she giggled and gave me a nudge.'

'Bingo, my foot! If you're in her lottery machine, your chances must be so low that your number will never come up. Not in a hundred years.'

'You think she'll never want me?' Michel looked deeply unhappy. 'But I want her! I want to hold her, make love to her . . . I need a woman in my bed!' he exclaimed.

Suddenly Anton chuckled. 'That shouldn't be too difficult. I've just read an article about a problem young Chinese men are facing. What with the one-child policy and parents' preference for boys, there are now about 10 per cent more young men of sexually mature age than girls in China. The article suggested an elegant solution to the shortage. Why don't you follow its advice? If you've got it so badly and absolutely want a woman in your bed, why don't you get yourself one of those life-sized inflatable rubber dolls?'

Michel turned bright red and kept silent for a while. Then he blurted out: 'It doesn't work! I've tried that already.'

Anton's mouth fell open. 'You haven't?'

'Yes I have. I . . . I bought a special model, one you fill with hot water. The shop assistant explained that the heat and bounce of a water-filled doll was so much more pleasant. Mind you, it was more expensive, too. Very nice she was, fair and all that; looked a little like Lottie. She came with clothes, too, so that you could undress her. When I got home I began to pour her full of hot water. You can't imagine the number of kettles I had to boil. It took me two whole hours. By the time I had filled her up I was so excited that I could hardly wait. And then . . .' Michel seemed to hesitate.

Anton sat there, gaping at his colleague. 'What happened then?' he asked, spellbound.

'When she was finally ready, lying in bed waiting for me all hot and enticing, I was so impatient to begin that I just pulled up her skirt, threw myself on her and started.'

'Yes . . .'

'You know that I'm quite heavy. I must have been moving a bit wildly and suddenly she burst!'

'She didn't!'

'Yes! It was horrible. It was days before the mattress dried out.'

'And what happened to the doll?'

'I took it back to the shop the next day. Wanted a refund. And they refused! They looked at me with horror in their eyes, as if I were a brutal caveman. Said the doll was guaranteed to withstand a thrust of I don't know how many newtons. Then they suggested that I take a super-resistant model! A sort of upscale version, they said. You should have seen the model they wanted me to take: an enormous hideous doll! So I left their shop slamming the door behind me. No! What I need is a real woman.'

18

'You know who's after me?' said Lottie as she sat down next to Pauline at the scanning tables.

'How would I know?'

Lottie blushed: 'Michel Legros . . .'

'What! That ugly fellow!'

'Well . . . he's besotted with me. And it sort of pleases me to have him stare at me with eyes like soup plates and to hear him sigh every time I pass him. It's . . . well . . . it's the feeling of unfulfilled romance that appeals to me.'

'Unfulfilled romance, my foot! The only kind of romance you can expect from him is caveman-style romance. Grabs you by the hair, pulls you inside his cave and jumps on you. Not for me the "Wham-bam-thank-you-ma'am" type. Thank you very much. I wouldn't have him touch me with a bargepole.'

'I don't intend to begin anything with him! I'm a serious girl.' Lottie seemed stung. 'I'm not obsessed with sex like you! Let me tell you that I remained a virgin until I married at twenty-one. Unlike you, who probably had your first affair when you left secondary school.'

'When I left school?' retorted Pauline, offended. 'Don't be ridiculous! I was only fifteen at the time.'

'What! Your mother must have been very upset. How did it happen?'

'My mother?' Pauline shrugged her shoulders. 'She'd gone to Brussels when it happened. She had found a job there and had left my elder sister and me behind in Paris while she was looking for proper lodgings in Brussels. In the meantime we stayed with one of her cousins. It was awful! They took us in, yes, but there was little room in their small apartment. And they never missed an opportunity to make us feel how good they were to us, and how grateful we should be. I hated them! I spent most of my time hanging about in the streets, looking in the shop windows, gazing at all the beautiful things people with money can buy.'

'OK, OK,' replied Lottie, trying to stop her. 'But you weren't going to tell me about your unhappy experiences with your family. You were going to tell me how you came to have your first affair at fifteen.'

'All right, all right, I'll come to that. I was at my wits' end when I happened to meet one of my best school friends. When I poured out my heart to her, she invited me to stay with her in her uncle's house. That's where it happened during my last two weeks in Paris.'

'You mean, with the uncle's son?'

'No, no, silly. With the uncle himself.'

'What! With an old man?'

'He wasn't all that old. I think he must have been forty or so. When I saw him, and he looked at me, we both knew immediately. I was supposed to spend the nights with my girlfriend in a room on the ground floor, but she was a sound sleeper and the moment she dozed off I sneaked out and crept upstairs to join her uncle in his bedroom. I stayed with him every night till four in the morning or thereabouts. He taught me all I know about making love. It was absolutely wonderful! I've never met a man like him since.'

Lottie sat there dumbfounded. 'And . . . and did you ever see him again?'

'No. When I was due to leave for Brussels, we went to pick up my sister and then the uncle drove us both to the station. He just kissed me politely on the cheek when our train arrived. My sister never realised what had been going on, and my mother never knew.'

'Gosh!' exclaimed Lottie. 'What a case you are. You're a real . . . what do they call it? A pathogenic case, or something like that.'

'Don't you try to be intellectual,' retorted Pauline sneeringly. 'No, I'm not a pathological case. I just happen to have a healthy sexual appetite.'

'Healthy appetite, pfft! You're obsessed, that's what you are! You think of nothing but men. All the time! It's unhealthy.'

'It's not! It's the essence of life.' In her frustration Pauline pushed the wrong button of her scanning table. 'See now!' she exclaimed. 'A fatal error. I've got to start everything again. Lucky Anton's on duty. He won't notice anything.'

'Don't be so sure. Maybe he can follow everything we're doing on his computer screen.'

'Well, he'd better stay in his office. If he dares come along to tick me off, I know how to make him forget what he wants to say.'

'Yeah, yeah. You too seem to have forgotten something.'

'I don't know what you're talking about.'

'Our bet.'

'Which bet?'

'The one we had three and a half weeks ago.' Lottie stared at her companion with astonishment. 'Don't you remember? You must! You sounded absolutely sure about it. Let me remind you of what you said. You said: "It won't take me a month." That's what you said.'

'What wouldn't take me a month?'

Lottie shook her head in disbelief. 'Anton, of course. You were going to seduce him and said that a month would be enough. Maybe you just pretend you've forgotten because you know you can't do it. That's it. Admit your defeat.'

'So, you think I'm not capable, eh?'

'Well, I must say you've got a way with men. They seem to fall for you. But Anton is more difficult than you thought, isn't he? You've been unable to get him and so you've lost the bet!'

'I haven't,' retorted Pauline. 'Three and a half weeks aren't a month. I've got seven days left!'

'And a lot of help that's going to be. If you haven't managed up to now you won't get any further in a few days. You've lost your bet. Admit it!'

'No I haven't!' insisted Pauline stubbornly. 'I've got seven more days, and that'll be enough. I'll make him come to my apartment tomorrow when my husband is off to his opera lesson.' And she bent down over her table and began to scan the pictures with a determined expression on her face.

19

It was exactly 7.30 p.m. when Anton arrived at one of those yellow brick buildings without a lift of which so many had been built in Brussels in the 1960s, and pressed the bell. He stood as close to the door as possible, waiting to speak into the entry phone, trying to shield himself from the snow which had begun to fall in the afternoon and was now blowing in gusts through the street. There was no answer but within seconds the front door opened automatically and he quickly slipped inside, shut the door, pressed the light switch and walked up the stairs of the four-storey building. He hadn't been very keen on accepting Pauline's invitation but she had insisted and told him that her husband was counting on him. He was going to sing for a few guests and wanted Anton as his guest of honour. Several times that day Pauline had passed him in the lab saying: 'Don't forget! Seven thirty. We count on you.'

When he reached the third floor, the door to Pauline's apartment opened and as he entered he found her standing in a bathrobe.

'Am I too early?' he stuttered.

'No, no,' she replied, smiling. 'Give me your coat. And take your sweater off. It's nice and warm in here.'

As he began to pull it off he felt a push in his back and heard Pauline say: 'Put everything in here.' When he had freed his head and was able to look around, he was surprised to see he was inside a bedroom. Then he saw Pauline, leaning against the doorframe. She was standing with the lights of the living room behind her, and at that very moment the bathrobe slid from her shoulders, revealing a semi-transparent champagne-coloured negligee. Anton could make out that she was wearing nothing underneath apart from very small panties, a suspender belt and stockings.

He stood there, gaping. 'But . . . but . . . your husband?'

She didn't reply but shut the door and started moving towards him.

'Where are the other guests?' mumbled Anton, feeling like a victim trapped in a spider's web. 'Where's the performance?'

'This is where we're going to perform, honey,' said Pauline in a sugary voice while she advanced slowly and sensuously.

'Ca . . . can't we sit down and have a drink or something,' stuttered Anton, desperately trying to put off the fatal moment.

'We'll have a drink later.' Pauline looked at him with sparkling eyes. 'Don't you want me?' She was now within inches of him and he smelled her strong perfume. 'You're a man and I'm a woman. And I've got what you need. Feel!' She took his hand and pressed it between her legs, moving it slowly back and forth.

Anton's mind wanted to pull back his hand but couldn't. His knees felt weak and shaky, his body trembled and, aided by Pauline, his hand continued to rub the strip of soft silky panties between her legs. It felt warm and alluring. This is it then, thought Anton, ready to accept the inevitable.

She now pushed him back till he tumbled on the bed. Then she began to pull off his shoes, socks, and trousers and within no time her expert hands had him completely undressed. As he lay there, staring with bulging eyes at her sexy body, she slid on top of him and began to kiss him passionately.

It was exactly at that moment that the bell rang, loud and insistent, and Anton felt her stiffen. She got up and stood there for a moment, undecided; then she said in an irritated voice: 'I'd better answer; maybe it's important.' She picked up a kimono that was lying over a chair, threw it around her shoulders and went out to pick up the door phone. Within seconds she was back, urging: 'Quick, quick! It's my brother-in-law. He's on his way up.'

She picked up Anton's clothes and shoes, threw them into his hands, pushed him out of the bedroom, opened the terrace door, shoved him into the outside broom cupboard, and slammed the cupboard door in his face shouting: 'I shan't be long!' Anton heard the terrace door close, and then everything was silent.

It was dark inside the small cupboard, and he would have been shut off from the world but for the muffled sounds of traffic in the streets, every now and then punctuated by the wailing sirens of an ambulance or a police car. Just my luck! thought Anton shaking his head, but as he did so the coarse hairs of a broom pricked his cheek. He was squashed between a vacuum cleaner, an assortment of brooms, buckets and mops, and the wooden door of the cupboard which pressed against his face, and he felt something bumpy sticking into his shoulder blades.

It was lucky he didn't suffer from claustrophobia, but that was about the only positive aspect of his situation. It wasn't long before the cold started to penetrate his body. He began to shiver and within minutes felt frozen to the bone. 'Hurry up, Pauline,' he implored. 'Come and deliver me or this will be the death of me.' But nothing happened and after a while he could stand it no longer. Damn, damn, he thought, I must put on my clothes. I must get out of here. He pressed against the door of the cupboard but Pauline had locked it from the outside and he was unable to open it.

Little by little despair took hold of him. I'm done for, he thought. I'll have to spend the night here. I'm going to die of hypothermia. Then, suddenly, he heard a sharp click and a second later the cupboard door swung open.

As Anton emerged on very stiff legs, Pauline pulled him inside the apartment, saying: 'Be quick! I've sent my brother-in-law out for cigarettes. Wasn't that clever?' She beamed. 'And he's gone down to get them. Lucky for you! But he'll be back within seconds. Come on!' And she shoved Anton's shivering body out through the door into the hall, pressed the bundle of clothes into his arms and began pushing him up the staircase to the top floor. 'Hide there till he's come in,' she whispered as she heard the street door open. The lights switched on and, as a blast of cold air shot through the staircase, Anton began to crawl up the stairway to the fourth floor as fast as he could. His legs almost refused to function but he managed to get there, leaning on one arm while holding his bundle of clothes in the other.

He lay down flat on his face in front of one of the doors, naked, with his clothes in a heap next to him, hoping that none of the occupants of the fourth floor would choose this very moment to come out of their apartments. When he heard the door of Pauline's apartment close he began to put on his clothes while rubbing his limbs vigorously. It was then that he realised that his socks and one shoe were missing.

He put on his one remaining shoe and stood there for a few seconds, uncertain what to do. Pauline must have discovered his missing shoe by now and surely would do her best to get rid of her brother-in-law. He would then sit on a radiator while she made him a hot drink. He could do with some warmth. As he sat down in the cold hall, waiting, he suddenly felt a sneeze coming and when it came it was no ordinary sneeze: it was a sound welling up from the deepest recesses of his lungs, shuddering through his windpipe and blasting out of his mouth and nose. It resounded in the hall like an enormous explosion and as Anton heard steps inside the apartment next to him, he wasted no time. He scurried down the staircase like a rabbit and was out in the street in no time. He ran along to where his car was parked and each time his bare foot splashed through the snow and touched the icy pavement he felt a bout of sneezing come on.

20

He sat in his car for some time with the engine running, hoping the interior would soon heat up: he didn't have the courage to go out and scrape off the snow. Instead, he switched on the fan to full heat and gradually the windscreen began to defrost. I must get home and have a hot drink, he thought, and he set off in first gear as soon as he could see enough to drive. The weather had turned really foul by now, sleet was coming down in great gusts, the windscreen wipers were working at full tilt and the steam coming off his wet clothes condensed on the windscreen, reducing visibility to a minimum. It was fortunate that there was very little traffic.

As he approached a main thoroughfare, he caught up with a car that was moving very slowly.

The driver was a thin middle-aged man of a nervous disposition; he had little self-confidence, especially when his wife was around, and at this very moment that wife was sitting next to him, lecturing him.

'Drive slowly,' she was scolding. 'How can you drive so recklessly? I'm a bundle of nerves. But you don't care about me, do you?'

The man shot an anxious sideways glance at her. 'Keep your eyes on the road!' she snapped. 'Look at the weather! It's dangerous! And you're such a bad driver. You're lucky I'm here to keep an eye on you. If it weren't for me, you'd soon have an accident.'

The traffic lights ahead of him had been green for a long time and the man eyed them warily. Were they about to change? Should he stop? But if he did, the lights were sure to remain green and his wife would snipe at him . . . The car carried on slowly and just as he was about to cross the thoroughfare the lights switched to yellow. 'Stop!' yelled his wife.

By that time Anton was no more than three feet behind, and just at that moment he felt a prickling in his nose. As he burst out in a tremendous sneeze, his eyes closed while his right foot was jerked onto the accelerator, and with a loud 'bang' he bumped into the car ahead.

The shock made the wife slide off her seat, and as she lay there in a heap she was temporarily silenced. Then she crawled back onto her seat and flared at her husband: 'You fool! Look what you've done! You nearly killed me. That's what you'd like to do, wouldn't you?'

'It's not me,' wailed the husband. 'It's not my fault. It's that car behind. It crashed into us.'

At once the woman shot out of her car and advanced threateningly towards Anton who was standing surveying the damage. The foul weather outside did nothing to improve the mood of the woman and as she faced Anton she began yelling: 'You idiot! You reckless fool! Look what you've done!'

Anton was about to answer as politely as possible when the sleet blew in his face and he was again overcome by a fit of sneezing. He stood there for seconds, his body shaking with bouts of sneezing while the woman was hurling abusive language at him.

When finally he was able to speak he said, as civilly as he could: 'It's not too bad. My front light is cracked but I haven't done any damage to your car as far as I can see.'

The woman took a long stern look at Anton's dishevelled figure, at his clothes that were completely in disarray, and at his sweater which was back to front. 'You're drunk,' she declared with disapproval in her voice. Then she looked at his feet and had a shock: he had no socks and one foot was bare. She rushed back to her own car in a state of great excitement, yelling: 'Edmond, I don't trust this. Call the police.'

Edmond who lay bent over the steering wheel, his head between his hands, looked up and said plaintively: 'How can I do that, honey. I haven't got their phone number.'

As fate would have it, a police car was just passing along the boulevard and pulled up to see what was happening. At the sight of the policemen getting out of their van and advancing towards the scene, the woman shouted: 'We were at a standstill and he crashed into us.' And without anyone asking for her opinion, she pointed an accusing finger at Anton, adding: 'I think he's drunk!'

The policemen now surrounded Anton who was trying to turn his back to the howling wind and sleet, and was sneezing constantly.

'May I see your papers, Sir,' said one of them.

'Yes, yes . . .' Anton began to search in his coat's pockets, inside, outside, until with a sinking feeling he realised that his wallet wasn't there. Oh my God, he thought, it must have fallen out at Pauline's and is now probably lying somewhere on the floor in her bedroom. Her husband is sure to find it. Oh my God!

'Well,' said the policeman, eyeing Anton with suspicion. 'Your papers?'

'I . . . I must have lost my wallet,' stammered Anton, excusing himself.

'Ah!' replied the representative of the law, putting a world of significance into the word 'Ah'.

Then he looked at Anton's feet, and his face showed even more disapproval. 'Where's your shoe?' he asked sternly.

'I . . . atchoo . . . I have lost it, too,' said Anton sheepishly.

'I see,' said the policeman with a face now ready to convict him.

'And what's happened to your socks,' the other policeman asked sardonically.

'Well . . . you're not going to believe this . . .' admitted Anton with a very guilty expression on his face, 'but I've lost them, too.'

'Is that so? Well, well. Is that so?' The two policemen stared at him without even trying to hide their suspicion, and one of them snorted derisively.

The woman, who had listened to the conversation with mounting excitement, now intervened. 'I think he's a criminal,' she declared. 'He's stolen the car and was fleeing the scene of the crime. He's a burglar, or maybe he's even killed someone; I wouldn't be surprised.'

Suddenly Anton felt a pair of handcuffs click around his wrists and he was shoved into the police van to the delight of the woman whose face expressed self-righteous satisfaction.

Inside, one of the policemen was calling up headquarters. 'No papers on him,' Anton heard him say, 'but we'll find out . . . What? Yes, probably a criminal . . . Yes, we'll lock him up for the night . . . All OK. I've already called up the towing service. They shouldn't be long. We'll leave when they arrive.'

21

While Anton was struggling with the inflexible arm of the law, Pauline was having a good time. Nothing of the inclement weather raging outside penetrated her apartment. It was warm and cosy, and she was sitting on a comfortable sofa next to her brother-in-law, sipping a glass of dry Martini. He was a dark-haired, clean-shaven, muscular man in his late thirties, and as Pauline looked sideways at him through half-closed eyes she couldn't prevent herself from thinking how attractive he was . . . and probably a good lover, too! Suddenly jealousy welled up in her. Why should my sister draw the lucky number? she thought. The cat! While I'm stuck with the biggest bore ever.

'Shall I put on some music?' she asked with a sensual smile. She went towards the CD player, moving voluptuously, and put on some pleasant background music. As she sat down again, the front of her kimono opened, revealing the dark edge of her stockings and suspenders. The brother-in-law swallowed a couple of times while staring as if hypnotised at the sexy legs within reach of his hand. The dimmed lights, the tickling feeling of the alcohol in his throat, the perfume, and next to him . . . it was almost too much to resist.

Just then Pauline put her glass down on the table behind her and as she stretched backwards, the kimono slid away from her legs and her seductive panties became visible. As she pulled her arm back, the wide sleeve touched his face and it was as if an electric shock went through him. Suddenly his lips were upon hers and his hand went over her legs, touching the stockings, the suspenders . . . Then he began to undress in a hurry while Pauline reclined on the sofa with a sigh of satisfaction.

22

'At last!' exclaimed Lottie. 'There you are.' She had been fiddling absent-mindedly with the buttons of her scanning table and now dropped all pretence that she was doing any useful work. 'Did you manage? I'm dying to know.' She turned a keen face towards Pauline.

'What's the matter?' asked Pauline somewhat sharply, taking her time as she sat down and settled herself comfortably. 'What is it you want to know?'

'I see.' Lottie hummed. 'Anton didn't show up, *n'est-ce pas?* Otherwise you'd already have been boasting about it.'

Pauline looked at her companion coldly, turned her attention to her scanning table and started working. About half a minute later she said: 'Don't talk nonsense. Of course he came.'

Lottie, who had been looking at her with undisguised contempt, suddenly felt much less cocksure. 'Oh . . .' she went. 'So you succeeded in getting him after all . . .'

'Well . . . yes and no.' Pauline seemed unwilling to reveal any more and carried on scanning.

'It's either yes or no,' protested Lottie. 'You've lost, haven't you? And you don't want to admit it. I knew you wouldn't manage. I knew it!'

'It's not like that! How can I explain it? I . . . I've lost interest. That's it.'

'You've lost your bet, that's what you've lost,' retorted Lottie.

'No I haven't! I could easily have won if I'd wanted. You see . . . I had him lying on the bed.' And she added triumphantly: 'Undressed! With me on top of him . . . So there!'

Lottie sat there gaping. 'And what happened next? Come on, tell me . . .'

Pauline seemed to hesitate. She was about to say something but kept silent.

'Nothing happened?' ventured Lottie. 'You found out that he doesn't like women?' She stared at her companion waiting for confirmation, but Pauline seemed unwilling to commit herself. 'So, that wasn't it,' concluded Lottie. 'No, it's more likely that he didn't want you. He decided against it after all and nothing happened. Yes, that must be it.' And she turned to her scanning table mumbling: 'You, the great seductress! I'm disappointed in you.'

Pauline felt stung. 'How daft you can be when you try to be intelligent. If you absolutely have to know, something did happen . . . the bell rang. There was someone at the front door.'

'Who?'

'Well, Daniel . . . my brother-in-law. You met him at my birthday party.'

'Yeah. Didn't have any chance of dancing with him. You kept him all to yourself after Anton left. I could tell your sister wasn't too pleased about it. You should have seen the murderous look in her eyes.'

'I didn't have time to look at her eyes.'

'*Cela ne m'étonne pas.* You were looking into *his* most of the time. So, what happened when that Daniel rang the bell? Was he pleased to meet Anton? Must have been a bit awkward for him to shake hands. With a naked man!'

'Don't be a fool! I wasn't going to let them meet. I quickly shoved Anton into the broom cupboard on the terrace and locked the door.'

'Lord almighty! You didn't! You mean that you pushed him in there naked? But it was freezing cold two nights ago. Poor man!' Suddenly she began to chuckle and then burst out laughing as she imagined the scene. 'I hope his dick didn't freeze off,' she managed to blurt out between loud hiccoughs of hysterical laughter.

At once steps resounded in the corridor and Stephen, a sleek geologist who had been called in to do the Thursday evening shift in Anton's absence, came in. 'What's happening here?' he inquired sharply. He looked at the computer screens and said in a stern voice: 'Is that all you've done so far? You're supposed to be working here, not chatting.' He hung around for some time while the two young women applied themselves to their appointed tasks with a great show of energy. Finally he left, satisfied that his intervention had greatly impressed these two female subordinates.

A minute or two after Stephen had gone Lottie leaned towards Pauline while continuing her scanning. 'What's happened to Anton? He's not still in your broom cupboard, is he?' She held her hand in front of her mouth to stop herself bursting out laughing again.

'Of course not,' whispered Pauline under her breath. 'You can imagine I was worried about him being out there. Just think: if he'd started to bang on the door of the broom cupboard, Daniel would have heard him and it would have been extremely embarrassing for me had my brother-in-law discovered him there, naked.'

'What did you do then?'

'I settled Daniel down with a nice drink and sat next to him, smiling and chatting while trying hard to think. Mind you, that wasn't as easy as you'd imagine. I'd thrown a kimono over my negligee and I could tell from the way he was looking at my legs that my brother-in-law was very keen on finding out what I was wearing underneath that kimono.'

'No!'

'Yes! And all the time I was racking my brain to find a solution. Then I had a brainwave: I asked Daniel for a cigarette, hoping that he'd left his cigarettes in his car as he usually does when he comes to visit us. My husband – the old fusspot – makes a point of not letting anyone smoke in the apartment; he claims cigarette smoke affects his voice. So Daniel went back to his car for cigarettes and I quickly let Anton out of the cupboard and pushed him up to the top floor before Daniel returned. Clever of me, wasn't it?' Pauline had a smug expression on her face.

'What! You pushed him out of your apartment without any clothes? I don't believe it.' Lottie looked shocked.

'You don't think I would do such a thing, do you? Of course he had his clothes. He carried them under his arm in a big bundle. But he had no time to put them on because Daniel was already coming up the stairs.'

'The poor thing.' Lottie shook her head. 'Poor thing. Did the neighbours discover him? What happened after that? Tell me . . .' She looked at Pauline like a small child waiting to be told an interesting story.

'I put on some soft music, and . . . and as we were sipping our drinks my brother-in-law . . . Daniel . . . discovered the sexy lingerie I was wearing under my kimono . . .'

'Gosh!' Lottie held a hand in front of her mouth and looked very much like a hen that had just accidentally swallowed a big pebble. 'You didn't . . .'

'I did!' Pauline's eyes turned dreamy. 'We did it . . . twice! It was wonderful.' An ecstatic expression came over her face. 'What a lover! I had to make a superhuman effort to tear myself away from him before my husband returned from his opera class.'

'But he's your brother-in-law . . . your sister's husband.'

'Serves her right, the cat,' said Pauline with determination. 'Anyway, after this I've lost interest in that silly Anton. So, now you understand why I haven't really lost my bet.'

'But what happened to poor Anton?'

'Oh, I suppose he'll get over it.'

'That's not what I mean. Did he get home all right? He must have been frozen, poor man.'

'Now you mention it, I did hear a terrific sneeze from the hall above just after I'd let Daniel in again. And you know . . .' she lowered her voice, 'he forgot his socks. And a shoe.'

'He had to walk home without socks and with only one shoe?'

'I suppose so. I put his belongings in a bag and brought them to the lab yesterday, but the idiot didn't show up. Now, where did I put that bag? I can't remember. Oh, and this morning I found his wallet under my bed. Must have fallen out of his pocket when I pulled off his clothes. It gave me such a shock when I saw it lying there. Lucky my husband didn't find it! I wouldn't have known how to explain what Anton's wallet was doing under the bed in our bedroom. My old man would have made a real fuss.'

'No wallet, no socks and only one shoe!' Lottie got up, took off one shoe and started hopping about, while pretending to sneeze. 'New fashion!' she exclaimed. The two women burst out in laughter, when suddenly a voice behind them said: 'You're supposed to work here. That's what you're paid for. This is a laboratory, not a theatre!'

'You're supposed to work here; this isn't a theatre!' imitated Lottie with a long face after Stephen had gone again. 'The skulking sneak.' And she bent down over her table mumbling: 'So much nicer the weeks before when Anton did our evening shift. Then it really was a theatre.'

23

It must have been the middle of the night when Anton woke up with a shock. He was having nightmarish dreams and it took him several minutes before he realised that the strange bed in which he was lying wasn't part of the nightmare. But it wasn't his bed either. Where was he? What was he doing here? Then he heard the sound of ambulances somewhere outside and he knew where he was: in a hospital in Brussels. That's how he'd got here. In an ambulance. Suddenly it all came back to him: Pauline and the broom cupboard; lying naked on the fourth floor of the apartment building, and next running through the slush in the streets with only one shoe. Then the accident, that awful woman, and the police. They had locked him up in a cell for the night and when an inspector finally arrived to interrogate him in the morning, he was shivering with fever. Checking his identity had taken an hour or two and by the time they had finished with him he was in such a bad state that they had thought it safer to rush him to hospital. And there they had diagnosed pneumonia.

He fell into a fitful slumber and woke up again, slightly delirious and wet with perspiration. This went on throughout the night. He was hallucinating, not asleep and yet not fully awake, and half the time he had no idea where he was.

At one time he thought he was again at his parents' home, an adolescent dreaming of life. One day, he knew, he would meet a girl, the girl of his dreams. She would be innocent like him; her face would be lovely and her eyes smiling. As they looked at each other they wouldn't have to speak; they would need no words. They would just look into each other's eyes and know. Yes, that's how he had always imagined it to be: he would see her face and know. And suddenly, in his feverish dreams, for an instant, he did see her face. Then it was gone, and he lost consciousness.

Over the next few days he gradually got better and as his head became clearer he had ample time to think. His parents had expected so much of him; had put all their hopes in him and surrounded him with love and care. And he had done what had been expected of him: he had kept his head in his books, worked hard and obtained brilliant results at the provincial university close to his parents' home. He had led a sheltered life where everything was perfect until he had gone to America and met Vivienne. That had been the fateful moment when his life seemed to have tipped over.

He had made a new start in Brussels, but what was happening to him now? There was no kindness in the city. And the women! No innocent girls of his dreams but grasping, experienced, self-assured creatures like Pauline: another Vivienne trying to get him! How was he to cope with women like her, pushy, bold, out to catch him in their nets? What would become of him? What was left now of the dreams of his youth? And lying there in his bed in the hospital he wondered how long he would be able to remain true to himself.

Part Two

1

It was Monday morning and Anton found it difficult to concentrate on his work. The laboratory felt stuffy after the long dreary winter, and every now and then the urge surged up in him to walk to the window of his office and look outside where the sun shone in a radiant blue sky. It was not really warm yet but there was definitely a feeling of spring in the air. The lab could do with a good spring cleaning, he thought. And so could my mind.

He was about to pick up his sandwiches and go down to eat them with the rest of the staff when suddenly he could no longer stand being shut up; and on the spur of the moment he decided to drive to one of the parks for his midday break.

As he arrived at the Bois de la Cambre he noticed that there were very few people about – it was still too early in the year for that. 'I'll stop here for a stroll,' he said to himself. 'It'll do me a world of good to stretch my legs and I'll have the park virtually to myself.' He remembered that there were lakes further along and at once set off. His blood was rushing through his veins and he felt as excited as a schoolboy who was playing truant.

The park looked extremely beautiful with its huge old beech trees, carefully spaced out amid closely mown lawns. How wonderful, thought Anton, these mighty trees going straight up to the sky. So strong, so unlike me. They seemed bare still, but from close up one could see buds everywhere. New life. If only my life too could start afresh . . .

He had been very ill, but he had pulled through. And he was well cured of that nightmare of a Pauline. No more senseless adventures for him, thank you very much. Those city girls were all the same: too sophisticated; just out for quick pleasure. No, from now on it was going to be only science for him. He would dedicate his life to studying, to discovering the secrets of geology. That was the type of adventure he was going to stick to. You did not risk finding yourself naked in a broom cupboard and catching your death doing science. Later maybe, when he felt up to it, he would go back to the countryside and meet the innocent girl of his dreams. Much later maybe . . .

He breathed in deeply and felt his head spin as the fresh air rushed into his lungs. The park seemed enchanted; the midday sun threw shafts of light between the huge old trees and there was a tingling of spring everywhere. As he wandered in and out of the trees, dreaming, looking up at the blue sky and the few puffy white clouds, he failed to notice a pair of legs sticking out from behind a big beech tree. He tripped over them and fell forward, his head struck one of the huge roots that stuck out from the tree, and he knocked himself out . . .

Minutes later, when he opened his eyes, the world seemed blurred. Slowly the haze cleared and then, to his utter astonishment, he began to perceive a dream face. He looked into a pair of anxious deep-blue eyes only inches away. Then his head began to throb, he nearly passed out again, groaned and shut his eyes.

He vaguely heard a voice pleading: 'Please, please, say something.' The urgency in the voice made him open his eyes and then he realised that a girl was bending over him, her arm under his neck.

'Thank God,' she whispered. 'Thank God you're alive. You've been ages . . . Is your head all right?' She sounded extremely worried.

Anton began to touch his head. The pain was excruciating, but nothing seemed to be broken. 'All OK,' he said in a thick voice.

'I'm so glad! You stumbled over my legs and banged your head on this root here. I heard a cracking noise. I was so upset! I thought you had broken your skull. I'm sorry, I'm so sorry to have done this to you.'

'It's all right,' replied Anton with difficulty while attempting to sit up, but as he did so a sharp pain shot through his head and he yelled: 'Awooh.'

'Lean against the tree,' ordered the girl, while she helped him to settle himself comfortably. Then she went to sit at his feet and began taking off his shoes and socks.

'Hey, what . . .'

'Just relax,' she said soothingly while she began to massage his big toes.

'But the pain is in my head . . .'

'I'm doing reflexology,' explained the girl quietly. 'Any pain you feel anywhere in your body you will also feel in corresponding points on your feet. And by massaging these points you can cure the body.' She pressed Anton's big toes hard and he cried out in pain. 'See how it hurts you!' she said. 'Just let me treat you for a few minutes and you'll feel much better.'

They sat there in silence while the girl massaged Anton's feet. His head still throbbed, but less so every minute and after a while he felt just heavenly. The girl had closed her eyes and was concentrating on her massage, but there was an air of great tenderness on her face, which was framed by fair hair falling in waves along the sides of her cheeks. As he looked at her, Anton wished that this would go on forever.

After some time she opened her eyes and asked: 'Are you feeling better?'

'Much better, thank you.' Then he added, smiling shyly: 'I never felt better in my life.'

Suddenly the girl looked at her watch. 'Goodness!' she exclaimed. 'I didn't realise it was so late.' She jumped up, picked up her small shoulder bag and before Anton had time to say anything she ran off shouting: 'Bye!' Within moments she had disappeared among the trees.

2

'You're late!' hissed Mr Vangroenten under his breath when Gael rushed into the shop. 'There's a customer. She's been waiting five minutes already and I've had to find all sorts of excuses to make her stay.' He seemed very displeased.

'I'm so sorry,' mumbled Gael while she hung up her coat. 'I'll attend to her immediately.' And she kept her head down and tried to be as amiable as possible when the woman made some sharp remarks.

After the customer had gone Gael went to her desk and started her paperwork. How rude that woman was, she thought while beginning to sort out the pile of papers Mr Vangroenten had dumped there.

She looked sideways at him. If he so wants to do business and I'm late, why doesn't he attend to the customers himself? she reflected. But she knew very well why. He was an uncouth man, good at bullying her but incapable of selling anything to rich women.

They were difficult; they wanted this and that and, when you showed them, they asked for something completely different. They could be so inconsistent. And trying! Most had no idea how to decorate their houses but, all the same, they would reject Gael's suggestions. Then it turned out that what they fancied was something they had seen in a friend's or colleague's home! They wanted something like it, but better and more expensive: they were out to impress. And they had the money to satisfy their whims – their own or, more often, their husband's.

What a life! Gael sighed as she thought of the four years of hard study she had gone through, of her high hopes when she had finished brilliantly. And then she had found out that there were no jobs for art historians. For more than a year she had tried to find work in a museum or anywhere vaguely related to her studies. Finally she had accepted work in this interior-design shop, which had just opened.

A job is a job, she had thought when she started. The shop was situated in one of the better areas of Brussels and from the start it attracted a high-class clientele. Gael's mother had married a French-speaking Belgian and Gael spoke French and English fluently. She had style and good taste, inspired confidence and devoted her energy to her work, and soon the shop became a resounding success. Two years on, Mr Vangroenten had made so much money that he began to talk of buying up the adjacent house to extend his shop and make yet more money. Gael said nothing, but she knew that her heart was no longer in her work.

This last year there had been days when she found it hard to accept her fate. There she was, stuck between four walls with a grumbling boss and difficult customers. At times, when she looked up towards the window through which some sunlight filtered into the shop, she wondered what she was doing here. What she was doing in Brussels, come to think of it? She should have been living in England. Wasn't the course of life pure accident? But what was she to do? The path of duty seemed to stretch before her as far as she could see . . . unendingly . . .

She had been playing with the idea of dropping everything and joining a medical aid project when suddenly, last Christmas, a miracle had happened. Trevor had asked her to marry him! Soon she would be gone from here. Just nine more months and there would be no more Belgium for her: in December she was going to marry Trevor and then she could at last live in England.

And tomorrow she would be off to England for the rest of the week. Just one more afternoon, she thought as she bent down and began to sort out invoices and enter them into her filing system. She was going to see Trevor in a few days' time. But first she would go to London for this reflexology course. She had nearly completed it by now. Maybe later on she could practise in England. They were so much more open to new ways over there.

Fancy that young man knocking himself out against a tree, she suddenly thought, and me being able to practise reflexology on him. Such a handsome open face he had. She liked him. A shame that she would never get to know him. But wasn't that how it was in life? Hadn't someone said that we were all ships in the night passing each other? What a beautiful image that was.

Tomorrow she herself would be on a ship, the Dover ferry. She didn't like the fast rail link through the Channel Tunnel. She preferred the slow approach. She wanted to see the white cliffs of Dover loom up through the haze; she wanted to feel her heart beat with expectation.

Trevor's family and hers had always been very close. In fact, Trevor's mother was her own mother's best friend. They had a beautiful old house in the countryside with a vast expanse of gardens. From early childhood onwards she had spent her holidays there and had always loved it. What a grown-up young man Trevor had seemed at the time. Who would ever have thought he would have waited all these years for her? And that one day, out of the blue, he would ask her to marry him? Of course she had said 'yes'. How could she have refused?

Solid, reliable Trevor. He was a lawyer and had recently become a partner in a well-established solicitors' practice. How pleasant her life would become. Everything was already settled. They would live in his parents' house . . .

She heard the doorbell and saw another customer enter the shop. Soon these awful women will be gone from my life, she reflected as she got up. Yes, marrying Trevor would be the end to all these problems.

She saw Mr Vangroenten spring to attention as the woman addressed him in an authoritative voice. These women had money, yes, but no manners. They expected you to jump at the slightest snap of their fingers. Look at him, she thought eyeing her boss while taking her time to go and rescue him. He's wringing his hands trying to be obliging, when what he would really like to do is wring her neck. But he wants her money and will contort his body like a serpent to get it out of her.

Money! That was all that counted nowadays. She had grown up with fairy tales, and when left alone she would often retreat into a dream world of her own. Where were the dreams nowadays? Was there no longer any place for dreamers in the world?

Once again she saw the face of the young man in the park. He had looked at her with such surprise and trust when he had opened his eyes. Yes, he had the deep eyes of a dreamer . . . There was a whole world hidden behind those eyes. A pity she would never know his dreams . . .

3

Back in his office Anton seemed unable to concentrate on anything useful. A big bump had appeared on the side of his head: it was painful to touch and he felt slightly dazed, but that was not what stopped him from working. He just sat there, staring idly out of the window to where a corner of blue sky and some white clouds appeared above the roofs of the ugly houses on the other side of the street. And in those clouds he saw a face . . . the face that had irrupted into his life.

It was a strange, almost ethereal face. Then, up there in the clouds, the big eyes suddenly sparkled, the lips parted and the face looked at him and smiled. Who was she?

The next midday, and the day after, Anton went back to the park and waited for a full hour but she did not appear. When he approached the tree on the third day he saw a pair of legs sticking out from behind the big old trunk. His heart began to beat wildly and he ran forward shouting: 'Hello!'

When he got to the tree, his face beaming, he saw a dark-haired woman looking at him in bewilderment.

'Oh, I . . . I'm sorry,' he stuttered. 'I thought you were someone else.'

'Yeah, that's what you would say!' replied the woman staring at him with a hard, suspicious look in her beady eyes. 'That's what they all say. Men!' she spat out. She got up quickly and removed her ungainly body from the premises before that nuisance of a stranger could make any further advances.

After she had gone Anton stood there for a while, speechless. A horrible woman here, he thought. Behind our tree! It's a sacrilege. And as he looked up at the treetops, at the sky which had abruptly darkened, he shivered, turned and left.

4

Extract from Anton's writings:

You came to me from the depth of my dreams. Heavy with sleep, you awoke me and I was filled with wonder.

In the secret gardens of youth, in images long forgotten, you had lain hidden. And then, one day, when I opened my eyes, the mist lifted and I saw the face, the one I had always seen in the deepest of my dreams – your face.

When you spoke, I knew your voice. When you smiled, the light in your eyes penetrated effortlessly into the most secret corners of my being. There you were, a stranger, yet I have always known you. When I was a boy, we ran off to the fields together. When I climbed trees, it was you who were up there with me, looking out towards the horizon and beyond, wanting to go to far-away lands together.

After all those years I found you . . . and yet you are as ephemeral as ever. You entered my world to disappear only moments later. Who are you?

To have seen the clouds withdraw for one fleeting moment, to have seen your face, to have been shown a glimpse of paradise . . . and then to see these clouds cover everything again and be thrown back into a world as dull and colourless as ever . . . it is more than I can bear . . .

5

Trevor was beckoning impatiently as Gael stepped down from the train. She had not seen him for several months and as she advanced towards him on the platform she was conscious that, for the first time in her life, she was looking at him with critical eyes. He was tall, yes, but thin and seemed rather colourless.

So this is my future husband, she found herself thinking. He's not really handsome. Then she felt ashamed to have let such thoughts enter her mind and immediately corrected them. But how distinguished he looks in his flannel trousers and blazer! And his face may be thin and his nose rather long, but he really has fine features.

'Here you are,' said Trevor, holding out his arms and giving her a peck on the cheek. 'At last! My dear, do you realise that you're late?'

'Oh, I didn't . . . am I really?'

'Yes, your train is late,' he repeated as he took her suitcase. 'Come on. I'm afraid we'll have to hurry. The car's just around the corner.'

'Of course . . . being a solicitor now you have lots of engagements. Sorry. I didn't think.'

'Well, no. That's not it. I have to dash off to a cricket match in Hampsworth. I'm going to be late . . . Your train, you see.'

'A cricket match?' asked Gael, bewildered, while they were tearing along one of the main roads.

'I couldn't possibly opt out, you see,' explained Trevor as he switched gears and turned into a narrow country road. 'They all count on me.' His face suddenly beamed with undisguised pride. 'I'm captain of my team, you see . . . I'm sure you understand . . .'

'Oh, it's that important!' she exclaimed with barely disguised sarcasm in her voice. 'Of course you must go!'

'Yes. It is a rather important match. But don't worry. The Mater is expecting you for tea. And I'll be back as soon as I can.'

They drove along in silence for the rest of the short journey. Trevor concentrated on manoeuvring the sports car along the winding country roads as fast as he could while Gael tried to look at the lovely landscape of trees and hedgerows which shot by all too quickly. Finally the car turned sharply into the drive of tall trees that led up to the imposing country house. Gael loved those trees. As long as she could remember they had always been there to welcome her into a world of which she considered herself a part. This time too they seemed to be waiting for her to come home.

As the car swerved along and stopped in front of the wide steps that led up to the house, the entrance doors opened and an elegant figure appeared.

'Hello, Mother!' shouted Trevor. 'I've brought Gael. Her train was late! Could you give her some tea? I must be off to my match.' He ran round the car, opened the door for Gael, lifted her case out, jumped into the driver's seat and was about to dash off when he suddenly paused. 'Oh yes,' he called out to Gael. 'I nearly forgot. We're expected at the Wallensteens' at nine o'clock tonight. A party for Bert. He's flying to

America tomorrow. Hope you don't mind.' As Gael nodded agreement, he revved up the engine, shouting over the noise: 'Wish me luck!' Then the car turned and he was off.

'Do come in, dear,' said Trevor's mother in a distinguished voice, but her attention was not with Gael. Her eyes followed the car until it had disappeared in a cloud of dust. Only then did she turn to Gael, saying: 'He's such a dear boy, but he worries me terribly. He drives so recklessly when he is pressed for time.' Then she added with a very slight hint of reproach: 'How unfortunate that you should be arriving on the day of his match. And, of course, you are late.'

'Sorry,' mumbled Gael apologetically. 'I didn't realise.'

'Well, never mind. You'll want to refresh yourself. You know your room. Tea will be served in half an hour.'

When Gael came down to the drawing room, tea was already served. The table was covered with an assortment of cucumber sandwiches, crumpets and fruitcake, but Trevor's mother was not alone. With her were three other women of indefinite age, and after she had introduced her future daughter-in-law, the women continued talking spiritedly without paying much attention to Gael. They all got up after tea, and as Trevor's mother went out with them she said in an absent voice: 'Would you mind looking after yourself, dear? I forgot to tell you, but I'm having a bridge party.' She followed the other women into the library and soon Gael heard animated conversation and laughter emerging from behind the half-closed doors.

She stepped out of the French windows onto the terrace at the back of the house and looked at the impeccably kept lawn surrounded by neat herbaceous borders, and at the pond overhung by the branches of a weeping willow. She had so often lain down behind the shelter of those branches, hiding from everyone, lost in dreams.

But this time, as she walked towards the pond, she found that strange thoughts were invading her mind. This was where she would soon be living. The house was beautiful; her future in-laws were rich and liked her; Trevor had a good position and was a kind man; her parents would be extremely happy; and all her problems would be over. Everything would fall into place. All appeared to be perfect. This was a world of order and security. But was it her world?

6

It was Monday again and well before midday Anton was sitting in the park with his back against the tree. He was watching tensely, looking at anyone passing between the tall trunks, hoping against all hope. And then, when he had nearly given up, he saw her. Her slender figure slid in and out of view, now hidden by a big tree, now visible as she approached without hurry.

'How extraordinary to find you here!' she exclaimed when she stood in front of him.

He gazed at her for a long while, his eyes misty with emotion. Finally he spoke. 'I've been waiting here every day since . . .'

'. . . since last Monday? You haven't!'

'I have. And I was getting desperate. I was afraid I would never see you again.'

'Oh, but . . . I had to go abroad.'

'How was I to know that?'

'I'm so sorry,' she said, and her voice expressed genuine regret. 'I shouldn't have run away so suddenly.'

'I wish you hadn't . . .'

'How's your head?' asked the girl, trying to change the subject.

'Oh, not too bad. Don't worry. I have fallen on my head before.'

'You sound as if you knock yourself out every other day!'

'No!' He laughed. 'It's not that bad. But I do stumble over things every now and then. You know, I once fell out of a tree when I was a boy. Straight on my head.'

'You fell out of a tree! How did that happen?'

'It was really my sister's fault. She always egged me on. I was up in a cherry tree and she wanted me to pick some very ripe cherries right at the end of a branch.'

'What did your sister do? Did she try to help you?'

'You must be joking! She just sat there in the grass, laughing her head off. Said I would have to walk for the rest of my life with a crooked neck.'

'How terrible. So what did you do?'

'I was determined to get those cherries and climbed up again, although my neck hurt terribly. I've always believed that, if you hurt yourself, you shouldn't sit there crying but get up straight away and carry on with what you're doing.'

'Isn't that extraordinary?' The girl looked at him with approval in her eyes. 'I loved climbing trees, too.' She chuckled. 'Once I was up in a horse chestnut tree and a policeman saw me. He was furious and told me I was a silly girl and that I was to come down immediately.'

'And you didn't?'

'Of course I didn't. Then he asked for my name but I refused to tell him. I thought that if he wanted to get me, he could jolly well climb the tree and come after me. He finally went away, muttering to himself, and left me in peace.'

Suddenly Anton stared at her with pleading eyes. 'Please tell me your name . . . You won't refuse to tell *me* your name, will you?'

She sat there for a few moments, looking out towards the lake. Then she said softly: 'I'm Gael. Gael Fernley.'

Anton didn't react but appeared absorbed in his thoughts.

'Don't you like it?' She seemed disappointed. 'It's a bit old-fashioned, but I can't change my name.'

'Oh no, I like it! It's a most lovely name. No, I was just putting the face and name together in my mind . . . something I've been longing to do the whole week. You see . . . you've never left my thoughts since you disappeared among the trees. Day after day your face was there in my mind's eye . . . the . . . the loveliest face I've ever seen. But then, as the days passed, it began to fade. In the end it seemed no more than a mirage because, you see, it was a face without a name. I didn't even know your name! It was disheartening. It was . . . how to explain it . . . like a book you're longing to read, a book that will reveal everything you ever wanted to know. But you cannot even begin to look for it because you don't know its title!'

He paused for a long moment while the girl stared at him with tenderness in her eyes. Then she sat down beside him and very gently put her hand on his arm, saying. 'Don't be so despondent.'

'A name is so important.' He shook his head slowly. 'You see . . . I've been trying out lots of names but none of them seemed to fit your face. But Gael . . . yes, that's you.'

'I'm so glad. I hoped you would like it.' She remained very quiet for a while, and then said: 'You haven't told me your name yet.'

'Oh, of course,' stammered Anton. 'How thoughtless of me. My name's Anton. Anton Felsen.'

'Anton,' she repeated as if weighing the name in her mouth. 'Anton . . . that's a nice name.'

Suddenly Anton looked at her with infinite longing. 'Day after day I've been wondering who you were,' he said, 'and prayed that you would return. I didn't know whether you would ever come back. I hoped that life wouldn't be so cruel . . . I was prepared to wait for you forever.' Then he smiled, a smile that lingered around the corners of his mouth and gradually lit up his whole face. 'But it no longer matters now. You have come back and whoever you are . . . to me you are the answer to my deepest dreams.'

His eyes shone as he put an arm around her. Then, without thinking, she leaned her head against his shoulder.

They did not move, they did not speak. They just sat there gazing over the grass towards the lake. Everything was perfect: the sun was shining on their faces, the ducks were dipping in and out of the water, and only their noisy splashing interrupted the silence. Time had lost its meaning.

7

When she looked at herself in the mirror, Gael was struck by the radiance of her face. It was still the same face and yet it wasn't. Even her mother had remarked upon it that evening when she got home. 'Is that what England does to you?' she had asked. 'Or is it Trevor?'

Gael had not answered. How could she have told her mother? She didn't want to talk about what had happened. She herself didn't know what to think. Why had she put her head on Anton's shoulder when she was going to marry Trevor? She didn't understand, and she didn't want to question her own behaviour. But she knew that it had felt so completely right, his arm around her and her head against him. And she just wanted to dream.

She looked again at herself. There seemed to be more of her than only a week ago: there was a glow that had never been there before. Her eyes were sparkling with life – life in all its strength. Everything of her recent past seemed insipid in comparison. She felt happy, absolutely and totally happy. And suddenly she realised: that's what love does to people.

8

During the following days Anton was in a state of euphoria. On Thursday he could stand the lab no longer. He jumped into his car and drove along, not knowing where he was going, until to his surprise he noticed that he had reached the park. He found an empty space for his car, got out and started walking towards their tree when the wind suddenly rose. Dark rain clouds were gathering, and the few people who had been strolling about began to hurry home, their collars turned up. The first drops fell, thick drops splashing on Anton's face. Then, without warning, the downpour started and the rain came down in sheets. He did not mind. When he reached their tree he suddenly burst out laughing, spread out his arms as if he were going to embrace the whole world, and began turning on his axis, round and round like a dancing dervish, laughing all the time till he was soaked to the bone.

The few people who rushed by, their open umbrellas stuck out like protective shielding, looked at him in surprise and then with suspicion, and gave him a wide berth. But Anton took no notice. There was sunlight and warmth in his heart and so much happiness that he felt as if his mind was going to explode. How could this have happened to him? After years of loneliness? To be suddenly two. To love and be loved. What had he done to deserve such boundless happiness? He didn't want to know. It had happened and that was all that mattered. Gael was all he had ever wanted. Nothing was missing in his life now. And slowly he kept turning round and round while the rain continued to pour down on him.

9

Extract from Gael's notebooks:

The road of life resounds eternally with the steps of people passing, passing . . . and then, one day, as you sit on your wall, waiting, a magician appears in front of you . . . his fingers touch you . . . and before your awe-struck eyes the petals of a thousand flowers open up, crystal-clear water bubbles below your feet, and life begins to glow with millions of bright colours.

'There are certain things I have to tell you,' said Gael, standing in front of Anton. 'You've got a right to know about . . . about my past.'

Anton looked at her with adoration in his eyes, and suddenly all her firm intentions melted away and she started off on a tangent, not knowing where to begin.

'You see . . . I've led a very sheltered life. I've always been moving back and forth between here and England . . .'

Anton caressed her hair and her voice faltered.

'. . . I just didn't like it over here. For several years now I have felt that something was missing and . . .'

He kissed her on her lips and suddenly her story became rather incoherent.

'. . . and I've been sitting on the wall around my garden, looking out . . .'

Anton laughed. 'You've been sitting on your garden wall?'

Gael began to laugh too, and buried her head in his shoulder. 'In the figurative sense of course, you silly one.' Then she looked up at Anton and suddenly blurted out: 'You see . . . I was hoping to find someone who would understand me without me having to explain myself.'

'You don't have to explain yourself. I understand you without words.'

'But I must tell you about my past!' protested Gael. 'There . . . there are things I ought to tell you . . .'

Anton put a finger on her lips. 'Not today. The past won't run away. We'll have plenty of time to talk about it later.' Then he held her at arms' length and, looking at her with shining eyes, he said softly: 'You exist, and you are here with me. Nothing else counts.' And he pulled her gently along towards the lakeshore.

10

Meanwhile, in his office in Moscow, Viktor Ippolitovich Boronov was staring out of the window. It was still freezing outside and the world was white as far as he could see, but he knew that the end of the cold season was nigh. Soon the winter, this interminable winter, would be over and spring would come with its exhilarating scents and its promise of new life. Maybe it would bring new life to him, too? Maybe he would have the time and courage to go for a day to the countryside? There would be wildflowers blossoming all over the meadows and in between the trees on the road to his dacha. He had occupied such a high rank in the Party that his years of outstanding service had been rewarded with a dacha. It had been no more than a small, weather-boarded wooden house with a single, rather dark room and a tiny kitchen, but it was his own dacha.

No, he thought suddenly, maybe it's better not to go that way. His dacha was no longer his. It had been taken away from him. Much worse: he had been told that it had become part of a building development for the new rich. For capitalists! He felt betrayed. The new bourgeoisie was devouring Russia and destroying everything he stood for. His old heart ached. The stable world of his past was crumbling around him.

Better not to think about what was going on. It was too painful. He turned resolutely to the task that had been assigned to him: he had to foment a revolution in Africa. He went to the map to put his finger on the spot where it was to break out, gasped and swore aloud. Once more he had forgotten what Africa had become: a huge red blot surrounded by a blue ocean. It had been the same every day since that fateful morning. Every time he stared at what his subordinates had done to his cherished map, he swore.

This very map had been the receptacle of his dreams. He had looked at it so often that it had become second nature to him to stand in front of it. In the 1970s he had followed the progress of communism with mounting satisfaction. In the 1980s there still had been hope . . . This map of Africa had been his treasure. And now! That unique, irreplaceable document had been ruined forever. He would never forgive those bastards for what they had done to his map. He would make them pay for this, oh yes!

Viktor Ippolitovich sat down, picked up his phone and began to dial a number. Then he realised there was no tone, and with a curse he slammed down the receiver. Out of order again! How could he organise anything when nothing functioned in this country? He needed to find small arms, ammunition and money, a lot of it . . . how could he get all this done before the summer? He sighed. There was so much to do and everything moved so slowly here. Then he pulled a folder with writing paper towards him. Even if nothing else functioned, the mail could always be relied upon. He picked up a pen and began to write, a resolute expression on his face, for he was determined to get everything ready by July. And then he would send those two bastards to the Sahara in the heat of the summer, and they would perish!

11

About a month later Viktor Ippolitovich was pacing back and forth in his office. He had felt so depressed during the winter that he believed he would never survive. But now at last spring had come, and as the skies cleared and a dim sun was shining, his spirits revived and his depression began to lift. He realised that he shouldn't have despaired. He had survived, and so had Russia: the snows were melting and the people were once more walking knee-deep through the muddy slush; everything was back to normal.

Russia . . . he thought, his face very solemn. Sacred Russia. Her history had been one long calamity. Here, on the very spot where this office block now stood, the Tatars once ruled. Like a hurricane they had swept over the country, trampling the people, enslaving them. It had taken centuries to get rid of them, but the Russian people had finally driven off the scourge. In the end, yes . . . in the end, we got the better of them. Viktor Ippolitovich smiled.

Then the French had come. Ah, Napoleon . . . he had marched into Moscow and burnt it! But the French, pooh . . . they had lasted no more than a few months.

The Germans now, they had been much tougher. Twice they had come and the struggle had been long and murderous. Russia had been down, but not out. And in the end the Russian nation had emerged victorious, strengthened by that terrible ordeal, and the Soviet Union had become a world power. Those had been the days! Tears welled up in Viktor Ippolitovich's eyes when he thought of those glorious years.

But now . . . Viktor Ippolitovich sighed deeply. Capitalism was doing away with all the good principles of communism. And the hated bourgeois were back, clogging up the streets with their big cars and flaunting their new riches around. And where had their money come from? They had stolen it from the State. From the Russian people! From people like himself who had lost nearly everything so that a few could be rich.

Viktor Ippolitovich shook his head. How he suffered for Russia. He was an old man already, and maybe it would be better for him to die rather than see Russia decline. He didn't want to witness the humiliating spectacle of the Americans basking in their victory, laying down the law and trampling upon the Russian people and all he believed in. Once again this seemed to be the end.

But then he remembered the past and he knew that he shouldn't lose hope. Russia had gone through worse than this . . . much worse . . . she had put up with the most terrible hardships. The Russians were a resilient people, and the Russian soul would survive intact, indestructible. No, he didn't want to die yet. He wanted to live long enough to see the Americans in turn kicked out, to see them disappear into the dustbin of history like the Tatars, the French and the Germans. No, he shouldn't despair. Russia would emerge victorious once more and be the mistress of her own destiny.

12

Viktor Ippolitovich was sitting behind his desk, vaguely looking at a point somewhere outside the window. At long last he turned, stared with undisguised disgust at the two subordinates who stood before him, their eyes respectfully fixed upon the tips of their well-polished shoes, and spoke.

'*Da, da* . . . we are getting on.' A flicker of satisfaction suddenly lit up his eyes. 'We've nearly got everything you need to take to Africa: the small arms, the money . . .'

At once the faces of the two men brightened up. 'Are you going to supply us with money, Viktor Ippolitovich?' asked Boris. 'How . . . how many roubles are we going to receive?'

'Boris Nicolaievich, you are a fool!' There was exasperation in Viktor Ippolitovich's voice. 'Roubles are good for Russia. But what can one do with roubles abroad, you ask me? You are going to receive dollars.'

'Viktor Ippolitovich . . .' Boris's tongue nearly hung out of his mouth when he heard the word 'dollars' and Igor was so excited that he began to hop up and down. 'Are you really going to give us dollars?' exclaimed the two men in unison, their voices thick with emotion. 'Can we first go and do some shopping in Moscow? Please Viktor Ippolitovich. You can buy anything with dollars. Our wives will be so happy.'

'No, you can't do that!' shouted Viktor Ippolitovich. 'You're not allowed to touch those dollars until you get to Africa.' He shot a reprimanding look at his subordinates. 'You can't use them in Moscow! They're right for Africa but not for here.'

'But . . . but . . . aren't those dollars good?'

'Of course they are good! Top quality even. All nice and crisp. In fact, brand new. Just printed in North Korea.'

After Viktor Ippolitovich had spoken, Boris stood there pondering, lost in thought.

'Well, what is it?' asked Viktor Ippolitovich, seeing that the man didn't move.

'Viktor Ippolitovich,' replied Boris, looking very confused, 'there is something I do not understand. Can I ask you a question?'

'No one expects you to understand anything, Comrade Boris!' barked Viktor Ippolitovich. 'That's not your role. You're here to carry out orders. That's your role.'

'But Viktor Ippolitovich . . . with all respect, my question is fundamental. If we can print dollars, why do we have to go to Africa to lay our hands on mines before the Americans get them? There's no need for that. Why don't we just print masses of dollars, and then we'll be much richer than the Americans?'

Blood rushed to Viktor Ippolitovich's face. He got up abruptly and pointed a trembling finger at the door. 'Out!' he screamed. And as the two grey men rushed out, nearly falling over their feet, he shouted after them: 'And don't ever try to think again. Just obey orders!'

After they had gone he sat down, shaking his head and muttering to himself: 'How can Russia ever triumph if she has to rely on fools such as these?'

13

'*Monsieur le Président,*' said the French President's political adviser, 'I have just received news from our African diplomatic services. It seems that Gwemboka is going to organise some special festivities and . . .'

'Who?'

'Well, Gwemboka, President of . . .'

'Oh, yes, yes . . . I remember. And what does he want?'

'He is going to celebrate his twenty-five years in power and intends to make it a very special occasion. Apparently he wants to invite several foreign dignitaries and . . .'

'Well, if we really have to, I suppose that we could send one of our diplomats . . .' He looked up from behind his desk and, noticing the look of disapproval in his adviser's eyes, he corrected: '. . . or maybe the Minister of Foreign Affairs?'

'*Monsieur le Président,*' said the adviser firmly, 'I don't think that will be adequate. I have been given to understand that he wants you in person. He intends you to be the star of the show.'

'What! He must be joking! That bloodthirsty dictator! There's no lack of tyrants in Africa, but in an open competition he would probably beat them all hands down. He should have been removed years ago. And think of the international repercussions if I went to his celebration! I can already see the headlines in foreign newspapers: French President supports murderous regime. No, that's out of the question.'

'But *Monsieur le Président*, we *do* support his regime. Only two years ago we sent French paratroopers to push back a rebel force that had surrounded his capital.'

'*Mon Dieu!* Why did we do that?'

There was discouragement in the adviser's eyes when he looked at his President but he carried on patiently: 'The rebels intended to nationalise all the mines. And let me remind you that most of those mines are owned by French companies.'

'Of course, of course,' muttered the President.

'So it is extremely important that the cordial relationship between Gwemboka and *la France* continues as always. We all know that he's a bastard, but to paraphrase an American President: he is *our* bastard.'

'But that's no reason why I should go there in person!'

'Allow me, *Monsieur le Président*, to give you an update on the situation.

Until recently our main competitors were American and Canadian and, so far, our special relationship with Gwemboka permitted us to advance the interests of our national mining companies. However, the era of special connections and easy contracts may be about to end. New bidders are looming on the horizon. The Chinese have launched a full frontal offensive – of the economic sort that is – and they have the funds to support their claims. The Russians, too, are moving in. From what I hear, important new deposits have recently been discovered and the Chinese may well lay their hands on these unless you accede to Gwemboka's demand. Going over there in person would allow you to put in a good word and might just tilt the balance in favour of our companies. On the other hand, I've been given to understand that your refusal to be present at his ceremony would have extremely harmful consequences for our interests in the country.'

'So that's how the matter stands?'

'I'm afraid, *Monsieur le Président*, that this is how the matter stands.'

The President tried one last objection. 'But it's an unsafe country! Haven't there been several bomb attacks recently?'

'I can assure you, *Monsieur le Président*, that there will be no reason to worry about your safety. You will be protected by French guards every minute of your stay over there.'

'All right then,' grumbled the President. 'If it's a question of national interest . . .' he threw up his arms, '. . . what can I do? But I count on you to make up a good story for the press.'

'That goes without saying, *Monsieur le Président*. Oh . . . there's one other detail. Gwemboka also wants de Lattignie to come over.'

'Who?'

'De Lattignie. He's a retired general.'

'What the hell does he want a retired general for?'

'It seems that long ago, when Gwemboka was a sergeant in the colonial army, he served under him. I suppose he wants to meet his old commander again, just to rub in how important he has become.'

'Well, if *I* have to go, this de Lattignie can damn well go, too,' said the President. 'And I count on you to arrange everything up to the smallest details. Oh, and I want a French chef to take care of my meals. Make sure fresh French food and wines are sent out every day for the duration of my stay.'

'*Bien sûr*,' smiled the adviser. 'That's the least we can expect you to request. A French President couldn't possibly travel in style without French cuisine.'

14

Every Monday Gael now set off from home well before midday to drive to the park, and when she got there she always found Anton waiting for her near their tree. The moment he saw her he would run towards her with outstretched arms and, as he lifted her high, she felt free as a bird, and laughed and laughed. Then they would stroll along the lakeside, or just sit together and look at the ducks.

At other times they would drive off to the woods and wander along narrow trails or simply find a sheltered place in which to lie down. And when they lay in the embrace of the woods, looking at the branches above through which the rays of the sun filtered like beams of light in a fairy world, they felt so close that nothing mattered any more. They just lived.

Extracts from Gael's notebooks:

An enchanted afternoon among the trees. Trees planted more than a century ago and now towering above us like mighty giants. We found a soft patch under the boughs. When I turned my head and looked far into the depths of the forest, I saw only beauty. The land seemed made for us. And we ourselves, were we not like the forest, too?

[. . .]

The life that lives in you echoes within me. From your hand a current of warm life flows into mine. At times it seems as if I carry your feelings within me, as if I am no longer myself, but you. Your eyes, alight with the radiance of your heart, hold my dreamland. There are so many things that come from you that I want to hear; so many things in me that I want to give to you. Let me try, just let me try to fill an empty space in your heart that perhaps no one else has ever touched.

Extracts from Anton's writings:

The world changed the day I met you. There wasn't a chance in a million that we would meet. It might so easily not have happened.

Not in this life. Not in a thousand lives. But it has, and I'm dazed with the sudden awareness.

How can I possibly tell you with words how much I love you? That my life would be a void without you? How much I miss you when you are not there? The words are unspoken, but I want to kneel down before you and tell you of my love:

I love you like dreams in the night; like the eternal rustling of the trees; like the clouds blowing through the sky. How could I not be affected when you stand before me?

Since you have come I'm no longer alone. Wherever I walk, you always walk beside me. I can almost touch you when you are not there, and I often talk to you. People must think me mad, but does it matter? Isn't it true that nothing is purer than pure madness?

Extracts from Gael's notebooks:

Months have passed by and yet the wonder of our heaven remains. How unbelievable! Before you came, the town seemed to have shattered my inner soul. For too many years I emptied into others the joy of living that flowed so strongly through me. Others lived my life for me. Then you came and showed me that the way I so strongly believed life and love to be – pure and absolute – was real and true.

[. . .]

Walking in the park on a misty afternoon, shadows flickered around our feet. Everything seemed enchanted and a fairy-tale veil covered the lake. Noises of ducks swimming, making small ripples as they dipped their heads under the surface and reappeared. The water lapping at the edge. The flight of geese, the perfection of their wings, so swift and firm. Standing with you along the lake's edge tightly locked together . . . how beautiful was this moment. And when you looked at me I knew we both desired the same thing.

When evening came, excitement awoke and rose inside like a warm glow. Every part of my body tingled with this curious rush of exhilaration. You asked me if I wanted to go to the forest. Yes, I would like to go. I have no fear of the trees at night . . . or of what may happen.

A small glen hidden in the forest. Birds and all the noises of the night. As I lay in the softness of the grass, I was aware of the strength of the trees; of your breath that flowed inside me; of the touch of your hands; of the trembling of your being. And I knew deep within me the feeling of life. Blessed was that night, for we were one of heart, and mind, and body.

15

And then it was summer. Gael had not wanted to think about it. She had simply pushed the thought back to the furthest recesses of her mind, but now the summer vacation was upon her. Every July she went to England with her parents. They always spent two weeks in a little cottage in Deal, a small fishing town just north of Dover, and the rest of the month with Trevor's parents.

How could she face Trevor? She had not written to him and had avoided any questions her mother had asked. But soon she would have to confront the decisions of her past and find an honourable exit.

She had hesitated to tell Anton about their coming separation – she hadn't felt up to it – but as the days advanced towards summer and July approached, apprehension rose in her. Then, a week before she was due to leave, she was unable to put it off any longer and told him that she had to go to England with her parents.

'Of course you must go!' Anton spoke jokingly. 'It'll be a nice change from having me around you all the time.'

'But . . . but it's for a whole month!'

Anton suddenly went very quiet and as she saw his face fall, she put her hand on his cheek and heard herself say in a choked voice: 'I'm so sorry to have to do this to you.'

'Don't worry. It doesn't matter.' There was a forced joviality in his tone. 'Just think how wonderful it'll be for your family and friends to see you. I'm sure they're counting on it.'

Gael froze when she heard his words. Anton didn't know anything about her predicament. She had tried to speak about it soon after they met but hadn't managed. And as the months flowed by, her promise to marry Trevor had seemed ever more unreal, something from a past life that had nothing to do with them. But now it loomed before her, very real, and the thought made her wince.

'Don't worry,' repeated Anton when he saw her distraught face. 'I'll just go to the lab and work. Don't bother about me. I'll manage. And with luck my detector will be functioning by the time you're back. I'll be so proud to show it to you.' Then he added, as an afterthought: 'Ring me or write to me if you have a moment.' It had been said in a light-hearted manner but she knew all too well that his feelings were different.

The separation hung over them like a black cloud and it saddened their last week together. When they said goodbye, panic rose in Gael's throat. A whole month without Anton! For the first time in her life her spirits did not lift at the thought that she was going to see the white cliffs of Dover.

16

Extract from Anton's writings:

You've been gone no more than a week – another twenty-four days before your return – and it seems an eternity already.

Your roots have grown so deep inside me that I'm no longer complete without you. Every nerve in my body is yearning for you. If only I could be with you – anywhere – but with you. I would rush over to England today if you wanted me, but I know that's impossible.

The days creep along like lazy tortoises. They hurry when I'm with you. Why can't they hurry now?

Letter from Gael to Anton:

Before, when I was with others, I was still alone. When their eyes smiled at me, the light did not enter me. When they wanted me, there was no response. There was no belonging. And now there is. Now I belong to you.

Before we met, we were two separate bubbles floating around on the sea of life, drifting on the currents, pushed now here, now there. We are still pushed about by the currents, by fate over which we have no control, but now we have fused. We are floating together like a single bubble.

Before you came I had my past and you had yours. We had no past together. And now we do. However short it is, however insignificant it may seem to others, it is our past.

Before, when I was here on the seashore, I was standing alone. But now I find myself speaking to you with words that do not end. And I want to tell you that anything I have ever said to you, any emotion I may have tried to express, is only a dim shadow of what I really feel. I am so much yours, my darling Anton. Much too much!

17

Nearly two weeks had passed by when suddenly the phone rang in Anton's office. When he picked it up, to his utter surprise, he heard Gael's voice, with seagulls crying in the background.

'Anton, darling, is it you?' And then without further ado: 'I'll be alone in Deal for four days. Would you like to come and join me?'

Anton sat there for a few seconds, unable to take in what Gael had said, while her voice was calling: 'Hello! Hello! Anton. Are you there?'

Then he blurted out: 'I'll come! Today?'

'No, tomorrow. There's a ferry that arrives in Dover at 2 p.m. I'll be waiting for you on the docks.'

'I'll be there. How marvellous!' Then a torrent of pent-up words poured forth. 'I've missed you so much. Day and night I've been thinking of you. I love you . . .'

Suddenly Gael heard a click and the connection was broken.

She felt elated. For the first time in their lives they would be together for four whole days and spend the nights together!

Extract from Gael's notebooks:

Your loving voice entered me, and for hours I felt weak. I could not go back to the house and see my mother, for my face read like an open book. I went to the beach and sat there for a long time looking out over the waves. You are there, somewhere on the other side of the sea, but you are woven around me.

Tomorrow you will be here. You are going to come to the land where I was born, to the cliffs that have always been part of me. I am thrilled, yet I am frightened. Will our love still be the same in this world of mine which I have never shared with any man? Nothing says that you will like England. Maybe you will be a stranger in a strange land. But I pray that you may be as much one with the cliffs, the peace, the flowers and freedom as I am.

18

Extract from Gael's notebooks:

England with you! Days of freedom, days of joy and discovery, of clouds and rain, of sun and moon. Days of understanding, of oneness, of the gentle meeting of our hands. Heaven, peace and happiness with you. Between us life itself seems to reach out, straining, longing to be joined.

We lay, our souls slowly opening to the swaying corn, to the rustling of the summer breeze. Wildflowers, raindrops, soft meadows . . . all these treasures the land offered to us. And you . . . you offered me the world of love that lay hidden deep inside you.

The happy, happy days spent with you overlooking the sea. The many grains of sand on the beach that felt our touch. The open spaces, the wind blowing through our hair. Like the wind, our minds flew outwards. One day we will travel together to the infinite.

Waking up with the glow of your warmth all around my heart and body, and your smile to open my eyes. How near is heaven in the morning.

Of your face I know each feature; of your face I love each line. And now, as you are asleep beside me on the beach, I want to look at you forever.

Today the waves carried away your shoes, and then brought them back. Tomorrow you will leave and carry away my heart. Will you bring it back one day?

Last evening: my love sits by the window writing a poem while he lets me just rest my tiredness and enjoy the little flowers of heaven.

Last morning: lying still and listening to the sounds of departure. Hearing the cupboard door open and feeling one by one small piles of clothes build up beside me on the bed. How strange to know the feeling of loneliness before you are really gone.

Last moments: sitting on the cliffs high above the harbour, speechless. I feel tears within us.

I drove you away and when you waved goodbye, intense sadness pervaded my whole being. How well you seemed to have become part of England, almost as if you were born on its shores.

Sitting high up on the cliffs I saw the ferry steam out to sea and my eyes followed it until it had become a small dot that disappeared in the haze. I wanted more than anything to be on that boat with you. Did you look at the white cliffs and feel the same?

I watched the waves at the foot of the cliff slowly cover the boulders, green with seaweed. Then I lay down in the grass full of the scent of wildflowers and closed my eyes. When I woke up I wanted to put my arms around you but you were not there, and the cliffs were covered in shadows. I long for you as I never dreamed I would.

The last four days were lived out of time. Days like these we will remember.

Anton's poem:

With You In Deal

1
We strolled into the dusk
of narrow winding streets
where the feet of countless lovers
had walked long before us.

2
Close to me you stood,
your eyes shining
with the light of many stars;
love was written all over your face.

3
And when I held you tight
longing rose in your eyes,
and your desire
ran through my veins.

4
In the depth of the night,
you, lying beside me,
arms searching for warmth,
our lips met.

         5
The passion of your youth
went through me like a wildfire,
lighting all my senses
with a devouring flame.

         7
You and me together,
in contracting convulsions,
exploded through age and time
like thousands of generations before us.

         6
From deep down inside,
welled up primeval lust,
and waves of utter feeling
obliterated all around us.

         8
Then, your face very still
in the hollow of my shoulder,
wonder came into your eyes;
slowly we were reborn.

19

'Did you have a nice holiday?' asked Lottie with eager eyes.

'No!' Pauline's face was long and sullen.

'You didn't? And I thought you had really enjoyed yourself. That's why you were a day late, I thought.' Lottie looked at her companion with surprise and disappointment. 'Why are you late then?' she said accusingly.

'It's all my husband's fault! He got lost in the mountains.'

'You mean on the way back from the Côte d'Azur?'

'We didn't go to the Côte d'Azur!' Pauline sounded bitter. 'If we had gone there, I'd have enjoyed myself.'

'Where did you go then? I don't understand. I'm sure you told me you were going to the Côte d'Azur.'

'We were but my husband changed his plans at the very last minute. "We're going to a wonderful place in Switzerland instead," he said. I expected a holiday resort with a swimming pool and lots of interesting men around, but Raymond was unwilling to tell me more. "It will be a surprise," he said. And when we reached our destination I can tell you that the surprise was complete: our home for the next two weeks was a chalet up the slopes of a mountain, miles away from a small peasant village somewhere in German-speaking Switzerland! Completely isolated! The only sound we heard was the tinkling of cowbells in the mountain meadows. I nearly had a fit!'

'And . . . and how did it go?' asked Lottie with growing curiosity. 'Did you turn into a cow girl?'

'Cow girl, my foot. I hate cows! Scullery maid was more like it. I had to do all the cooking, the cleaning, the upkeep . . . Not that there was much to keep up: it was a very small chalet, just a sitting room, kitchen and bedroom combined. And the bed! A rustic narrow wooden structure in which there was hardly room for two!' She shuddered at the recollection. 'Twice a week we drove to the nearest village for bread, meat and vegetables, and to a farm for eggs and milk. And the people spoke only German! My husband thoroughly enjoyed it – he sings a lot in German – but I was left high and dry. I've never been so bored in my life! Just imagine: I had only my husband to talk to because he was the only one who understood French. Dreadful, absolutely dreadful it was!'

'At least, with no one else around you must have turned all your seductive powers on him.' Lottie was unable to suppress a giggle. 'He must have been in heaven!'

'Oh he was in heaven! Every morning after an early breakfast he climbed up the mountain . . .'

'Is he a hiker?'

'No, I wouldn't say that. After a few days he told me that he had discovered a spot a mile up where the acoustics were simply fantastic. And there he spent his time . . . singing. While I was left behind in the chalet, alone with nothing to do!'

'You should have gone with him. Then at least he would have had an audience.'

'I went with him once out of pure boredom, but I don't like opera. I like modern music. Dance music. But opera! What's the good of that? It's loud and so old-fashioned. And it doesn't make sense. He did have an audience, though. The cows all stopped grazing and looked at him with surprise in their big bulging eyes. They even approached him and stood in a semicircle around him while they were chewing.'

'Do you think cows like opera?'

'I wouldn't be surprised. Cows!' she snorted. 'That's about the level of interest he's capable of awakening. Anyway,' she continued with a vengeful expression on her face, 'on his last evening he was chased by a bull. He escaped, but got lost in the mountains and spent the night shivering up a slope. We set off a day late as a result, and that's why I was late for work.'

'Hey,' asked Lottie, 'and what's happened to your great affair? You know . . . your brother-in-law. He must have had a quiet time these last few weeks?' She laughed shrilly, like a whinnying horse.

'Daniel? I'm going to see him today. Oh, I can't wait. All these weeks of pent-up feelings. You can't imagine how frustrated I felt when I thought of him up there in that chalet. What a waste of time! But I'm determined to catch up. I hope he's saved up. It'll be double and triple portions from now onwards!'

20

The day after Anton's departure Gael cleaned the house that had been their lovers' nest for four short days, and by midday she was ready. She was not looking forward to facing Trevor and his parents, but she forced herself to do what could no longer be put off.

It's up to me to know and decide what I want, she thought, trying to give herself courage as she drove along slowly. But I must tell the truth to Trevor. I owe it to him.

It was early evening by the time she turned into the drive that led to the big house. There seemed to be no one around, but as she entered the hall she bumped into Trevor.

'So there you are,' he said as he kissed her on the cheek. 'Late as ever. You must learn to be more punctual, my girl. We expected you yesterday . . . to celebrate our engagement, you know. I had the ring ready.' He tried to sound light-hearted but she felt he was very displeased. Then he added: 'You'll have some explaining to do to the Mater.'

Gael did not seem to show any remorse. Instead, she said with great urgency: 'Could we go outside for a few minutes? Walk to the pond or somewhere? There's something I must tell you . . .'

'Can't it wait till after supper? I've still got to change, and . . .'

'No, it can't wait!' There was a firmness in Gael's voice that made Trevor look up.

'All right, all right. No need to get on your high horse.' He seemed surprised by her unexpected recalcitrance. 'If you must talk, do so by all means, old girl. But don't be too long.'

'So I mustn't be too long . . . all right.' She looked him straight in the eye and said: 'Trevor, I can't marry you.'

'Don't be ridiculous! I know women are prone to nerves before the great day. But you mustn't be frightened. Everything will be fine, dear.'

'But I'm not frightened! I'm just trying to tell you that I can't marry you.'

'I won't accept it!' Trevor's face had hardened, and his lips had tightened. 'You will have to give a valid reason for refusing me! What exactly do you mean by "I can't"? Can you explain yourself more clearly, please?' His voice sounded admonitory, as if he were speaking to a stubborn child that needed to learn to act within the confines of the law.

Suddenly Gael felt very annoyed with Trevor, and she blurted out in a defiant voice: 'I can't marry you because I belong to someone else. I love another man. There! Now you know why. Have I explained myself clearly enough this time?'

'What!' Trevor's face went pale and anger flashed in his eyes. 'You have dishonoured me! When I've always respected you. How could you?' And without further ado he turned away and stormed into the house.

By suppertime the whole household knew. Trevor had not come down. 'He doesn't feel well,' his mother explained, giving Gael an icy look.

The supper that followed was the worst of Gael's life. A funeral would have appeared lively in comparison. Conversation was limited to 'Can you pass me the salt, please,' and other such cheerful exchanges. Every now and then Gael's father sighed deeply, while Trevor's father coughed a couple of times to brighten up the atmosphere. Worst of all were the women. Trevor's mother resembled a vengeful Greek goddess, her mouth drawn in a thin line, and her eyes like cold steel. Gael's own mother didn't even try to participate. She barely touched her food and looked pale and drawn. When the dessert was brought in, a big cake in the shape of two intertwined hearts, she broke down and rushed out of the dining room. The meal ended in confusion after that. The ordeal over, Gael withdrew immediately to her room. She left early next morning without so much as a cup of tea, and set off for London to follow another two weeks of her reflexology course.

21

Anton's poem:

Summer Fields

I shall sing and I shall dance
till the moon is full again,
till like an enchanted flower
you come back to me again.

On the fields is still the shadow
that a bird's song threw on them
when they were so full of flowers
on the day we lay in them.

Never was your smile so sunny,
never were your eyes so bright,
like blue cornflowers reflecting
a part of the golden shining light.

Silence filled the afternoon,
was woven in the ripened fields;
like a string of coloured flowers
summer lay over the hills.

Now you've gone but there's a longing
for the touch of gentle hands,
for the scent of those wild flowers
and the warmth of summer lands.

After he had returned from England, Anton was bursting with energy. He had never felt so well in his life. For months his scientific work seemed to have remained stuck in a quagmire. Solving the problem on which he had been working for the last years – the creation of a mobile detector for discovering deposits of special metals – seemed beyond his capacity. Maybe it was simply a pipedream, an undertaking that was scientifically impossible.

But now, to his amazement, he found that every morning as he woke up, new ideas came tumbling out of his mind. He seemed to be guided by some supernatural inspiration. Yes, he would reflect, this ought to work. It's really simple. Why didn't I think of it before? All the obstacles that had loomed so large for many months gradually melted away and, one after the other, the pieces of the puzzle began to fit together.

The lab was very quiet now that most people were away on holiday. Anton was free to do as he liked, and he clocked up weeks of eighty hours and more, and enjoyed every moment of it. Sometimes he was still busy in the workshop after midnight, testing bits and pieces of electronic equipment and adding them little by little to his detector. It felt like the conception of a new life, and as he saw his detector grow he became increasingly excited. By the end of July he had completed his special miniaturised echolocation system and took it home to his parents' garage where he began installing it in his Land-Rover. Then he started writing the computer programs that would analyse and interpret the data. Another few weeks of this, he noted with surprise and satisfaction, and everything will be ready.

22

When Gael finished her course she felt relieved. She would only have to return once more at the end of August, and then she would be a full member of the British Reflexology Association and be allowed to practise her new skills.

As she was driving towards Dover it suddenly dawned on her that this was the first time she had ever wanted to leave England and cross the Channel. But so great was the urge to be with Anton again that nothing else mattered. She kept hurrying as if pulled by an invisible string from over the sea.

She had been home for no more than a few hours when she realised she would no longer be able to live with her parents. Her father just said 'hello' when she arrived and then quickly withdrew to his study, but her mother wouldn't stop hurling abuse at her.

'How could you have done such a thing?' she kept reproaching her. 'Throw yourself at a stranger when you had promised to become Trevor's wife? After he did you the honour of proposing! His mother no longer speaks to me. You've ruined my life forever!' Whereupon she sat down, her head buried in her hands.

Then she flared up again: 'You must be mad! Haven't you got any sense in that head of yours? Everything was so nicely arranged. And look what you've done! How could you? You'll come to regret this, my girl! That man will soon abandon you for another, and then you'll bitterly regret this!' And between these accusations she ticked her off for all kinds of imaginary faults, as if she were a badly behaved child needing constant correction.

When Anton saw her the next day he couldn't fail to notice how unhappy she looked. He took her in his arms and simply said: 'What's happened? Come on, out with it!'

She had made up her mind not to burden him with her troubles, but when he held her tight, her unhappiness overflowed, and between sobs she began to tell him. And once she had started, it all poured out like a great flood: Trevor; what had happened in England; how upset her parents were with her . . . 'And now I've no longer got a home . . .' she finished, looking completely desolate.

'But you *do* have somewhere to live!' exclaimed Anton. 'My room is yours. I know that it's an ugly little room, but I'm sure you can easily make it look more attractive. If you'll accept, it'll be our home until we find a better place . . .'

She returned to her parents' house the same day, packed a few essential belongings in a suitcase and moved in with Anton. It was the first time she had ever lived away from her parents.

They spent a few happy weeks together in the little room and then, towards the end of August, she left for England to complete the last week of her course.

23

'There's not a word coming out of you this morning,' said Lottie. 'What's wrong with you?'

'There's nothing wrong with me!' retorted Pauline.

'Well, you look as if you'd drunk a pint of vinegar.'

Pauline didn't reply. For a while she continued to thumb the buttons on her scanning table with vicious movements. Then she blurted out: 'It's all their fault! Damned cat of a sister. And that awful husband of hers. He's the worst of them all!'

'Daniel? I thought you liked him? Adored him? Not so long ago you were simply praising him up to the skies. What a good lover he was . . . how well you hit it off . . .'

'You stop it, will you!' interrupted Pauline sharply. 'Don't you dare pronounce the name of that bastard again in my presence.'

'I don't understand,' muttered Lottie. 'Wasn't Dani . . . sorry, that bastard, the one who made you scream with pleasure? The one you couldn't get enough of? Every day you had to have him! Two, no, three times in a row he did it. Superbastard . . . I mean, superman!'

'That's all finished.' Pauline's face looked like thunder.

'But why? Was it too much strain? You couldn't keep up?'

'Don't be stupid! It's him . . . he couldn't keep it up! His balls cracked under the strain.'

'What!' Lottie began to chuckle and her whole body seemed to go into spasms of laughter. 'No ammunition left . . . hahaha.'

'Don't laugh! It was no joke. Two days ago he woke up at home and found that his testicles had swollen to the size of small footballs. He couldn't go to work like that! They had to call in an ambulance and he was rushed into intensive care. The doctor concluded that it was a case of extreme overexertion and prescribed a few months of absolute rest without any sex . . .'

'So it's going to be a quiet period for you?'

'Quiet period, my foot! There's a hurricane blowing. And all because of that cat of a sister. When the doctor sort of accused her, telling her that her husband needed a quieter sex life, she flared up, saying that if he went to bed with her twice or three times a month, she could count herself lucky. The doctor wouldn't believe her. He didn't call her a liar straight to her face, but he snorted, saying that two or three times a day was more like it. That kind of set her thinking. She remembered how I had danced with him at my birthday party, and that he'd always found excuses every time she'd suggested visiting us since. Also, he was often away on work assignments, or so he had claimed. But after what happened she decided to ring up his work and found out that it was all a lie. She ended by putting two and two together, picked up the phone and began to shout insults at me . . .'

'Gosh!' interrupted Lottie. 'How did you get out of that?'

'I denied it all! What else could I do? But she put the pressure on her husband and what with the state he was in, heavily drugged and all that, he caved in and admitted everything, putting all the blame on me. Pretending he was the poor innocent victim and that I had seduced him! That I was an impossibly demanding woman, forcing him to perform! Would you believe it? The monstrous pig! How could he? After all I've done for him. But that's men for you.' She slammed her thumb on one of the buttons, pressing it furiously, repeating: 'Horrible, horrible pig!' until the button nearly broke under the strain. 'And you know what he told my sister? He told her that he had wanted to end the affair a long time ago, but that he hadn't dared because I had threatened to make a big stink and tell her everything if he did. Think of that. The lying pig!'

'So your sister has blown a fuse?'

'And that's not the end of it. She told my husband!'

'So the great Raymondo knows, too!' exclaimed Lottie who seemed to be fully enjoying the latest developments.

'Yes.' Pauline sighed. 'He is still debating whether or not to throw me out . . .'

'Let him throw you out! Good riddance I would say. Such a ponderous, deadly serious fellow. Years older than you. Cares for nothing but singing arias from stuffy old operas. No fun for a girl. I wouldn't trouble myself with a man like that – wouldn't want him if they offered him on a silver platter. Now, my Eddy, he is fun. Plays the guitar; sings love songs to me. We have wonderful evenings together laughing about silly things. But your Raymondo? Why do you care for such a dull husband? I've never understood what you could possibly see in him.'

'You wouldn't, would you? You, who have always been spoiled, always had enough of everything!'

'I don't see what you're aiming at. You're turning very unpleasant.'

'Unpleasant!' Pauline snorted. 'You don't know what it is like when the other girls at school have nice clothes, go off on holidays with their parents, have everything . . . the rich spoiled bitches!' She sounded very resentful. 'While you have nothing but worn second-hand clothes, never a holiday and very few friends at school because you live in a poor neighbourhood. All that because your father ran away when you were a child, and your mother has to do cleaning work to keep her two daughters alive!'

'My, oh my! I . . . I didn't realise . . .'

'I had the intellectual capacity to study,' went on Pauline with bitterness in her voice. 'I wanted to study literature. But there was no money, and not the slightest hope I would ever get out of the hole we lived in, in Brussels.' She sat there for a few seconds while long-suppressed painful images of her youth came to life again. 'And then, one day, I met this man and he took pity on me. He wanted to save me. I was such an innocent, pretty girl, he said. He was years older than me, but I had only one idea: to get away from the awful situation in which fate had put me, whatever the cost. He came from a wealthy old family and married me against the wishes of his parents. He has been my security ever since. He dotes on me and gives me everything I want.'

'I am sorry,' mumbled Lottie. 'So what are you going to do now?'

'I want to keep my husband. I'll deny everything. He'll believe me. He's never liked my sister.'

'So no more affairs?'

'You must be joking! I need something spicy to look forward to. I need men . . . but I'll have to be very careful in the future. I'll have to find myself a quiet, unmarried man.'

24

'I've been thinking about your problems,' said Lottie the next day.

'Well, I'm sure that's really going to help.' Pauline's voice sounded unmistakably sarcastic, but any sarcasm was wasted on Lottie. She always continued with her own train of thoughts.

'Yes. And you know what you are?'

'I may have some vague idea about that after twenty-nine years, but do tell me if you like . . .'

'You're a loser.'

'What! Let me tell you that I haven't lost my husband. I made up a story about my sister, about how jealous she was of our perfect marriage. I told Raymond that she had always wanted a nice, quiet husband like him, but that her own husband was an impossible man, always running off to other women. That she couldn't stand it any longer, and had decided to do all she could to try and separate us out of pure spite. I cried a good deal on his shoulder. Said how unhappy I would be if he left me. And he believed me. Overflowed with apologies in the end.' She looked triumphantly at Lottie. 'So there! I'm a winner.'

'No, you're not! Keeping a husband like your Raymondo is no great feat. Anyone could do that. But you weren't even able to get Anton.'

Pauline shook her head in pity. 'You know . . .' She lowered her voice and approached Lottie's ear: 'If you ask me, I don't think he's really a man. I doubt whether he's capable of . . . you know what I mean . . .'

'But that's completely wrong! I saw him the other evening when I was walking to my car. Arm in arm with a girl!' Lottie's eyes shone. 'And very pretty she was, too. All fair. You should have seen them. They looked so happy. And just as they arrived at the house where he has a room, I passed them and he didn't even see me. He only had eyes for the girl. He took her by the hand and pulled her inside. I heard them laugh as the door shut behind them.' She looked triumphantly at Pauline.

'You don't say!' For once Pauline seemed to have lost her cocksureness. 'Who would ever have believed that he takes girls to his room. The sneaky devil! Is it really true? I haven't noticed anything.'

'Of course you wouldn't have noticed anything,' sneered Lottie. 'You were too busy with your Daniel to have eyes for anything else, weren't you? And see the mess it's got you into? Serves you right!'

Pauline didn't reply but sat there as if lost in thought. Then she exclaimed suddenly: 'But that changes everything!'

'What changes everything?'

'That he's for women after all.' She suddenly brightened up. 'That would solve all my problems. He's unmarried and he would certainly keep quiet about our affair.'

'Your affair!' Lottie snorted. 'Put it out of your head. You'll never get him.'

'And may I ask you why not?' Pauline drew herself up and gave Lottie a cold look.

'Because he's like me.'

'He's like you?' Pauline stared at her companion with disbelief. Lottie was dressed in frilly romantic clothes and had a daft expression on her pretty face. Pauline didn't see much likeness, apart maybe from the daft expression.

'Well yes . . . we're both the faithful type. I'm happy with my Eddy and don't want any other. And he's in love with that girl, I can tell you, because only faithful love makes people really happy. So, however much you try, you won't stand a chance.' She defiantly stuck out her chin.

'What do you bet?'

'I'm no longer betting with you. You don't pay up.'

'All right. Then I'll do it just to prove that you're wrong. You know what? I'll go and ring his bell. Where exactly does he live?'

'In the street just round the corner. In that blue-painted house. But you can ring his bell as much as you like, it won't get you anywhere.'

'We'll see,' replied Pauline brazenly. And she started scanning her satellite pictures, keying in the information with a determined expression on her tanned face.

25

Sitting in the early train from London back to Brussels, Gael was unable to read the book lying open on her lap. She felt too excited thinking of how surprised Anton would be. He didn't expect her back until tomorrow but then . . . the week had been long and her presence on the last day wasn't really essential – there was only an end-of-course party for all the students.

Anton had given her a poem when she left Brussels. She had been reading it every day, and longed to be back in their room.

Anton's poem:

Early Mornings

The early mornings
with their early noises:
cars in the streets
and voices in the other rooms,
while slowly I wake up
between the white of the sheets
where you have left your warmth
and the scent of your body.

Your smile is on the pillow.
If I stretch out my hand
I'm sure I can touch you.

Your laughter is in the air,
and the echo of your voice.

Your wavy golden hair
is woven in the blanket.

Your footprints are on the floor,
your jewels hanging on a chair,
and, in a corner, one of your skirts.

You've gone into the noisy streets
and the dim light of early morning,
but in the silence of this room
you are everywhere.

26

Around eight thirty in the morning Pauline advanced along the pavement in her high-heeled shoes, dressed in a miniskirt and a light blouse that showed her firm breasts. A man who passed her turned his head, unable to keep his eyes off her long shapely legs, but she paid him no attention: she was concentrating on what she was going to say and do. She stopped in front of the house Lottie had described, looked at the names on the bells, and found Anton's. Then, just as she was about to press the bell, the front door opened and a middle-aged man appeared, ready to go out. A waft of Magie Noire, Pauline's perfume, hit the man's nostrils and before he realised what he was doing, he stepped out of the way and motioned her to enter the house, almost bowing low. Pauline bestowed her most engaging smile on him and as she lifted a leg to put her foot on the doorstep, the man gasped and nearly turned to follow her inside. Then, with a superhuman effort, he controlled himself, looked at his watch, and strode rapidly away along the street.

Now that she found herself so unexpectedly inside, Pauline had no idea what to do. She checked the doors on the ground floor first, then she went hesitantly up the stairs and her eyes quickly scanned the names there until she found Anton's. For a moment or two she stood immobile in front of his closed door. Was he still asleep? Or much worse: what if the girl Lottie had seen him with was in bed with him? She no longer felt so sure of herself. Maybe she'd better turn back and drop the whole thing.

Finally she made up her mind and knocked softly on the door. There was no answer and she knocked again, a bit louder this time. Then she crouched to look inside through the old-fashioned keyhole, and, as she steadied her hand on the handle, it moved, the door flew open and she fell flat on her face inside the room. She got to her feet, flustered, and then realised that Anton wasn't there.

'Damn, damn!' she swore to herself. All this effort for nothing. Dressing up, putting on pretty lingerie and using her expensive perfume. She fumed. Then, as her eyes went round the room, she noticed some photographs stuck to the wall, and loathing came into her eyes. That must be that stupid girl, she thought. How can he possibly be interested in such a childish grinning face? No sex appeal. Just fluffy hair and an ethereal look in her big silly eyes. And that's what he falls for. Men are hopeless!

And the state this room was in! Clothes were lying everywhere, even a skirt! The room could do with a good tidying-up. That Anton needed a real woman to keep everything in order. She walked over to his cupboard and peeped inside. There were woman's clothes in there, too!

She turned in disgust, went to the window and stared at the street below. As she did so she saw a fair-haired girl approaching on the opposite pavement, about to cross the street.

At once a diabolical plan formed in her mind. Quick, quick, she thought. I'm sure I can pull it off.

27

Gael had parked her car near the lab and walked light-footed, almost skipping, to the house where she now lived with Anton. He always got up late, and she would slip quietly into his room and kiss him while he was still asleep. She imagined the look of utter surprise on his loved face and then the joy, the glory, as he folded his arms around her. And they would laugh and laugh . . .

She reached the house, let herself in with the key Anton had given her and silently slipped upstairs. It was then that her acute sixth sense picked up a disturbing sensation. There was a malevolent atmosphere in the house, and she hesitated halfway up, her hand on the banister. Her intuition was warning her to turn back. It was as if a red signal flashed up, telling her not to go any further.

No, she decided, this is ridiculous. I haven't come all the way from London to turn back at the last second. No, nothing can go wrong. And she continued slowly, quietly up the stairs and into the corridor to their room.

When she got close she seemed to hear voices. Then she noticed that the door was ajar and heard a woman speak. She advanced like a moth drawn towards a bright light, till she stood in front of the crack and peered inside. From where she stood she couldn't see the bed or Anton, but she observed, not four feet away, a naked woman. Suddenly the woman turned her head and Gael quickly withdrew. Had she seen her? Then she heard the woman say in a sexy voice: 'Oh Anton, you're such a marvellous lover. Shall we do it once more?'

Gael's hand swung to her mouth to stifle the cry that escaped from it. Her blood started throbbing in her ears, hot flames of disgust shot through her head and she began to tremble. Then she turned around and rushed down the stairs in a daze, slammed the front door and ran along the street blinded by the tears that streamed from her eyes.

28

Pauline was extremely pleased with herself. What a quick-witted mind is capable of doing, she thought. How clever I was to think of saying what a marvellous lover he was. That finished her off! As she heard the door slam downstairs she looked out of the window and saw the girl run away. 'Goodbye,' she said, a look of satisfaction on her face as she followed the rapidly retreating shape of the girl until it disappeared around the corner. 'I don't think that one will come back,' she congratulated herself. 'The coast is clear now.'

Then she turned her attention to the room. Just look at this, she thought as she stared again at the photographs of the girl. That stupid girl! Love and happiness. Pfft! And it took all her self-control not to snatch the pictures off the wall and tear them up.

What shall I do now? she pondered. Shall I wait for him here? She stood there for a few minutes, looking out of the window, undecided, when she noticed Anton, appearing round the street corner with a shopping bag and a long French baguette under his arm. So that's where he's been, she thought. To the bakery.

Suddenly she made up her mind: if he finds me here and realises what I've done, he won't be pleased. He can be such a donkey! Much better that he doesn't know anything. The girl will break off the relationship, and soon I'll have him crying in my arms. But I must leave him some time.

She dressed quickly and just as she pulled the door of his room shut and rushed up to the top floor to hide, she heard Anton come in and walk up the stairs, whistling to himself.

29

'I saw Anton pass by a few minutes ago,' said Lottie later in the morning when she was sitting next to Pauline at the scanning tables. 'And he didn't seem to be in a state of shock.'

'Why should he?'

'Well . . . didn't you say yesterday that you were going to ring his bell and let all your charms loose on him?'

'If you really want to know, I did go to his house this morning . . .'

'And that's all the effect it's had?' interrupted Lottie mockingly. 'Oh I know . . . maybe he isn't yet aware of the spell you have cast on him. Maybe you're like those bombs . . . now, what are they called again? They don't go off immediately. They produce . . . that's it . . . they produce deranged action!'

Pauline shook her head in pity. 'You mean delayed action.'

'That's what I said! He doesn't yet realise what you've done.' She laughed out loud. 'The shock will come later, but when it comes, *oh là là!*' She vigorously shook her hand *à la française* with her fingers spread out.

You couldn't be more right, reflected Pauline. Then she looked again at Lottie's jeering face and felt stung. Idiot! she thought. I'll tell you what's happened. That'll shut you up! She opened her mouth, ready to boast about her triumph, but held back. No, maybe it's better not to say anything, she pondered. The little chatterbox would waste no time telling everyone what I've done. The news would soon get to Anton's ears and all my plans would be ruined.

She quickly made up her mind and spoke in an absent-minded way: 'If you really want to know, I intended to ring his bell, but as I walked along I thought better of it. I'm not interested. After all, there are other, much more fascinating men around.'

'I told you it was useless, didn't I?' Lottie hurled the words at Pauline who sat there in silence, biting her lip in her effort to shut up. 'Good! For once you listened to what I said and gave up. I told you seduction isn't everything. It will never triumph over real love.' And as she spoke these last solemn words, Lottie looked mighty pleased with herself.

You believe whatever you like, you dumb blonde, thought Pauline. But we'll see who has the last laugh.

30

After she fled from Anton's room, Gael drove straight to her parents' house and broke down in front of her mother, blurting out everything about Anton and the naked woman. Then she rushed up and shut herself up in her room.

Extract from Gael's notebooks:

Wednesday. Tonight my heart is dark with the ashes of our love. How could you have let a vile woman enter where only I belonged, and desecrate the room and the bed where we loved? When I saw that woman my world crumbled. In one moment she tore down our dream castle and wiped out my faith in love. How could you have done this, Anton?

[. . .]

Thursday. I gave you all I cherished in life: my dreamland of adventure; my inner joy and the roses of my garden growing wild with love. Now I'm one of those lifeless, empty shells, left stranded among the pebbles high upon the beach when the sea has retreated. Why did I need to look so high? Why did I have to reach for the sky? I will never, ever search for another one to walk this shining path of love together.

[. . .]

Friday. How terrible to have felt so much one with you and now to be so incomplete. It is frightening. All is darkness without you. How can I retrieve the pieces of my broken heart? I could easily go beyond the gates of life on this earth. If you no longer care, there is no reason for me to stay.
[...]
Saturday. There is a strange, dull ache that clings to me through the silent days. The days turn into nights and the nights bring no oblivion, only shadows, grey, shapeless and viscous, that surround my heart.
[...]
Sunday. Lonely nights have come, long hours of sleepless torment. How my eyes have learned to cry. Something evil lies encroached in my flesh. Why did this wicked woman have to worm her way into our lives? Why was this forced upon us?
[...]
Monday night. From the depths there rose a tide of anguish until all seemed to break inside and great waves welled up and overflowed in streams of rolling tears, purging me of all illusions. Only weakness and change are to be found in men. The love that I believed in, fool that I am, this word that means heaven, only exists in my mind. Just forget the dreams now and cry alone in the night.
[...]
Tuesday. I fight no more. I feel I can never believe again. Sad, sad is the day that killed our love.
[...]
Wednesday. There is a wound in my heart that will not heal. Every breath is painful and inside me a sickness is spreading that is slowly numbing my whole body and mind. I am so weak that I can hardly stand up.

Several times a day during that week Gael's mother had implored her to come out of her room, had brought up food, but her daughter just remained locked inside. In the end the mother feared that she might die. Then, unexpectedly, Gael came down and her mother was so relieved that she no longer even thought of scolding her. The situation seemed to have returned to normal: through a great effort of will-power Gael managed not to show any of her anguish; and her mother no longer criticised her. But the strong bond that had always united them, the tacit understanding, had gone.

31

On the Thursday when Gael was supposed to have returned from London, Anton had asked for a day off and was waiting for her in his room. The coffee was percolating, its aroma filled the room and his heart was full of expectation.

By eleven he had finished laying out the table and putting candles around the plates – Gael loved candles – and begun to prepare a small meal. By midday everything was ready and he listened anxiously for her step on the stairs but she hadn't come. He waited through the long hours of the afternoon and well into the evening. Had she been delayed? He lay awake for hours that night and then slept in fits and starts.

He had to go to work the next day but had pinned a message above the table in his room in case she arrived. 'I love you', the message said, and underneath: 'Waiting for your smile to cheer me.' At noon he rushed over to his room but she hadn't come, and when the day was over and she still wasn't there, waves of panic welled up in him. He had been unable to sleep after that and tossed and turned until a bleak light announced the breaking of a grey day.

Extracts from Anton's writings:

Saturday evening. I've been sitting in my room the whole day, trying to ring you on your mobile but it seems to be switched off. Ten, twenty times I walked to the window to look out into the street below, hoping to see your car but the hours passed by very slowly. Yet I keep hoping.

[. . .]

Sunday evening at my parents. I went for a walk to calm my feverish brain. All around me I felt the peace of the expanse of heather and smelled the scent of pinewoods. For a long time I looked at the lighter patch in the western sky where the sun had just gone down. Are you still in England and are you, too, watching the sunset?

[. . .]

Monday. As I drove to town my heart was filled with expectation. Will you be back today?

It is evening now and you have not come. Every nerve of my body is longing for you so much that my skin almost aches.
[. . .]

Wednesday. I saw your car in one of the side streets near the lab and my heart almost stopped. But of course it wasn't your car.

I can't understand the mystery of your disappearance. How can I find out what's happened? You never gave me your address.
[. . .]

Friday. The most horrible week of the year! Day after day I've tried to call you, but you seem to have vanished from the Earth. I'm frantic with worry. I'm so very tired and cannot sleep. Life no longer has any sense. This uncertainty is killing me.

Days of despair, days of bitterness. Who would have expected this, when the air is heavy with summer? How empty Brussels is without you! I feel utterly alone.
[. . .]

Another evening of terrible loneliness. This night the rain has started falling, rain, rain, endless rain, dull and dreary like my heart, washing everything away. An unending wheel of sadness has begun to turn inside me.

32

Anton sat staring out of the window of his office when there was a knock on his door. As he said, 'Come in,' the door opened slowly and Pauline's head appeared in the opening. She gave him a warm, sympathetic smile and then proposed in her sweetest voice:

'Is there anything you'd like me to do for you?'

He gave her a brief look, mumbled a 'No thank you,' and motioned her to go with a wave of his hand.

'But . . . but . . . you're so quiet these days . . .' There was concern in her voice. 'Are you unhappy?' She gazed at him with tenderness.

Suddenly he stared at her with hostile eyes and spoke sharply: 'Would you please mind your own business?'

'Well,' she insisted, 'if there's anything I can do for you, just tell me.'

'I told you I don't need anything.' His voice sounded barely civil. 'Just shut the door behind you, that's all.'

When she had shut the door, the expression on her face changed. I'll get you! she thought. No man I've set my sights on has ever resisted me for long, and you'll be no exception. You'll end up in my arms and then I'll teach you!

33

Gael was in limbo. Sooner or later she would have to go somewhere else. On no account did she want to stay in Brussels where she risked running into Anton. She must leave Belgium. For a while she thought of going to England but somehow the idea no longer appealed to her. England was where Trevor lived, and where she had been so happy for a few short days in July. No, she wanted to be far away from anything that reminded her of Anton. To start anew without any links with the past.

And then she remembered Dr Wilbert. She had met him last December at that medical convention where he had talked so enthusiastically about his involvement in medical projects in Africa.

For a couple of weeks after that meeting she had played with the idea of going to Africa. Then she had gone over to England to spend Christmas with Trevor's parents and to her surprise Trevor had asked her to marry him. She had said 'yes' and had forgotten all about Africa.

But she still had Dr Wilbert's card. She found it and made an appointment. The next morning she was talking to him, forcing herself to be cheerful and interested.

'So you have done some first-aid training,' he said. 'And you've also completed a training course in London. Hmm . . . all very good.' He picked up a list and started scanning through it. 'There are several possibilities . . . all in relatively safe spots. But you'll have to wait a couple of months for a place to become vacant.' He looked at her with questioning eyes.

She didn't want to wait a couple of months. She wanted to go now and told him so.

'In that case there's only one possibility. I'll have to send you to our project near Bobodiou.' He said it mockingly.

'Why is that?'

'Because we've been waiting for a whole year to fill the post of assistant there.'

'Doesn't anyone want the job?'

'No. You see . . . it's an unstable country – much too dangerous. And I don't think you would want to go there either.'

'I don't mind,' she objected. 'I'm a tough girl. Have you got a contract? I'll sign it now.'

He looked at her with undisguised admiration. Such a slender young woman. And so brave!

'Right!' he said. 'Phone back tomorrow. Be ready to leave within a few days.'

34

Do women have a sixth sense? wondered Anton. Time and again these last two weeks he had run into Pauline. He hadn't seen much of her during the past six months and that had been a relief, but now they would bump into each other at least three or four times a day. She seemed to have changed, though. She was no longer pushy or obnoxious in any way. She just appeared to be concerned about his well-being and smiled encouragingly at him every time he passed her in the corridor.

Lately she had got into the habit of sticking her head inside his office to inquire whether he was all right and if there was anything she could do for him. Once she had even brought up a cup of coffee when he hadn't gone down for the coffee break.

He'd rather she left him alone, but after he had been so rude to her some time ago he hesitated to send her away again. After all, it wasn't her fault that he was so unhappy, and there was no reason to hurt her. He was sure she had the best of intentions, but he didn't want to be consoled by Pauline, or by anyone else for that matter. He just wanted to be left in peace. Only one girl could make him smile again, and that girl had mysteriously disappeared from his life.

35

Gael's poem:

Illusions

Illusions . . .
like multi-coloured bubbles
floating in the air . . .
I so admired the sparkling,
I so desired the warmth.

And then,
in front of my very eyes,
they burst
scattering sticky droplets
all over my face.

Illusions . . .
blurred reflections
of images from my youth.
So many things
I always dreamed of.

And then
the dreams were broken,
and the pieces
carried away
by the wind.

Illusions . . .
the world we shared
collapsed around me
and now I'm left behind in darkness
where there's no place for love . . .

Extracts from Gael's notebooks:

Now comes the time when I must think of things I've never had to face before. I stand at the frontier of a new world and have to enter it, alone with my thoughts and this great pain.

I have bought a ticket with no return. I will leave this place to fight somewhere else, far away from you, Anton.

As Gael was packing her clothes, a few books and some photographs into a small suitcase, she felt a great sense of relief. Today she would be away from it all. No more fear of running into him. No more illusions. Just doing good work. That was the life she had dreamed of in her youth; that's what she should always have chosen. The short period of knowing Anton had been no more than an interlude. It hadn't been real. Now her real life was about to start. Her days would be filled with work; it would be hot, there would be many discomforts, but she wouldn't mind. She could see herself going on her daily rounds through the villages. The people would surround her when she arrived, and she would help to save them. But she would be more than just useful: she would love those people and in turn be loved by them.

When she was sitting in the taxi that took her to the office of the aid organisation where Dr Wilbert was waiting to give her his final instructions and some parcels for the project, her spirit lifted. Tomorrow she would be in Africa.

Part Three

1

These last days, when Pauline passed Anton's office and saw him sitting quite still, staring absent-mindedly out of the window, she felt tenderness well up in her. He looked so forlorn, so vulnerable, and yet impressively beautiful. He was like no other man she knew. There was something indefinable about him, a quality of innocence that he alone seemed to possess. Yes, he was very special. How else could it be that he did not seem to see her, unlike other men she had set out to attract?

She now often found herself daydreaming about him. What he needed was a woman, one who would put her arms around him, in whom he could lose himself, discharge all his pent-up feelings. And she wanted to be that woman. How well they would hit it off together! She would free him from his inhibitions, from his shyness. In her experienced hands he would come to life. What they could do together! He was made for her, she was sure of it. And one day, as she looked at him and felt butterflies move inside her lower belly, she thought: this must be love!

As the days went by she felt ever more drawn to him and yet she didn't know how to approach him. This was a totally new situation for her. Patience, she thought. He isn't ready yet. But she was not one to be patient. If she wanted anything, she wanted it immediately. Having to be patient was torture to her.

After a few weeks she could hardly contain herself. When she dreamed of Anton now she had to exert all her self-control to suppress the intense need for sex that devoured her. At times she felt she was going to explode, especially at night when she lay awake in bed while her husband was peacefully asleep next to her, breathing deeply and regularly. She would fantasise that Anton was lying with her, and when she imagined how she would arouse him and what he would do to her, her whole body would begin to itch with desire. And she would toss and turn, unable to quench the fire that raged inside her.

She couldn't stand this any longer. Tomorrow, she thought. Tomorrow I must risk my all. He must succumb or I'll go crazy!

2

Anton wasn't happy. For weeks now he had been unable to keep his mind on his work and lately he had begun to close the door of his office. Day after day he was just sitting behind his desk, staring out at the small patch of grey sky above the roofs on the other side of the street with eyes that failed to see. His world had disintegrated since Gael had so inexplicably disappeared from his life. And with her had gone those bright endless days without a thought for the morrow.

He forced himself to carry on and, with difficulty, managed to add a line or two to the text he was writing, but within minutes his attention wandered again and he sat staring at his computer screen with blank eyes. Almost without thinking he clicked on to a file labelled Photos, and suddenly there was Gael, standing on the beach with the white cliffs of Dover rising behind her . . . As he zoomed in on her, the picture of Gael filled up his screen. There she was, her eyes shining and a smile like no one else's . . . He stretched his fingers to touch her beloved face but all they touched was the screen. And he repeated the question he had already asked himself a hundred times: 'Why hadn't she come back?'

It had started to rain an hour ago and now it was pouring down. A wild wind blew the rain against the window pane and from there it streamed down in rivulets, blurring the outside world like a wet moving curtain of tears – tears outside, tears in his heart. 'Gael!' he cried. 'Where are you?'

He had been living in a nightmare ever since she had vanished. How could he find her? It was incredible but she had never given him her address. He had tried the phone directories, searched for her name on the Internet, but drawn a blank. Had she died? When he thought of that he became frantic. He felt lost, totally lost.

3

Just then there was a knock on Anton's door and a second later Pauline entered – long legs and a miniskirt as short as could be. Not again, he thought and sighed. What did she want this time?

A strong scent of heavy perfume had wafted in with her and he instinctively recoiled as she came nearer with voluptuous movements, a beguiling smile on her face.

'I just wanted to see how you're feeling this morning,' she said with a voice like honey. 'Here's something to cheer you up.' She put a cup of steaming coffee on his desk and kissed him warmly on one cheek and next on the other.

'Don't you like my kisses?' she asked mischievously when Anton didn't react. 'Aren't they sweet enough? I can do much better. Wait.' And with a quick movement she bent over and kissed him sensually on the lips.

Anton stiffened in his chair and then, abruptly, he pushed her away with such force that she tumbled over the waste-paper basket and landed on her back on the floor. She lay there for a few seconds, an expression of utter surprise on her face, while Anton averted his gaze from her legs. Then she steadied herself on her elbows, crawled up and advanced threateningly towards Anton, wild rage flashing in her eyes.

'You'll pay for this!' she yelled. And with an impetuous gesture she knocked his papers and the cup of steaming coffee off his desk and ran out of his office slamming the door.

4

As she stomped along the corridor, she fumed. She had been so patient. She had gone out of her way to be sweet to him, and he had ignored her. And finally, when she had made up her mind to do him the favour of giving herself to him, he had pushed her onto the floor! Was that all the thanks she got for her efforts?

The ungrateful man! She had wasted her time dreaming of him when she could have had any man she wanted. Three weeks! Bitterness welled up inside her when she thought how pleased other men would have been to hold her in their arms. But that uncouth brute had just shoved her away with disgust on his face when she had offered herself on a silver platter. How dare he!

She felt betrayed. Was it possible that he was still pining for that shit of a girl? You wait! she thought. You wait for what I've got to tell you. She was about to turn back and scream in his face how she had ruined his silly love affair, when she hesitated. No! Better to leave him wondering what had happened. Let him be devoured by uncertainty. That would be much greater torture. It would serve him right. And every time she saw him, sighing and miserable, she would feel great satisfaction.

Then she could contain herself no longer. Revenge! all her thoughts screamed. You'll come to regret this. I'll ruin you! Yes, she would scheme until she brought him down . . . until he came to her crawling on his knees, begging for mercy.

5

Gael had desperately wanted to put as many miles as possible between herself and her past life; to go somewhere out in the bush where no one would ever find her; where she could forget about everything. But when after a long journey the Land-Rover that had picked her up at the airport wheeled into the enclosure of the dispensary of Kanibasso and the African driver dumped her luggage in front of a low adobe house, she was no longer so sure that coming to Africa had been such a good idea. Here she was, in the very place she had agreed to go to, and suddenly she felt lost in this strange new world.

As she was gazing around an older woman came out of the low house, her arms stretched out towards her, exclaiming: 'You must be Gael. Welcome!'

She took Gael by the hand and sat her down on a chair, saying: 'Poor dear. We've been waiting for you for hours. But you've arrived, at last! Oh, by the way, I'm Marie. We're going to live and work together. I hope you won't mind. If at any time you feel bothered by my presence and want peace, just tell me, will you?'

Gael stared at her, somewhat bewildered, and then looked questioningly at her surroundings. 'Where are we?' she asked.

'In the dispensary, of course.'

'I didn't realise. Where are the patients?'

'They've all gone home by now. Don't think about them for the moment. You'll see plenty of them tomorrow.' She chuckled. 'More than you bargained for, I dare say.'

'And . . . and where am I going to live?' The question sounded somewhat abrupt and Gael hastened to add: 'I . . . I feel a bit tired.'

'No need to excuse yourself for that,' replied Marie. 'Of course you're tired. You've come all the way from Brussels. And it's such a long drive from Bobodiou. Right! Pick up your bag and follow me.' And she led the way inside.

Gael hesitated. 'But . . . but you said that this was the dispensary.'

Marie smiled. 'Yes. And our house, too. That's how we live in Africa. There's no money for luxury. Just for the bare essentials. We have to survive on a shoestring budget.'

She led Gael along a corridor to a small room closed off by a curtain. 'Your bedroom,' she said.

Gael looked at it with apprehension. There was a low wooden bedframe on the dirt floor, some crude shelves and a built-in cupboard with curtain. 'And . . . where do I wash?' she inquired shyly.

'Oh! We've got all you need. There's a small hosepipe sticking out of the kitchen wall. You can shower there if you want to.' Marie gave her a good stare. 'Don't look so shocked,' she commented. 'That's more comfort than most Africans have, I can assure you.'

'And . . . and . . .' Gael seemed to hesitate even more, 'where's . . . the loo?'

'Oh that! You go outside for that.' Marie made it sound as if this were the most natural thing in the world.

'Do you . . . do you mean that I have to go and crouch behind a wall?' Gael's voice sounded panicky.

'Of course not!' Marie laughed heartily. 'We do have a toilet. But it is not what you're used to in Europe. It is . . . let's call it . . . French colonial style.'

'Do you mean to say that there's no proper toilet?'

'My dear girl . . .' Marie sounded sarcastic. 'You didn't expect European plumbing and five-star bathrooms in the African bush, did you? Didn't they explain everything to you before you came?'

'No . . . noo . . .'

'All right. I'll show you then.'

They went out to a small adobe outhouse stuck in a corner of the low wall that surrounded the compound.

'Here we are,' said Marie. 'All very private. Away from the main house, and it's even got a wooden door, though it doesn't shut properly. You'd better shout when you approach in case there's someone inside. Loud and clear! Somewhat like this.' She cupped her hands in front of her mouth and produced a loud hoot. 'And if you happen to be inside and you hear someone call, you shout "engaged".'

As no one replied to Marie's hooting sound, she opened the creaky wooden door, which hung limply from its hinges. Inside it was quite dark and the smell was far from pleasant.

'See!' Marie stepped aside to let Gael have a look. 'This is an original colonial-style French toilet.'

Inside the small house a latrine trench had been dug over which two five-inch-wide wooden boards were placed. 'You put one foot on each of these boards,' explained Marie, 'crouch down and aim for the latrine underneath. It's very simple. You'll soon get the hang of it.'

Gael felt slightly nauseated when she looked at the two flat wooden boards, which were about a foot apart, and at the dark smelly pit underneath. She recoiled visibly. 'But . . . you said that this was a French toilet. I've used a French toilet once . . . in an old house in Normandy. It had a proper ceramic base with two places to put your feet on. And it had a chain which you pulled. Mind you, you did have to jump out of the way not to flush your feet!'

'I told you that this is French *colonial* style,' said Marie firmly. 'It's much simpler! It has been adapted to African conditions. No chains . . . no moving parts . . . so it never breaks down.'

'And where's . . . where's the toilet paper?'

'No toilet paper here. Can't find it outside the capital. Remember, we're in the bush here. But there's a tin with water if you want to clean yourself afterwards. Always use your left hand for it, as your right hand is for touching food and shaking hands.'

Gael now looked completely bewildered. 'How deep is that trench underneath?' she asked apprehensively.

'Oh, that could easily be seven or eight feet deep. These trenches have been dug to last a long time before they fill up completely. So, when you go to the loo you'd better make sure you put your feet on the boards and not in between,' commented Marie with a straight face.

Gael shuddered. 'There aren't any other dangers, I hope?'

'Well, you've always got to be careful, of course. Especially at night. Take a torch and look well in the corners of the toilet: there might be scorpions; they like warm places. Snakes have been known to hide there, too. But you'll get used to that. Always carry a stick at night. But enough of little details. Let me show you the more important parts of the house: the kitchen and sitting room.'

After Marie had finished the guided tour of the house she took Gael to her room, saying: 'So, let's recapitulate, because you seem to be worrying. We do have bathroom facilities. The shower is outside the kitchen wall and the toilet is in a corner of the enclosure. When you go out to the toilet at night, it's important to take a firm stick with you and a properly functioning torch. Shout when you approach. Watch out for scorpions and other undesirable creatures that crawl out of the bush at night. Once you're inside and there's no snake hiding in the dark and you've checked that there's water in the tin, be very careful where you put your feet. Put them on the boards, not in between them. Don't ever slide down into the latrine pit underneath because you're not going to like it. You're not very tall and I can't guarantee that your head will stick out above the mess.'

And at that she turned and went, leaving Gael gaping.

6

A few days later the two women were seated on a couple of reclining chairs made from welded pipes, sipping a glass of boiled water, when Marie suddenly chuckled. 'The other day, when I showed you the toilet, I told you that African loos never break down . . . well, that's not quite true.'

'I can't really see what could break down,' replied Gael, confused.

'No? Let me tell you then.' Marie made herself as comfortable as possible in her iron chair, settled a cushion behind her back, and began.

'It happened many years ago when I was a young girl of about your age. I was just married and had joined my husband who was working in one of the African colonies. Those were the dying years of the French Empire but, still, they deemed it wise to send us a new District Officer, fresh from the Colonial Institute. You should have seen him when he arrived: impeccably dressed in his uniform, his shoes shining, proud of himself, cocksure. The local expatriates had organised a welcome party and were going to offer him a lunch befitting his rank. And when asked what he wanted to eat, guess what he asked for?'

'I can't imagine,' replied Gael, all ears. 'Something very French? Snails?'

'Tuna steak he wanted.' Marie let out a deep snort. 'Tuna steak! A thousand miles from the sea! The Europeans all got into a terrible state but the African cook, resourceful as ever, had a solution. A big python had just been caught and he assured everyone that, prepared the right way, the important Bwana wouldn't be able to tell the difference.'

'And did he?' asked Gael.

'He thoroughly enjoyed his meal! So much so that he asked to see the cook, wanting to congratulate him. And when the African was brought along and the DO inquired if there was any tuna left, the man was so pleased that he said: "At your service, Bwana. Come along." And before anyone had time to stop him, the cook led the DO outside, saying: "I'll cut some more for you. There's another twelve feet of it just lying behind the shed." When the young administrator saw the bloody leftovers of the giant python – quite impressive they were – he became violently ill. His face turned white and he began to vomit and asked for a toilet. He was rushed to one of those outdoor houses, exactly like ours, and had only just disappeared inside when we heard a terrific cracking noise as of breaking wood, immediately followed by the most awful collection of French swear words. Moments later the young administrator crawled out of the toilet in front of a spellbound audience. He was covered in excrement. It appeared that one of the two footrests had been rotten and had given way under the jerky movements of his violent vomiting.'

'No! What happened next?'

'I don't really know. My husband immediately led me away. First the swearing, and now this! It was not what well-brought-up young women should be exposed to, he claimed. But I really enjoyed everything tremendously.'

'Did you tell him?'

'Of course not! It's no good telling husbands what they don't want to hear.' She laughed heartily. 'I learned afterwards that they had to take the poor man to the local cleaners – meaning the open-air washing place along the river – where he was thoroughly scrubbed by a few Africans, and his clothes washed. I never saw him again. Later I heard that he had gone back to his home country. I think his dignity had suffered irreparable damage. A shame, really, because my instincts told me that he was accident-prone, and we could have done with some fun in that God-forsaken hole where we lived.'

She sighed and sat for a while in silence, no doubt seeing other interesting stories in her mind's eye. Then, almost unwillingly, she got up, looked at Gael and said: 'Come on, let's make supper.'

7

As the days went by Anton sank into a deep depression; he had never been so unhappy in his life. He tried to turn his attention to his work but just wasn't interested. What was the point of sitting in his office pretending he was working? He couldn't stand it any longer. He refused to accept that he would never see Gael again; he had to do something.

Then, suddenly, he had an idea. He went to his director, Mr Briart, and asked him if he could take a few days off. The next morning he took the train to England and went to Deal, the small fishing town near Dover where he had spent four happy days with Gael in July. By late afternoon he stood in front of 40 Duck Street, the small house where they had stayed.

What a difference between July and the end of September! And what a difference these few months had made to his life. Then everything had been bright and beautiful. Now there was nothing left of that sun-drenched summer. Even the weather was in a sombre mood. A cold wind came sweeping in from the sea through the narrow streets, and the grey sky was hanging low over the roofs.

He stood there for some minutes, undecided, looking at the house wondering what to do, when the door of number 42 opened and a platinum-blonde woman of about fifty appeared, dressed in a thick overcoat, a shopping bag in her hand. The mop of unnaturally fair hair struck a chord of remembrance: he had met her once with Gael in one of the side streets. He stepped forward and as he greeted her heartily, she stared at him with only half-disguised suspicion. Then a vague look of recognition came over her face.

'You do remember me, don't you?' Anton asked anxiously.

'I'm sure I've seen you before, young man,' she said hesitantly, 'but I'm not certain when . . .'

'Last July,' said Anton. 'With Gael.'

'Oh yes, of course! That's when I saw you. How is she?'

'I don't know,' replied Anton. 'I had to go abroad and have only just come back. I thought I'd find her here.'

'Oh but you won't!' exclaimed the woman. 'She and her family only come here to spend the summer holidays. Didn't she tell you?'

'Well . . . no. We had just met and then I had to return urgently to . . . to America,' replied Anton, quickly making up a story and trying to speak with an American accent. 'I didn't even have time to say goodbye because you see . . . I had to rush back to America because . . . because my father died. Poor Gael,' he added, seeing the eager look in the woman's eyes. 'I don't know what she must have thought when I disappeared so suddenly.'

'Oh dear,' replied the woman. 'Oh dear. I'm sorry to hear that your father died.' But she looked more thrilled than sorry. She was used to the twists and turns of the romantic soaps she constantly watched on the telly and would have believed any incredible story in which fathers died and young lovers were separated. 'And what happened next?' she asked with barely concealed excitement at the thought that here she was, participating in a real drama herself.

'The burial ceremony was very sad but at the same time very beautiful,' went on Anton, trying not to blush at having to invent such overt lies. 'I intended to come back once everything was finished, to apologise to Gael, but as it happened I had to stay over there to . . . to wind up the family affairs. You see . . . sorting out the inheritance took much longer than I imagined.'

The woman nodded in agreement, understanding fully what that meant. America and a dying father! 'Was there some disagreement about the inheritance?' she asked, her eyes alight with curiosity. 'Excuse my asking you, but . . . was there a lot of money involved?'

'A great deal,' replied Anton, looking away, trying to appear unconcerned. 'But the family lawyers finally managed to settle it all. I came back as soon as I could, and now . . . and now she's no longer here and I haven't even got her address . . .' He turned to the woman with a look of genuine desolation on his face. 'What am I to do?' he asked. 'We got on really well together and I was so looking forward to seeing her again . . . It never occurred to me that she didn't live here.'

'Dear, oh dear!' The woman was visibly impressed by the quantity of money she saw in her mind's eye. But she also felt great pity for this young man who had lost his girl in spite of being so rich.

'You wouldn't have her name and address so that I can go and find her?' Anton asked imploringly.

A smile of sympathy came over the woman's face. This was romance. She could see it in the man's eyes. This was true romance. He, very rich now, but unable to forget Gael, dreaming of her all the time he had to stay in America. And Gael. She liked her a lot. The girl had always been so polite to her. She imagined her at home dreaming of him, wondering what had happened. And they had been separated by a cruel turn of fate!

She made up her mind. From the way the man stood there in front of her like a dog waiting for a bone, she could tell that he counted on her to save their love. Such a well-behaved handsome young man, too. So different from some of the rough fellows she knew around here. Yes, she was going to do what he expected of her. She was going to give fate a hand and help these two lovers to meet again. It needed just that little push, and hers would be the hand to give it!

'I think I've got the address,' she said, smiling benignly on him, and disappeared inside.

She came back after a few minutes with a small piece of paper and handed it to Anton. He took it and read: Gael Fernley, avenue des Hirondelles 84, Brussels.

'Oh, thank you, thank you very much!' he exclaimed. He felt so relieved that he gave the woman a big kiss on both cheeks. Then he turned and rushed off.

A deep blush coloured the woman's face. She straightened her ample bosom, touched the platinum blonde mop of hair that crowned her head, and sighed as she eyed Anton's disappearing shape. If only I were young again, she reflected. The charming men that would fall for me. Then, with a brisk step, she set off on her errand to Doreen's shop. Wait till she hears the story I've got to tell her, she thought. Green with envy Doreen is going to be when she learns what's happened to me. I've played a major part in a love story. I've saved the romance of two young people!

8

Within twenty-four hours Anton was back in Brussels and standing in front of Gael's house. It was a large house surrounded by a hawthorn hedge, and he paused for a while on the opposite pavement. So this is where she lives, he thought, looking at Gael's home with a mixture of tenderness and awe. At last he plucked up enough courage to push open the gate. He walked across the front garden, stepped on to the veranda and hesitantly pressed the bell.

For a while nothing happened and he was about to press the bell again when he heard steps inside. The door opened and a slim, well-dressed woman stood looking at him enquiringly.

Anton had prepared a little speech but when he saw the woman staring at him, he forgot every line of it. He felt his heart beating in his throat and for a moment or two was at a loss for words. Then he blurted out: 'Gael Fernley? She lives here?'

The woman seemed surprised. 'Yes,' she replied after a slight pause. 'Yes, she lives here, but she's not at home.'

'Will she be back later?' Anton's voice sounded strangely choked.

'No.' The woman gave him a stern look. 'Why do you want to know?'

'Oh! I've . . . I met her in England and she gave me her address, so I thought I'd look her up. Are you her mother?'

'Yes.' After a few seconds the woman continued with a touch of mockery in her voice: 'If you want to see her, come back in a year. She's gone to Africa.'

Anton stood there gaping at her, incapable of taking in what Gael's mother had said. Then he stammered: 'But why? Why would she want to go to Africa? I . . . I don't understand.'

Suddenly a look of suspicion shot through the woman's eyes. 'You're not Anton, are you?' she asked bluntly.

'Ye . . . yes, I am,' admitted Anton.

'So it's you!' She stared at him with undisguised antipathy.

'Well . . .' mumbled Anton, not knowing where to look. 'Well yes . . . it's . . . it's me.'

'You!' she hissed. 'It's men like you who destroy happiness. Men like you should be locked up!'

Anton was stunned. 'But I haven't destroyed anything,' he protested feebly.

'How dare you come here after defiling all that's sacred!' the woman exclaimed furiously and attempted to shut the door, but before she could do so Anton had stuck his foot in the entrance.

'Please, please,' he pleaded. 'Tell me where she is, please. Where can I find her?'

The woman seemed extremely upset. 'Will you remove your foot immediately,' she commanded.

'I will do everything you say, but please tell me first what's happened. She's not unwell, is she?'

'Not unwell!' Gael's mother repeated in a voice thick with rage. 'How can you ask such a question when you've broken her heart? When you first seduce my poor innocent child and then abandon her for another woman? You devil! You womaniser. How could you do a thing like that? She was such a cheerful girl, and now you've ruined our happiness. If you absolutely want to know, she has run off to Africa because of you. Because she never wants to see you again!'

'But I haven't done anything!' shouted Anton, frantic with misery. 'I love her with all my heart and miss her dreadfully. Please tell me where she is . . .'

'Go away, you horrid man! She'll never forgive you for what you've done and neither will I. Oh I'm so cross with you. You wicked, devious man!' And she gave his foot a hard kick and slammed the door in his face.

9

Extracts from Anton's writings:

My darling Gael, have you really left me then? How could you have done this? Didn't you know that your image would haunt me? That I would wait for you, search for you, day after day? I saw love being born in you, I saw you become a woman. And I, who needed no one, can no longer think of a life without you.
 [. . .]
Last night, in the depth of my sleep, you came to me and I tasted your lips and smelled your perfume – wild roses and honeysuckle.

It was strong and real and I was overcome with joy. But when I stretched out my arms to hold you, I woke up . . . and you were not there. How could you have left me behind in a world of blurred dreams? In a world that's empty whenever I wake up?
[. . .]
Your absence affects me terribly. The colours have faded from my life. The world has lost its brightness and the streets are full of faces I don't want to see. The Earth is spinning on its axis; tomorrow is another day that must be lived.
[. . .]
Slowly the hours grind on. I try to work but when I look out of the window, the windswept clouds carry away my thoughts. How can I ever find you? When I stare at those clouds I feel the emptiness of many, many miles between us. I despair . . .
[. . .]
This morning the sky is blue, so blue . . . Far away an airplane leaves a long white trail. If only I could be in that plane and fly to where you are. Oh the joy of holding you in my arms! But of course, you have run away and never want to see me again.
[. . .]
Today is Monday. I drove to the park and went to see our tree; it looked just as cold and miserable as I did. I called your name but nobody answered. The days when you were here with me, those days of lightness and laughter, seem far away. The cold has taken possession of my heart. Only sombre shadows remain.
[. . .]
I've just put your photographs away and all those things that remind me of you. It hurts me to see them, and it hurts to enter my room without any hope of finding you there. I wish I were in some other room, one that had never known your presence. And yet my love for you has such deep roots that my body screams when I try to pull them out . . .

10

Monsieur Briart sat in front of his desk thinking of all the things he still had to do. Today was his last day in the lab. A shame, but that's the way it was. He had been promoted to the post of rector of his university. Such a fitting culmination to his career! He smiled contentedly. But the work there was, trying to wind up the affairs here! Staring at the piles of documents on his desk he realised that he would never be able to finish it all. There was one thing in particular that kept nagging at him. He had been trying for some time now to recall what it was, but the more he had tried, the deeper it had seemed to sink into the recesses of his brain. And then, suddenly, as he bent over the pile of documents and no longer made any effort to think about it, it flashed into his mind. That conference! Yes, that was it. Anton! He needed to see him urgently.

He called out to his secretary in the adjacent office and told her she was to go and find Anton immediately.

When Mrs Vanabel returned a quarter of an hour later she had an apologetic look on her face. 'I can't find him anywhere,' she said.

'Who can't you find anywhere?' inquired the director, looking up from his papers.

'Well, Anton.'

'What do you need him for?' he asked absent-mindedly while continuing to sort his papers into different piles: one to throw into the waste-paper basket; another pile for Mrs Vanabel to file away; and a third one he wasn't sure about.

How irritating Mr Briart can be when he sets himself to it, thought Mrs Vanabel, but she had learned a long time ago not to express personal opinions. Instead, she reminded her director that he himself had just told her to go and find Anton.

'Ah, yes, of course, of course. Now what did I want him for. Wait, it's coming back. Yes, yes. That conference somewhere in Africa. That's what it was. Where is he?'

'I don't know. Just a moment, please. Let me check the files.'

She got busy checking Anton's file on her computer, while the director continued to sort out his papers. Finally Mrs Vanabel said: 'You've given him a few days off. He'll be back tomorrow.'

'But this is my last day. What a nuisance. A real nuisance! I need him this very moment.'

'What did you need him for, Monsieur Briart? Maybe I can help you?'

'I wanted to tell him to go to that conference in my place. He's got some very bright new ideas and I think he deserves to get some international recognition. Have you still got that letter?'

'I beg your pardon?'

'Well, the letter. The letter of invitation to the conference. From my esteemed colleague . . . the director of the French Geological Institute. I promised him I would give a talk at that conference in Bobido . . . Bobodi . . . well, in that African place with an unpronounceable name. Or that I would send one of our researchers in case I couldn't go myself. And, obviously, I won't have time to go to that godforsaken place once I'm rector. So I thought of Anton. He would fit the bill perfectly. And can you believe this? I'd forgotten all about that conference until now!'

The secretary was about to reply that she had no trouble whatever believing it, but she wisely abstained. Instead, she replied: 'I don't know anything about that letter.'

'Oh hell!' exclaimed Monsieur Briart. 'It wouldn't surprise me if it were in here.' And he thumped the huge pile of documents he still had to sort out.

'You know what?' he said suddenly. 'I've got an idea.' He gathered all the documents in his arms, walked over to Mrs Vanabel's office, leaving a paper trail from his own desk to the secretary's, and dumped whatever he was still carrying on her desk. 'You sort these out in the next few days. I'm sure you'll find the letter somewhere in here and then you arrange everything. I just haven't got the time for it.'

He was ready to turn away when the secretary asked: 'Who's going to replace you, Monsieur Briart?'

'Oh . . . yes . . . now, what's his name again? I've forgotten . . . to tell you the truth, I don't know him. As a matter of fact, I've never even heard of him.' A deep frown creased his forehead when he went into his office and the secretary could hear him say: 'I do hope that the laboratory will be all right with that new man . . .'

11

Some five days later Emile came rushing into the workshop of the Geological Institute, fuming. 'Twenty-seven years I've been working here,' he yelled, 'and I've never seen anything like it!'

'What's happened?' asked Jean Gaillard, one of the technicians.

'Twenty-seven years!' repeated Emile, red-faced. 'Six different directors I've known. Some were nearly impossible. Remember Monsieur Depage? But at least he and the others were scientists and kept themselves busy with the work they were qualified for.' Emile seemed extremely agitated. 'They would never have got it into their heads to stick their noses into my kitchen to check up on my coffee!'

'Is that what that new fellow's done?'

'Yeah. Imagine! There am I, preparing the coffee for the ten o'clock break as usual, when that little weasel walks in and begins to snoop in my cupboards. I wasn't too pleased and asked him what the matter was, and you know what he said? That I was spending too much and that he was going to check whether my purchases corresponded to the expenses I had claimed. He wanted to see my accounts for the last month. And he's only been here a few days! I nearly had a fit. And then he told me in an offhand way that I would have to halve my expenses.'

'He must be off his nut.'

'That's more or less what I told him. But he just replied that I could easily buy cheaper coffee and make it less strong. No one would notice the difference, he said, with a smug look on his face. And if they did and no longer liked their coffee, so much the better. All they did down here, he said, was waste their valuable time chatting instead of being productive. He'd also brought a notice stating that the coffee break was to last for no more than fifteen minutes and that by 10.15 everybody was expected to be back at work. And I've had to fix that hateful notice on the door. It's disgraceful!'

'Why don't you put poison in his cup? Maybe he wouldn't notice the difference?'

'Our little *Monsieur* doesn't come down for coffee,' said Emile in a scathing tone. '*He* is not going to mix with the crowds. He has his own coffee. It's prepared by the secretary in her office next to his, didn't you know? And I bet you that he doesn't drink the cheapest and weakest. No, it would be difficult to poison him, and anyway, that's not my style.

I'm more for direct action, like hitting him with a blunt object. I would find that much more satisfying. A good whack on the head, that's what that little weasel needs. And then good riddance . . .'

'I haven't seen him yet.'

'You'll see him soon enough when he comes down to the workshop, as he is sure to do, and starts asking you to account for the screws you have used up.'

'Surely, he wouldn't do such a thing?' objected Jean.

'You wait! From what I've heard he's already been round to the library. He told Marion to take down the name of anyone who wants to make a photocopy, and if they can't justify that they absolutely need it for their work, they'll have to pay for it out of their own pockets. Marion was in tears about it; told him that she couldn't do such a thing, but he wouldn't budge.'

'*Quelle horreur!* Are you sure he's a scientist, not an accountant?'

'I don't know. Where they dug that little ferreting weasel out from is beyond me. And I bet you he's mighty pleased with himself. Those people think that their role is essential to the proper functioning of an institute or a department of the civil service, or wherever they happen to be harassing other people. I don't know where all this will end.' Emile sighed deeply.

'Maybe he's just a temporary replacement until they find the right candidate?' Jean looked at Emile with a glimmer of hope in his eyes.

'I'm not sure. He may be here to stay.' Emile had a sombre look on his face. 'This lab was such a nice place. Everyone was happy. We all got on well together. And look what's happened now. They sent us an undersized specimen. A smally!'

'A smally? What's that?'

'That's the little weasel. I've been given to understand that that's his real name. Would you believe it? Jack Smally. That's what he's called!' And he returned to his kitchen, shaking his head.

12

Looking at his big desk Jack Smally was mighty pleased with himself. How he had come up in the world! His paternal grandfather had worked for a pittance in a textile factory, and his grandmother had been a charwoman, but they'd saved every penny they could in order to send their son to the military academy. And the son had worked hard and become an officer. He was not very bright but had always carried out the orders of his superiors unfailingly. He had steadily risen through the ranks, and now he was a colonel!

When the time came, the officer had sent his own son to university. And through sheer hard work Jack Smally had managed to finish his studies. He had already begun to cultivate political connections during his student years. The political party he had chosen was not in power but political fortunes come and go and it was on the cards that his party would one day participate in a government coalition. In the meantime Smally had worked his way up through local councils, never missed a committee meeting, taken on tasks no one else wanted, and had finally become the trusted aid of one of the big shots in his party.

And then his moment had come: after a particularly successful election his party was left holding the balance of power and had been asked to participate in a government coalition. Naturally, they had insisted on some top jobs. Jack Smally had been extremely lucky. One of the members of his party who was better placed than him had died in a car accident a month before the elections and another one had recently landed a well-paid job in the private sector. So he'd just made it into the list of those who were going to get good jobs in the public sector, and they had rewarded him with an administrator's post in the Ministry of Labour.

Then, within months, the directorship of the Belgian Geological Institute fell vacant. Several Ph.D.s had applied, and even a couple of professors from different universities but, as it transpired, those top scientists had no political connections while for many years he, Jack Smally, had been the right hand of Dufour, the man who was now Minister of Education. Smally's scientific references were not up to much but when the selection committee had been unable to reach a decision, the Minister had intervened, throwing all his weight in the balance.

Raising scientific productivity within an existing budget, the Minister of Education had pleaded, was as important as, or even more important than, great scientific ideas. What, he wanted to know, was the good of nominating someone as director who might be a good researcher but would be unable to run the institute on a sound financial basis? It was common knowledge that doing research and running a public sector needed two different mind-sets. Researchers lived for their research, dwelt in the clouds and had no idea of how to handle a budget and stay within its limits. In the past that hadn't mattered too much but, the Minister pointed out: '. . .we can no longer afford to let dreamers make a mess of budgets. We have entered an era of budget cuts and saving. Spiralling debts are the bane of any government, and one of the main tasks of responsible politicians should be to keep the budget under control.'

Did he need to remind his audience that this research laboratory was an official institute paid for by the government? What was appropriate now was someone able to run a laboratory efficiently, and even cut the budget while keeping scientific productivity at a good level. And he happened to know someone just like that. The man had the necessary qualifications to oversee research but, more importantly, he had excellent administrative capabilities. The Minister could vouch for this since he had been watching the achievements of that competent man for years. Even better, he was already a civil servant and was used to running a department with great efficiency.

And so, after a lot of haggling and with the Minister's weight behind him, Smally had been chosen as a compromise candidate. And now he, Jack Smally, was sitting behind a big teak desk smiling contentedly. He had succeeded and he was only just forty! Who would ever have believed that the grandson of a factory worker would one day become the director of a national laboratory? That he would lord it over doctors in science? He remembered his years at university, the frustration, the fear of not being able to pass the exams while all those clever guys had looked down upon him, the plodder. And now here he was, the boss, reigning over bright doctors in geology who wouldn't have considered him worthy of their attention.

He straightened the notepad in front of him, put pencil and pen just above it, and turned the photograph of himself and his wife so that it made an angle of exactly forty-five degrees with the corner of the desk. He liked order and neatness. He liked rules. That was just what this laboratory needed: rules and regulations. A good dose of them! He had noticed in no time that all the scientists were lax, never arrived on time, hung about in the corridors chatting with each other and with the technical staff, stayed too long at coffee breaks and left at irregular hours. And the lack of formality! Everything was too informal here. The young women were particularly easy-going in their day-to-day interactions with the men. When they met they kissed almost as if they were on intimate terms. It was improper! How could an organisation be run efficiently when such attitudes were rampant? He hated disorder and loose behaviour. And he especially loathed the total lack of respect for authority that was all too evident here.

The whole set-up was intolerable. This called for a new approach. A cultural revolution was what they needed here. Years of permissive attitudes would have to be not just reversed, but wiped out. He knew he was going to face stiff resistance but he was determined. From now on zero tolerance would be the rule. That was it: zero tolerance! Even in the smallest details. He would impose new rules, stick to them and make this laboratory run like clockwork. The Minister had made it clear that he expected no less of him. He knew that he could do it, and he would.

13

Jack Smally had married the daughter of a general. His wife was a rather bulky – some would have said ungainly – woman. He was a lean, rather small man, and she was a good four inches taller. When she drew herself up to her full height and looked down on him as if he were a worm, he felt overpowered by her presence. In addition, she was several years older than him and it was definitely she who was in command. She didn't tolerate any opposition and on the few occasions when he had dared stand up to her she had cold-shouldered him for a week or two and hadn't even prepared his supper. He had learned his lesson and did not wish to go through such a harrowing experience again.

Their love life had been a very tame affair but they had managed to have one child, a daughter. She was a miniature edition of her mother and was now the centre of his wife's world. And it was with the greatest reluctance that his wife submitted to his weekly sexual overtures after that. The week was for working, Sundays for family visits, and Saturday morning for shopping. But Saturday afternoon was the appointed time for lovemaking.

After the wife had put her little daughter to bed she would lower her bulk next to her husband on the sofa in front of the telly. Then, little by little, while she was watching the programme, Smally would move up until he was sitting close to her. Next he would look at her with expectation in his eyes while stroking her arm. It was a sign she knew all too well but, still, every time she would stare at him with feigned surprise and exclaim: 'What! Not again!' Finally she would sigh, get up and go to their bedroom with him trailing behind, to submit herself to the inevitable. But before they started she would always hiss: 'Don't make any noise or you'll wake up Cherry.' And it would all be over in five minutes.

Yet his marriage had been advantageous. He had been able to make ample use of his father-in-law's connections. And the order established in his life left him time to concentrate on his career. No, all in all the marriage had been relatively successful. All had been plain sailing once routine had taken over. There was no longer any room for deviations or creative impulses. Everything proceeded with clockwork regularity and he had come to like it, or at least accept it where his love life was concerned. His sexual impulses had been reduced to five minutes every Saturday afternoon. Except of course on those Saturdays when his wife had her periods. It was true that there had been times when he'd felt that maybe this was less than he had expected. Three Saturdays – fifteen minutes – per month . . . it was not much.

Still, it had all turned out for the best. The lack of opportunity to expend his energy elsewhere had enabled him to focus on his boundless ambition. And look what he had achieved: he had become the director of a prestigious laboratory! And that was just the start. He felt that he was cut out for even loftier tasks. He, Jack Smally, was not a very tall man but, then, Napoleon hadn't been tall either. And look how far that great man had gone!

14

'I'm fed up with all this snooping!' announced Guy Lefranc, one of the technicians. He was sitting at the table in the coffee room looking very agitated. 'You should see that little fellow, the way he strolls in surreptitiously and then begins to ask questions. I just can't stand it! I hate snoops!'

'Then you'd better watch out for someone else, too,' warned Didier Verenikov, one of the brightest young scientists in the lab. He took a sip from his watery coffee, pulled a face and said: 'At least, the liquid in this cup is warm. That helps on a cold day.'

'Don't blame me!' came Emile's voice. 'I've had to halve the quantity of coffee. I'm following written instructions laying out in detail the quality and quantity of coffee I'm allowed to use every day.'

'What were you saying just now?' asked Michel Legros. 'Do you mean we've got a second snoop? One is already more than I care for.'

'I think you'd better watch out for Stephen,' replied Didier. 'If you ask me, he's hand in glove with little Smally. Don't let him poke around in your office.'

'Not Stephen!'

'Yes, that innocent-looking Stephen!' Didier nodded. 'Haven't you noticed? When little Smally passes by, Stephen is like a doggie wagging his tail, eagerly waiting for a pat on the head. I bet you he does his share of snooping.'

'I don't believe that he would betray us.'

'Yes he would! Yesterday I was in the library when he sneaked by. I saw him disappear into Smally's office with a furtive expression on his face.'

'But why would he do such a thing?' asked Michel, shaking his head.

Didier began to rub his hand over Michel's sleeve, the French gesture to indicate that he was a *frotte-manche* – a bootlicker. He was about to make a rude comment when Stephen walked in, a smug smile on his face.

'You seem pleased with yourself!' exclaimed Pauline as he sat down beside her.

'Well . . . I've just finished some very important work,' said Stephen, patting the pocket of his jacket.

'What have you got in there?' asked Pauline. 'Something for me?'

'Don't be stupid!' He dipped his hand in his pocket and held up a little stick.

'Is that all,' said Pauline, disappointed. You said it was something important. And this is just a small piece of black plastic. Pftt . . .'

'You don't realise of course,' said Stephen, speaking down his nose. He drew himself up, tapped the memory stick with his forefinger and said, trying to look very important: 'I've got the whole lab in here.'

'The whole lab?' parroted Pauline. And before Stephen could do anything she snatched the stick from his hand.

'Hey, careful!' yelled Stephen. 'Give it back!' But Pauline had already passed it on to Lottie who'd been nudging her, exclaiming excitedly: 'Give it to me!' Lottie now held up the stick and began to sing: 'I've got the whole la . . . ab in my hand, I've got the whole whole la . . . ab in my hand . . .' swinging the stick back and forth.

With a quick movement Stephen tried to grab the stick from her but their hands collided and the stick flew out of Lottie's fingers and rolled under the table.

'Oh!' she exclaimed, holding her hand in front of her mouth. 'I've dropped the lab.'

'Careful, careful!' warned Stephen while he dived under the table to retrieve the memory stick. He almost laid his hand on it, but Guy Lefranc's foot had been quicker and kicked it away.

Stephen now started moving rapidly on all fours under the table and a great confusion ensued.

'Eek!' screamed Lottie as he bumped into her knees. 'He's looking under my skirt!'

'He's pinched my leg!' yelled another girl.

'There he goes running on all fours under the table!' shouted Didier. 'Just what I told you: he's a dog. Careful he doesn't bite.'

Stephen was crawling about frantically, and had nearly got the stick when Michel bent down and picked it up.

'Give it back!' screamed Stephen getting up, but Michel had already thrown it to Didier.

Stephen began to advance threateningly, but Didier was much bigger and stronger. He held up his arm, shouting: 'Come on, doggie, higher!' while Stephen was jumping up like mad trying to grab the stick, yelling: 'Give it back!'

'The dog is barking!' screeched Didier. Suddenly he ran to a window, opened it and called out: 'Shall I drop it?'

'Noo!' came Stephen's voice. 'Yeeees!' shouted everyone else.

Stephen now seemed to lose all self-control and went for Didier. As they collided, the stick shot out of Didier's hand and flew through the open window. It described a big arc in the air, bounced off the top of a parked car, fell onto the tarmac and rolled towards the middle of the street where it came to rest.

'An accident!' exclaimed Didier. 'The laboratory has fallen out of the window, haha . . .'

Lottie yelled: 'Quick! We must save it,' and everyone rushed to the windows. Then a car appeared round the corner of the street and ran over the stick with a crunching sound. 'Too late!' shrieked Lottie with a heartrending sigh. 'A car has just driven over the lab.'

When he saw what had happened to his memory stick Stephen began to tremble with rage. 'I'm going to tell the director!' he shouted, wagging a threatening finger at Didier, 'and you'll be punished.' And he left the coffee room, slamming the door.

'I'm going to tell the director . . . and you'll be punished . . .' repeated Michel in a high-pitched mocking voice. 'You'd think this was a primary school!'

After Stephen had left the kitchen he stomped straight up to the second floor and knocked on the door of Smally's office. Unfortunately, Jack Smally was having his coffee and was not to be disturbed. He did not receive visitors during the coffee break. It was a rule – one he himself had recently established – and he wasn't going to tolerate any infringement. So he ignored the knocking and carried on ignoring it for a good ten minutes longer. That'll teach them a lesson, he thought to dare come and interrupt my activities during the coffee break.

While Stephen was impatiently pacing up and down in front of Smally's office, Didier had a brainwave. I bet you he was going to take that stick to Smally, he thought, and ran quickly to the scientists' offices on the first floor. He found Stephen's door unlocked, went in and rushed over to his computer. Stephen had not switched it off, and within seconds Didier discovered what he was looking for: a folder named Laboratory. He clicked on it and to his horror he found files with descriptions of all the scientists, the work they were doing, their characters, and details of all their real and imaginary misdeeds. 'I don't believe this!' he exclaimed and set to work with determination. He deleted the folder, clicked on the recycle bin icon, emptied the recycle bin, punched in a few instructions and was gratified when the screen began to flash and a warning message appeared: 'A fatal error has occurred'. He opened the door and looked left and right. There was no one. He quickly pulled the door shut, rushed to his own office and went inside with a satisfied smile. When that snoop reboots his system, he thought, he'll find that he's lost all his data! And the vision of a desperate Stephen trying to recover the unrecoverable cheered him up no end.

15

'I always imagined the Sahara to be like an oven,' said Gael. 'Boiling hot. And now that I'm here I find it quite pleasant.'

Marie shook her head. 'Don't be silly.'

'Why? What's wrong with what I'm saying? It's true it gets rather warm in the afternoon, but I must admit that I never thought the nights would be so cool. Last night was even chilly. Towards five this morning I felt so cold that I started shivering under the sheet and had to put on a sweater. Imagine that! In the Sahara.'

'That's because we're going towards the winter. And don't call this the Sahara. This may look arid to someone like you who comes from a rainy country but there is scattered plant cover and low shrub here; there are even thorn trees. This is bush area, not desert. We are in the Sahel, several hundred miles south of the Sahara. Up there temperatures are much more extreme. By January the thermometer often drops below zero just before sunrise. You wouldn't believe how cold the nights can get in the Sahara in the middle of the winter, especially in the mountainous areas. Freezing!'

'How incredible!' exclaimed Gael. 'To freeze in the Sahara.'

They sat sipping their tea, warming their hands on the hot cups, watching the sun rise slowly above the wall of the compound, waiting for its heat to diffuse through their bodies.

'This is how I imagine lizards must feel in the morning,' said Gael. 'Waiting for the solar radiation to penetrate their skin, waiting till they are loaded up with warmth and ready to start moving.'

'At times you look a bit like a lizard yourself with your languid movements,' replied Marie. 'And the way you soak up the sun! Maybe you've been a lizard in a previous life. If so, you won't mind the summer.'

'Why?'

'You'll find out. Let's hope you've become even more of a lizard by then.'

'You mean to say it gets very hot?'

'You wait till May–June just before the rains come – if they come that is. When afternoon temperatures run up to nearly fifty. That can be quite unpleasant.'

'What! You call that *quite* unpleasant? I can't imagine it getting worse than that.'

'Oh but it does further north,' commented Marie calmly. 'One year my husband and I had to cross the Sahara in the summer. We drove only during the night, and that was hot enough. But in the daytime! I remember being stuck in a sandy outpost in the middle of nowhere. The stupid local police commander was being as obnoxious as petty officials can be in Africa when they want to throw their weight around. He claimed our papers were not in order and took his time to check them. Then the police post closed for the afternoon, and they just left us sitting there in the full sun. By early afternoon the temperature had shot up to nearly seventy. I thought I was going to die!'

'Goodness me!' Gael looked at Marie in awe. 'That's why you think nothing of the summer here.'

'Well, it isn't pleasant. It's not just the sweltering, oppressive heat while you're waiting for the rains to break and clear the atmosphere. It's also the time when water runs out and there are flies, millions of them. But you'll see,' concluded Marie. 'You'll get used to it. You'll be surprised what one can get used to.' She looked appreciatively at Gael. 'And I can tell that you're a tough girl, fragile though you look.'

They had finished their cups of tea, it was pleasantly warm now, and Marie got up. 'Come on,' she said encouragingly. 'We'd better start. There are about fifty sick and wounded to get through before we can have lunch.'

16

'Can't we do anything about those flies around the children's eyes?' asked Gael a few days later, rather upset. 'There are so many eye infections that it's incomprehensible no one does anything about it. Even mothers don't bother when their babies' faces are covered in flies.'

'They've got enough to do as it is without constantly chasing the flies away from a fourth or fifth baby they're carrying on their backs,' replied Marie. 'And we can't do much about it either. Our stock of medicine is very limited. We just hope that the children develop a natural resistance.'

'But there must be a simple means of getting rid of those horrible flies. Why don't doctors try to find a local plant flies abhor? Then we could extract the juice from it and smear it on the children's faces.'

Marie shook her head. 'The few doctors around here have enough work already. And it's not their role to develop medicines for Africa. That's something the research laboratories of pharmaceutical companies do.'

'But why should Africans have to rely on pharmaceutical companies? From what I've read, many African plants possess beneficial medical properties. Witchdoctors healed with plants for centuries. So why can't we use indigenous plants to cure illnesses? Or why doesn't anyone extract a concentrate that would do the job more efficiently?'

'You're right that there are many valuable herbs. African ginger, for instance, is good for relieving headaches. And there are plants that cure rheumatism, heal wounds and all sorts of things. Herbal medicine was certainly used extensively in the past, although I don't know how efficient it was. When I arrived here as a young women many years ago, the knowledge had not yet been lost completely. Unfortunately, with the coming of European medical practices, herbal medicine gradually fell out of favour. People over here now believe in popping pills. The problem is that pills are too expensive to pop for most Africans.'

'Isn't that all the more reason for Africans to turn back to herbs? If these are so potent, why don't people study the medicinal properties of local plants and develop, for example, a cheap juice that would keep the flies away from children's faces, as I said?'

'The simple answer, I guess, is that collecting African plants and studying them isn't high on anyone's agenda. The pharmaceutical industry would not be interested in your proposal of developing a cheap juice against flies. Pharmaceutical laboratories basically want to develop synthetic blockbuster drugs that turn huge profits for their companies, for example, pills that cure illnesses such as diabetes, which afflict affluent societies.' She sighed. 'And there's very little we can do about that . . .'

17

'I've been thinking,' said Gael the next day. 'Why doesn't the world do more for Africa?'

Marie sighed. 'If you have no money and can't pay, no one is interested in you. There is no profit to be made from doing anything for Africans. In our world very few people care about the poor. And so Africa falls along the wayside . . .'

'But that's cruel!' Gael looked very upset.

'That's only one of the many cruelties Africans have to live with.'

'But we must change that! People here are unhappy, and we ought to do something about it.'

'What makes you think that Africans are unhappy?' Marie cut in sharply. 'There you are, no more than a few weeks in Kanibasso, and you are talking as if you already knew all about how or what Africans feel. But you don't know anything yet. You're just dishing up preconceived Western ideas and think they apply to Africa. Let me tell you that people here are not unhappy. They are poor, but when it comes to happiness I can vouch that they're much happier than most spoiled rich Westerners will ever be. You hear more laughter in this poor, harsh land than in our Western cities which are bulging with goods and riches.'

'But . . . but look around,' protested Gael. 'All those sick and wounded and . . . and those flies . . .'

'The flies are just a part of daily life here. People have to put up with them as they put up with so many other things. But they are not unhappy. They're just fatalistic about everything.' Marie sighed. 'That's the only way to cope with things in Africa.'

She looked at the day's patients who had gathered outside the compound, waiting to be attended to. 'Obviously, life here is totally different from what it is in modern Europe. It's hard and insecure. Here you're alive today, but maybe gone tomorrow. The fleetingness of your existence is always on your mind. Human life is insignificant. Nothing is eternal here but the heat, the star-spangled sky and the endless expanse of sand and rocks . . .'

She sat there for a while, staring out towards infinity. Then she continued: 'Africans know that they can't do much about their difficult living conditions. That's far beyond their limited power. There are so many problems that it's hard even to know where to begin. Everything here is beyond comprehension. Not only the overpowering vastness of space or the harshness of life, but also the cruelty of men towards one another. And yet Africans carry on stoically and smile. They smile when you are kind to them, and even when you are not, because they don't count on kindness.' She looked at Gael and her eyes softened. 'So don't judge life here with Western ideas but open your heart and then, after some time maybe, you'll begin to understand.'

18

Jack Smally was pleased with himself. He had spent the first month trying to put some order into this laboratory. He had begun by examining each part of the organisation and had checked up on every detail, however minor. Next he had drawn a map of the structure of the organisation. There he was in a square at the top labelled: Director. From that square a number of lines of command went down to the different departments and he had pencilled in the names and tasks everyone performed. He had filled in all the relevant technicalities and had next started on the budget, drawing flow charts with all the ins and outs. After two weeks of incessant work he finally had the whole organisation in front of his eyes. And once he had mastered the general picture, got it all under control, he had embarked upon drawing up restructuring plans. That was the part he liked best. That was where he excelled: in devising clever ways of cutting the budget. In the previous few weeks he'd pried into every little nook and cranny. Nothing had escaped his attention. He had diminished expenses here, halved costs there . . . It might not seem much but it all added up. And the end result was very satisfying. When he'd finished, he had cut 20 per cent off the running costs.

Then he turned his attention to the travel budget. When he looked at last year's expenses he knew at once that he had put his finger onto something really big: he'd unearthed a clear case of abuse of government funds, there was no doubt about it. All those scientists seemed to have been rushing off left, right and centre without any justification. How the previous director could have tolerated this state of affairs was beyond him. This was simply over the top! He decided there and then to cut an arbitrary 50 per cent off the travel budget, and he'd particularly enjoyed doing so. Conceited blown-up frogs! he thought. Why those spoiled scientists should think that participating in international conferences in fancy places was absolutely essential to the good functioning of the institute was beyond him.

Listening to them one would almost believe it was their God-given right to travel as much as they chose to. He had told them in no uncertain terms that from now on, if they wished to go abroad or anywhere else, even to a Belgian university, they would have to apply to him in writing at least a week ahead of time. And they would have to give solid justification for wanting to be absent from the lab, and especially for wanting money for their trips. The researchers had been up in arms, but he didn't care. He'd made his decision and it was irrevocable. Serves them right, he reflected. Those arrogant fellows who think the world of themselves!

Until he'd come along, everyone seemed to have been using up money as if they couldn't have cared less. Had it been their own money, they would no doubt have been much more cautious, but it was government money. It was this kind of behaviour that led to budget deficits, and in the end caused governments to fall.

Last night he'd read an article on the butterfly effect. Isn't it interesting, he had thought, how small causes can bring about a great calamity? The article said that the butterfly effect could happen anywhere at any time! But he was going to make sure that such a calamity wouldn't happen in his laboratory. He was going to keep every little component of his organisation, however unimportant it might seem, under strict control. He was not one of those irresponsible scientists. He was a responsible administrator, and the government could count on him to act in its best interests. Government services were like a sieve with a thousand holes that had to be plugged, and he was determined to plug the hole he was responsible for. Wasn't that why the Minister had chosen him for this job?

When he'd finished, he leaned back with a sigh of satisfaction. He'd plugged the hole, and more! He had thought out dozens of new rules and regulations, jotted them down on pieces of paper and handed them to the secretary who'd typed them in large print. They had been put up all over the laboratory, in the corridors and inside the different services. And all the staff, including the scientists, now had to clock in their times of arrival and departure. He himself was there before eight every morning, standing by the entrance to check up on arrivals, and he remained at the helm till well after 6 p.m. And during the day he constantly prowled around the laboratory to be certain that everyone was at their jobs instead of chatting.

19

When Pauline entered the scanning room she saw Lottie quickly trying to hide a magazine and starting to work assiduously.

'So that's where you are!' exclaimed Pauline.

'Oh it's you!' Lottie turned around with relief. 'I thought it was that new director.'

'Well, you're lucky it wasn't him. You weren't quite quick enough when you tried to hide that magazine just now. By the way, why weren't you at the meeting?'

'What meeting?'

'Didn't you know? We all had to go and listen to the director. As some of us apparently still go about as if nothing had changed, he drew our attention to the fact that new rules and regulations are stuck up all over the lab and that we should all read them and stick strictly to them. He particularly warned us against the butterfly effect . . .'

'I don't know what you're talking about.'

'You would if you'd been there,' retorted Pauline. 'I found this butterfly effect very interesting. You see, something or someone can be like a butterfly beating its wings and . . .'

Lottie cut her short: 'I'm not interested in butterflies.' Then she grumbled: 'I wish I were working somewhere else.'

'But you so liked it here!'

Lottie pinched her lips. 'It's that new director.' Her face looked sombre. 'What that man needs is an affair!' she blurted out. 'That would keep him busy.' Suddenly she brightened up. 'Oh . . . I've got a brilliant idea. Why don't you try your charms on him?' She giggled and nudged her elbow into Pauline's side.

'Don't be daft!' Pauline shrugged her shoulders. 'He would have to stand on tiptoe to kiss me with my high heels on!'

She turned to her scanning table and began to measure her pictures when all at once a strange expression came over her face. Maybe there was something in what Lottie had suggested? Ever since Anton had pushed her onto the floor, she had been thinking about revenge. If only she could pay him back for what he had done to her. The bastard! she thought. It enraged her that he was here, in the same building. That when she ran into him he systematically passed her pretending not to notice her, as if she were thin air. It made her blood boil. She was ready to do anything to harm him.

And on the spot she began to conceive an audacious scheme. It was a long shot but it might work. Yes, she thought, that's what I'm going to do. Yes . . . that would open up a world of possibilities; and there might be fun in it for me as well. Then she said softly to herself: 'My girl, you'll have to play this very astutely, but you've got the talent and can pull it off.'

20

The last touches to the reorganisation plan had been put into place more than a week ago. The laboratory should have been functioning like well-oiled clockwork and yet something was wrong. Smally had the impression that he wasn't entirely in control. There was a sense of unease in the atmosphere that even he had perceived. The technical staff seemed to avoid him and the scientists hardly acknowledged his greetings, however cheerfully he tried to say good morning in order to encourage them to work. They now kept the doors of their offices shut and this bothered him because he didn't know what they were doing behind those closed doors. If he knocked and entered one of their offices, the reception was invariably icy. The scientists just answered his questions with a yes or a no, and showed him in a thousand ways that he was interrupting them and that they were thinking, please could you leave me alone so that I can carry on with my work.

He fumed. Despicable fellows! Who did they think they were? After all, he was the boss and they were his subordinates. He wasn't going to take this lying down. Pretending they were busy! He would teach them. So he had a message sent to all the scientists ordering them to submit a detailed report on what they were doing. And would you believe it! So far only one of the scientists had filed in his report. Only Stephen had obeyed his orders.

Stephen! He was the exception. When Jack Smally thought of him he felt gratified. Stephen really was a good fellow, always ready to do as he was told, always receiving him with proper consideration. He even reported on remarks the others made during the coffee break. But he was the sole positive element in a sea of gloom. No . . . maybe one of the female technicians wasn't too bad either. Recently he had begun to notice that she always greeted him politely, smiling cheerfully as she did so. She, at least, seemed genuinely pleased to see him. When he unexpectedly entered the scanning room she was always working efficiently and never minded him checking up on what she was doing. Instead, she seemed to enjoy his presence. If only the rest of the staff were like her. What was she called again? Pauline something. For a fraction of a second a vague smile hovered around his lips when he thought of her. But the rest! He sighed.

Even his secretary, Mrs Vanabel, had started giving him trouble. He'd been very careful to keep their relationship on an impersonal footing. He didn't want any familiarity and had refused to call her Rosemarie as the previous director had apparently done. To him she was just Mrs Vanabel, a colourless character, employed to pick up the phone, type letters and make his coffee in the special machine in her office. Everything had gone well for the first couple of weeks, and he hadn't given it another thought. But lately she had been *distraite*, mislaying papers and making several major typing errors. Yesterday afternoon, after he had come back from an inspection tour of the laboratory, he found her staring vaguely at the wall in front of her. She hadn't typed the letters he'd given her and when he made a sharp remark she had suddenly burst into hysterical sobs, picked up her coat and rushed out slamming the door. This was unheard of! He had remained behind in the gloomy half-darkness of the late October afternoon. What had come over her? He had been ready to report her to the Ministry of Education but on second thoughts had hesitated. She'd been efficient most of the time. All right, he reflected, I'll give her a second chance. See what happens tomorrow.

21

If yesterday had been a bad day for Jack Smally, today was worse. It was already 9.45 a.m. and the secretary hadn't turned up. Why hadn't she phoned? The personnel knew that if they were ill and unable to come to work, they had to ring the secretary first thing in the morning and follow it up immediately with a doctor's report. He'd established this rule not two weeks ago. So why hadn't Mrs Vanabel phoned?

As he was pacing up and down between his big office and the secretary's smaller one, he realised why. There was a serious flaw in the rule he'd established. What happened if the secretary herself was ill? How could she phone herself when she wasn't in her office? Maybe she had phoned. He had heard the phone in her office ring several times, but he wasn't going to pick it up. He wasn't a secretary. He was the director, and only the calls he wanted to take were put through to him.

While he was pondering over this dilemma, another problem loomed up in his mind. It was nearly ten o'clock now, and there was no one to prepare his coffee. What was he to do? Even if he had been willing to do the job himself, he didn't know how the coffee machine worked. He could go down to the kitchen, of course, but that would be a comedown. He'd been told that the previous director had had no objection to mixing with the crowds, but no, he couldn't possibly do that.

Just then there was a gentle knock on the secretary's door.

'Come in!' he shouted, upset at being interrupted in his musings on the relationship between director and subordinate.

The door opened slowly, and Pauline's face appeared surrounded by her luscious brown hair. She smiled apologetically.

'Ahem, yes . . .' said Mr Smally, mellowing slightly when he saw it was her.

'*Monsieur le Directeur*,' she said in a mellifluous tone, 'please do excuse me for barging in like this . . .'

'Ah . . . oh, well . . . it's all right. What's the matter?'

'My scanning table is going to be serviced after the morning break and I thought . . . I wondered whether there was any work you wanted me to do?'

Jack Smally was pleasurably surprised. Instead of profiting from the occasion to fiddle her time away, this girl was asking him what he expected of her. Had she gone to one of the scientists, he would have put her onto something useless, and she would have wasted her time. But no! She'd come to him instead. So responsible! This was the right attitude. He beamed at her.

'If you'll allow me . . .' She seemed to hesitate.

'Yes, tell me . . .'

'Well, seeing the secretary has abandoned you . . .'

'You have news of her then?'

'Yes . . . as I went down for my coffee break I heard that she hadn't come, and I immediately thought, what about our director? He is alone up there without any coffee while we are enjoying ourselves. It's not fair. So I came straight up and . . . Would you allow me to prepare your coffee for you?'

This was totally unexpected. As he looked at the young woman standing there in front of him, her eyes full of goodwill, Jack Smally was really touched. He vaguely indicated the coffee machine. 'Do you know how to make coffee?'

'Naturally. You'll let me? Everything is in the cupboard, I suppose?' She went over to the small cupboard next to the coffee machine. 'How do you want your coffee? Medium? Strong?'

'Strong,' he replied. 'With milk and sugar.'

'How many cups?'

'One.' Suddenly he paused. This girl was sacrificing her coffee break to help him out and would be foregoing her own coffee. He thought for a while. It was a difficult decision to make. Then he added, as if it was something wrenched out of him: 'And add a cup for yourself, too.'

She smiled at him gratefully, measured out the right quantity of coffee, poured water into the machine, switched it on and set to work laying out a tray with two cups.

'It'll be ready in five minutes,' she said. 'In the meantime, can I do anything else for you? Would you like me to type some letters?'

'Can you type?'

'Of course. I've done secretarial courses and can use the computer. But it's so difficult to get a secretarial job nowadays. All I managed to find was a part-time technical job here in the lab.'

This girl really is a godsend, thought Jack Smally. So deferential, so helpful! And a good worker.

'Come, sit here,' he said with a large smile, indicating the secretary's chair. And before he realised what he was doing, he actually held the back of the chair and pushed it forward as Pauline sat down. 'Do you think you can type these few letters? They're really urgent. I hope you can read my handwriting,' he added in an almost apologetic tone.

Pauline looked at the handwritten pages. 'Oh that's no problem at all. You write very clearly. And such nice writing, too. You should have seen the handwriting of some of our teachers on the secretarial course. You simply wouldn't believe it!'

Jack Smally now no longer attempted to hide his pleasure. What a difference to that Vanabel woman, he thought. Come to think of it, I never liked her. A tall gloomy stick she was, never even pretending to be willing to please me; always looking down at me along that long nose of hers. And there and then he began to form a plan in his mind to keep Pauline as his secretary.

22

'I won't be able to stand this much longer!' exclaimed Didier Verenikov, slapping his cup down with a bang during the ten o'clock coffee break. 'It's getting worse every week. This is no longer a laboratory for postgraduates. It has become a primary school! You hear nothing but *"Monsieur le Directeur*, can we do this?" and *"Monsieur le Directeur*, are we allowed to do that?" And who or what is that fellow, I'd like to know? He hasn't even got a Ph.D. And he wants us to write a report on the scientific work we're doing! When I'm certain he doesn't understand even half of the research that's going on here. What a joke!'

'A school!' snorted Guy Lefranc, one of the technicians. 'You say that this is a school? A prison would be more like it! Day after day that little *monsieur* comes along snooping around in the workshop, and then he stands behind us looking over our shoulders to check on what we're doing. I bet you that, when we're gone, he sneaks back inside to count the screwdrivers – just in case we've taken one home. Nothing but checking . . . as if we were ready to commit a crime if he didn't keep controlling us.' Suddenly he hit the table with the palm of his hand. 'In fact, that's exactly what I'd like to do! Let me tell you that when he stands there behind me, I have to assert all my self-control not to commit a crime. I would joyfully stick a 380-volt cable up his arse and electrocute him!'

'I'll come and give you a hand,' proposed Emile. 'I'll pull his trousers down for you if you like!' Everyone laughed, even Lottie who burst into loud giggles as she visualised the scene.

'Would serve him right!' exclaimed Jean Gaillard. 'Damned little asshole! Look what we've had to put up with since he's come along: nothing but rules and regulations. We've got to account for every minute of our time, and receive watery coffee as a reward. Bah! All the fun has gone out of working here.'

'Rules and regulations!' snorted Michel Legros. 'Judging from what's happening here one would think that communism is still alive and kicking. It wouldn't surprise me if the fellow had been educated in Moscow. We ought to call him Smalski.'

'Let me tell you something,' interjected Didier. 'I got an email yesterday from the American mining company I've been trying to set up a collaboration with for some time now. They wrote to say that they're interested in my proposal, and asked me whether I could please come to London to discuss everything with one of their top geologists who'll be there for a couple of days. So I went to the little asshole and told him about it. And you know what he answered? You're not going to believe this: "If they're so keen on having your opinion," he said, "why don't they invite you and pay all your expenses." And that was that! I could have murdered the bloody idiot. How am I going to explain to an American mining company that we can't discuss the project unless they pay all my expenses? And that I have to write a report beforehand on all we're going to say and do? In duplicate because that little jackanapes wants a copy for himself! Wonderful for our international reputation, isn't it? We'll become the laughing stock of Europe. The proud Belgian Geological Institute, known for its original ideas and brilliant research results, is ready to slide into the dustbin of scientific history.' And he stared sombrely in front of him.

'That's exactly what's going to happen,' agreed Michel. 'We were so proud of working here. We felt like the chosen few and did what we could to uphold the reputation of our lab. But who wants to stay here now? Better to leave the sinking ship, I say.'

'Hey, you can't go and leave us behind with that little weasel!' exclaimed Guy Lefranc. 'If you scientists leave, what's going to become of us technicians?'

'Sorry,' interrupted Emile suddenly, 'but it's 10.15. Out of the canteen, all of you.' And as everyone looked at him with furious eyes he explained: 'The rules and regulations of the house say so. And they must be obeyed,' he added with barely hidden glee.

23

The next morning Jack Smally found a letter on his desk certifying that Mrs Vanabel had had a nervous breakdown. In a separate note the doctor stated that he was unable to tell when she would be able to return to work. Had this occurred two days ago Smally would have been up in arms, but now he was rather pleased. In fact, when he thought about it, he never wanted to see that long face again, and good riddance! What luck that she had gone and that he would be able to replace her with Pauline.

From that time onwards Pauline came in every day to offer him full-time secretarial assistance, and he found her presence extremely pleasant. Such an obliging girl, always ready to carry out his orders with a smile! Always looking up at him with barely hidden admiration. So different from that stiff stick he'd had as a secretary before her. And, to top it all, she was very nice to look at. In fact, she was really rather pretty. Twice he had found himself standing beside her dictating a letter, when a waft of her perfume had hit his nostrils, stirring something deep inside him.

With every passing day he had felt closer to her, felt as if an intimacy was growing between them. Just now he was standing behind her, holding on to the back of her chair. It was somehow symbolic. It established some sort of physical contact between them, a contact he feared, and yet . . . He looked at the top of her head while he was dictating a letter, at the brown hair which fell in a neat wave to her shoulders. He gazed at her firm little breasts, sticking out under her tightly fitting silky blouse; and then he looked further down at her miniskirt, which left a lot of her slim legs visible . . .

The perfume is so strong today, he thought as he stared at those attractive legs and forgot the text he was dictating.

Pauline waited a few seconds but when nothing more seemed to come she turned her head up towards him, revealing a pair of shiny hazel eyes. They smiled at him as if they wanted to say that she liked him being there.

Smally blushed slightly and suddenly lost some of his aplomb. 'How . . . how far did we get?' he stuttered, trying to regain control over his senses.

Pauline looked at him with concern. 'Would you like a short rest, *Monsieur* Smally?' she asked politely. 'You have been working so hard the whole morning.' She said it with what sounded like admiration in her voice.

'What about you?' he inquired unexpectedly. 'Aren't you tired?'

'Don't bother about me,' she replied. 'I'm here to serve you. I don't mind anything you say or do . . .' She looked at him expectantly – or was it invitingly – swivelled around on her chair and continued: '. . . as long as you are pleased . . .' when the chair abruptly wheeled away from underneath her. She slid helplessly to the floor and landed at his feet, lying on her back, her legs spread wide open.

Without thinking he knelt down and clasped her hand but as he gazed at her transparent underwear, so near and so enticing, he felt bewitched. He tried to pull her up when suddenly he seemed to be catapulted forward and before he realised what was happening he was lying on top of her. A wave of perfume hit his nostrils and, as he felt Pauline wriggle underneath him, his senses took leave of him. His hands grabbed her soft, warm body, and as she began to respond passionately to his kisses he made love to her there and then on the floor of her office.

He felt very awkward when it was all over. It was a complete deviation from his perfectly ordered existence, from all the rules of conduct he himself had laid down. One of these rules was that interactions between the staff, and *a fortiori* between the director and any member of the workforce, should remain on a strictly professional level. And there he was, having broken this rule in the most scandalous way. What would happen to him now?

He was at a loss for words and very shy, but she just pulled down her miniskirt, straightened her blouse and sat down again as if nothing had happened. Then she gave him a conspiratorial look and said: 'Shall we continue the letter?'

He was determined never to repeat this, to keep himself under control, and was glad when the day was over.

When he drove to the lab the next morning he felt very apprehensive, but there she was, already in the secretary's office, as good-humoured as ever, smiling as if nothing had happened. What a great girl she was! He felt relieved and thankful and retired into the inner sanctum of his own office.

He was pleased that the day had passed uneventfully and yet, when he drove home, he felt a deep disappointment. She had kept herself at a respectful distance. Why had she not even kissed him? And he had been in a foul mood at home throughout the evening.

24

The next day he found himself revolving around her chair while he was dictating letters. Once or twice he had stood behind her and had nearly put his hands on her shoulders. When he smelled her perfume he almost went wild and was aching to touch her breasts, but with a great effort of will-power he held back.

And then it happened. A sheet of paper escaped from her hand and when she got up and bent down to retrieve it from underneath the desk, the back of her short miniskirt moved up her thighs to reveal the edge of her underwear. He stared at it like a mouse hypnotised by a snake and knew that he was no longer in control. His hand shot forward, unable to resist, and touched the bottom of her panties. A shock like an electric current now went through him. He grabbed her, turned her around, pushed her onto the floor, pulled up her skirt and threw himself upon her. And he had gone completely mad: his hands were like claws around her buttocks, while her hot body lay underneath him, wriggling like a harem girl's trying to pleasure her master.

That's how it had all begun, his slow slide downhill towards pleasure seeking and the neglect of his duties. He had been unsure at the start, wanting quick sex, but once he had yielded she guided him and gradually took over.

He became hooked on her body. Every time he saw her pass by with swaying hips, when he looked at her alluring legs or at her pert breasts, he felt a sexual surge come up. And he would touch her breasts or squeeze her buttocks when she stood close by. She would let him do anything without any inhibition and responded with an expression of ecstasy on her face.

He was impatient now to get to his office in the morning. When she finally entered she would brush up to him while taking off her coat, rub her body against his and kiss him, let her hand wander over his crotch and arouse him. And he needed her, needed her every day, no, two or sometimes even three times a day. He always made sure that the doors of their offices were carefully locked, and he had also removed the photograph of himself and his wife: he certainly didn't want her to see what was going on! And what he was doing was something he would never have imagined. They had sex in the most unbelievable positions, not just for a few minutes, but sometimes for a full half-hour.

It was all so new to him, this incredible world of the senses. She had opened the gates that had been closed until then, and there was no stopping the flood now. He could touch her, grope her whenever he liked; she was always willing, always arousing him. And her perfume! Magie Noire it was called, and it worked magic on him; it stirred up his desire. It made him go crazy, and he was able to give free rein to his wildest fantasies, was encouraged to do so. He had never been so pleased with himself! He felt like a victor who had conquered everything that stood before him. And when she lay helplessly underneath him, trembling, squirming with pleasure, he, Jack Smally, knew that he was a great man.

25

In his office on the fifteenth floor of an old KGB building along one of the main avenues of Moscow, Viktor Ippolitovich Boronov was pacing up and down agitatedly, a prey to black thoughts. He had planned everything so carefully, had worked overtime till all was ready: the money, the small arms, the ammunition, it had all been there by the end of June. And those two men, whom he loathed with all his heart, had been waiting to fly off. It had been very warm in Moscow, and he reflected with great satisfaction how much hotter it would be in the Sahara. It must be scorching hot over there, he had thought rubbing his hands. And the thirst! He'd read somewhere that you needed to drink at least ten litres of water every day to survive the summer in the Sahara.

And soon those two men would be in Africa, driving a truck crammed full of arms, ammunition, and all sorts of things except water. They would set off and follow the map he had supplied. And that map would be their undoing. He had not smeared red paint over it as those uncouth subordinates had done to his precious map of Africa. No, he had acted much more subtly than that. He had carefully tinkered with it, and as they followed that map they would drive straight into the Sahara and get lost. He could see them in his mind's eye, crawling up one of those high sand dunes, looking frantically for water. And the despair when they got to the crest, their tongues hanging nearly down to the sand, and saw nothing but dunes stretching endlessly before them! He had been unable to hide his contentment when he thought of the agony they would feel. A few more weeks and those bastards would be in the Sahara in the middle of the summer. And they would perish of thirst.

Then the incredible happened. One morning he had received a phone call from headquarters to tell him that the ammunition had been sent to Chechnya where it was urgently needed. It would be replaced as soon as possible, they said, but he was given to understand that ammunition factories were working full time to supply foreign customers who paid in hard currency, and that his project was low priority. Then, a week later, when he'd gone to the depot where the crates with weapons were kept, he discovered that they were no longer there! The soldiers on guard didn't know anything – or so they claimed. A few days later one of his sleuths had told him that there was suddenly an influx of small arms for sale in the black market run by the Moscow mafia.

Soon after that the cash – the stock of crisp new dollars, carefully locked up in a safe in his own building – had mysteriously disappeared. He had all the personnel interrogated, but no one had pleaded guilty. It had been a pitiful sight, all those low-rank officials being marched in front of him without showing even the slightest sign of remorse. It had been so much simpler in the past. Then the police had had the means to extract confessions from people. And all those brought up for interrogation had freely admitted to their misdeeds, even before they had been properly accused.

So the dollars had vanished without leaving a trace, but some time later one of his undercover agents heard rumours from a dealer in the black market. The man had said that it wouldn't surprise him if those dollars were now circulating in Moldova, supporting the trade in arms and prostitutes.

This would never have happened in the good old days, thought Viktor Ippolitovich. This was surely another consequence of that hated capitalism. Corruption seemed to have spread to all levels of the government. No one was safe from it now, not even those who had been in the inner sanctum of the Party.

He had spent the summer in his derelict apartment in one of those building developments dating from the Stalinist era, which were crumbling by now. It had been swelteringly hot, the hottest summer on record, it was said. There was not a breath of air and day after day he lay on his bed, perspiring profusely, while the water supply was cut off for hours on end. And every time he thought how much hotter it must be in the Sahara, and that those two men, Boris and Igor, were not there but had gone instead with their wives to the Black Sea on a government-sponsored holiday, he groaned, and finally he had a nervous breakdown.

26

The summer had passed, Viktor Ippolitovich had recovered, and Boris and Igor were back in service. Whenever they smiled at him obligingly he found himself grinding his teeth. He had tried to have them sent to Chechnya but no, it seemed that the plans for fomenting a revolution in Africa had been approved and signed by the proper government services, and that nothing could be changed now. He had been given to understand that a cargo plane would soon be ready to fly mining material and trucks to Bobodiou, and that the requested arms and money would go on that plane, too, together with his two subordinates. The Russian Embassy in Bobodiou had been briefed and the officials over there were on full alert.

By now Viktor Ippolitovich hated the whole enterprise. What use was it at present to send those two imbeciles to Africa? It was late October already and by the time they would get there driving through the Sahara would be a pleasure trip. Still, the orders from headquarters were sacred: he had to do his duty. With reluctance he applied himself to the task that had been allotted to him, but whenever he stopped and happened to look up at the red stain his map of Africa had become, he was overcome by despair. And then, suddenly, his dull face lit up as a diabolical plan began to form in his mind.

27

It was one of those Monday mornings in early November when the gods responsible for the weather – in as far as there are any such gods – seemed to find a devilish delight in creating the foulest possible conditions for people having to drive to work. No one in his or her right mind would have chosen to leave their cosy homes of their own free will on such a morning, and maybe not even their beds, but those people who were now creating huge traffic jams on all the approach roads to Brussels did not have the choice. Thousands upon thousands of cars were crawling forward at a snail's pace, every now and then shaken by a strong gust of wind, while the rain was pouring down on this bleak November morning.

Among the many drivers biting their nails because they were going to be very late was Anton. He had just reached that mental state of mind where he was reproaching himself for not having set off an hour earlier, when he looked up at one of the bridges that crossed the motorway. He had been slowly approaching it for the last quarter of an hour, and now began to make out the graffiti which had been scribbled all over it months ago and seemed to remain there forever. Then he noticed that there was something new: a line that had not been there last Monday. He tried to read it but the bridge was still too far away, and the dark morning and the water running over his windscreen obscured much of what was written. When the bridge was nearly overhead, the rain stopped abruptly, there was a hint of light in the sky and suddenly the words stood out clearly. They read: 'Why are you doing this every day?' The message only increased Anton's state of extreme irritation. He shrugged his shoulders and said to himself: 'It's useless to ask that kind of question. It's better not to think about such things at all.' And he gripped the steering wheel again, hoping that the cars in front of him would move on.

Three-quarters of an hour later Anton clocked in at the lab, ran up to his office and sat down behind his desk in a foul mood. That Smally is not going to be pleased, he thought. I'd better finish the report he wants. He picked up a sheet of writing paper and a pencil and began fiddling with it, but not a single idea came to his mind. He stared again at the paper in front of him, sighed and gazed absent-mindedly out of the window. Gael! As the weeks had passed by he had felt ever lonelier and more desolate.

There was nothing to cheer him up in the lab either: the atmosphere was frankly bleak. Everyone wandered about as though they were getting ready for a funeral, and, indeed, it seemed as if the lab was being buried. Didier had left a week ago, just like that. He had taken the train to London and been hired on the spot by the representative of the American mining company he'd met there. And two technicians had also handed in their notice. It was whispered that Didier had poached them for his new company, but the rumour was not confirmed. Anyway, it was obvious that the lab was heading for a major crisis.

Anton had avoided his new director as much as possible. He had taken a dislike to the fellow at first sight; he particularly hated the man's unpleasant remarks when he was late, which he usually was on Mondays. Still, he did his best to comply with the new directives and for the last two weeks he had applied himself to write a report about his activities. But, however much he exerted himself, he'd been unable to produce anything he considered up to standard.

He switched on his computer and moments later the report appeared on the screen. He scanned through it with disinterested eyes. How useless this was! What was the point of writing it? Why make any more effort when his heart wasn't in it? The report was going to end up in the dustbin anyway, like those of all the other scientists. Let's get rid of it, he thought, clicking on the print icon. He picked up the printed pages, stapled them together and set off for the second floor dragging his feet.

A minute or two later he was outside the secretary's office. Then he hesitated. He hadn't been there since Mrs Vanabel had left and that awful Pauline had become the new secretary. I must get this over, he decided, plucked up his courage and knocked.

There was a shuffling behind the door and then silence. Anton was about to knock again when he heard the key turn in the lock, and the door opened slowly.

He found Pauline staring at him with undisguised hostility.

'Can I . . . can I see Mr Smally?' he asked, taken aback.

'What do you want him for?' Her voice sounded short-tempered.

'Well . . . it's about my report . . .'

'Mr Smally cannot see you at the moment.' She spoke with authority in her voice. 'Right now he is busy with important matters. Come back another time.' She was about to shut the door when he repeated, holding out the pages tentatively: 'But . . . but what about the report? He wanted it.'

'I'll handle this!' she said sharply, grabbed the papers from his hand and slammed the door in his face.

28

'Who was that?' asked Smally, reappearing seconds later in the doorway between their two offices, zipping up his trousers.

'Oh, that annoying Anton.'

'Who? Oh yes, that inconspicuous fellow. Why do you say he's annoying? I haven't seen much of him.'

'You are lucky then, Jacky,' she said in a honeyed voice. Ever since they had been on intimate terms she'd called him 'Jacky' when no one else was around. 'I've seen more of him than I wanted.'

'What do you mean by that?' Smally was barely able to hide his suspicion.

'Well, I just can't stand him any more. You naturally think very highly of your scientists, but you have no idea what we innocent girls have to put up with. Not all the scientists are bad, of course, but some definitely are.'

Smally was getting more and more agitated. 'If that fellow has done anything to upset you, you must tell me about it!' he said in a commanding voice.

'I don't know whether I should. It would put him in a bad light and that wouldn't be good for his career, would it?'

'What has he done? I want to know. I insist!'

'If I really must tell you . . .' She sighed deeply and paused for a few seconds as if she were unwilling to speak. 'He . . . he often bothered me when I was working at the scanning tables. In fact, he . . . he never left me alone.' Pauline spoke hesitantly, as if the words were dragged out of her with hot irons. 'He tried to lay his hands on me . . .' She sat down and her face took on a tormented expression. She even managed to produce a tear in the corner of her eye. 'In the end I didn't know how to keep him away.' She now hid her face in her hands.

'This is outrageous! The scoundrel! The womaniser! And to think he looks so innocent.' Smally's face was contorted with rage. He had never given it a thought, but it was obvious that some of the men in the laboratory must have been after his prized possession. Suddenly he looked up sharply. 'Nothing of consequence happened, did it?'

'No, but it was not for want of him trying. One evening, when I was scanning and he was on duty, he told me to come to his office after I finished at nine. And when I was inside he locked the door and tried to grab me. He was going to rape me! But I was too quick and escaped with a few bruises.'

'What! The rotten devil! To attack a defenceless girl like you. How dare he? I'm going to call him in right now and give him a piece of my mind. And refer him to the ministry for improper conduct!'

'Oh, please, Jacky, don't do that,' pleaded Pauline. 'It will create a big scandal. You know what people are like. Always saying there's no smoke without fire. Always out to sling mud and ruin the reputation of defenceless girls like me. And my husband will imagine that I was involved. Aren't there ways to punish him that wouldn't involve my name?'

Smally stood there for a while, turning this over in his mind. Pauline is quite right, of course, he reflected. He didn't want her husband to become aware of what was going on in the laboratory. From what she had told him, he had got the impression that he was a quiet fellow who was too old for any sexual activity and had no idea what a treasure he possessed. Everything was working out so well. Pauline was safely married and made no demands. She did not want him to separate from his wife, nor did she even ask to see him outside office hours: she never pestered him to waste his money on taking her out to restaurants, as other women would have done. Her only demands were of a sexual nature and here he fully collaborated. It was an ideal arrangement for him and he didn't want to upset the apple cart.

At last he spoke. 'Right. We are going to leave you out of it, don't worry. But I have to do something about that wolf in sheep's clothing. He needs to learn a lesson. We can't close our eyes to his vile conduct.'

Pauline looked up at him with eyes full of gratitude. 'It's so wonderful for a girl to know she can count on a real man to protect her,' she said and kissed him on the mouth. Then she continued, as if with the greatest reluctance: 'I know I can trust you and depend on you, Jacky. That's why I think I should tell you what he's got on his mind . . .'

'Tell me. Don't hesitate!'

'He said that he was determined to get me. That he wouldn't give up till he'd reached his goal.' She shivered. 'I know he'll try again. I'm afraid to have him around here . . . he gives me the creeps. Can't you send him away to some other place, please?' She looked at him expectantly.

'So that's what he intends to do, the evil schemer!' hissed Smally through clenched teeth. 'That menace needs to be thrown out! I would do it today if I could. Ah! I have an idea. How long has he been here in the laboratory?'

'About eleven months I think.'

'Less than a year? But that's wonderful! Ministerial contracts are not permanent for the first two years. And the second year's renewal is subject to evaluation by a committee . . . over which my friend the Minister presides.' He rubbed his hands. 'That'll teach him, the dirty swine. Nothing but sex on his mind, eh! Some men are like that, but we definitely don't want that sort in a decent institution such as this, do we?'

'Will I be safe then?'

'Don't you worry,' said Smally, patting Pauline on the head. 'That menace won't be here much longer. By the way, what did he come for?'

'He just brought this report.'

Smally picked up the report and disappeared inside his office. He had barely gone when a devilish grin appeared on Pauline's face. She had done it! She was so pleased with herself that she went to the small mirror on the wall in her office and as she looked at her reflection she said: 'Mirror, mirror on the wall, who is the cleverest of us all?'

29

After Pauline had slammed the door in Anton's face he walked back to his office as if he were living a bad dream. That's what his life had become: a dream turned nightmare. He had started here so full of hope less than a year ago, so full of enthusiasm. And now there was nothing left. The bubble of illusions that had floated so brightly in front of his eyes when he had come to work in the lab had burst. A little weasel was now his director and that ghastly Pauline was the new secretary.

He went into his office, shut the door and sat down, his head between his hands. Everything seemed insipid now: getting up in the morning, going to work, his life in Brussels, everything. It was more than he could stand. And out of the blue the message he had read on the bridge that morning resurfaced and hit him with full strength. Yes, he thought. Why am I doing this every day?

30

Anton had been in an unspeakably bad mood for the last few days. He no longer saw any purpose in staying in Brussels or in doing his job. He hated being in the lab, hated it intensely. He felt like a tiger locked up in a cage, longing for the wilds, dreaming of breaking out.

What am I doing here? he asked himself again, sitting at his desk in front of his computer. Why should I continue to stay in this lab where not a single cell in my body wants to be? When Gael is somewhere in Africa. What's holding me back? Can I not sever the ties life has imposed? Why can't I do the only thing I really want to do?

He got up so brusquely that he knocked his chair over. 'I'm not going to accept this,' he said to himself, pacing back and forth agitatedly. 'To hell with the lab! And to hell with my career, too! I'm going to search for Gael. I'll find her if it takes me a lifetime!'

In a flash he remembered her interest in medical aid. She had told him that she'd been to a convention on medical aid, and had been toying with the idea of going out to Africa a few months before they had met.

That's what she's done, he thought. I bet you. She's gone to Africa to join a medical aid project! Let's see what I can find on the Internet. There can't be many organisations in Brussels that do that sort of thing. After half an hour of searching he had unearthed a couple of organisations that ran aid projects in Africa. 'Tomorrow I'll go and talk to them,' he said to himself with a determined expression on his face.

He got up and stood in front of the window, his hands clasped behind his back, thinking of the tasks that lay ahead of him. Then, as he looked up at the sky above the rooftops, at the ever-changing shapes of the clouds, a patch of the sky was lit up by a beam of sunlight and for one short moment the clouds took the shape of the face he loved. And he looked at Gael's face up there in the clouds and cried out: 'Wherever you are, I will find you.'

31

Anton's poem:

Longing

Now that the wind is howling in the chimney,
and the sun is disappearing in a sea of fire,
I stand before the window
and look towards the south
where you must be.

I wish I were that bird up there,
its outspread wings a deeper dark
against the fading light of the sky.
Would its wings take me
to you?

I wish I were the ground
on which you walk,
the garden in which you like to rest,
the pillow
on which you lay your head.

> My body is pulling and straining;
> the waves of longing are growing stronger.
> Will they pull out my roots
> and carry me
> to where you are?

32

As she looked at the patients who had gathered outside the wall of the dispensary, Gael felt her spirits sink. She turned round and retreated to the breakfast table.

'Hey, you don't look very cheerful this morning!' exclaimed Marie, helping herself to some more steaming pancakes. 'What is it? Are there a lot of sick today?'

'Oh, the usual fifty or sixty.'

'So why do you look as if the sky has fallen upon your head?'

'I don't know. There are days when I just don't feel up to it and I suppose that today is one of them.'

She sat down and poured herself another cup of tea. It had seemed such a grand idea, back in Europe, to dedicate a year of her life to medical aid in Africa. She had felt that she was going to do something really worthwhile, something good. And what better remedy to forget her own problems than go and help the needy? But the daily fight to cure the ill and wounded was taking its toll. Lately there had been nights when she had collapsed into bed in a state of utter exhaustion, too tired even to eat.

This morning, suddenly, she felt incapable of facing her patients. Her stomach seemed to turn at the idea of another day of wiping off blood, cleaning deep wounds and bandaging them; of putting ointment on burns; or of giving injections to people shaking with fever. Her whole being revolted against it. She wanted to see nothing but beautiful, healthy men and women. People who had not cut themselves with their pangas or fallen into the fire. Wives not beaten up by drunken husbands. Children not shaking with malaria and without bloated tummies. She had been here a mere ten weeks and had already seen enough human misery to last her for a lifetime. And she had signed up for a year! How could she possibly stick it out for another nine and a half months?

Why had she come to Africa? What was she doing here? I'll be lucky, she thought, if I get away from it without my health being permanently damaged.

33

'So you're worrying about all the dirt here?' remarked Marie one morning soon after.

'Why do you think so?' replied Gael evasively.

'Don't deny it. I've been watching you for a few days now, and have seen you boiling the boiled water again. For minutes at a time.'

'Oh! I just think that you can never be careful enough over here.' She looked uncomfortably at her cup of tea. 'You must agree that the river water is not very clean. I have noticed people crouching in the water to relieve themselves.' She blushed slightly. 'They wash in it, too. And then the women go down to the river and fill their calabashes with that same water to take home. Do you think they drink it?' There was an expression of repugnance on Gael's face.

'I see what's bothering you. The river water is not particularly clean. But it's not the local pollution that's the worst. The worst polluters are the mining companies further upstream. But where else can most people get their water from? Some health projects do try to sink wells, but human beings do not easily change their habits. As long as the elders survive and dominate, they want the younger generation to act as they themselves have always done.' She grinned. 'Often with little or no success, thank God. Still, if grandmothers had their say everyone would still be drinking water from the river.'

'There you are,' said Gael. 'And that's what we have to live with!'

'Not you, silly girl,' said Marie. 'We've got our own well, and the water we pump up goes through a filter, as you may have noticed. On top of that we boil it for our tea. And our meals are thoroughly cooked, so much so that all the taste has gone out.'

'That's rather a relief. From what I've learned so far, most of the illnesses people pick up here come from what they drink and eat.'

'Well, it pays to be careful. You're quite right there. Still, a little bit of dirt doesn't do any harm. Your body has to build up a natural resistance.

It needs to get used to bacteria and viruses. The more you fight them with modern medicine, the worse it gets, I think. Your body has to learn to live in symbiosis with them.'

Gael shuddered. 'I'm not very keen on bacteria.'

'But we've got to live with them! Whether we like it or not, they're everywhere: on our skin, up our noses, inside our stomachs and guts. And a good thing, too. We couldn't survive without bacteria. They help us to digest foods and to perform vital functions. It's a symbiotic relationship that has worked well for hundreds of millions of years. We are floating in a world of bacteria. We live by their grace. They are the ones that tolerate us, not the other way around. We are wedded to them, as are all other animals and plants. We've had to adapt to them, even co-opt many of them to survive. Yet we look upon bacteria as enemies, just as we look upon the natural environment as something hostile that we have to tame.'

'But so many bacteria are detrimental. I think it's fortunate that we have antibiotics.'

'Some bacteria are bad for us, of course, just like some plants are poisonous or some animals are dangerous. But that's no reason to attack the lot. And, unfortunately, that's what many people in modern society are doing: they are fighting an escalating battle with all the power our medical technology can muster. But that's one of their greatest delusions! They cannot win that battle. And one day they may push the bacteria too far, and they will strike back and wipe us off the face of the Earth. That is . . . if we don't wipe ourselves out before that time, of course.'

Marie sat there pondering for a while. 'Bacteria . . . they were already around billions of years before we humans appeared. And they will still be around billions of years after we have disappeared. It's a certainty that they will outlive us.'

34

In his office in Brussels Jack Smally picked up Anton's report and read the title: A NEW METHOD TO DETECT DEPOSITS OF RARE METALS. That sounds interesting, he thought and began to read the ten-page report.

It took him a full two hours to work through the pages. He didn't understand all of it, but his sixth sense told him that here was something of exceptional interest. He called in Pauline.

'Do you know anything about this?' he asked, holding up the pages.

'That's the report that awful Anton brought in, isn't it? What's it about?'

'He seems to have found a clever new way to detect metal deposits. I have a feeling that the geological community will go wild when they hear about it.'

'The geological community, you say? What a strange coincidence. I've finally had time to look through the pile of unsorted documents Mrs Vanabel left behind, and I was just about to tell you what I found in there: an invitation to an international geological conference!'

'An invitation?'

'Yes. For the director of the laboratory. He has been invited to give a talk.'

'Give a talk?'

'Well, that's what the invitation says.'

'But I don't know anything about this.'

'Of course not. The letter arrived before you became director. Maybe Mrs Vanabel knows. Why don't you leave this to me?' suggested Pauline, smiling. 'I've got her phone number and I'll find a way to squeeze the information out of her.'

35

Half an hour later Pauline entered Smally's office, radiant. He affectionately laid his hand on her bottom as she stood next to him and said: 'Yes?'

'I've got it. The invitation was for Monsieur Briart, but once he'd been made rector he was no longer interested. So he thought of sending Anton instead to talk about his new method to detect metal deposits.'

'What! And does the scoundrel know this?'

Pauline smiled reassuringly. 'No. That's what's so wonderful. Monsieur Briart forgot to tell him. And when finally he remembered about the conference on his last day at the lab, he couldn't find the letter and Anton wasn't there either. So he told Mrs Vanabel to arrange everything. But she never got around to doing it and never told Anton anything! You kept her too busy, she said.'

'I kept her too busy? How dare she!'

'Still, it's lucky for you, isn't it?'

'Why should that be lucky for me?'

'Well, as you're the director now, I think you should go and give the talk.'

'How can I give a talk? I haven't got a subject.'

'But you do have a subject!' She pointed at Anton's paper lying on Smally's desk.

'I can't do that! It isn't my paper.'

'Of course you can! Those puffed-up scientists jolly well ought to submit all their ideas to you first. They should respect the hierarchy! You are the boss. You're doing them a favour by presenting their ideas. And remember, you're the one who's been invited to give the talk.'

'There's something in what you say,' admitted Smally. 'Yes, there is . . . But won't Anton kick up a fuss when he finds out?'

'I wouldn't bother about him if I were you,' suggested Pauline. 'As you're not going to renew his contract he'll be out of the way and won't even know. And it would really boost your career if you went. It's an extremely important international geological conference from what I understand. The directors of all the world's mining companies will be there to listen to you. You'll become famous. Oh, I would be so proud of you if you became famous!'

Smally now began to smile to himself. 'Where does this conference take place?' he asked.

'Somewhere in Africa. In one of the capitals called Bobodiou.'

'In Africa? Do you mean to say that I would have to go to Africa?'

'I can't see any problem there. I think you're made for adventure. I'm sure you'd enjoy it enormously. The only thing that would make me terribly sad is that you would be away for such a long time. Even now I find the weekends dull and long. I don't know how I'll survive here without you. I wish I could go with you.'

All of a sudden Smally had a vision of the two of them in a tropical country spending wild nights together, and before he had time to stop the words, he blurted out: 'That can be arranged. Why don't we go together?'

Pauline's mouth fell open, she looked at him with sparkling eyes and cried out: 'Yippie!' With a quick movement she pulled up her miniskirt, flung herself on his knees facing him, one leg on each side of the chair, and began to kiss him.

Smally suddenly realised the implications of his promises and he made one last attempt to wriggle out of them. 'It's a complicated subject,' he mumbled between two kisses. 'I don't know whether I'll be . . .'

'Nothing is beyond your capacities!' she cried, taking his hand and thrusting it between her legs. 'Feel how hot you make me, just thinking of going to Africa with you. You can do anything you set your mind to. Even make love in this position on the chair. Just unzip your trousers.'

Twenty minutes later when it was all over and he lay back on his chair gasping for breath while Pauline was lying limply on top of him, her head on his shoulder and her arms hanging down, he said: 'Yes, I'll do it. We'll go to Africa and I'll give the talk.'

36

Africa! When Gael thought about where she was, she recoiled. Nothing in her life had prepared her for this. In fact, she hadn't really given it a thought before coming here. Back in Brussels she had just imagined dedicating her life to a good cause; that was all. And, of course, she had desperately wanted to get away from Anton. She never wanted to see him again.

But then . . . the shock of Africa! It had been much worse than she could ever have imagined. The primitive living conditions, the absence of even the most basic things she had been used to all her life, the isolation, the filth, the masses of sick and wounded. It was too much for her. She just couldn't cope and gradually she had begun to withdraw. She lived, ate, worked and slept, and took care of those who needed her. Her body was in Africa, but her mind wasn't there. It was the only way to prevent herself from starting to scream, from going mad.

Then, little by little, she felt that the outside world was creeping in through the defences she had erected around herself. The first time she had become aware of her surroundings was when Marie had taken her to the local market. At first Gael had refused but Marie had insisted.

'Come on,' she'd said. 'It'll do you good.' And finally Gael had followed Marie like an obedient dog, not wanting to upset her.

The local market was a world of smell, sound and colour, vibrating with life in all its strength. Walking past the stalls, scattered bits of conversation, light-hearted African music and carefree laughter began to penetrate Gael's soul. The warmth, the vitality of these people somehow managed to seep into her. Children surrounded her, staring at her with eyes full of natural curiosity. Then a little girl touched her arm and put her small hand into hers and suddenly, with a pang, Gael sprang into life again.

For the first time, there in that market, she began to take an interest in the world around her. She touched the woven tapestries, felt their texture, let her fingers wander over the smooth curves of wooden sculptures . . . She gazed at the bright colours of the women's dresses and returned the women's shy smiles. And when she looked at their smiling faces, she knew that her long nightmare had come to an end. She had resurfaced into a world of colour and sunshine.

Her mind had lain dormant and her heart had been closed. Now a ray of light had touched her and all at once life began to flow through her again. But later, as she was lying on her bed, aware of these new feelings, listening to the sounds of the night, suddenly the pain reappeared. Images of the past that she had suppressed for so many weeks kept sliding into her mind. Once again she saw her dreams lying in broken pieces all over the floor while a naked woman trampled on them with a triumphant sneer on her face. I must exorcise this suffering, she thought. Pull out these images by the roots. She no longer wanted to be numb; she wanted to have feelings again – but not the pain.

She wanted to live once more with wide-open eyes, feel the warmth of the people around her, open up to them, return their shy attempts to meet her as a real person. For that was what they wanted her to be. Here she was not just an official figure doing her job, employed by someone for a salary, faceless and interchangeable. Here she was a real person. When local people greeted her they addressed themselves to the human being she was, not to the aid worker. And when children took her hand, they took the hand of Gael, that strange-coloured young woman who had come to them from another world. Here everything was personal, direct, human.

The touch, the light, the colours . . . they were so different here from anything she had ever experienced. They were so much more intense, so vibrant, bursting with life and yet gentle, more enveloping than intruding. She soaked it all up like a sponge that had lain dry for a long, long time, and as life flowed into her again, the light in her eyes softened, a smile began to colour her lips and her face radiated back some of the warmth her heart was receiving.

37

Her medical work, too, was becoming more rewarding. Marie reckoned that Gael had acquired enough experience to do things on her own, and every now and then she sent her off on inoculation campaigns into the outlying countryside. On such occasions Bamboko, a huge coal-black man, was her driver, mechanic and medical help combined. He was kindness itself, very protective and always concerned about Gael's comfort.

There were no Europeans in the outlying hamlets and when they arrived, women and children would press in on her, wanting to touch her. At times it became uncomfortable and then Bamboko would move about like a guardian, keeping them at a distance. He seemed to feel a personal responsibility for Gael's well-being and was constantly on the watch lest anything should happen to her. He would hop around like a mother hen fussing over its little chick, almost making clucking sounds. And, indeed, Gael looked like a small being next to him.

He always insisted on carrying everything. The first thing he invariably did before they began was to install a folding chair for her to sit in the shade. Then he would turn to the mothers with babies waiting to be inoculated and line them up outside the field hospital – which was usually no more than a somewhat bigger hut. Next he would call them in one by one, ask for the name of the child, write it on a card, and after the child had been inoculated he would hand the card to the mother, to hang on to as if it were a precious document. It was like a ritual in which Gael played the most important part: that of giving the crying babies an injection that would protect them from some devastating illness.

38

Little by little Gael began to adapt to Africa. There was no need to rush out to the yard in the morning and start taking care of the patients. They didn't expect to be helped straight away; there were no appointments. If people were sick, they had been so for several days already, and if they had wounds that needed attention, they would not come immediately. They always hoped that their condition would improve of its own accord and would wait until the wound got so bad that they could barely walk. They would sometimes try folk remedies or go to the witch doctor first, which more often than not made things considerably worse.

Those who had already arrived from the neighbouring villages at this early hour had often walked through part of the night, and once they reached the dispensary they sat down leaning against the wall, resting with outstretched legs.

From where she was sitting at the breakfast table, holding a cup of boiling tea in both her hands to warm her fingers, Gael could hear their voices, chatting quietly just behind the wall as they were waiting patiently till Madame and her new young help were ready to start their day's work and look after them.

Time . . . thought Gael as she stared dreamily at the tops of the thorn trees outside the enclosure and at the sky which was getting brighter every minute. Time feels different in Africa. It flows slowly here, like water trickling out of a fountain. You can almost feel it running through your fingers, bubbling. Or maybe it's like a pebble which you hold in the palm of your hand. You can look at its shiny, gleaming surface, touch its smoothness, turn it over and then see its shady side. Yes, time is like that. No rush. Turn it over in your mind, look at its multiple facets, slowly. Just savour it.

'You're very quiet this morning,' came Marie's voice. 'What are you thinking about?'

'Oh! Nothing special . . . about time. It's so different from what it was in Europe. It's such a luxury to have time.'

Marie smiled. 'It's one of the few luxuries Africans have. They have time, African people. Plenty of it. If time had been money, as some in the West claim, all Africans would be millionaires.'

'That's exactly how I feel this morning!' exclaimed Gael. 'Like a millionaire. I have time on my hands. I no longer rush. That's one thing Africa has taught me: that time doesn't matter. But . . . but also that one must be in harmony with it. One must let it pass freely, slowly, without disturbing its flow. Maybe there's a contradiction in what I'm saying?' She looked at Marie with questioning eyes.

'*Ma fille*, how you have grown in wisdom in these few months!' Marie smiled affectionately at Gael. 'If other Europeans who work here could learn a fraction of what you have learned, they would be so much happier.'

'Don't they keep their eyes and minds open then?'

'If only! Most Europeans can't be changed. When they come over here they import not only their technology but also their Western lifestyles, their rushing, hurried attitudes. I have been to some of the mining settlements for expatriates. You should see them in their walled compounds. They can't live without all the comforts they've been used to; without electricity and air conditioning; without timesaving equipment and time-wasting entertainment. They need to remain connected. They create a small artificial island for themselves with a high wall around, a surrogate copy of a Western city, and don't want to look out over that wall. They're not interested in what's on the other side; they don't want to feel lost. "And isn't that the right attitude," they argue when you try to talk to them. "Africa has got everything to learn from us, hasn't it? We've got the knowledge; we've got the technology. What could we possibly learn from Africa?" Anyway, they're usually only here for a few months, or a few years at most, and when they go back home they count themselves lucky to have survived the terrible ordeal that staying in Africa represents for them.' Marie sighed deeply.

'But when you are an old Africa hand like me things are different. You learn, year after year. You may not realise it, but every time you return here you compare. And every time you feel less European and more African. Somehow, you grow in strength, in wisdom. You whittle down your necessities to the bare minimum. Little by little, all the things you needed in the West, all those comforts and luxuries you thought you couldn't do without, seem to become unimportant. And suddenly you are free. You find that you can live easily in Africa, that you are happy in Africa. And that, maybe, the superiority of Western life is one great illusion – the illusion of the century.'

39

'So it's important to have time?' ventured Gael. It was still early and she didn't feel like starting her work yet. She was used to Marie by now and knew that it only needed the slightest encouragement for a whole new story to pop out of the multi-coloured kaleidoscope that Marie's life had been.

'Of course. It helps a lot to have time,' replied Marie, her fingers wrapped around the warmth of her cup of tea.

'Tell me how it helps . . .'

'Well, you can avoid a lot of unpleasantness when you have time. I'll just give you a little example from Africa, shall I?' She glanced expectantly at Gael.

'Yes, please.'

'I've often had to cross borders in Africa, and what with being white and therefore rich in the eyes of Africans, and the border officials having power and wanting to get a small share of your wealth . . . It's quite understandable, really . . .' Marie sat there for a while, thinking and nodding to herself. She was liable to be sidetracked by any new thought that crossed her mind – and her mind was a storehouse of varied thoughts. Finally she carried on: 'But I do object to such practices because whatever these men wrench out of you does not go any further than their own stomachs. It is immediately converted into beer and food, not into anything useful for their wives and children. They spend it all on themselves. Or else it goes to keeping up an expensive mistress, a *bureau* they call it – an office. "I'm going to my second office," they say, or "to my third office," if their position permits it. No, I don't want to give to government officials.'

'Goodness me, I never imagined that it could be as bad as that.'

'It's not bad. Don't judge,' warned Marie. 'No, that's just the way it is. Anyway . . . the border guards know they can't actually stop you if your papers are in order, but they can be extremely slow in processing them and giving you exit stamps. That's their strength and also the weakness of Europeans. They have time – Europeans don't. Western people in general want to get on; they want to arrive somewhere at a given hour. They plan their trips; they have a schedule to follow; and they end by giving the guards money to speed up their work. But I, I am no longer European. My outside looks white but my mind has become African. And so, when they tell me that I may have to wait for several hours, maybe a whole day, I don't protest. I pretend that I don't know about bribes. I just say: "Fine, I shall wait then, here in my car," and I install myself comfortably and fall asleep.'

Gael laughed aloud. 'I can just see you doing that sort of thing. You would think of it. And I bet you they don't like it.'

'They don't.' Marie smiled contentedly. 'No, that really gets their goat. After a while they come to the car and knock on the window. I wake up all smiles, exclaiming: "Are you ready? How nice!" Then they go away grinding their teeth and I fall asleep again. After an hour they can stand it no longer. They come over to where the car is parked, wake me up, thrust the papers into my hands and tell me to move on. I can see that they're not pleased, but I thank them profusely for their speedy work. Yes,' said Marie as other pleasant memories drifted through her mind. 'That's what happens if you move over to African time.'

40

That same morning in Brussels Anton turned into a quiet side street leading off one of the main roads. It was one of those typical streets with houses built in a row in the French style, as had been the fashion around 1900. Minutes later he stood in front of a house bearing a plaque with the inscription: Brussels' Section of the African Medical Aid Organisation.

He had already been to two aid organisations and had drawn a blank. This was his last chance, and he pressed the bell with some apprehension. After a while the door opened slightly and the head of a woman of around forty appeared. She peered at him suspiciously but seeing that he looked respectable, she said: 'Yes?'

'I'm so sorry to bother you unannounced,' said Anton, doing his very best to smile and be friendly. 'You see . . . I'm shortly driving to Africa in a Land-Rover and I thought that I might as well contact some aid organisations to offer my help. Do you have any parcels or medical supplies that need to be taken over there? I've got lots of free space and it would be a shame to waste it. I'd be delighted to be of any help to organisations like yours which support such a worthy cause.'

The woman visibly mellowed. Still, the man might be anyone; you could never be careful enough. 'How do you know about us?' she wanted to know.

'Oh, a very good friend of mine told me about it,' he replied, seeming to exude confidence. 'I do hope I've got the right address . . . she's joined one of your projects in Africa.'

'What's her name?'

'Gael Fernley. You have got someone of that name working for you, haven't you?' He said it with an even face, bluffing for what he was worth. 'A young woman, fair, not very tall . . .'

The woman reflected while Anton held his breath. 'Of course . . .' she said finally. 'Gael Fernley. Yes, yes . . . she left for Africa, oh . . . several months ago.'

Anton felt his head spin and was barely able to hide his relief, but the woman was no longer looking. She had already turned round saying: 'Do come in,' and led him along a corridor into a small room next to her office. 'Please sit down here,' she said. 'What's your name?'

'I'm Dr Felsen, geologist,' replied Anton with as much aplomb as he could muster and, trying to keep the woman talking, he added: 'I'm really glad that I remembered the name of your organisation. Gael was so enthusiastic about what she was going to do that it stayed in my mind. Where did she go again? Wasn't it the Congo?'

'No, no. We haven't got any projects in the Congo. She flew to Bobodiou.'

Anton's heart beat so hard that he was hardly able to hide his excitement. He had discovered where she was! 'Isn't that in Central Africa?'

The woman smiled, as a teacher would have in front of a slightly dumb pupil. 'No! It's in the Sahel. In fact, it's not too far south of the Sahara.'

'She's working in Bobodiou then?'

'No, no. Bobodiou is the capital. The medical centre where she's working is somewhere east of the capital. What's the name again? Let me see ... I think it's called Kanibasso or something like that, but I'm not quite sure.' She looked at him apologetically and added: 'You'd better ask the director, Dr Wilbert. He'll be arriving soon. He'll know.'

Just then the door swung open and a tall strong man walked in.

'Oh, here's the director himself,' said the woman.

'Yes?' said the doctor while Anton got up to say hello.

'This is Dr Felsen, a geologist,' said the woman. 'He's driving to Africa and is offering to take medicine and other aid materials for us. He's a friend of Gael Fernley ...'

At once, suspicion spread over Doctor Wilbert's face. He motioned to the woman to follow him to the next room and closed the door, but Anton could hear them speak.

'What's all this?' barked the doctor, short-tempered. 'Who's that man?'

'I don't know him,' replied the woman taken aback. 'He just rang the bell and said he was a friend of Gael Fernley.'

'Didn't I tell you that she gave us strict instructions not to reveal anything about her whereabouts to anyone?'

'Oh, but ... I forgot and ... and seeing that he offered to help the project ...'

'You stay here. I'll handle this!'

He entered the room where Anton was sitting and stood squarely in front of him.

'Thanks for proposing to help us,' he said in a cold voice, 'but I'm afraid that we have no use for your offer. I'm flying out to Africa myself within a week or two and will take whatever is needed.'

The doctor now turned to the woman, who had reappeared, red-faced. 'Will you please let the gentleman out,' he instructed. Then he disappeared upstairs.

41

'I'm thinking of leaving,' said Anton as he sat down on Michel's desk.

'What!' exclaimed Michel. 'Why?'

'Because I'm totally fed up with the whole caboodle. And with my life.'

'Didier has already left and now you! You can't do that to me! I don't want to stay behind with that little weasel. If you're going to leave I'm leaving, too.'

'I thought that you had your eye on Lottie . . . wasn't she a goddess on Earth?'

'I'm no longer interested!' Michel spoke firmly. 'I'm not going to wait for her. If I do, I'll wait forever before my number comes up. You were quite right.'

'But isn't there anyone else? You're always so interested in women.'

'Don't talk any more about women! They just take one look at me and run. No, I'm through with those impossible creatures.'

Anton shrugged his shoulders. 'If that's the way you feel about it, why not? But what are you going to live off if you leave the lab? Don't you need a job?'

'I think I may have a job.' Michel gave Anton a conspiratorial look. 'You know . . . Didier? I've just spoken to him.'

'He phoned from America?'

'Yeah. He's working for a mining company over there at triple his previous salary, imagine. And it's interesting work, too.'

'He's pleased then?'

'Yes, he is. And you know what he proposed? That I join their company.'

'You're really serious about leaving then?'

'And why shouldn't I leave? What is there to hold me back here, I ask you? If that asshole of a Smally thinks I'm going to run around for him as if I were his little poodle, he's badly mistaken.'

'So you're going to America?'

'Not at all. I'm going to Africa. Didier told me that they're looking for someone with exactly my qualifications for a job with one of their mines over there. It pays very well, but he told me to go there first to find out how I liked it. The political situation is kind of unstable, you see. But if I don't mind he'll arrange for me to be hired on the spot. So, if you leave, I'm off, too. I'm going to try my luck. Anything is better than vegetating here.'

'Whereabouts is that mine of yours?'

'It's near a town called Bobodiou. Lot of mining going on around there it seems.'

'No!' Anton's mouth nearly fell open. 'Not Bobodiou! But that's exactly where I'm going to drive to.'

'What! You're going to drive there? All the way from here! You've got to cross the Sahara, you know . . .'

'I know. That's no problem. I've got a fully equipped Land-Rover. And how did you think of getting there?'

'I haven't made any plans yet. I haven't even agreed to go there yet. But it would be great fun if we went together. How long would it take to drive from here to Bobodiou?'

'Probably two weeks at the most. I've just bought a map of Africa and there seem to be several roads through the Sahara. It's a long way, of course, but if you come with me, we can take turns at the wheel. And it would be interesting, too. We'll pass through some really out-of-the-way places . . . And you know what? You can take as much luggage as you like. And we can share the cost of the petrol and that'll make it really cheap.'

'Sounds good to me,' nodded Michel. 'Hey!' he suddenly exclaimed, pointing a finger at Anton. 'What about you? What are you going to live off in Africa? Don't you need a job?'

'I think I've saved up enough to survive for a year in Africa. I can live on very little if I need to.'

'Well, if you say so . . . Anyway, I like your idea of driving to Bobodiou . . . I like it very much indeed, setting off just like that. I've always dreamed of doing that sort of thing one day but . . . to be honest, I don't think I've got the guts to do it alone. Well . . .' he extended his hand. 'I'm your man.'

'Wonderful!' Anton looked relieved. 'All we need is a week to get the necessary visas and pack our luggage, and off we go.'

'A week for the preparations and two weeks for the trip, that's three weeks in all. OK! I'll ring Didier tonight, so that he can arrange a meeting for me in three weeks from today.' And as he shook hands with Anton he called out: 'Bobodiou, here we come!'

Part Four

1

Gael had been living in a time capsule since she had moved to Africa. She was oblivious to what went on in the wider world. She was not aware of the wars that were always raging in one spot or another; she had no idea of decisions taken by world leaders, although these were of vital importance – or so they claimed; neither did she read about the glittering lives of celebrities, nor see on a screen the smug, self-congratulating faces of certain public figures. She was cut off from it all.

She no longer thought of the far-away world. It was out there, somewhere, but to her it wasn't real. The dispensary had become her real world. She just got up each morning, set about her daily routine, was busy from daybreak till nightfall, then ate, talked or gazed at the stars, and dropped into bed.

There was so much suffering to alleviate, so much misery to look after. And yet Gael had never seen so many smiling people. Her patients, even when shivering with fever or hardly able to stand up because of deep painful wounds, all looked at her with trust. And they smiled at her, almost apologising for bothering her. In a thousand ways they showed her that they cared for her, that they wanted her to feel happy. They were worried about her comfort, they, the sick and crippled!

The villagers, too, showed their affection through many small gestures. Women brought her little things they had made, or gifts of food. Men sometimes waited outside the compound and when she came out they would ask her if she wanted any work done. And the children . . . so many children. They fell into step with her as she walked, shyly sliding a little brown hand into hers, smiling at her out of big shiny eyes. Such beautiful sunny faces they had!

Everyone knew her now in Kanibasso and for miles around. Finding Gael, her real name, too difficult to pronounce, the Africans had given her a name of their own, referring to her English origins. They called her 'Missie' – 'meaning *petite* Miss' – and pronounced it with an African intonation. She was accepted and felt secure wherever she went. She was never alone and felt happier than she had ever been back in Europe, with the exception of those few months which she tried to shut firmly out of her mind.

2

Marie and Gael were sitting in the enclosed yard of the dispensary; work was over and they were having cups of steaming tea and eating some coarse homemade cakes, which Marie had taught the cook to produce after long and patient tutoring.

As she was sipping her tea Gael found herself looking at Marie with interest. She must have been a very beautiful woman once, she thought. Marie had kept very fit for her age, but her hair was turning grey and had lost its lustre, fine lines had appeared in her delicate face, and the skin under her chin had begun to sag. She always wore long trousers and blouses that covered her arms. It was a sensible way of dressing in the fierce African sun, but it also hid the ravages of time. How cruel life is, mused Gael. Marie should never have aged. She should have remained young and beautiful.

'What are you staring at me for?' came Marie's voice abruptly.

'Oh!' Gael blushed. 'I'm sorry, I didn't realise . . . I didn't mean to be rude.'

'Who cares about being rude? You can look at me as much as you like. I don't mind that. But I saw a whole world of thoughts whirling behind those deep blue eyes of yours and I just wondered what you were thinking.'

'I was . . . I was thinking that . . .' Gael's face expressed indecision.

'Come on,' urged Marie. 'Out with it. I won't take offence.'

'Well . . . I thought that you . . .'

'Yes . . .'

'. . . that you must have been very beautiful once and that it's a great shame you had to age. I think ageing is highly unjust . . . especially for women!'

Marie didn't answer for a while. Then she nodded. 'Yes, I was beautiful once . . . yes . . . I was a very pretty young girl like you . . . I would have liked youth to last forever . . .' her voice seemed to falter, '. . . and now it seems so far away . . .' She paused and sat there for some time without moving, her eyes turned inwards, deep down where the memories lay. Finally she continued: 'It's amazing how fast everything has gone. It's a shame really, but I wouldn't call it an injustice. That's the way we all go.' And she repeated very quietly: 'That's the way we all go . . . much too quickly . . .'

'I don't want to get old!' Gael suddenly blurted out. 'I . . . I'd prefer to die young.'

'Don't be silly!' Marie looked at her with disapproval. 'Mind you . . . I do understand your feelings. Ageing is hard to bear, especially when for many years you've been used to seeing men following you with their eyes as you pass by, staring at you with longing. And then, one day, you realise that they no longer pay any attention – even men older than yourself, much older . . . that they prefer to look at young girls . . . at fresh, pretty things. It does hurt, I can tell you, when you discover that no one seems to want you any longer . . .'

Tears came into Gael's eyes. She had thought of Marie as a somewhat distracted, even scatter-brained older woman. Now she saw her as a sad human being that seemed to have outlived its reason for existing. She put her hand on Marie's arm and whispered: 'I'm sorry.'

Her words made Marie look up.

'Whom or what are you sorry for?'

'That you're so sad . . . that you no longer want to live . . .'

'What are you talking about? Who says I no longer want to live? I love life, even though I know that I mustn't expect too much from it now. But I'm certainly not complaining. I've had more than my fair share of fun and happiness. My past will never come back; there's no way it ever could. But even if I can no longer relive the passions of the past, there are still lots of things that give me happiness. And I want to feel useful.'

'So . . . that is why you're out here?'

'In part. But there's much more . . . I just couldn't stay in Europe after my husband died ten years ago. I wanted to return to Africa. You see . . . it's only in Africa that I have experienced the true measure of our existence. It is only here that I've felt the immensity of space, the sheer strength of life, harsh and unadulterated.' Marie sat there for a while, staring at the lonely sky. 'Every time I had to leave Africa – and my husband and I left it many times – part of me always refused to come along. It was as if I were torn in two. My physical half went back to Europe, old Europe with its culture and man-made history, its well-dressed people and rich cities. And I would attend dinners and go to parties, and talk, and talk. But my spiritual half, my heart as one might say, was not there. It had remained in Africa. Sometimes I felt like a split personality, like someone schizophrenic. I once or twice tried to explain myself, but found no one to be a sounding board.'

'A sounding board?'

'Well, yes. Only if the other person is like a sounding board, giving back the sounds you produce, can you really be sure that you're understood. You see, music . . . you have to make it together, in unison. That's the basis of African music. I don't have to explain that, do I?'

'No, no. I see what you mean.'

'So, when I wanted to return to Africa after my husband's death there was no way I could explain myself to my family or my friends. I was worried that they would think me strange, and they most probably did. "You never know what to make of her," I sometimes heard them say softly; or: "I wonder if she's really all right up there?" I once noticed a man I had sat next to during dinner, tapping his temple with his finger. "Probably too much sun," he whispered to his neighbour.'

'It must have been very difficult for you.'

'For the first five years or so, yes. After that people no longer try to understand, or even bother if you make strange remarks. That, I found out, was one of the few advantages of getting older. I got used to saying just what I thought, even if it upset people. I seemed to get away with it because people didn't want to be rude to me.' Marie laughed out loud at her own remark. 'But you must have had enough of my chatter by now. It's your turn to talk. I'm curious to know why a pretty girl like you came out here to bury herself in a godforsaken corner of Africa. That's what I've been asking myself ever since I set eyes on you, and as tonight seems to be a night of confidences, you might as well tell me something about yourself.'

Gael seemed strangely reluctant to do so. 'Well,' she said after a few moments, 'I wasn't quite happy in Europe. I thought that there must be more to life than work and earning money. And I suppose I wanted to dedicate my life to a worthwhile cause.'

'Is that all?' asked Marie, disappointed. Gael's reluctance brought home that she knew very little about her. The girl had in fact been extremely good at turning attention away from herself and avoiding any personal questions. 'I'm certain that there is much more to your coming out here than that. Why don't you tell me?'

When Gael didn't answer, Marie became even more insistent. 'I have a feeling that there's something you're trying to hide. You're pushing it away inside you, hoping that it will disappear, aren't you? But it won't. Wounds can leave deep scars. You will find out that when you expect it least, the old wound starts bleeding again and I can tell you that it hurts nearly as much as it did the first day. The truth is that some wounds never heal.'

Gael turned away and as Marie looked at her face, at her profile traced so beautifully against the rapidly fading light of the sky, she was struck by the expression of deep unhappiness that passed over it for a short moment. It seemed so much at odds with her cheerful nature, her willingness to put up with the most awful circumstances, and her unfailing desire to alleviate the suffering of others.

'You said a moment ago that you thought I no longer wanted to live,' remarked Marie. 'Maybe it's *you* who no longer want to live. Is it broken love? I think that you're unhappy, very unhappy. I can read it in your eyes. It hangs around your body like a dark cloak.'

Gael had been listening with growing unease. Then she seemed to come out of a profound trance and cried out: 'I don't want to talk about it!'

Marie looked at her, surprised at such a violent reaction. 'All right,' she acquiesced. 'But remember: it's no good keeping unhappiness locked up. When the poison stays inside you, the cancer spreads. A conflict like the one I feel you're carrying with you must be resolved. You must talk about it. You must flush it out of your system. Maybe not today . . . but another day when the moment is right for you. Come and find me when you're ready.'

Night had fallen, stars began to twinkle and suddenly, from the oasis somewhere further along the river, voices rose, accompanied by the clapping of hands. Slowly, in fits and starts, a deep timeless song rose up and began to drift in and out of the palm grove like the wind of the desert. The sound gradually enveloped Gael and penetrated into her heart – into the wound that had not healed. And one after another, tears dropped from her eyes onto the dry sand at her feet.

3

When the big Russian cargo plane landed in the freight area of Bobodiou airport and Boris and Igor set foot on the tarmac, they recoiled. The heat was overpowering. They immediately removed their heavy overcoats while three Africans in uniform, who had leisurely strolled up to them, looked on in amusement. Soon the two Russians were standing in the bright sunlight in their shirtsleeves; then they sat down and started to take off their thick boots while keeping a wary eye on their heavy shoulder bags filled with documents and dollars.

Within no time several African vendors turned up, all wearing mobile phones hung from nylon cords strung around their necks, and they began to press brightly coloured T-shirts on the Russians; hats; sunglasses, and anything else those new customers might conceivably be willing to buy.

'Want hat?' said one man, literally shoving a hat on Igor's head. 'Good fit. Cheap. Keeps sun away.' And when he saw Igor's dollars: 'You got dollars? Very good! We accept any money.' And before the Russian could stop him, he had grabbed a handful of notes and shoved another two hats on Igor's head.

Within no time the Russians had their arms full of goods they would never have dreamed of buying only ten minutes ago. To their surprise, they found that they each had three or four wristwatches in their hands or around their arms; hats on their heads and others hanging from strings on their shoulders; four pairs of shoes; jackets and trousers; a suitcase; bed linen; forks and knives; three pairs of sunglasses; fishing rods; a portable radio/CD-player, and a medley of other goods. And all the time they were desperately trying to cling on to their money bags, which were the centre of attention of ten pairs of eyes and as many hands.

Meanwhile the unloading of the cargo plane was in full swing. A few officials from the Russian Embassy had arrived and were supervising the operations: one after the other, big mining trucks rolled out of the belly of the monstrous plane and were lined up neatly next to each other; then four huge crates slid out of the aircraft; finally the doors were shut and the now-empty plane began to taxi to the airstrip, preparing to take off.

Boris and Igor stood there, feeling lost. Back in Moscow they had been thoroughly briefed by Viktor Ippolitovich but this was the first time they had been given a responsible role, and it was all a bit too much for them.

'Where . . . where is security?' they asked bewildered. The three uniformed Africans, who had been there from the start, strutted forward and stuck out their chests saying: 'We are airport security.' But all the same, the lively trade around the two Russians continued unabated for another quarter of an hour.

Suddenly a military jeep appeared round the corner and came to a halt with screeching tyres. As the armed guards jumped out, the African vendors scattered and disappeared as mysteriously as they had come, leaving the Russians with a pile of cheap goods at their feet but without their boots and overcoats, which had vanished together with a wad or two of dollars.

One of the military men now stepped forward. 'Have you got anything to declare?' he asked sternly.

Boris and Igor remembered what they'd been told. 'Act as if you've got nothing to hide,' Viktor Ippolitovich had instructed them. 'They can check all the mining equipment. Pay the import taxes straight away in dollars. Don't discuss. Just pay anything they want. But don't let them touch those four crates! They contain the weapons and mustn't be opened on any account. Tell them they contain diplomatic material and that they have to go unopened to our embassy. Defend them with your lives. You've got nothing to fear. You're protected by diplomatic immunity. So be firm. The success of the revolution depends on your steadfastness!'

As they faced the military, they were slightly nervous. Their command of French was far from good and they found the African accent difficult to understand, but they managed to convey the gist of what they had to say and didn't budge when the military began to circle the four crates with suspicion.

Two of the guards finally drove away, to return a quarter of an hour later with a customs officer. The man strutted towards them, took one look at the trucks and shouted: 'What! Six big new trucks loaded with drilling equipment. You want to import these? That's going to take a long time. And cost a lot of money!'

He motioned to the Russians to follow him to an office, but only Boris went while Igor stayed with the crates. As he sat down in front of the customs officer, Boris remembered the good old Communist practice when dealing with a difficult official situation. He passed a large wad of brand-new dollars under the table into the hand of the man and waited. The officer took one look at what he had received, smiled contentedly and shot into action. He dug a sheaf of documents out of a drawer, filled them out and began to stamp them energetically, trying to get everything over before other customs officers arrived. Boris paid the huge import duties without so much as blinking an eyelid and the import formalities were over in less than a quarter of an hour. The officer didn't even bother to check the trucks and soon the heavily loaded vehicles began to leave the compound with African drivers hired by the Russian Embassy behind the wheels, and a man from the embassy in the cabin of the first truck.

All that remained now were the four huge crates, but here the customs officer was adamant. No amount of dollars could bribe him to let these go. He told Boris that the *brigade spéciale* was going to come and that he would have to wait.

As he walked back to the crates, which were standing on the hot tarmac where they had been dumped, Boris felt worried. Things were definitely not going to plan. The embassy people had gone instead of defending them, just leaving them some food and water, but Boris and Igor remembered their strict instructions and remained behind with the crates, leaning protectively against them. They waited for several hours but no special brigade turned up. Then darkness fell and the compound was locked up for the night. And slowly, as the mosquitoes began to descend in swarms on any uncovered part of their bodies, it began to dawn on the two men that they had been abandoned to their fate.

At the same time some sixty miles from there, the convoy of trucks was stopped by a small rebel force. 'Which trucks contain the weapons?' asked the leader.

'These two,' replied the man from the Russian embassy.

The rebels set to work at once, and quickly and efficiently they began to transfer the arms and ammunition to the fleet of small jeeps that were waiting behind a dune.

4

'Mr President! Mr President!' Gwemboka was having a nap in his big chair on the terrace of the presidential palace when a voice woke him up. And lately, when he woke up, he was invariably in a bad mood because he slept badly.

He had always slept so well in the past. Years ago, when he had been a rebel in the bush, he would just close his eyes and fall asleep the moment he lay down, whether in the sand behind a thorn bush, or on a slab of concrete. And his sleep had been deep and dreamless. But now! His whole body ached when he woke up, especially if he'd fallen asleep as he had this afternoon, slumped in his chair, his head hanging down on one side.

And his joints were painful, almost all of the time. His doctor had said it was because of his great weight, and that he would have to slim. How dared he criticise him, the President! Tell him what to do! And he had ordered the man to be thrown into prison.

The doctors he consulted had overflowed with amiability ever since, as doctors jolly well should. After he'd made this example, they had all obeyed his orders without exception and just given him pills. He had to take heaps of pills now: purple pills, yellow pills, round pills, oblong pills . . . some in the morning and others in the evening; some before and others after meals. It was getting too much for him.

Gwemboka just lost count and usually forgot to take most of his pills, or else took them twice. It had been very difficult until he had struck upon the solution: he had raised one of his trusted subordinates to the rank of 'Guardian of the President's pills'. It was the man's responsibility to keep track of everything and make sure that the President took his pills in the right order and at the appointed times. Mind you, he always had his pills cut in half and obliged the man to swallow the other half first before he took his. One could never be careful enough.

Today he had had a particularly bad nap. He had dreamed that a huge crocodile was pursuing him. He had run as fast as his great bulk had permitted, but had finally been cornered and stood there, panting, staring with terror at the monstrous crocodile which was slowly advancing upon him, hissing threateningly: 'Misster Pressident! Misster Pressident!'

When he opened his eyes in deadly fright, he realised that it was his Minister of Home Affairs and Internal Security, standing there in front of him saying: 'Mr President . . .'

He felt relieved that he had escaped the crocodile, but furious that the stupid Mamboulou had dared disturb him while he was having his nap. And then the thought flashed through his mind that maybe this man was the crocodile trying to swallow him. Maybe his dream had been a premonition!

He now stared at his Minister of Home Affairs and Internal Security with undisguised suspicion. 'What is it?' he barked.

'Mr President . . .' Mamboulou made himself very small. 'I've just caught two foreign spies.'

'How do you know they're spies?'

'They came from Moscow on a big cargo plane,' replied the Minister in a whining voice. 'It was loaded with trucks and material for a Russian mining company up country and . . .'

'Trucks for that Russian company! You didn't let them in, did you? We want the Chinese to get the concession.'

The Minister stood there, visibly shaken. 'I . . . I didn't know anything about this,' he mumbled apologetically.

'You wouldn't! I kept it secret so far, but all the same. You should have stopped those materials from entering the country!'

'But . . . but it all seemed above board. The customs officer made them pay huge import taxes, which they settled on the spot in dollars. And they paid stamp duty, too.'

'Well . . .' Gwemboka waved his hand. 'It doesn't really matter. They will learn in due time that all their attempts are useless. Then they'll have to leave those trucks and all the mining equipment behind, and we'll sell the whole lot to the Chinese.' The President rubbed his hands. 'But why are you gibbering about spies?'

'There were four huge crates on that cargo plane, Mr President, and those two Russians refused to have them checked. They claimed that the crates contained diplomatic documents for the Russian Embassy. They called it a diplomatic bag and invoked diplomatic immunity.'

'A diplomatic bag? Four huge crates!' The President's eyes bulged out of his head. 'This is unheard of! You didn't swallow that story, did you?'

'Of course not. I always think of your safety. That's my mission in life,' Mamboulou hastened to add. Then he continued: 'So we put them under guard for two days until we managed to assemble our rapid intervention team and were ready to investigate. And would you believe it! The two men literally stood in front of the crates, refusing to have them opened. They said it would create a major diplomatic incident. They threatened us! Said we still owed their government a lot of money. But we did open them and . . .'

'And what did you find?' The President looked like an eager child waiting to be told the rest of the story, his mouth half open.

'The crates were full of documents, yes, but not of a very diplomatic nature. They were . . .'

'Come on, come on, tell me!'

'Well, one could call them revolutionary posters.' The Minister had to exert all his self-control not to burst out in loud guffaws when he thought of some of the caricatures of Gwemboka he had just seen. He would gladly have posted them all over Bobodiou himself, but there were limits to what a man in his position could enjoy.

'What do you mean, revolutionary posters? What was written on them?'

'It was awful, Mr President.'

'But I want to know!'

'Well . . . they said really offensive things such as . . . no, I don't dare . . .'

'I order you to tell me!' The President was nearly screaming by now.

'All right. But I want to make it clear that I highly disapprove of what was written there.'

'Tell me!' This time Gwemboka screamed.

'They said . . . they said, "Down with the fat ugly pig!" and other even nastier things.'

'What! What!' The President got up in a state of extreme agitation. 'A fat ugly pig! They dared call me a fat ugly pig!' Gwemboka started to foam at the mouth. 'They must be crushed! They must be burned!'

'We've done that already, Mr President. The crates have been taken away to be burned.'

'You idiot! I mean those two spies! Where are they?'

'They've been thrown into prison, Mr President,' replied Mamboulou, trembling. 'We are awaiting your orders.'

'I want them brought here! Immediately!' He was shaking with rage. 'Dare call me a fat ugly pig!' His huge fat fingers made a wrenching movement as if they were strangling someone, and his eyes bulged out of his head, when suddenly a sharp pain shot through his chest. He gasped for breath and sank down in his chair.

Mamboulou stood there looking at the fat man, holding his breath. Had he had a heart attack? Or a stroke? That would be too good to be true. Then, to Mamboulou's disappointment, the President seemed to stir into life again. He sat there for a while, dazed, staring out into the garden. Finally he noticed his Minister and asked: 'How are the celebrations coming along?'

The Minister was surprised. 'Oh!' he said. 'Well . . . everything is fine. The first foreign dignitaries are already here. And you know who'll be arriving in a few days' time: General de Lattignie.'

'Oh, de Lattignie. Now, that's good news.' The President rubbed his fat hands. 'Bring him to the palace the moment he gets to Bobodiou, will you?'

'All right, I will. But . . . but what about those two spies? What shall I do with them?'

'Which spies?'

'The two Russians we caught.'

'Russians?' asked the President absent-mindedly. 'Oh, by the way . . . has the Russian Ambassador been invited to the celebrations?'

'Of course. But those two Russians?'

The President made a great effort to remember what it was all about, but didn't manage. But a president should never lose face, and Gwemboka spoke with determination. 'We don't want to create a diplomatic incident right now, do we? We'll deal with this problem later when the celebrations are over and everyone has gone home.' And with a wave of his hand he motioned the Minister to leave him alone.

5

'Good news!' exclaimed Marie. 'Our headquarters in Bobodiou have received a telegram from Brussels. Dr Wilbert is going to come out and he wants to visit our dispensary.' She looked at Gael. 'That's going to be really nice for you. We're so isolated here, and you're just stuck with me. It's a miracle that you're not fed up with it by now. He'll be a welcome change for you. He's a man, and good company, too.'

'I've met him,' said Gael without so much as a glimmer of enthusiasm in her voice.

'Didn't you like him?' asked Marie, surprised. 'I've always thought him such an attractive man.'

'I liked him well enough at the beginning, but not on the last day.' Gael seemed to hesitate. 'I'm not sure whether I ought to tell you.'

'Oh, but you can tell me. If there's any problem, it's better for me to know.'

Gael stared out towards the horizon, making a great effort to recall memories that were clearly distasteful. 'You see,' she said after some time, 'the day I left for Africa I had to go to his office to collect the final instructions. As I was leaving he leaned forward to wish me good luck and then, without warning, he flung his arms around me and then began to kiss me on the mouth while I felt his hands slide over my bottom. I stood there for seconds, frozen. Then I wrenched myself free and ran out towards the taxi which was waiting in the street.'

'Goodness me!' exclaimed Marie. 'I can understand men losing their heads over you – you're a very attractive girl. But still . . .'

'And now he's coming here. I'll be at his mercy . . . he's such a strong man.' She looked imploringly at Marie: 'Please, help me . . . I don't want to see him.'

'Don't worry, my girl,' replied Marie with a twinkle in her eyes. 'I'll arrange for you to go off on an inoculation round to an oasis up north while I pick him up in Bobodiou. You won't have to see him.'

6

When Gael returned two days later she found the dispensary in a state of great upheaval. It seemed that Madame had not returned from Bobodiou with the great Bwana. They had sent a car to the capital to find out what had happened, and it appeared that the Bwana and Madame had set off the day before and hadn't been seen since. Everyone feared the worst, as there'd been rumours that rebels had been spotted in the area. Some people came up with the most extraordinary plans: send for the army; order a helicopter, and even wilder suggestions. Gael decided to give it another day. If there wasn't any news by then, she would go and search for Marie herself.

Then, during the afternoon of the following day, Marie drove into the yard of the dispensary at the wheel of her Land-Rover.

When the commotion caused by her arrival had died down, Gael sat her in a chair and soon appeared with two cups of steaming tea.

'We were all so worried,' she said as she handed a cup to Marie. 'We were sure that something awful had happened to you. And where's Dr Wilbert?'

'I've driven Dr Wilbert back to Bobodiou,' replied Marie, looking as if this were the most natural thing in the world. 'I really can't understand what you've been worrying about.'

'But what happened? Why didn't you arrive here the day before yesterday?'

'Oh, we got lost . . .'

'You got lost? How can you have got lost? You know every stone and each patch of sand for hundreds of miles around.'

'Well . . . you see . . . when we set off from Bobodiou, one of the first things Dr Wilbert did was ask for you. And when I explained that he wouldn't be able to see you because you weren't at the dispensary but had gone up north on an inoculation campaign, he became very short-tempered. He ordered me to drive straight to where you were. He insisted that he particularly wanted to see you . . . to find out how you were getting on with your work, he said. And so I took a shortcut through the desert and lost my way . . .' Marie seemed unwilling to elaborate on the subject, and continued: 'And then, towards late afternoon, as the sun began to set, the engine suddenly came to a standstill. I don't know how it happened . . .' She looked puzzled. 'But there you are. That night we

185

slept in the sand and the next morning Dr Wilbert tried to start up the engine, but he doesn't know much about car mechanics and couldn't bring it to life . . .'

'But don't you know a lot about engines?'

'Well . . .' said Marie with an even face, 'I didn't intervene. You know, men don't like women to show them how a car functions. They've got their pride. After that we tried to doze off lying in the shadow of the Land-Rover. At least I did, but when I woke up I found Dr Wilbert standing about, staring at the horizon. I told him that he'd better lie quietly in the shade like me; that way he would perspire less, lose less water, and need to drink less. I explained that we had to drink sparingly to make our water supply last, but he wouldn't listen and became more frantic with every passing hour. He just kept staring at the empty expanse in front of him. When he asked if there was any chance of vehicles passing by, I told him that we could easily be stuck here for a week or more before anyone found us. Then I added that he needn't worry about what would happen in a week's time because, the way he went at it, our water supply would run out within a day. That didn't cheer him up, and when the sun set the second evening with us still in the same spot, he was pretty desperate, I can tell you. When I saw him sitting there looking utterly miserable I felt really sorry for him and put an arm around his shoulders to console him. And then . . . I don't recall exactly how it happened, but I found him kissing me madly and before I could do anything he made love to me.'

'He didn't!' gasped Gael, flinging her hand in front of her mouth.

'I can assure you that he did,' said Marie calmly. 'And when it was all over and I lay there on my back, staring at the stars in wonderment, he suddenly crawled up to me, put his head on my shoulder and started to cry. And I understood him. Such a young life, and so many things that still remained to be done – that he still wanted. And now this: to die here in the desert, unexpectedly, in the prime of his life. And I tried to console him, whispering sweet words to him, telling him that all would be all right, and suddenly he began to kiss me and made love again. It was as if he put all his life's strength into that last act of his – as if this was the ultimate thing he would ever do. And when it was over, he cried again while he lay on top of me. It was so moving.'

'Oh my! How awful!' Gael stared at Marie with horror in her eyes. 'Weren't you shocked? How can you sit there with a contented expression on your face when a man has done such a thing to you?'

'My dear girl,' said Marie firmly. 'You don't know what you're talking about.'

'But . . . but . . . to be assaulted by a man much younger than you!'

'There's nothing to be shocked about. How can I explain this? You see . . . at my age you no longer take things for granted. You simply can't imagine what it felt like to be a woman again after ten barren years. It was wonderful, absolutely wonderful! To be desired again . . . even if the circumstances were a bit unusual. I often hoped that fate would be good to me and let me make love once again before I died. And now it has happened. I will treasure this memory for years to come . . .' She suddenly looked uncertain. 'At least I hope that there will still be many years to come.'

Gael sat there very quietly, making a great effort to take it all in. Then she asked, trying to change the subject: 'And how did you get away from there?'

'Oh, that wasn't difficult. Later in the night when Dr Wilbert was fast asleep after all his exertions, I quietly opened the driver's door. Hidden underneath the dashboard is a small switch they installed at my request some years ago to prevent my Land-Rover from suddenly disappearing in Africa. You see . . . if you flip it, it cuts the electrics and the engine can't start.'

'My goodness . . .' Gael's mouth fell open. 'So you set the whole thing up?'

'Well . . .' continued Marie, 'I rather liked the idea of spending the night alone with Dr Wilbert. Anyway, next morning, when I told him to try one more time, he found to his utter surprise and delight that the engine shot into life. He couldn't understand why, but I told him that this sometimes happened in Africa. Sand might have got into the filter or something, and it had probably settled during the night. And when I proposed slyly to try and find you, he said: 'No!' He wanted to return immediately to Bobodiou. He was adamant! So I did as he asked and would you believe it? He kept up an embarrassed silence all the way! When we got there he disappeared into the Riverside Hotel without even kissing me goodbye; he just left me the parcels he had brought! That's why I've come back alone.' Marie looked at Gael with a stern expression on her face. 'I knew I had to return quickly because I felt that you might get it in your head to organise a rescue expedition and I didn't want you to get lost. You're so inexperienced, really.'

'But why did you do all this?'

Marie's eyes twinkled. 'Sometimes you have to give fate a helping hand, don't you? And didn't you tell me that you didn't want to see him?'

Gael looked at her with emotion in her eyes. Then, without further thought, she threw her arms around Marie's neck and kissed her warmly on the cheek.

7

Anton and Michel had set off from Brussels a week ago. So far their journey had been pleasant and relatively uneventful, but now they had reached the last oasis and were facing the formidable expanse of the Sahara.

They drew up at 'Your Last Chance', which was not a proper petrol station but a small shop with two petrol pumps standing proudly in front of it. After checking oil levels and loading up with diesel fuel and water they were told that two pickup trucks were about to drive south, and that they had better form a small convoy. They found the pickups just around the corner, busily arranging their loads for the long drive south.

'Yes, you come with us,' said one of the drivers, staring at Anton's valuable Land-Rover with appreciative eyes. He had a round swarthy face and smoked non-stop.

'You know the way?' asked Anton.

'Yes. I drive many times.'

'Is the road in good condition?'

'Oh, track? Not bad. Normal.'

'How long will it take to get to the other side?'

'Maybe couple of days, maybe more. Depends.'

'It depends on what?' Anton wanted to know.

'Oh! If we drive part of night. And especially if Allah is willing . . .'

The men now began to stow a load of bulging sacks in their pickups. Then a few women, wrapped in black, appeared out of nowhere and climbed up on the sacks with their children while the men shouted orders. When everything was arranged to their satisfaction, the men climbed into the cabins and the small trucks set off at a good pace.

Anton did his best to follow but the two pickups drove next to each other, throwing up a huge cloud of dust behind them.

'We'll have to let them go,' he coughed after a short while. 'The inside of the Land-Rover is completely covered with fine dust. It's like driving in a sandstorm.'

They fell back to a respectful distance, following the cloud at about a quarter of a mile, and drove on like that over an unchanging flat expanse for what seemed hours. Dusk came, and still the cloud ahead of them kept moving. Then the sun disappeared beyond the horizon in a burst of flaming red fire, and the dust thrown up by the pickups rapidly dissolved into the setting darkness.

'We've got to stop,' urged Anton. 'We don't know where we're going. We can't even see their taillights. It's too dangerous. There may be ruts in the track, or deep holes, and I don't want to risk breaking the suspension.'

'But we'll lose them,' argued Michel.

'They're sure to stop, too, and we'll catch up with them tomorrow morning.' Anton spoke with assurance, but when they stopped and got out to make their camp, they both knew they wouldn't see the pickups again. Their lifeline had gone. They were alone, abandoned in the middle of nowhere.

8

They had stopped next to a high dune and as Anton looked up at its sandy slopes he suggested: 'How about climbing up before having our meal? It'll give our legs some exercise. We've been sitting cramped up in the cabin the whole day. And the view from there must be magnificent.'

'I don't want to exercise my legs,' protested Michel. 'I want to exercise my stomach.' But in the end he followed reluctantly.

They found that walking up the dune was hard work. The sand kept slipping away from under their feet and by the time they reached the top the light had nearly gone out of the sky. Only a thin strip of the south-western horizon remained dimly lit and, one after the other, stars began to shine. There was no moon and gradually, as the last glimmer of light faded and the sky became a deep velvety blue, more and more stars appeared.

They lay down in the sand on the crest of the dune and as they gazed at the infinity of the expanse above them, its immensity became overpowering. Everywhere they looked they saw nothing but stars, millions upon millions of them, some bright yellow, others just about visible. It was like a fairy tale, this vast expanse overhead spangled with twinkling stars. And through the sky, in a wide sweep from Cassiopeia in the northeast to the southwest where the sun had set, the Milky Way ran like an irregular stream of pale white light.

'Look!' Anton pointed at it. 'Our galaxy.'

They lay there for a long time, staring into the infinity of space. They had never seen anything like it. It was awe-inspiring. Here, in the middle of the desert, for the first time, Anton became aware of the vastness of the cosmos, and at the same time of the fleetingness of his own existence in the face of all this infinity. And he sensed something else he had never felt before.

'Listen,' he whispered.

Michel pricked up his big ears, cupping his hands behind them and turning carefully in all directions. 'I can't hear anything,' he said. 'There's no sound at all. Absolute silence. It's incredible! This is the first time in my life that I'm somewhere and hear absolutely no outside sound. All I can hear is my voice and the blood rushing through my head. And that suddenly sounds like a steam train.'

'Shht . . . be quiet and listen.'

They sat there for a few more minutes until Michel shook his head. 'There's nothing,' he said.

'The cosmos . . . the stars,' whispered Anton.

'You're joking. Stars don't make a noise.'

'They do! I once watched a documentary on stars and they broadcast the sound of a fast-rotating neutron star. It made such an impression on me to hear the sound of stars that it obsessed me for a long time.' Anton spoke very softly, as if he were unwilling to break the silence of the desert and the spell the vision of the night sky had cast. 'But that's not what I heard just now. It was something of a different order altogether. You see . . .' he turned hesitantly towards Michel. 'The cosmos is so near here that I felt the throbbing of deep space.'

'Come on now!' exclaimed Michel, shrugging his shoulders. 'I think it's time we went down and had something to eat. You may be hallucinating about hearing stars, but what I heard very clearly a moment ago was the rumbling of my belly and that's not a hallucination. I can feel great pangs of hunger, and that is a very real feeling, I can tell you!'

9

The first rays of sunlight woke them up next morning and they immediately looked out towards the southern horizon. Michel even climbed up on the roof-rack but there was no sign of the pickups anywhere.

'They must have driven on,' said Anton as he saw Michel's gloomy face. 'We're in it alone now. Anyway,' he added to reassure his companion, 'we can't go wrong. If we just keep heading south we'll eventually get to the other side. And I've got my GPS system.'

'Yeah, I guess so,' replied Michel somewhat unconvinced, as he began to prepare tea for breakfast. The warm tea and sandwiches gradually cheered him up. 'That feels better,' he sighed. Then he looked at Anton, almost apologetically. 'Last night . . . well . . . don't take the remarks I made too much to heart, old man. I admit that I was impressed. The sky was so clear! And the Milky Way . . . I've never seen it before.'

'That's not surprising. There's massive light pollution in Europe,' explained Anton, warming to one of his pet subjects. 'The light from towns and houses is scattered through the atmosphere where it creates a luminous background that crowds out the light of all but the brightest stars. It's like trying to see faint stars when there's a bright moon. In Europe one has to go far away from the cities to have any chance of seeing the Milky Way at all. I've been lucky enough to live in the countryside for most of my life but, even so, I've never seen a sky like the one we saw last night. Here we're hundreds of miles away from any artificial lights, and there's no humidity in the air either . . .'

'No wonder I've never seen anything like it before.'

'Of course not. We've become city dwellers and are used to having everything lit up at night. It wasn't so when my grandparents were young. I remember them telling me stories about the dark winter nights.'

'Same with mine. And they didn't seem to have liked the dark nights.'

'I think most humans like the security of light. It's because we're afraid of the dark. The moment modern sources of energy gave humans the power to do so, they began to produce ever more light. And now . . . do you think we've gone too far? I've never really given it a thought before.'

'Can we talk about this later?' interrupted Michel. 'Look, the sun's already well above the horizon. We can't sit here the whole day philosophising. I've got an appointment to keep, remember.'

By seven thirty they were packed up and set off towards the south. The map of Africa had shown a road leading south from the last oasis, but there was no man-made road, only the flat expanse of the desert marked by the tracks of dozens of trucks and other vehicles, until a sandstorm eventually obliterated these. They drove wherever they liked, as there was no one in view. They might even have closed their eyes for all the difference it would have made. The probability of colliding with another vehicle was nil. The surface was hard, they were moving at a fast pace, and Anton had begun to relax when, without warning, they struck a sandy patch and the Land-Rover suddenly slowed down; then it came to a standstill.

'If you'd swerved to the left, you would have avoided this,' commented Michel acidly. 'Why didn't you pay more attention?'

Anton didn't reply but switched into four-wheel drive mode and revved up. The only result was that the Land-Rover dug itself deeper into the sand, and after a while he gave up.

'You fool!' shouted Michel as they got out. 'See what you've done! We're completely stuck.'

'Easy to know what I should have done after it's happened!' Anton shouted back. 'You'd better help to dig us out of here instead of lecturing me!' And he threw a spade in front of Michel's feet.

They started swearing at each other, but in the end Michel began to dig out the front wheels while Anton unfastened the metal sand ladders that were bolted on to the roof-rack. A quarter of an hour later they were dripping with sweat but had managed to shove the sand ladders under the wheels. As Anton got behind the steering wheel and switched into first gear, the vehicle moved forward with a jerk, but immediately got stuck again, and they had to start everything all over. After repeating the operation three times, Anton finally gathered enough speed to leave the sandy patch behind.

By the time they'd struck another sandy patch or two, they'd got wise. Anton would immediately climb out, shove the sand ladders under the front wheels, let the clutch in very slowly and when the Land-Rover started moving he would suddenly rev up and keep the vehicle going in four-wheel drive mode until he got on to firm soil again. If it was a long sandy patch, Michel would keep moving the sand ladders as many times as needed till the Land-Rover was on firm soil, then collect them, throw them onto the roof rack and they would set off again.

By noon they had got the knack of it, scanning the terrain in front of them and working as a team, and they were even able to spot most of the sandy patches before they got stuck, giving them a wide berth. They were more relaxed now, taking everything in their stride, and were beginning to enjoy the challenge.

After a few hours they left the sandy area behind. They were now driving over a particularly firm stretch of flat desert and were feeling less stressed.

'I've been thinking about what we discussed this morning,' said Michel after a while. 'You may be right about the pollution the bright city lights create. It's true that we rarely see the moonlight in Europe and, even less so, the stars. But I must admit that I like city life. It's so much more varied than life in the countryside. You meet so many people, you see pretty girls . . .' he sat there dreaming for a while. 'I especially like the Internet, and even the virtual world of games . . .'

'Yes, but don't you see where this is leading us?' interrupted Anton. 'The result is that the connection with nature has been severed. Most people now live in cities. I'm not judging whether that's good or bad. That's the way it's become, and there isn't much we can do about it. But I think we're in danger of losing our bearings in modern society because the artificial man-made environment we have created has shut out the natural world.'

'And why would that be bad?'

'Well, the longer we live in urbanised surroundings created by ourselves, for ourselves, the more we humans imagine that we're the centre of the universe. We live at a time of rampant individualism. We are the important ones. The natural environment, where it still exists, now seems a strange, hostile place to us, lacking everything we're used to. How can you expect people to care about something they don't know, or don't even want to know? And so we've become indifferent to what we're doing to the environment, and we no longer care about our planet. We're just taking from it and destroying it. I've been thinking about this for some time, and I'm very much afraid that one day our greedy indifference is going to backfire.'

While they were pondering over some of the deep questions the desert tends to bring out in people, they advanced southwards towards the ever-receding horizon without meeting anyone, without seeing anything but a few sand dunes and some low hills far away. Hour after hour, mile after grinding mile, the Land-Rover kept moving forward towards an unseen goal, at times reaching a peak velocity of fifty miles per hour, but more often struggling for minutes to cover a few hundred yards during a sandy patch. If someone had observed it from a space station circling the Earth, the Land-Rover might have looked like a small beetle, crawling slowly and erratically over the surface of the planet.

For the first time in his life Anton realised how vast the Earth was. Back in Europe there was variety. There were smaller or bigger towns every few miles, or at least isolated houses. Driving through America, the UK, France or any Western country, you nearly always noticed signs of human interference. The European landscape in particular was man-made. Distances were no obstacle either. You could drive through a European country in a day, and fly to another continent in less than a day. Everything seemed so easy in Europe or America.

But here, in the greatest of all deserts, Anton began to experience the real meaning of distance. Here nothing had been smoothed out artificially. It was true that he and Michel no longer had to cross the Sahara on camel back. That would have taken them fifty days or so. But all the same, even in a four-wheel-drive vehicle, it was a slow and difficult process, and struggling with the sandy patches in the hot afternoon slowly wore them out. It was man against the untamed elements. How many more days before they reached the other side? This was not the pleasure trip Anton had so foolishly imagined it to be when he had planned the journey. This was a long, tough fight, and either they would win, or else the desert would come out on top and they would perish.

10

'So there are still things you'd like to do in life?' asked Gael while they were having breakfast.

'Does that surprise you?' replied Marie, blowing at her steaming tea before taking a cautious sip. 'You never manage to do all the things you dream of. We have so many dreams when we are young. At least, I had. And to think that in all the years of my existence I've been unable to fulfil most of them. I know now that I never will. A single life wouldn't be sufficient for that.'

'Are you dissatisfied then?'

'Oh, no! I told you I've been lucky. I've led a very full life.'

'Maybe it would be better not to have dreams at all,' suggested Gael with a slight bitterness in her voice. 'Then, at least you're not disappointed when things don't turn out the way you expected them to.'

'But it's good to have dreams! The more outlandish, the better! How mediocre our lives would be if we didn't have such extravagant dreams.'

'I'm not sure,' replied Gael

Marie looked attentively at Gael. 'You're not going to tell me that you don't have dreams? You must have dreams!'

'What's the good of having dreams? I don't want to live a life of illusions.'

'But it's good to have illusions!' objected Marie. 'What would life be without them? A bleak affair, not worth living.'

'What's the good of having illusions if all your hopes end up shattered in a thousand pieces?' Gael looked miserable. 'What's the good of running after love?'

'Oh, but that's different. One must never run after love. That's no good. When you really want it, when you try for it with all your will-power, desire it, it won't come.' Marie sat there, nodding to herself.

'How do you know that?'

'I have found out. Life has taught me.'

'Then, what do you do when you want love very dearly?'

'My girl,' said Marie slowly, 'you are contradicting yourself. First you tell me that you don't want to have dreams. And now you say that you want love very dearly.'

Gael blushed. 'It's . . . well . . . just tell me what you do when you really want love.'

'Stop wanting it. Free your mind. Liberate yourself from longings.'

'But that's easy to say! How can you do that? And if you stop longing, you'll miss out on everything.'

'No you won't! If you're destined to have love, it will come. If not, it will pass you by, and when you're detached that doesn't really matter. And then, one day, when you least expect it, there it is. That's the way it is with love. It will come of its own accord, stop in front of you smiling, and offer itself. Only, be sure to be ready for it, to recognise it when it comes.'

'You're right!' exclaimed Gael. 'That's exactly what happened to me!'

'Yes . . .' Marie waited expectantly.

'Oh, nothing . . . It's not important,' said Gael evasively, and she went into the house and started rummaging through her things.

11

Gael had driven to one of the oases up north for an inoculation round, leaving Marie to cope with the sick and wounded on her own. By the time Marie had finished, sat down, had some tea and a snack to eat, it was too late to go out to Kanibasso. As she had nothing in particular to do – which is what usually happens in the evening in those places in Africa not yet touched by modern life – she wandered aimlessly through the house, thinking of Gael. How could she help her if the stubborn girl didn't want to tell her anything? As she went past the entrance to Gael's room the curtain was slightly open, and she saw a small notebook lying on the bed. She hesitated for a moment but it drew her like a magnet. Here, at last, was an opportunity to pierce the mystery that surrounded her companion. Before she could stop herself she went in, sat down on the bed and opened the little book.

Little by little, as she turned the pages and read slowly, the book began to reveal a whole hidden world to her: Gael's feelings in Brussels, then England and Brussels again. She had added very little since. Only one poem, probably written shortly after arriving in Africa:

The Spell That Can't Be Broken

> All around
> the desert stretches endlessly,
> empty
> like the desert in my heart
> which is blank and terrifying,
> a wordless, unending agony
> ebbing back and forth
> till my feelings burst
> and an all-pervading pain
> takes possession of my inner self.
>
> A spiteful mocking woman
> peered through the crack of your door,
> and a face that was so trustful
> became a mask of horror . . .
> My face . . .

Nights used to be
togetherness and belonging;
and the mornings . . .
you, sleepy with deep dreams
till you woke up
looking at me
with wonder in your eyes.
But with each morning now
begins another dreary day
through which I do not want to live.

What have you done, my love?
What have you done?
Didn't you know that I needed
the love that filled me with warmth?
Your warmth . . .

For deep down in my heart
the passion for you
burns as strongly as ever
and my body aches with longing.
I want to hold you tight again,
touch you, kiss you,
let love flow from me to you,
from you to me,
just like before, my love,
just like before.

When she had finished, Marie sat there for a long time, the little book in her hands, while outside the shadows kept lengthening. 'Poor Gael,' she murmured. 'How could such a thing have happened to her? How very sad. Poor, poor girl . . .' And then she thought: I must do something about this, but what can I do?

12

Anton and Michel had been going onward for hours when around 5 p.m. the engine began to splutter. 'What's that?' asked Michel, alarmed.

'I don't really know.' Anton looked concerned. After a few hiccoughs the engine once more began to run smoothly but Anton kept listening nervously for any unusual sound. Then, sometime later, the irregular noise started again.

'There's something definitely wrong.' Michel's voice was tense.

'Can't you be quiet for a second!' shouted Anton, irritated. 'I'm trying to concentrate on the sound!' He felt exhausted after a whole day of driving and this unexpected problem was the limit.

But Michel kept insisting: 'It's not something serious, is it? You ought to know. It's your car.'

'Oh, it's probably nothing important,' replied Anton hoping that this would reassure his companion and keep him quiet. 'I'll have a look at it when we stop.'

He had hardly finished speaking when the engine began to move in fits and starts. Then it stalled altogether and the Land-Rover ground to a halt.

Michel stared accusingly at Anton and screamed: 'You just said that it was nothing important, and now look!'

Anton didn't reply but jumped out, lifted the bonnet and began to look inside. While he was examining the engine, fiddling with the tubes and cables, Michel kept nervously hopping up and down, asking: 'Have you found it yet?'

Anton merely grunted while he continued to check different parts.

'Can you repair it?' Michel's voice sounded panicky. 'You've got to repair this.'

Anton emerged from under the bonnet, his hands greasy and a black smear on his tired face. 'It's probably the fuel pump. It's given me trouble before, in Belgium. That's the sort of breakdown it creates. Don't worry. I've got a spare.'

Anton's soothing tone seemed to have the contrary effect on Michel. 'It's all your fault!' he yelled. 'You assured me that this car was in good condition when we set off, didn't you? You should have told me that we risked this sort of thing. If I'd known this, I would never have come with you.'

'Oh, shut up!' Anton's nerves were totally on edge by now.

They began to shout at each other and were nearly coming to blows, when suddenly they heard the sound of an approaching car. As they looked up they saw a vehicle coming towards them at high speed.

Within seconds a powerful four-wheel-drive car with French diplomatic licence plates drew up next to them and a well-dressed man climbed out, extending a hand. '*Enchanté* to see someone around,' he said. Then he noticed the open bonnet. 'A problem?' he asked.

'Oh, it's nothing serious really,' muttered Anton, trying to minimise the gravity of the situation. 'I can repair it.'

The man gave Anton's old Land-Rover a good look and then asked disdainfully: 'Are you trying to cross the desert in that old pile of rust?'

'But this is a perfectly good car,' replied Anton, offended. 'It's been doing very well up to now.'

'Is that what you call a perfectly good car?' The diplomat snorted. 'And it's not moving very much right now, is it?'

'Quite right,' cut in Michel, fuming. 'He never warned me about the risks, and I trusted him blindly.' He pointed an accusing thumb at Anton. 'And here we are, stranded in the middle of the Sahara when I have to be in Bobodiou by December 6th.'

'Why is that?' the diplomat wanted to know.

'Because I've got an appointment with a representative of the mining company I'm going to work for. I don't dare think what's going to happen if I don't turn up in time, as I most likely won't! I'll probably lose my job.' He shot a furious look at Anton as if he were the cause of all his troubles.

'I told you not to worry,' said Anton, his mouth pinched, trying to calm the situation down in front of a stranger. 'I'll fix the problem first thing in the morning. With luck we'll get there in time.'

The diplomat looked mockingly at Anton's old Land-Rover. 'Luck is what you'll need,' he said in a voice heavy with sarcasm. 'I wouldn't trust my life to that old banger if they paid me for it.' He spoke with contempt. 'Now, when I travel, I take precautions.' He pointed at his gleaming four-wheel-drive vehicle. 'My car is brand new; powerful; it's got specially reinforced suspension; air conditioning . . .' He spoke with pride. 'The sort that will get you through the Sahara without any trouble and in comfort.'

'My Land-Rover will get us through the Sahara all the same!' retorted Anton.

The diplomat snorted. 'I can't understand what pleasure people find in driving through the Sahara.' He shook his head in commiseration. 'I can assure you that you wouldn't have seen me here if I hadn't been obliged to go to France to buy this car. You see . . . by driving it down myself I avoid paying huge import taxes.' The man seemed mightily pleased with himself. 'But why you chose to drive through the Sahara in an old pile of rust is beyond me.'

'And why you need such a huge car is beyond me,' sneered Anton, vexed by the man's arrogance.

The diplomat gave him a withering look. 'I couldn't make do with anything smaller.' He drew himself up. 'I need a car befitting my status . . .'

Michel went up to the big vehicle and looked at it admiringly. 'I'd like to be in there rather than in Anton's old Land-Rover,' he said wistfully. 'What a smashing car . . .'

'Well, if your friend says he can fix the problem, why don't you come with me?' proposed the diplomat. 'I've got to start work again at my embassy on the sixth and am certain to be in Bobodiou the day before that. In fact, I would rather enjoy having someone to talk to. Driving alone for a whole day has been a real bore.' Then he added, as an afterthought: 'And that way your friend here won't have to worry about getting to Bobodiou in time. He can drive on quietly at his own pace once he's repaired his car.'

'Would you really take me?' Michel looked extremely pleased. 'What do you think, Anton?'

Anton was about to shout: 'No way!' Instead, he heard himself say: 'But of course you must go.' He even insisted: 'It's really important that you don't miss your appointment.'

'Wonderful!' exclaimed Michel. 'That's all settled then. Let's eat something, shall we? I'm ravenous after all this.'

'What are you going to eat?' the diplomat asked warily.

'Oh, some tinned food. And we've still got an old loaf of bread left.'

'Is that what you call having a meal?' The diplomat looked down his nose. 'I couldn't eat that!' Then he went to his car, opened the back door and got out a huge picnic basket containing an assortment of prepared French dishes, cheeses, and even *paté de foie gras*. Next he dug out a couple of bottles of French wine, napkins and a folding chair and table. 'Come along,' he said invitingly. 'Let's have a proper meal. We need to keep up our morale, especially here in the middle of the Sahara.'

13

'Are you sure you can fix it?' asked Michel the next morning with an anxious face. They had finished their breakfast and Michel had just transferred his luggage to the diplomat's vehicle.

'Don't bother,' replied Anton with forced cheerfulness. 'It'll be all right. I know what it is. It's only a minor problem and I've got the spare part. You carry on. You mustn't miss your appointment.'

'Well . . .' said the diplomat, his voice heavy with importance, 'if we haven't heard from you in a week from now I'll alert the authorities.' He sounded reassuring. 'Come on then,' he motioned to Michel. 'We've got to go.'

'All right,' nodded Michel, moving towards the diplomat's gleaming new car. Suddenly he turned round, rushed up to Anton and gave him an affectionate hug. 'Good luck, old chap,' he said, his voice thick with emotion. Then he ran back to the big car and the diplomat set off in a cloud of dust.

Anton had kept up a brave face so far, but as he eyed the car that carried off his companion, his spirits sank. There was no longer any need to pretend and suddenly he screamed: 'Don't! Come back! Don't leave me behind!' But the cloud of dust did not seem to feel his anguish. It just kept moving away, shrinking with every passing minute. Anton stared at it, his eyes wide with fear. They followed the plume of dust, which was all that remained of his companion, until it became a mere dot on the horizon and then disappeared altogether. Then he sank down against a wheel of his motionless vehicle, put his head on his knees and abandoned himself to despair.

Why does this have to happen to me? he asked himself while waves of panic went through his body. Why had he insisted that Michel go with the diplomat? Always ready to say what's expected of me, he thought. That's my problem. Always doing my very best not to make others feel uncomfortable.

'I should have put my foot down!' he shouted to himself. 'I should have told them: "Don't even dream of it! You're jolly well going to stay with me until we're sure that I've repaired this. What do you think you're doing?" I should have said to Michel: "To hell with your appointment with that mining company!" And that diplomat with his smug face, mumbling about being expected at his embassy. I should have yelled at him: "What's the rush? Who cares if you arrive a day late? It won't kill you! But abandoning me to my fate could well kill me! You can't leave me behind just like that. My life counts for more than your stupid appointments!" That's what I should have screamed in their faces.'

Instead, he had meekly assented, as he had always done. No, worse: he himself had insisted that they go. 'When will you ever stand up for your own interests instead of letting others ride roughshod over you?' he said to himself. 'Must you die first before there's any hope you'll change?'

How could he be such a mentally deficient being, so absolutely daft? Who was to be blamed for that? His parents? His education? Whoever or whatever it was, he was saddled with the most stupid character anyone could have inherited or acquired. And where did it leave him? In a big hole! And who was going to help him out of that hole? No one.

Damn, damn! Everything had looked so promising: his studies; his scholarship in America; his job at the lab in Brussels. And then he had met the girl of his dreams. But now! He just couldn't believe the bad luck he'd been having in the last few months. First I lost Gael, he thought, and I still don't know why. Then that idiot of a Smally became director. And now, to top it all, they've abandoned me in the middle of the Sahara. How did I get myself into a situation like this? I'll be lucky if I come out of it alive. And I'm only just thirty. Was it worth being given life for this?

After a while he began to feel hot and thirsty and looking up he realised he was sitting in the full sun. It was only eight in the morning and yet the heat was already beginning to be very uncomfortable. He went inside the back compartment, took a swill from a water bottle and started to take stock of his situation. There was nothing cheerful about it. Who could he turn to for help? Then he remembered that his car was fully insured, and that the insurance included legal assistance, breakdown and pickup service worldwide, and he burst into hysterical laughter. Where were all those pickup services, repair people, insurance men and medical services he had always taken for granted? They must still be there, far away in our cities where everything is arranged by humans for humans. But as far as he was concerned they didn't exist. Who would appear over the horizon to rescue him here in the Sahara?

For the first time ever he realised how precarious everything was. All the stability, the solid foundations on which he had based his opinions and his life, seemed to have collapsed around him. What was the value, here in the middle of nowhere, of laws and regulations? Where were all those humans with their immense pride in their achievements, their great sense of importance and the well-functioning societies they had created? They had abandoned him, and it angered him.

Then a strange thought went through his mind: I'm thinking of people as if I begrudged their having abandoned me. But they didn't. It was I who decided to cross the Sahara. It is I who went away and turned my back on other people. As far as they are concerned, I am the traitor. And now I might just as well not exist for all they care. If I died today, people would just carry on as usual, as they do when any human dies. They would fill up the vacancy I left in the blink of an eye. Yes, that's what would happen.

Suddenly rage surged up in him. 'I'm not going to give them that pleasure if I can help it,' he shouted aloud. 'I will not let them defeat me!' And with a determined expression on his face he climbed on to his Land-Rover and began to search for tools and spare parts, which were stored in a big metal box on the roof-rack.

He was certain that the fuel pump was the cause of all his troubles. Within an hour he had taken the defective pump out, fixed the spare and connected it. Then he climbed behind the steering wheel and pressed the starter. Nothing happened.

While he had been busy he had never doubted that he would be able to repair this breakdown. He had not given a single thought to the fate that awaited him in case of failure. Now the reaction set in and he found himself shaking. His legs suddenly refused to carry him and he had to sit down. 'I can't believe this,' he muttered to himself. 'This just can't be true.'

After a while he began to calm down. I had better make some tea and eat something, he decided. As he sat chewing a sandwich made of tinned sardines stuck between two slices of rather stale bread, he began to ponder the different possibilities. If your car breaks down in the Sahara, he reflected, there are only two possibilities: either you manage to repair the breakdown, or you don't. And if you don't, you die.

After he had finished his frugal lunch he looked up. Only the sun has been moving in these last few hours, he thought. And the wind has been blowing. If I die, the wind will keep blowing and sand will cover me until I am buried and have completely disappeared. And after a while, who will remember me? Who will remember me anyway in a hundred years from now? I'm not one of those famous fellows they mention in history books. I'm not irreplaceable. I'm interchangeable, disposable. Like most people, I might as well not have existed for all the difference it will have made to the planet.

If you think of it, Anton mused, we are just pure accident. For every sperm that fertilised an egg to become a living baby, there were millions that never got there. Millions of potential humans with their very own characteristics that were never born. It was just sheer luck that I was in a combination of egg and sperm that made it – I and all the others who are alive today. No one would ever have missed us if we hadn't been born, so we cannot be all that important.

'But I *do* exist!' he suddenly exclaimed. That was probably the most extraordinary thing about him: that he existed at all; that life flowed through him in all its strength. 'No!' he cried out, 'I may be unimportant, but I'm not going to let myself die. I want to live! I have given myself a mission: to find Gael. And that's what I'm going to do. I will get this Land-Rover started, if it takes me days.'

He set to work again, determinedly, and began to check all the electric circuits. After two hours he found it: one small wire had been chafed through. He linked the two pieces together and as he pressed the starter the engine shot into life, and the Land-Rover vibrated with movement. Waves of emotion went through his body. Victory! He had done it! He slammed down the bonnet, climbed inside the cabin, slid the stick into first gear, and slowly the Land-Rover moved forward.

Yes, he was alone now, with only his wits to help him survive, but he was determined to keep going. His survival depended on a ton of metal transformed into springs, axles, pistons and all the rest of it. With luck, if he managed to repair any breakdowns, it would carry him to the other side of the desert. And then he would search for Gael, and he would find her.

14

Marie came strolling into the yard, holding up a small envelope. 'A letter for you,' she called out when she saw Gael. 'From Brussels.'

Gael looked at the postmark: 15th of October. 'Would you believe that?' she asked while she began to tear open the envelope. 'One and a half months for a letter to get here!'

'You're lucky it got here at all,' remarked Marie philosophically. 'At least half the mail gets lost.'

'It's from my mother,' said Gael, unfolding the letter.

Marie gave her an affectionate look. 'It's always so nice to get news from your family. It makes you feel you're not alone in the world. I know you're a brave girl and you don't complain, but I'm sure that the isolation here must sometimes be a bit hard to bear.'

Gael just shrugged her shoulders and began to read:

Dear Gael,

We haven't had any news from you yet. Maybe it's too early for that with all you have to do over there, and having to adapt to a new world.

Everything is as usual in Brussels apart from one dreadful incident, which I must tell you about. You'll never guess who had the audacity to come to our house and ring the bell. When I opened the door I stood face to face with a man I'd never seen before. He tried to find out about you without telling me his name, but I soon realised who he was: that awful philanderer who seduced you!

I told him in no uncertain terms to go back to his other women and leave you alone, but he pretended not to understand what I was talking about and kept pleading: 'I haven't done anything!' He looked such a miserable sight that anyone else would have taken pity on him, but I knew better. I said you never wanted to see him again, and to get rid of him I added that you'd gone to Africa where he'd never find you. And you know what he answered? 'But why? I love her.' You just wouldn't believe it. He screamed it in my face, the horrid man. You should have seen him: he looked desperate, but I wasn't going to fall for that. All a big show, that's what it was! I got quite upset with him and told him he was a monster who had broken your heart and wrecked your happiness and mine, but he kept protesting his innocence and begged me to tell him where you were. So I told him to go away and slammed the door in his face.

He stood there in the front garden for ages, his head hanging low. I watched him from behind the curtains and was afraid he'd never leave and I'd have to call the police. I got quite alarmed, alone in the house with that dangerous man outside, unwilling to move. I still can't think how he got our address. But finally he did go. Walked away as if all the sorrows of the world were weighing on his shoulders. Serves him right, I thought. I wish I could have done much more to him than slam the door in his face.

For a week or so after that shocking episode I felt quite insecure. What if he came back? But he hasn't yet, and I hope he'll never turn up again. It's lucky for you that you're far away in a place where he'll never be able to find you, because I wouldn't put it past him to pursue you as far as Africa if he knew where to find you.

Anyway, enough of that. We hope you are well and that you are careful with what you eat and drink. I've heard stories about people who got seriously ill in Africa because of food and drink. And do take your malaria pills and . . .

Gael couldn't read any further. She stood there, the letter trembling in her hand.

'Are you all right?' Marie had watched Gael's face pale while she was reading the letter, and now looked at her with concern. 'Bad news?'

'No, no, don't bother,' mumbled Gael. 'I . . . I just need to be on my own for a while . . .' And she rushed out of the compound and disappeared into the nearby dunes.

Extracts from Gael's notebook:

Today they brought me a letter from my mother in Brussels. She said that you'd been to the house and were trying to find me. The news had a devastating effect on me and I couldn't stay with Marie any longer. As I read the letter again in the dunes, I somehow felt your anguish scream from the pages. I don't know what to do. How can I ever believe in you again?

[. . .]

Anton, what are you doing to me? This morning I dreamed that your hands were caressing my body and I woke up shaken to the core. Why aren't we together? Why am I here when you are there? Everything I'm doing seems meaningless.

[. . .]

I'm sitting on the flat roof of our house, looking out over the desert. You would love it here. Somehow I feel very close to you. I've been thinking so much about you in the last few days. Sometimes I talk to you and imagine that you can hear me. I must be daft.

[. . .]

This evening, as the sun set and the first stars were beginning to twinkle, I went alone into the dunes. There was not a whisper of wind; everything was so quiet that I could hear the silence. Suddenly a great urge came over me and I called your name across the dunes. And then, from somewhere far away, the sound of music and voices floated up to where I stood: the Tuaregs had begun to sing. It moved me so much that I had to sit down and weep. How I wish you were here to share these precious moments with me.

15

Slowly, very slowly, mile after grinding mile, Anton kept moving through the immensity of the desert. He clung to the wheel, constantly scanning the uneven surface in front of him, and every time the wheels banged into a rut, every time the frame of the Land-Rover shook, he felt vulnerable.

There was nothing to block Anton's view in the vastness of the landscape around him, nothing to remind him of life. Just bare rocks and a flat expanse of yellow sands that stretched all the way to the horizon under the deep blue of the endless sky. The colours were so dazzling that he had to shield his eyes, and the loneliness was intense. Was there anything beyond the horizon? Could it really be true that somewhere far away, beyond the edge of this world, people lived, ate, slept, dreamed, worshipped, loved and hated?

Hours later he stopped, glad that he was able to relax at last. He walked to a big boulder some hundred yards away to give his legs some exercise and looked around. Earlier in the day the yellow of the sands and the blue of the sky had dominated, but now the sun was about to set and the surface of the desert began to turn a soft orange. Soon it would be blood red while the blue of the sky would change to indigo and then to a deep violet as night fell. Red, orange, yellow . . . blue, indigo, violet. All the colours of the rainbow were there . . . all except one: green – the green of life.

Is this planet Earth, thought Anton, or is it another strange planet somewhere far away in the universe. A lifeless planet of which I am the only inhabitant?

He stared at the unyielding outcrops of darkening rock many miles away, just visible above the flat empty space around him. Or maybe, he reflected, I am on planet Earth, but I've been taken back to some primitive era four hundred million years ago. That's what the planet's surface must have looked like before green plants moved out of the sea and began to colonise the land. There had been nothing to cover the Earth's nakedness then. Just bare, rocky landscapes like the ones he saw now, and grains of dust blowing freely in the wind.

The wind . . . yes, it was still there, blowing through gullies and over the endless plains, moving the dunes and grinding down the rocks . . . slowly, very slowly. What was a million years for the wind? What were ten million years? Who could stop the wind? It had blown yesterday; it would still be blowing tomorrow. Long after humanity had come and gone like a mere blip on the cosmic timescale, the desert would still be there, indestructible. The mighty desert and the wind blowing through it freely . . .

16

As he sat down to a frugal supper of tinned food and tepid water, barren landscapes stretched everywhere around Anton as far as he could see. He was no more than a small speck of life alone in the middle of a lifeless plain limited only by the horizon. There was nowhere to hide; the endless sky was his shelter.

It made him realise the fleetingness of his existence. In our cities back home we imagine that we are the masters, he thought, but how could one possibly believe such a thing here in the desert? How can we be masters over our fate when we are but grains of cosmic dust blown about by the winds of time?

I'm thinking of humans as if I were on the side of the desert, he suddenly reflected, and maybe I am. Do I really respect people who spend most of their life jostling for position, for power, for money? For money! What can money buy here in the desert? And what is the value of fame here in this bare, harsh environment where human life is so insignificant?

'I, too, have been running about like everyone else . . . after money and maybe fame,' he said to himself. 'I, too, have been in bondage all my life: by being busy; by doing what was expected of me; by living the way others wanted me to live; by hiding from myself . . .

But here you are stripped of all the coatings that seem to make you important. One by one, as you penetrate deeper into the desert, the layers of make-believe are scraped off until you stand alone in your naked skin; until there is nothing left to hide behind; until there is nowhere to go and only yourself to turn to; until nothing but the core remains: you, weak and frightened, or resilient and trusting . . .'

All at once it dawned on him that this, maybe, was the secret of the desert. And then, in a flash, the thought came to him: I'm no longer going to run about and hide from myself! In the short time allocated to me on Earth, I'm going to live a life worthy of the name. He was infused with the sudden awareness of self-realisation and felt elated. For the first time ever, here in the desert, he was free.

17

Supper was over, and while she was sipping her tea in the falling dusk Gael was conscious of how close she had grown to Marie, closer maybe than she had ever been to her own mother. She looked for a moment at Marie with trust in her eyes. It was not just that they were thrown together in a medical outpost in the bush. There was more to it than that: it was something particular about Africa, something it did to you.

Human contact was so much easier here than anywhere else, especially when the day's tasks were done and the body began to relax, leaving the mind free to expand, to start wandering on its own and reach out towards the vastness of the sky. The evening was a time for confidences and Marie, whose wisdom had grown during her years in Africa, sensed that this was the right moment to talk.

'So when are you going to clear your heart?' she asked, looking at her young companion with great tenderness.

Gael took some time to reply. Then she answered softly: 'I don't know.'

'You loved a young man?' suggested Marie, pretending she didn't know anything. 'And you fell apart?'

'Something like that,' replied Gael after having gazed for a minute or two at the first bright stars that had begun to twinkle overhead.

'That's often the case,' said Marie, trying to draw Gael out. 'There's a bit of physical attraction to start with, yes . . . but when that peters out there's nothing left.'

'But it wasn't at all like that!' protested Gael. 'We got on very well. But then . . . but then . . .'

Marie gently touched Gael's arm. 'What happened?'

Was it the longing to share her torment with someone else after bitterness had been devouring her inner self for months? The intimacy of the African night? The small fire of dry twigs crackling close to them? She didn't know why, but staring into the mystery of the dancing flames, Gael finally began to speak.

'We got on very well together . . . no . . . more than that . . . being together was a long string of moments of total joy, of pure happiness.' Her voice came slowly, hesitantly, as if it was extremely painful to speak of what she had been trying to push back into the deepest recesses of her memory. 'There was no past and no future. We didn't think of it. We didn't think of anything. We lived for the moment. We just wanted to be together. It was so strong that nothing else mattered . . .' Her voice trailed off in the growing darkness. 'That was how I always felt true love should be. He was . . . Anton was like no other man . . .'

'So you still love him?'

Gael didn't reply. Instead, she asked: 'Do you remember the letter I got from my mother?'

'Yes . . .'

'She said that he'd been to the house . . . that he was trying to find me and . . . and that he screamed in her face that he loved me . . .'

'But do you still love him?' repeated Marie.

Gael hesitated. 'I don't know. I've been thinking about it ever since that letter came.'

'Why don't you try to make it up?'

Suddenly Gael blurted out: 'How can I ever believe in him again after what he did? After that horrible morning?'

'Tell me about it.'

'I can't.' Gael's voice rose. 'I can't! It's too awful!'

Marie slipped her arm around Gael's shoulder, putting all the warmth of her heart into that simple, ageless gesture of compassion. 'Come,' she said, 'tell me about it.'

When Gael finally spoke, her voice was almost inaudible: 'One morning I went to his room . . . you see, he didn't expect me . . . I had gone to London and was supposed to have stayed there for another day. I thought I would surprise him . . .' For a few seconds she stared into the flickering flames. Then she carried on: 'I went up and when I got to his room he . . . he was in there with a naked woman!'

'No!'

'Yes! The door was slightly ajar and I saw her through the crack of the door.'

'Did they see you? What happened?'

'The woman turned towards the door for an instant. I'm not sure whether she saw me . . . I didn't make a sound and stood there, unable to move. But she had a triumphant expression on her vulgar face. And then . . . and then she said to Anton what a good lover he was and . . . and she added: 'Shall we do it once more!''

'But him? Did you see him? Did he say anything?'

'No! I wasn't going to wait. When I heard what she said I ran off as fast as I could. I never wanted to see him again.'

'But you just told me that he loved you; loved you truly. Otherwise, how could you have felt the way you did?'

'That's why it was all so horrible! Why I will never believe in him again.' Gael's face was contorted with anguish.

Marie shook her head. 'There is something wrong with this story,' she said firmly. 'Are you sure that what you saw wasn't all make-believe?'

'Make-believe?' Gael spoke with bitterness in her voice. 'I can tell you that that vile naked woman and her awful voice were very real.'

'But are you quite, quite certain that your interpretation is right? There is often more than one interpretation for what one thinks one observes.' Marie shook her head. 'What you saw and heard doesn't fit with the feelings. It sounds all wrong to me. So it must have been like . . . like a stage. I think that what you saw and heard was what that woman wanted you to see and hear.'

'Don't you try to whitewash him! I've been thinking a lot about this and I'm not going to fool myself!'

'My girl, I think you're making a big mistake.'

'No I'm not!' protested Gael stubbornly. 'He's the one who made a big mistake. And there is no turning back now. My dreams are dead. And I don't want you to argue with me about this. It's my life we're talking about, and I alone will decide what I do with it.' At this she turned and resolutely went to her room.

18

Pauline was lying in an easy chair under a sunshade beside the swimming pool of the Riverside Hotel. The vast pool was set in a garden of palm trees and tropical flowers, and as she looked around she sighed with satisfaction. This was the life she had always dreamed of. Back in her youth, when those spoiled rich girls in her school told her about how their parents had taken them for their holidays to Thailand or other exotic places, while she had spent her time helping her mother to clean houses, she'd been green with envy. And now, here she was herself in a tropical paradise. All paid for by the government! She sighed again contentedly while taking a refreshing sip from her ice-cooled long drink.

She'd already spent several days with Jack Smally in Bobodiou, and had enjoyed every moment of it: the luxurious hotel suite, the copious meals on the terrace, the exotic dance groups. And then, the evenings on the dance floor followed by sultry nights making love under the mosquito netting while the sounds of the African night filtered into their room. And having lazy mornings in bed while their breakfast was brought up to them on a silver tray. What more could a young woman desire?

Jack Smally, too, was happy. He, the grandson of a factory worker, was living the life of the super-rich, a life which had been far beyond the modest means of even his father. Here he was on a dream holiday with a woman in a thousand, a woman who was sitting at his feet, looking up at him in admiration. And there was much to admire in him. There he was in the pool, and he had already been swimming back and forth in front of her, showing off his firm breaststroke. And she had looked at him with encouragement, nay, with adulation. What about a bit of diving? he thought as he swam underneath the diving board. Must be easy. That'll be sure to impress her.

He clambered out of the pool and marched towards the diving board with measured steps, his chest stuck out, just like he imagined Napoleon to have done as he marched towards Moscow, set to conquer. He climbed up, stood at the end of the plank, which was precariously swaying up and down, and turned towards Pauline. Then, just as he called out: 'Look at me!' he lost his balance and, arms spinning wildly, he landed with a loud splash flat on the water.

Pauline immediately got up to rescue him, but the big African who was on pool duty had been quicker. He dived in like lightning, caught

Smally by a leg as he was sinking, pulled him up, dumped him on the edge of the pool and then jumped out himself. He bent over Smally trying to apply mouth-to-mouth resuscitation, but when Smally felt the man's lips on his he came to with a shock and pushed him away rudely. He lay there for a while, regurgitating water, and then crawled up and slowly began to walk back to Pauline shaking his head in disgust, looking like Napoleon must have looked when he retreated from Moscow.

'Are you hurt, Jacky,' inquired Pauline, seeming very concerned.

'I'm all right,' grumbled Jack Smally. 'Just a moment of inattention. I'm a good diver really. One of the best!' And he inflated his chest defiantly.

'Of course, Jacky. You are the best!'

They lay down on their deckchairs, sipping their drinks for a while, when Pauline said: 'There's a notice in the hotel announcing that they're organising an excursion tomorrow to one of the animal reserves some sixty miles south. Why don't we sign up and go on a sightseeing tour? Wouldn't that be a welcome change from the swimming pool?' She looked eagerly at her boss.

'I don't want to go on an excursion with a group!' Smally had a stubborn expression on his face. 'Mix with the common people? Not me.'

Pauline's face fell and she mumbled: 'I was so looking forward to seeing wild animals . . .'

When he saw the disappointment in her face, Smally felt remorse. 'I know what we'll do,' he said after a while, raising a finger. 'We'll hire a big four-wheel-drive vehicle and I'll drive you to that animal park myself. No need to rely on African drivers. They can be so reckless. And that way we won't be stuck for a whole day in a hot coach with people we don't want to be with.'

Suddenly Pauline hesitated. 'But . . . but can we afford to rent a big car all for ourselves? Isn't that going to be too expensive?'

'Don't you worry,' replied Smally, putting a reassuring hand on her arm. 'I've got the lab's credit card with me. There's still a lot of money left in the travel budget thanks to my careful management.' He smiled at her generously.

'Oh Jacky!' exclaimed Pauline, throwing her arms around his neck. 'Are we really going? Just the two of us? How wonderful!' She looked at him with admiration. 'You're such a great man. How lucky I am to be with someone like you.'

Jack Smally was lapping it all up. By now he had forgotten the miserable performance he had offered the public, and the painful contact with the water's surface. He drew himself up. 'Just leave it all to me,' he said firmly. 'I'll be in the driver's seat. I'll be in charge. That'll be much more fun.' Then he added magnanimously: 'I'll show you all the animals you want to see: lions, elephants, tigers . . . anything you fancy. Just tell me which animal you want to photograph and I'll stop in front of it to let you take its picture.'

Pauline was about to say that there were no tigers in Africa, and also that wild animals were unlikely to pose for a picture, but she was a wise girl and abstained from making comments.

That afternoon she lay naked on the bed, fast asleep, trying to catch up after the wild exertions of the previous night, but Smally couldn't afford such relaxation. Another couple of days and he would have to give his talk at the conference. No, no leisure for him. He had set himself a task. He had a mission to fulfil. He was to be a famous scientist, the focus of the world's admiration. He had brought several textbooks with him and was now plodding through Anton's report trying to understand it. And as he got stuck again on that difficult formula, he ground his teeth. Why had the fellow not been more explicit? I should have been firm with him, thought Smally. I should have called him into my office and made him explain everything clearly. But no, that unreliable subordinate had disappeared without so much as a goodbye and without any official permission. And where did this leave him now? Him, the great Smally.

Next morning a taxi drove them to the town's only car hire company, Happy Bobo Cars, and Smally set about hiring the most powerful four-wheel-drive vehicle they had. After the manager had explained the functioning of all the knobs, buttons and sticks twice, Smally heaved himself into the driver's seat of the big vehicle while the manager assisted Pauline to get in on her side. As they set off, the vehicle began to move in fits and starts but soon Smally got the hang of it and started to enjoy himself like a small child who'd been given a big toy to play with.

As they left the town and turned onto a dirt road, Pauline remarked: 'This is only the second exit. Didn't the man say we had to take the third?'

'He said second,' corrected Smally with authority in his voice.

'OK, OK . . .'

They advanced for some time with the sun behind them, when Pauline spoke again. She sounded worried. 'Do you think we're going in the right direction? Aren't we heading north? I read in the brochure that the animal reserve is somewhere south of Bobodiou.'

'We are heading south,' countered Smally in a tone that tolerated no contradiction.

'OK, Jacky. You're the boss.'

'Yes I am,' affirmed Smally as if this were the natural, God-given state of affairs.

They drove on for half an hour while the vegetation around them became thinner with every passing mile, but Smally didn't pay any attention. 'Look,' he shouted, 'seventy miles per hour!' The car was bumping and banging, but he kept his foot down on the accelerator. 'I could easily take part in the Paris-Dakar Rally,' he yelled over the noise. 'I would be extremely good. Maybe I would even win the rally.'

After another half-hour of racing along the now almost non-existent track, swerving around potholes and banging into ruts, they got to a landscape of weirdly shaped dunes. Pauline was not feeling very well by now. All this shaking and swerving had upset her stomach, and she was just about to suggest that they stop for a while when Smally exclaimed: 'Hey! Let's see what this car is capable of doing in the sand,' turning the vehicle towards a nearby dune. It shot up the steep slope at full speed and then the sand seemed to give way. As Smally pulled hard on the wheel, trying to turn back, the vehicle leaned sharply to the right at an awkward angle, toppled over, slid down a few feet and came to rest on the passenger's side. Pauline screamed as Smally fell off his seat and landed on top of her. Then the engine stalled and there was complete silence.

19

'Am I speaking to René Hautbois? Yes? Look, I've got a big problem and I don't know how to solve it. I'm getting pretty desperate.'

René Hautbois reflected for a second or two, holding the receiver in his hand. Then he said: 'Is that you, Jean-Marie?'

'Who else?'

'Indeed! Who else would have the cheek to phone me at home early on Saturday morning?'

'Listen, I'm not in the mood for small talk. I'm at the end of my tether. It's about the festivities they're organising for the twenty-fifth anniversary of the reign of one of those African tyrants . . . a certain President Gwemboka. The fellow thinks himself so important that he's invited lots of foreign dignitaries and, first and foremost, the President of France. And our president is going, would you believe it? Now you may wonder what that has to do with me, but these festivities are supposed to mark the union between Europe and Africa. The Africans will present some of their dances and music, while Europe is expected to supply a selection of European culture. And our president had the *wonderful* idea of proposing an opera singer and made me responsible for finding a tenor to sing a few arias . . .'

'Don't tell me that you haven't been able to find anyone . . .'

'I had someone lined up, *mais vous voyez*, his wife rang me a week ago to tell me that he had gone down with the flu and couldn't possibly fulfil the engagement. I don't know whether what she said was true or just an excuse, but that leaves me high and dry, doesn't it?'

'I don't see what the problem is,' interrupted Hautbois. 'As director of the Paris Opera you can't have had any difficulty in coming up with a suitable replacement.'

'You couldn't be more wrong!' retorted Jean-Marie d'Arembère. 'I've personally contacted at least fifteen tenors so far, offered them the most juicy contracts, and they've all refused!'

'But why?'

'They say they already have other engagements, but I suspect that's not the real reason.'

'Why would they lie?'

'Don't you know? The political situation over there is most unstable. There've been several terrorist attacks around Bobodiou recently and it looks as if rebel troops are closing in on the town. I can't really blame those tenors for not wanting to stick their head into the lion's mouth. But it leaves me with a big problem. The President has insisted that I come up with a tenor. He counts on me. I can't let *la France* down! And we're Saturday today, and the fellow has to perform on Tuesday! The whole thing is becoming a nightmare.'

'And where do I come in?'

'You're my last resort! Isn't there anyone in Brussels who is able to sing a few arias? I'm not even holding out for a professional at this point. The situation is so critical that anyone will do, even an amateur capable of pulling it off more or less reasonably. You wouldn't know of a tenor who could do the job, would you?'

'Well, I don't know . . . just like that . . . on the spot . . .'

'Please, don't let me down. Anyone, anyone . . .'

'Wait . . . maybe . . . there's that amateur. He comes here for lessons. I've heard him sing a couple of times and his voice isn't bad. He isn't really all that young: he's maybe forty-five or so, but he's quite shy. And I don't know whether he's free and willing to rush over to Africa at such short notice. I think he's married.'

'That doesn't matter. Have you got his phone number?'

'I think I can find it for you if you give me a few minutes. Which number are you on right now?'

René Hautbois noted the Paris number on a piece of paper and then said: 'Stay where you are. I'll call back straight away.'

20

Saturday morning was a time of the week Raymond d'Elbreux particularly liked. He always switched his alarm clock off on Friday night and stayed in bed as long as he fancied the next morning. He had not slept particularly well though the previous night because he was worried about Pauline: he hadn't seen her since Monday. She must have gone to her lab in the morning as she always did, about half an hour after he had left for the insurance company he worked for. As usual on Monday evening he'd gone straight from the office to the Brussels' opera where he took singing lessons. When he got back at 9.30 he found the apartment dark and empty. It was a nuisance because he was tired and had expected to find supper ready.

Then he discovered a small note on the table. It was in Pauline's handwriting and said that she might have to go on a trip with the lab for a few days. Apparently, she had scribbled it down quickly before leaving in the morning. He supposed that they had organised a coach trip to some other laboratory, maybe abroad, but why hadn't she told him so the previous evening? She surely must have known about it? As he went into the bedroom he discovered that her suitcase had gone and some of her better summer clothes. She had taken summer clothes! And it was the beginning of December! Then he remembered that she had gone into town the previous Saturday to buy a safari outfit. He didn't understand it.

Well, she was sure to phone within a day or two, and would soon be back. No need to call the lab. She wouldn't like that. He didn't want to upset her more than necessary.

She had become quite short-tempered after the row she'd had with her sister last summer. That had been a really nasty business. The sister had rung him, accusing Pauline of having an affair with her husband. Vicious she had been. He had almost believed her, but fortunately he had never liked her very much, and had had the good sense to trust his own wife. Naturally, Pauline had been extremely upset and had cut off all contact with her sister after that. How that woman could have been so mean to Pauline, her own flesh and blood, was beyond him.

No, it was best to wait for Pauline's return. She would tell him all about the trip when she got back. She was always so enthusiastic about her laboratory. Lucky she'd got a job there because he felt that life with him was no fun for a young lively girl like Pauline. But he was good to her, and he was sure that she loved him.

But it was Saturday now, there was still no sign of her, and he was getting worried. He put on the coffee machine and went to have a shower. He had just switched the water full on and was soaping his face while wondering whether he wouldn't have done better after all to call the lab during the week, when the phone rang loudly and insistently. 'Pauline!' he exclaimed and in his agitation the piece of soap slipped into his mouth and he bit off a sizeable chunk.

He rushed out of the shower tub, stumbled over the edge, pulled down the shower curtain trying to steady himself, fell on his knees, clambered up, ran into the hallway, picked up the receiver and held it against his ear, saying: 'Pauline?' while breathing heavily and dripping water all over the carpet.

An unknown man's voice said: 'I beg your pardon. Am I speaking to Monsieur d'Elbreux? Raymond d'Elbreux?'

'Yes, yes,' replied Raymond, disappointed that it wasn't Pauline. He already began to regret that he had rushed to the phone instead of staying under the shower. 'What is it you want?' he asked in a peeved voice.

'I am Monsieur d'Arembère, director of the Paris Opera,' replied the ponderous voice.

When Raymond realised who was speaking to him he stood there, speechless. He would never have dreamed that Jean-Marie d'Arembère, one of the most famous opera singers of the past and now director of the Paris Opera, would ring him. Imagine that! The great maestro whose records he had listened to a hundred times. Whose voice he always tried to imitate. He was so impressed that he straightened himself up, military fashion, and almost saluted. He pressed the receiver against his chin and stammered: 'Oh . . . ah . . .'

'Are you all right?' inquired the voice.

'Am I all right? Yes . . . yes . . . very much so . . .' An expression of beatitude slowly spread over Raymond's face.

'Listen then, what I wanted to know is: are you free?'

'Am I free?' repeated Raymond mechanically, trembling with emotion that he had the honour of speaking to the great d'Arembère.

'It is not for me to know that, dear man,' replied the ponderous voice somewhat sarcastically. 'You yourself ought to know whether you've got engagements for the next few days or not. But if you have, you must cancel them.'

'Yes, yes, I'll cancel them . . . I'll cancel everything . . .'

'Good. Now listen carefully. I have recently talked to Monsieur Hautbois . . . you know, René Hautbois, director of the Brussels Opera . . .'

'Yes, yes . . .'

'. . . and he specially recommended you. He said that your voice was exceptionally good and that you would be the right person. We are in fact looking for a tenor to sing a few arias for a very special occasion. You are a tenor, aren't you?'

'Oh, ah . . . yes,' came Raymond's voice. He was so impressed by now that he almost began to stutter.

'You're sure that you're a tenor? Your voice seemed slightly deeper, especially in the beginning.'

'That's because I had a piece of soap in my mouth,' explained Raymond, somewhat confused.

'Never heard anything so strange,' commented the director. 'A most extraordinary way of training your voice. I suppose it makes it smooth. I must try it out on my singers.'

'Euh, oh . . .' replied Raymond.

'So you are free for the next few days and willing to come? Good, that's settled then.'

'Ahem . . . would it be too much to ask you to be more specific?' asked Raymond as politely as he could.

'Specific? Oh? Yes, of course. There's a performance to be given by a famous tenor in an African country for the occasion of the twenty-fifth year of the presidency . . .'

'But I'm not a famous tenor . . .' Raymond's voice was hardly audible.

'Well, I've been given to understand that you are. And if you aren't yet, you certainly will be afterwards. The President of France will attend, and lots of foreign dignitaries. And the event will be transmitted on world television . . .'

Raymond felt his head spin. The French President . . . world television . . . he a famous tenor . . .

'Are you still there?' asked the director who suddenly feared his hopes might yet be thwarted.

'Yes . . . yes. What do you want me to do?'

'Well, you're supposed to sing a few arias. Can you manage that?'

'I . . . I suppose so,' replied Raymond hesitantly.

'You don't know three or four well-known arias?'

'Of course I do. Sometimes I sing for three hours.'

'No one wants you to sing for three hours. Your performance is scheduled to last only a quarter of an hour. So, what can you sing? Puccini?'

'Ah . . . oh . . . yes . . . shall I sing "Che gelida manina"?'

'*La Bohème*! Excellent. Anything else?'

'"Nessun Dorma"?'

'*Turandot*! Wonderful! Any Donizetti maybe?'

'"Una furtiva lagrima"?'

'From *L'Elisir d'Amore*. Extraordinary! What about Verdi? We must have some Verdi!'

'Maybe something from *La Traviata*: "Brindisi"? Or *Rigoletto*: "La donna e mobile"?'

The director was now almost overcome with joy. 'Fantastic!' he exclaimed. 'Fantastic! Let's have "Brindisi". That'll bring the total to about fifteen minutes. That's an excellent cross section of opera arias.'

'But what about the orchestra?' inquired Raymond hesitantly. 'Will they know what to play?'

'There won't be an orchestra. I'll have the music copied on to a tape right now, and you'll do the singing live. All right? So you have no objections? You're going to do it? I do hope that you fully realise that you've been specially chosen among many possible candidates. This is the opportunity of a lifetime! You can't possibly refuse it.'

'No, no . . . but it's such a great honour for me. I don't feel sure that it's right to accept.'

'You must accept,' insisted the director. 'We all count on you.'

'Of course. If you all count on me . . .'

'That's settled then. And how's your wife?' asked the director as an afterthought.

'Well . . .' Raymond seemed to hesitate. 'She's not here. She . . . she has disappeared.'

'Good!' The director seemed relieved. 'That's all for the best. She won't object then. Could you pack your suitcase straight away and hop on the next train to Paris? Oh, and don't forget your passport.'

'Right, I'll do that.'

'What's the weather like in Brussels?'

'Oh . . . normal . . . just as awful as ever.'

'You'll be pleased, then, to get out of it all and go to sunny Africa. Your train stops at Charles de Gaulle Airport. That's where you'll get off. Once you're there, go to the Air France desk and someone will take care of you from there on and put you on the next plane to Bobodiou. All your expenses will be paid, of course, and you'll be handsomely rewarded. By the way, your performance is scheduled for Tuesday afternoon.'

'Thank you, thank you,' stammered Raymond. 'I'll be in Paris as soon as I can . . .' Then he heard a click: the communication was cut off.

As the director put down his phone he sighed: 'Ouf! At last! That's a load off my mind.' He rubbed his hands. Only fools dare tread where reasonable men won't go, he thought. And I've found my fool. I hope that his handsome reward doesn't include a coffin. With the situation as it is in Bobodiou one never knows.

Raymond stood there for several minutes, motionless, dazed. Then a smell of burnt plastic brought him back to reality. The coffee machine! When he got to the kitchen he found that the coffee had completely evaporated. Only a foul brown stain remained in the bottom of the coffee jug.

Oh . . . well . . . no time now, he thought. I'll have coffee and breakfast on the train. He switched off the coffee machine and rushed back to the bathroom. Quick, quick! My clothes . . . call a taxi . . . oh, and leave a message on the answering machine of my insurance company . . .

Fifteen minutes later he jumped into the taxi which had drawn up at the front door of his apartment block and was on his way to the station.

Part Five

1

The lounge of the Riverside Hotel, the only hotel in Bobodiou worthy of its name, was dominated by a huge portrait of President Gwemboka. It showed him in military uniform, his broad chest hung with colourful decorations like a Christmas tree. To his left was a much smaller photograph of General de Gaulle, a leftover from the 1960s when the hotel had been built. It had been placed somewhat lower and been slightly tilted, creating the impression that the famous general was looking up at Gwemboka who was towering above him. On the right of the President's portrait, smallest and lowest of all, hung a black-and-white photograph of Mao, staring towards nowhere with unfathomable eyes. The impassive face of the venerable leader looked somewhat out of place in Africa. No one knew what he was doing there. Maybe it was all because of his Little Red Book. At one time it was whispered that Gwemboka was writing a booklet that was going to eclipse Mao's red book – and *a fortiori* Gaddafi's green booklet – but the subject hadn't been brought up for a long time. The booklet was a mystery like so much else in this country, and in those rare moments when people discussed it in secret, it was simply referred to as 'the black book'.

Portraits of the 1960s . . . time seemed to have stood still here. Only Gwemboka's portrait had been replaced by a more recent edition every few years, unlike the rest of the hotel and most of the country's infrastructure. Only the President seemed to have flourished. He had put on more weight with each year in power and now literally bulged out of his uniform. He needed ever more decorations to cover his chest, and his portrait an ever-larger frame to enclose the bulk of his expanding body.

Michel, who was sitting in the lounge with a drink in his hand, had been staring for a while at Gwemboka's impressive figure. At last he put down his glass, turned to the representative of the mining company with whom he had been discussing his future employment, jerked his thumb up and asked: 'Who's that fat ugly pig up there?'

'Shht!' warned the man. 'Be careful no one hears you! The walls have ears over here. Don't talk politics.'

'Oh! I didn't realise this was politics. I had no intention of talking politics. I'm not even interested in it. Never been. I just wondered who that . . .'

'Shht! Don't. Don't ask questions here.'

Michel picked up his glass and turned away, an offended look on his face. 'Tell me,' asked the mining representative to defuse the situation, 'what are you interested in?'

'Not in politics,' replied Michel grumpily. Just then a smartly dressed African hostess passed by, slightly swaying her voluptuous hips. Michel nearly dropped his glass and his eyes followed her every movement till she disappeared through the door.

'No need to tell me any more,' laughed the man. 'I know what you're interested in!'

'Well . . .' Michel still seemed under the woman's spell. 'I dare say she's the goods.' He looked apologetically over his glass. 'I can't deny it, can I? Yes, that's what I'm interested in!'

The man smiled. 'That at least is a safe preoccupation over here.' Then he hesitated, thinking of Aids. 'Up to a point, of course. One has to take certain precautions. But having female company is easy enough to arrange.'

'You think you could arrange something for me?' asked Michel eagerly. 'It wouldn't be too difficult?'

'Today if you like. After we've settled the business part of our meeting.'

2

'What's this?' barked de Lattignie, standing in front of what looked like a giant version of a round African hut with an extremely low doorway. He was eyeing the structure of straw and branches with undisguised suspicion. It appeared to have been erected in a hurry and seemed totally out of place in the beautiful garden of the presidential palace in Bobodiou.

The government official who had guided him through the palace and out into the garden looked ill at ease. 'Mr General,' he said in an apologetic voice, 'you're expected in there.' And he extended an inviting arm towards the hut's entrance.

'What? In there? You're not serious. Why should I go in there?'

'Because that's where the President is waiting for you . . .'

'In that dark hole? You must be off your rocker!' The general was a tall upstanding man and, although he was nearly eighty, he still radiated authority. He was used to shooting a withering look from underneath his big bushy eyebrows when something displeased him, and this had stood him in good stead in the days when he had led an army brigade. His subordinates had invariably trembled in their shoes when that furious gaze had flashed from his steel-blue eyes. Age had not diminished his powers of command, and the official visibly shrank when the general stared at him as though he were no more than a despicable worm. He would have backed away had the fear of Gwemboka not been stronger.

'Please, Mr General,' implored the official, extending his arm, 'please do enter.'

De Lattignie gave the man one more pulverising look. Then he shouted: 'All right!' and moved forward with stiff steps. The President of France had sent him on a mission: to go and see Gwemboka, and he would fulfil that mission. If this was the lion's den, he didn't fear the lion, and he was determined to face whatever lay behind that dark entrance.

He tried to bend down to enter the hut, but his back was too stiff and he didn't manage. Why the hell did they have to make this so low? he thought. But a mission was a mission, and he was not to be stopped. He went down on his knees and crawled forward until he had cleared the entrance. Then, holding on to the doorpost, he steadied himself with difficulty, got up and tried to look around.

As his eyes got used to the semi-darkness he began to make out a huge shape in the centre of the hut, not ten feet away, and suddenly he perceived the flashing of white teeth. His throat went dry and he recoiled against the doorframe. Then de Lattignie heard a low growl and his heart started to beat rapidly . . .

3

It was early morning in Kanibasso and Gael had just begun her daily round of the sick and wounded, when two small army jeeps drove into the enclosure of the dispensary and several armed Africans jumped out. They rushed forward, Kalashnikovs pointed threateningly towards the group of people gathered in the courtyard, and grabbed Gael by the arm shouting: 'You! Come with us!'

When they heard this, the forty or fifty patients who had been standing around her waiting to be treated immediately shot into action. Without hesitation they threw themselves on the ground face down to make sure that they wouldn't see anything or be able to recognise the intruders afterwards. They held their hands on top of their heads to show that they had no bad intentions while the armed men kept swinging the barrels of their assault rifles over the mass of bodies lying in the dust, bellowing: 'One movement and we'll shoot!'

Gael stood there in a state of shock, unable to take in what was happening while an African stuck a rifle in her back hissing: 'Take medical bag and move, quick.' The man's eyes kept going nervously from left to right as if he expected the police to be lurking behind the low adobe wall that surrounded the dispensary, ready to shoot at any moment.

Just then Marie, alarmed by the unusual sounds, appeared in the doorway of the house. Before she had time to say a word, two rebels rushed forward yelling: 'Quiet!' while pointing their Kalashnikovs at her. But Marie was not to be silenced so easily. She faced the men without a trace of fear and said calmly: 'What is it you want?'

'Who are you?' shouted one of the men.

'I'm the boss here,' replied Marie. And without so much as batting an eyelid, she repeated: 'What do you want?'

'We want medicine,' shouted the man who seemed to be in charge, sticking his assault rifle in her face. 'Get tablets and syringes. All you have against fever. Hurry!'

'I'll get what you need,' said Marie quietly, pushing the barrel of the rifle aside. 'And I shall come with you.' She pointed at Gael. 'You leave her alone. She's just an assistant.'

'Woman,' screamed one of the men threateningly, 'you shut up! She come, too.'

Marie walked slowly over to where Gael was standing, seemingly fixed to the soil and trembling slightly. 'Don't move or try to talk to them,' she whispered. 'Don't make any sudden movement. They're very nervous. Don't even look at them. Stay absolutely calm. Just follow me when I tell you.'

Then she turned to the armed men. 'All right,' she said. 'We'll both come. I'm now going to collect the medicine. It's inside the house. Will one of you accompany me to check on what I'm doing?'

A minute or two later Marie emerged carrying a few large boxes and deposited them in her own Land-Rover.

'What you doing, woman?' yelled one of the men.

Marie spoke soothingly: 'There won't be enough room in your small jeeps for the two of us and the boxes of medicine.' Seeing the African hesitate she added: 'We'll follow you, don't worry. And if you don't trust us, there's room for a couple of your men in the back of our Land-Rover.'

The one who seemed to be the leader made up his mind. 'Right!' he yelled. Then he pointed at two of his men. 'You go with them,' he ordered.

Seconds later the small jeeps left the dispensary, with Marie's Land-Rover stuck in between. When the patients, who all that time had lain motionless on the ground, finally dared to look up, there remained nothing to be seen but a big cloud of dust that began to settle slowly.

Soon the sick and wounded set off towards the little town of Kanibasso. While they stumbled along, talking excitedly about this unprecedented occurrence, some claimed that they had only pretended to lie face down but that in reality they had been observing everything. The number of rebels they alleged to have seen grew steadily as they proceeded along the dusty track. When they got to the town's central palaver place and recounted the trauma they had been through to a duly impressed audience, the tale had become so enlivened that the people gave them beer and food so that they could relate the whole story all over again.

By the time the local police appeared on the scene two hours later, the dispensary's patients declared that there had been at least a hundred rebels who had turned up in fifteen heavily armed vehicles. Of course, they had resisted vigorously trying to protect Madame and Missie, but the rebels had carried such huge guns that any opposition to those brutal men had been useless. And when the policemen heard the tale their eyes widened with terror, and they were all too happy that fate had been good to them and spared them an encounter with such fierce bandits.

4

In the centre of the hut in the garden of the presidential palace Gwemboka sat perched on a kind of throne, staring at the man who had been his commander so long ago. He had observed the slow painful progress of the old man as he crawled forward on his knees to clear the low doorframe and at first had felt immense satisfaction. He had planned this very carefully: he had wanted to humiliate his old commander and scare the wits out of him, and he had done so. Then, to his utter surprise, a sense of shame came over him – a feeling he hadn't experienced for a very long time. He turned his head towards the subordinates who were waiting at the back and hissed: 'Take it away!'

They immediately rushed towards a cage which had been standing at Gwemboka's feet and started to pull it away. It contained a big black panther, which growled loudly and menacingly as the men wheeled it out through the back of the hut.

The moment they had gone Gwemboka lifted his huge bulk out of his improvised throne and stepped down to meet de Lattignie. This upright man, old now but still dignified, had been his commander and somehow the respect Gwemboka had always felt for him was still there. He couldn't call him Sir, or Lieutenant, but when he blurted out 'de Lattignie!' there was a hint of respect in his voice.

De Lattignie came forward, slowly, as if he found it difficult to walk after the unexpected events. 'President Gwemboka?' he asked, clasping the President's outstretched hands. The President now took the general by the elbow and led him gently out of the dark hut through a much bigger exit at the back. De Lattignie was a tall man, as tall as Gwemboka, but he had remained lean – was it the Mediterranean diet? – and seemed unimpressive next to the African's great bulk. As they emerged into the sunlit garden, Gwemboka clapped his hands and servants started to run about, bringing chairs, tables, drinks and succulent titbits to eat.

When they were seated under the big shady trees, they stared at each other for some time. De Lattignie was the first to break the silence. 'I've always known that you were brave, and I was certain that you would go far in life,' he said looking affectionately at Gwemboka. 'But who would have thought that one of my men would become President? It has warmed my old heart. I'm proud of you.'

There was emotion in Gwemboka's eyes when he heard these words. De Lattignie had not cowed down as all men around Gwemboka had done for years. His old commander had not tried to flatter him. Instead, he had spoken as a father would have to his son, simply, with words that went straight to the heart.

All at once the years seemed to drop off Gwemboka. In his mind's eye he saw himself again as a young, ambitious sergeant in the colonial army, standing behind de Lattignie, all together saluting the flag as it was hoisted up the flagpole while the sun rose behind the barracks in a sea of flames.

And they began to talk about the time when they were both agile young men, when they were not full of all the aches and pains they now felt, when they didn't fear what the future would bring but lived each day as it came.

The army had not been a place for weaklings: de Lattignie's platoon had trekked through desert and bush with barely enough to eat and drink. At night the men had slept in tents or just under the starry sky, and sometimes they had reached the limit of what they thought they were able to endure. But always de Lattignie had pushed them on to go beyond what they would have imagined possible. The lieutenant had been a severe commander, tolerating no weakness or transgression, but he had been just and had cared about his men. And they in turn had not feared him but respected him, and had become deeply attached to him. They had lived in comradeship and enjoyed each moment they had spent together.

Gwemboka's eyes clouded over. He was carefree then. His life had been in his commander's hands and he had trusted him blindly. He had believed in ideals then, in the future. Those had been times of dreams and expectations . . . the best years of his life. I would give up everything to return to those days, mused Gwemboka. My presidency, my wealth . . . everything . . . to be young again.

'I'm so glad to be back,' said de Lattignie as he looked at the tropical flowers and experienced once more that indefinable sensation of lightness and warmth that envelops you in Africa. The colours are so much brighter here, he thought. Everything is different in Africa. He sighed and turned to Gwemboka: 'Oh, to live those years again . . .'

He gazed at the President almost with tenderness, not seeing the fat ugly man he had become but the young, muscular athlete he'd been long ago. The one who so often had taken upon himself the most difficult and dangerous missions . . . the survivor.

Gwemboka swallowed hard a couple of times. The emotion was almost too much. Yes, those had been the days . . . the days when Africa had been young and beautiful, had looked promising like a maiden ready to blossom – not the mess it had become today.

They sat there, talking over and again of all they had done, of small anecdotes that would have seemed unimportant to anyone but these men who had lived them together. For a long, long time neither of the two men had spent such a wonderful afternoon. They continued to reminisce about the good old days until the shadows began to lengthen. Then, with difficulty, they got up and stood there for a while, holding on to each other's hands as if they were unwilling to let go of the link with the past.

At last the President took the general by the elbow and accompanied him through the palace to the exit where the presidential guard sprang to attention and formed a line of honour as they passed by. At the gate he made a sign to one of the officers to accompany the general, not to the car in which he had come, but to the big presidential stretch limo which drew up to the edge of the steps just as the general went down. De Lattignie turned and looked at Gwemboka one last time before he was helped into the presidential car. It drove off the moment he was comfortably seated, and as Gwemboka eyed the disappearing car he sighed heavily. Then he turned around and withdrew into his palace so that no one would see the tears that welled up in his eyes.

5

When Gael and Marie arrived at the rebel camp, the armed men led them straight to their leader. They found him unconscious and delirious with fever. Marie took one look and told Gael to give him an injection of antibiotics immediately; to keep watch over him, and give him an extra shot every two hours.

While they had been rushing towards the camp Gael had felt extremely frightened, but the moment she saw the rebel leader she understood the nervousness of his men. As she sat there on an improvised camp chair hoping that the medicine would take its effect, she was very worried. The man's condition didn't seem to improve. He just lay there, sweating and trembling. Had they arrived too late to save him? Then, to her great relief, the fever started to abate and little by little her patient began to breathe deeply and regularly.

While she was waiting for him to regain consciousness, Gael was looking appreciatively at Amadou Sékouré, the rebel leader who was lying in the shade, his eyes closed. He must be nearly forty, she reflected, yet he looked surprisingly young and lean as he lay there. Life in the bush doesn't allow you to put on any weight, as Gael herself had experienced, and gazing at the man she felt great empathy for him.

She had just put a hand on his forehead thinking how much cooler it felt now, when suddenly he opened his eyes and stared in surprise at her worried face so close to his.

'At last,' she whispered. 'You've pulled through!'

The rebel leader looked around startled, saw his guards standing close by and relaxed.

'Who are you?' he asked.

'I'm Gael. I'm a medical assistant.' She smiled at him, relieved that the medicine had taken its effect. 'You got me really worried. You had such a high fever. I had to give you several shots of antibiotics.'

Amadou Sékouré seemed to remember. 'Yes, yes . . . I wasn't well. But . . . where do you come from? How did you get here?'

'Your men came to our dispensary in Kanibasso and forced us to accompany them at gunpoint. I was rather scared,' she admitted. 'They were in no mood for discussion and ready to shoot if we'd so much as protested.'

'They didn't harm you, I hope?'

'They were a bit rough but I'm glad they made us come. You were delirious with fever and might not have lived another day.'

Amadou Sékouré now leaned on his elbow, attempting to sit up to thank her. She immediately reached her hand out, saying: 'You're not yet well enough to sit up,' and held him back. As she did so two guards ran forward, caught her by the arms and began to pull her away while Gael called out to the rebel leader: 'Please, tell them not to interfere.'

'Leave her alone,' ordered Amadou Sékouré, waving the guards away with a faint movement of the hand.

'But, Boss,' they objected, 'she's mistreating you.'

'I was just trying to make you lie down,' protested Gael. 'You must remain quiet for a while,' she insisted.

'All right,' Amadou Sékouré consented in a weak voice.

The rebel leader lay back for some time, exhausted. Then, gradually, he started to feel better and while Gael took his hand and felt his pulse, busily consulting her watch, he found himself looking at that strange being so close to him. She noticed it and smiled at him as if they had been old friends, and he spontaneously responded with a wide grin. Suddenly he felt embarrassed and to hide his discomfort he asked: 'So you work in the dispensary of Kanibasso?'

'It's not real work,' she replied quietly. 'I've enlisted as a volunteer.'

'Are you a doctor?'

'Oh, no! Not at all. I had very little medical training before I came to Africa a few months ago. But I've learned a great deal since. I may not look strong, but I'm capable of doing a lot now.' She looked at the leader with undisguised pride.

'You like your work then?'

'Well, to be honest, not at the beginning.' She blushed slightly. 'Right from the start I had to treat forty or fifty sick and wounded every day, and some of them were really horrible cases.' She shuddered. 'I must admit that for a long time I didn't know how to cope. Everything was so different from what I'd expected. There were times when I thought I wouldn't be able to carry on. But then . . .' Suddenly she looked at the rebel leader. 'You must think all this very silly,' she said humbly. 'It's nothing compared to what you've got to put up with, I'm sure. Your life in the bush is much tougher than anything I've had to go through . . .'

'Oh! Life in the bush isn't really so bad,' replied Amadou Sékouré, taken aback by the sudden change of subject. 'One gets used to it.'

'Fancy you saying that. That's exactly what I've been thinking. One gets used to anything. It's really surprising what we're capable of putting up with.'

'So you're out there in the dispensary . . . alone?' asked the rebel leader, trying to turn the conversation away from his own life.

'I'm not alone,' protested Gael. 'I'm with Marie, who is a qualified nurse. I'm her assistant. She's the one who's in charge of the dispensary.' And Gael pointed to her companion who had made herself comfortable on an improvised chair and seemed to be having a heated discussion with one of the men.

Seeing her movement, the guards, who had been standing at a respectful distance, now approached again. 'Are you OK, Boss?' they asked. 'You don't need any help?'

'I'm feeling better every minute,' replied Amadou Sékouré, waving the guards away. 'Just leave us.' And he tilted his head again towards Gael. It was clear that he was beginning to enjoy the conversation, and Gael's company.

After the guards had retreated Gael carried on: 'Anyway, how can you ask me if I'm alone? You ought to know that it's impossible to be alone in Africa.' She looked at him almost as if she were ticking him off. 'The people here wouldn't allow it.'

Amadou Sékouré smiled. 'You seem to have found out a lot about Africa in such a short time.'

'That's because of Marie. I owe a great deal to her. She has taught me so many things. She's been in Africa for many years . . . in medical aid projects . . .'

'And now you want to help, too?'

'Someone has to help . . .'

'Well, not everyone would be willing to do what you're doing. That's why the people over here appreciate it . . .'

'They do, but that's not what I meant when I said that it's impossible to be alone in Africa. There's much more to it than that. You see . . .' She stopped for a second and looked at him, wondering whether she should reveal her deepest feelings. Then she made up her mind. 'I've discovered that I love Africa . . . and when there's love in your heart and you open it, warmth comes to you . . .'

The rebel leader stared at her in wonder and no longer interrupted her.

'When you open your heart,' continued Gael, 'the people over here surround you with unfailing support. Never before have I experienced anything like it.' Her eyes began to shine. 'The rewards of working here are tremendous. I'm not talking about money because there's no money involved. In Europe you work for money, but not here. How could people pay for anything here?' She shrugged her shoulders. 'Here you give, and those who receive give you whatever they can in return. And they give you their affection, which is worth more than all the money in the world . . .'

Amadou Sékouré looked at Gael with admiration in his eyes. 'My dear Gael,' he said quietly, taking her hand, 'it's a privilege to have been saved by you. I'm like all your other patients. You have my affection, too.'

6

Meanwhile Marie had been talking to a man who appeared to occupy a high rank in the revolutionary hierarchy. The strange thing was that he was white. He had dark shiny hair, black eyes, and a short pointed beard that made him look like a Spanish hidalgo. With her usual flair for establishing friendly contacts, Marie was soon talking to him and it turned out that he was indeed Spanish. His name was Juan Rodriguez and when Marie addressed him in his mother tongue his joy knew no bounds, and soon he was talking excitedly about everything and nothing.

It is always useful to know people but also to be aware of what's going on, and this is particularly the case in Africa where possessing the correct information can make the difference between life and death. In no time at all, therefore, Marie was applying herself to extracting information in her own innocent way.

'How did you end up here with the rebels?' she asked. She had no trouble feigning surprise, since she was indeed surprised.

'Oh, I've known Amadou, the rebel leader, for a long time. We met in Paris. We both studied political philosophy at the Sorbonne.' The man lit up a cigarette and puffed on it for a while before continuing: 'Exciting years those were! The discussions we students had! Night after night we gathered together in small groups, talking about the world; about how we were going to change it. Yes, we were going to fight and improve everything. We had so many bright ideas . . .' His eyes clouded over. 'And then . . . you would never believe what happened to all those young idealists. Guess what most of those fellows talking about *la révolution* till daybreak have become?' He looked at Marie with eyes full of loathing. 'Businessmen!' he said, spitting out the word. 'And worse: civil servants! With high-ranking jobs in ministries, imagine that! And yes, they're all fighting to improve things,' he sneered. 'For themselves! They're elbowing others out of the way to promote their own careers within the existing social order. What a let-down!' He shook his head in despair. 'Only Amadou and I have stuck to our principles. Together we're strong. We, at any rate, intend to change the world. And we're going to begin with this country.'

He took a deep drag from his cigarette and the pause gave Marie the opportunity to ask: 'But to overthrow a regime you need arms.'

'Oh, we're well armed,' bragged Juan Rodriguez.

Marie pointed at the assault rifles the rebels were carrying. 'They're all brand new,' she observed. 'Where did you get those from?'

'We got a tip-off from someone in the Russian Embassy who told us to wait at a certain spot for the arrival of some trucks. They brought the ammunition and arms, cleverly concealed among the equipment for a mining company. And this time the Russians got it right.' He chuckled. 'This time the ammunition fitted the rifles. Unlike what happened during the Spanish Civil War when the Republic bought loads of Russian weapons, paid for it in gold, and when everything arrived, the ammunition didn't fit!'

'How do you know that?'

'Because my grandfather told me. He fought in that war. On the Republican side, of course. What a shambles! It was not just the arms deliveries that went wrong. The Republican troops were totally divided, too. No wonder they lost against a well-organised and well-armed fascist force.' Juan Rodriguez sat there for a while, grieving as he remembered the painful stories his grandfather had told him.

'But we're not ones to give up easily. My father carried on the revolutionary tradition.' Juan looked up proudly. 'He fought with Che Guevara. A great man, Che. But once again we were betrayed. By capitalists this time.' He stopped for a while, took a few more drags from his cigarette and threw away the stub carelessly without extinguishing it. Then he continued: 'But we shall overcome. Look at the revolutionary enthusiasm of these men here.'

Marie looked around and seemed duly impressed.

'Yeah,' said Juan Rodriguez. 'As you see, there's progress. This time we're going to win and throw the tyrant out. Hang him.'

'So you are revolutionaries from father to son?' asked Marie, interested in the man's unusual life story.

Juan Rodriguez nodded his head. 'Yes, yes . . . we Spanish like revolutions.' Suddenly a painful expression came over his face. 'At least . . . that's how it used to be. But now . . . the Spanish have betrayed the revolutionary ideals! No more guts. No more fight in them. All that counts now are cars and money. I can only weep over Spain today.'

Then he brightened. 'But I'm not giving up. In our family we never give up! Look at the rebel army we've assembled! And when this is over I'll go to Latin America. That continent is ripe for a revolution. And I'll find myself a woman over there who has the same ideals as me, and have a son with her, and he'll carry on the struggle. Yes, there are great improvements. Another fifty years or so of this and we're sure to win!'

He stared at Marie expecting admiration, but she was looking with apprehension at what Rodriguez called 'the army'. Could one really call this band of young men with sunglasses, jeans and T-shirts an army? she mused. She had no idea whether or not there were other rebel camps around, but in this camp there were at most a few hundred men, leaning against their jeeps while carelessly handling their Kalashnikovs, or sitting in Peugeot sedans. A few machine guns were mounted on the back of pickups and there were two or three bigger vehicles carrying equipment, food and water. If this was an army, it was no more than a ragtag army. They're young and enthusiastic, thought Marie, but how can they ever succeed against Gwemboka who can spend millions on the defence of his regime and keeps everything under tight control?

When he noticed that Marie seemed to be evaluating the strength of the rebel forces, the expression on Juan Rodriguez's face changed abruptly. He regretted that he'd talked so much. He got up brusquely, turned his back on Marie and walked away. His lips were pressed tightly together when he thought of the valuable information that woman had wormed out of him. She's a spy, he thought. As likely as not, she's a spy. We can't run the risk that she passes on the important information she now possesses. Anyway, Amadou seems to be getting better, and soon we'll no longer need these two women. A hard, set look appeared in his eyes. They must be silenced as soon as possible.

7

Day was breaking when Anton woke on the third morning of his solitary journey. He climbed out of the Land-Rover in the faint light of early dawn and noticed that the rim of the sun had only just appeared, glowing brightly. As he stared at it like a hypnotised worshipper of some primitive religion praying for the new day to come, the sun seemed to grow rapidly. It kept moving upwards until it detached itself from the horizon and hung low in the sky like a huge burning ball, staining the east with flames of red. The silence was eerie and it was still chilly, but as the fiery ball rose further, its rays warmed the Earth and touched Anton's face. The sun's life-giving warmth began to envelop him, an incredible lightness lifted his spirits, and suddenly he felt bursting with life.

This is a new beginning, he reflected, starting to boil water for tea. All my troubles are behind me. As he was munching some biscuits smeared with stale jam, his thoughts went to the project he'd been working on for endless months: he had prepared a prototype of a metal detector and installed all the scientific equipment inside the Land-Rover. All this time the detector had been sitting underneath the board on which he had slept, and he hadn't dared to try it out because he'd been afraid it might have exhausted the batteries. Until now he had just been attempting to survive. The tension had been so great that he had been unable to think of anything else.

But today was different. Now, with the desert nearly behind him, he felt much more confident. He had always thought that one day he would test his equipment in the Sahara or somewhere like it. And now he was in the Sahara. Why not test it while he was driving? He began to rummage inside the Land-Rover, got out the equipment, switched on the detector, and set off.

He had covered no more than ten miles when the landscape began to change. At first he didn't notice it, concentrating as he was on the stretch of track just ahead of the wheels, but then it struck him that a few scattered low bushes had appeared. So this is the area where the Sahara ends and the Sahel begins, he reflected.

It wasn't clear at first that life had really managed to get a foothold. After a while the Sahara seemed to regain the upper hand: all traces of plant cover disappeared completely and once more there was nothing but bare soil and rocks. Then sparse vegetation became visible again here and there. By early afternoon the plant cover had become more abundant and there were even a few small thorn trees. Yes, this was definitely the Sahel.

Then Anton perceived a cluster of black dots on the horizon. Was it a mirage? A few minutes later he had got close enough to notice that the dots were moving, and as he drew nearer he understood what they were: camels! A herd of maybe twenty scraggy animals was moving slowly over the vast expanse of sand and coarse gravel, led by a man accompanied by his young son. Anton was overjoyed. At last, here was someone to talk to. He drew up next to the small caravan, jumped out and, waving his arm, shouted: 'Hello! Pleased to meet you!'

The man stared at him with incomprehension. He was barefooted and dressed in baggy black trousers over which he wore a blue-and-red striped garment, held together at the waist by a belt from which hung an impressive curved dagger. A blue turban surmounted his brown face, which ended in a pointed, slightly greying black beard.

Anton advanced, his arm stretched out ready to shake hands but the man recoiled, put his right hand on his heart and bent his head slightly forward. Only then did Anton realise that the man didn't understand his greeting and that they had no common language. He racked his brain, trying to think of a possible conversation. Ah, he thought. I know.

'I . . . go . . . Bobodiou.' Anton spoke slowly and clearly, first indicating himself and then pointing at the southern horizon.

There was no reaction; the man just stared at him impassively. Anton repeated the word Bobodiou. The man seemed puzzled and made a wide sweeping movement around himself.

Surely, he must have heard of Bobodiou, thought Anton. How was he to convey that he was driving there? Suddenly he had an idea. He drew two crosses in the sand, quite apart. He put his foot near one cross and pointed a finger at the man and then at himself. Next he indicated the second cross, saying 'Bobodiou,' and then walked over while holding an imaginary steering wheel in his hands and imitating the sound of a car engine.

While this was going on, the man's son had retreated and was now hiding behind the camels. The camel driver himself eyed Anton with the utmost suspicion and slowly his hand went to his dagger. Anton, who was quite close to the man by now, recoiled, climbed quickly into his Land-Rover, started it and drove off.

8

The encounter between Anton and a man from the desert seemed to be symbolic. How am I going to make contact in Africa if I cannot speak to anyone? he thought. If people mistrust my most innocent gestures? He didn't know the language of the man he had met. In fact, he didn't have the slightest notion of any of the hundreds of languages spoken outside Europe, but he had been sure that he would get along anywhere in the world with the few European languages he'd mastered.

Somehow he had always assumed that other people would make an effort to understand him and his ways. That Western symbols and reasoning were relevant to all and universally appreciated. And now, for the first time in his life, he had stood face to face with another human being with whom he didn't have a single word or symbol in common; and his Western ways of making contact had failed abysmally.

If he, who was so full of goodwill, hadn't even managed to communicate, let alone establish a friendly connection, what chance was there for people from different cultures ever to get along? Distrust seemed to be the usual reaction between strangers. Thinking about it, Anton could come up with many reasons for such a reaction. People are not at ease with those who don't speak their language; and they're generally suspicious of those who don't share their culture.

He had never given these questions much consideration but as he drove along, gazing over the empty landscape that stretched as far as the eye could see and beyond, he realised that most people tend to see others from their own narrow vantage point. Yes . . . he thought, people are generally convinced that their ways are right . . . even that their system of values is absolute! But how, he wondered, can belief systems be absolute when humans are no more than a mere blip in the geological history of the planet?

All the same, Anton became aware that a void had opened beneath the system of rational thinking that had always guided his reasoning. The shock of meeting a stranger with whom he didn't appear to share a single mental process had somehow kicked the pedestal from under it. Were Western systems of thought really as superior as he'd always held them to be? Or were there other ways of living and reasoning, totally different from the ones he had learned, other perceptions of time maybe, which were just as valuable, or maybe more?

Suddenly it dawned on him that he might have to reconsider many concepts that had seemed obvious to him. That maybe he would have to discover totally new ways of looking at everything. He instinctively felt that it was important to approach the unknown world that lay on the other side of the Sahara without prejudice or preconceived ideas and he realised that, as long as he saw things through Western-tinted glasses, there was no chance he would ever understand Africa. But he also knew that it was going to be very difficult to take those glasses off because they were the only ones he'd got, and he had been wearing them from a very young age; in fact, ever since his parents had begun to educate him.

9

He had driven for maybe half an hour through a stony landscape strewn with strange boulders when he heard a faint beeping sound. It was so unusual that at first he couldn't think where it came from or what was happening. Was anything wrong with the Land-Rover? 'Not again!' he exclaimed.

He immediately stopped but the sound continued. Then he realised what was emitting it: the detector! He was so excited that he ran to the back door, pulled it wide open, crawled inside and threw out his cooking equipment and the board on which he slept, to get at the detector. There it was, beeping and LEDs flashing.

He attached his laptop, opened some files and began to read the detector's information with great interest.

How can that be? he reflected. Surely, this is a mistake?

He reset everything and started again but the peaks in the chart on his screen remained in the same position. He began to twiddle with the detector's knobs and settings and continued for maybe half an hour till he was satisfied that there was no mistake possible: the detector had discovered a combination of very rare and extremely valuable metals.

The radar attached to his detector was pointing at some darker rocks towards the southwest. He drove a few miles further south, leaving the rocks behind, and repeated the whole operation. The results were the same, except that this time the radar pointed north-northwest, towards the same formation of dark rocks. So that was it! That's where the metals were located. The rocks looked so different from all the rest that he wondered what could possibly have thrown them up here in the middle of nowhere. Were they leftovers from an ancient volcanic eruption? That might explain their strange content.

He switched on his GPS system to determine his exact location and looked at his large-scale map of North Africa. For several days he had just carried on over the flat featureless expanse of the desert and hadn't noticed how far he had strayed off the beaten track. Now he realised that he was at least fifty miles away from the line that was marked as 'the road' crossing the Sahara. That would explain why this unusual rock formation had never attracted any attention before. Camel caravans might know about it, but no modern vehicles or explorers from mining companies were likely to stray into this inhospitable region. He carefully jotted down his position, saved all the information, switched off his computer and detector, and set off at an angle to join the track that would eventually take him to Bobodiou.

10

Some seventy miles north of Bobodiou a big four-wheel-drive vehicle lay on its side on the slope of one of those high sand dunes that are scattered across the Sahara. Absolute silence reigned, outside and inside the vehicle, until one of the occupants stirred into life. When Jack Smally opened his eyes it took him quite a while to come to his senses. He had been dreaming that his wife had given him a whack on the head, and that he had escaped her and was hiding in a small cupboard, sitting in a most uncomfortable position. As he looked around he couldn't think where he was or why he was there. Suddenly he became aware of a body underneath his own and it all came back to him. Pauline!

He began to nudge her, but she didn't move. And then he realised that she was dead. Dead! She must have broken her neck. How could she have done this to him? He lay there for a while trying to take it all in, feeling trapped like a fish in an aquarium but without the water. Water! His throat felt so dry that his tongue literally stuck to his palate. Water. He must find water or else he, too, would die. Then he remembered the bottles they'd brought with them and he began to search around while waves of panic surged through him. At last he found the bottles, opened one of them with shaking hands and took a long gulp.

He felt better after that and began to review his situation. It was clear that this was Pauline's fault. Why hadn't he stayed safely in the hotel? Instead, he had given in to her unreasonable demand and look what he got in return? Nothing but trouble. What was he to do now?

He thought for a while. What would Napoleon have done under these circumstances? He would have kept his head cool, of course, and his eyes riveted on his main objective. And what was the main objective in this case? The conference! That's what I've come to Africa for, reflected Smally

He quickly began to conceive of a plan of campaign, just as the great Emperor would have done. First of all he must get out of this vehicle. He straightened himself and, standing on Pauline's body, he started to push against the door on the driver's side, which was right above him, until it opened sufficiently to throw out the water bottles. Then, climbing up on the back of the passenger's seat and pressing a foot against the steering wheel, he put his shoulders against the heavy door and with great effort began to slide his head and torso between the half-open door and the side of the car. He kept moving until his legs and feet were free and the door slammed shut again. Then he picked up the bottles, slid down the slope of the dune and started the long walk back to Bobodiou, following the tracks he had made himself only a few hours ago.

He kept on marching at a steady pace through the night, and through the morning and late afternoon of the next day, certain that he would reach Bobodiou. But when the sun began to set for a second time, nothing seemed to have changed. The landscape was as barren as ever, there was still no sign of human presence anywhere, and tomorrow was the day of the conference!

He hadn't eaten for a day and a half, had already emptied one of his two bottles of water and felt worn out. He decided to lie down where he was and try to sleep, but lying on the coarse gravel was no fun. He kept thinking of the horrible situation in which Pauline had put him. She with her wild animals! Suddenly he thought of the wild animals that were sure to be prowling through the night looking for a victim; for something to eat. What if a hungry hyena found him? Or a lion? He began to panic and stared into the darkness. What was that? He was sure he had heard something . . . He didn't dare shut an eye after that and kept peering around, alarmed by the slightest real or imaginary sound. By the time morning broke he was completely exhausted, stiff, shivering with cold and so hungry that his belly kept rumbling constantly. But at least he had survived the night.

He was trying to get his legs to move again when he heard the faint sound of an engine. The noise gradually became louder and then a lorry appeared on the horizon, coming straight at him. This was maybe his one and only chance to be rescued! He jumped into the middle of the track and started to wave his arms wildly.

When the driver saw a diminutive white man pop up from nowhere, his heart nearly stopped beating. This could only be a malevolent jinni! He was about to accelerate when the man knelt down, throwing up his arms in entreaty, and he had to jam his foot on the brake not to flatten him.

The lorry came to a halt within inches of Smally while a cloud of dust enveloped him. When the dust settled, the driver got out and went hesitantly to where the little man sat, trembling. Suddenly he pinched him hard in the arm, making Smally yell. Satisfied this was no jinni but a real being of flesh and blood, the driver was all smiles now.

Smally seemed to be in a state of shock and it took him some time to recover. Finally he asked in a shaky voice: 'Bobodiou? Can I come?'

The man nodded agreement. 'Yes. You come. You go in back.' He pointed apologetically at the two men who were already sharing the driver's cabin with him.

Smally breathed a sigh of relief that the driver was willing to take him, but as he went to the back of the lorry he recoiled. It was filled with goats!

He quickly ran to the driver who was already behind the wheel. 'I can't go in there,' he objected. 'It's crammed full of goats!'

'Then you stay here,' said the man, lifting his arms in a fatalistic gesture.

'All right,' grumbled Smally, and he heaved himself up onto the back of the lorry and pushed forward through the tightly packed goats.

The driver now wanted to make up for lost time, the lorry started off with a bump and, as it did, Smally lost his balance and disappeared amid the mass of legs and hoofs. One of the goats panicked and gave him a kick in the side while another one emptied its bowels over him in fright. He swore, got up and tried to hold on to the goats' scraggy coats while the lorry heaved and banged its way along the potholed track, but it was almost impossible to remain standing, the stink soon became unbearable, and Smally decided to push his way towards the front of the lorry. When he got there he steadied himself against the driver's cabin and stuck his head forward as far as he could to be out of the foul smell. Then he began to think.

What would Napoleon have done in a situation like this? As far as he could remember, the great Emperor had never had to share close quarters with two dozen filthy, bleating goats. No, this was a totally new situation that required careful consideration.

Smally was just debating the different scenarios when he was rudely interrupted in his reveries by one of the goats, which began to tear pieces off his trouser leg and was clearly enjoying the taste of it. He gave the goat a vicious kick but at precisely that moment the lorry hit a deep rut and Smally lost his balance again.

This was intolerable. To put an important man like him in such a situation! All because of that Pauline. She was the one who had wanted to see animals. She should have been stuck here with those filthy, smelly goats! I must get out of this or I'll go mad, he thought. Then he had an idea. With great difficulty he climbed to the top of the cabin and lay there, clinging on for dear life. The metal of the cabin was scorching hot, the sun bore down upon him like a blazing fire and every irregularity in the track reverberated through his body, but at least he was out of reach of the goats and away from their repulsive stench. By the time the lorry got to Bobodiou and the driver dumped him not too far from the hotel, he was grey with dust that had mixed with his sweat and stuck to his face and body; he had blisters on his hands, and slight sunstroke. But he was alive!

11

When the early light woke him that same morning, Anton knew that this was going to be the last day of his solitary journey. He had consulted his GPS system the previous evening and estimated that he was less than a hundred miles from Bobodiou. Only three days ago he had wondered whether he'd ever be able to cross the Sahara on his own; even whether he would survive. And now he had done it!

As he breakfasted on the little food he had left he felt so excited he was almost unable to eat anything. He, the shy fellow who'd always let others take the limelight, had vanquished every obstacle fate had put in his way. Against all odds he had overcome being abandoned; mechanical breakdown; despair and loneliness. And he had at last tested his detector. It had functioned perfectly and he had located some rich deposits of extremely rare and valuable metals! Whatever obstacles he might encounter from now on, he would face them and fight to surmount them.

An hour or so after setting off, he entered a landscape of weird, strangely shaped dunes and noticed a bright shiny point halfway up one of them. He swerved to have a look at it and as he approached he realised that what he'd seen was the sunlight reflecting in the windscreen of a car. How the hell did that get up there? he wondered.

As he didn't want to be trapped in the sand like that car he stopped well away from the dunes and began to walk to where it was stuck on the slope of a high dune. As he got closer he saw that it was a powerful, brand-new four-wheel-drive vehicle lying on its side.

Whoever drove that car up this dune must have been a total nitwit, he couldn't help thinking. And what a state it's in!

The two wheels that were accessible had gone and everything that could be taken apart or was of any value had been ripped off. He saw the footprints of many camels and understood. No need to hang around any longer, he thought. That's what happens in Africa when you abandon a car.

He slid down the dune shaking his head, and set off again towards the south. Some twenty miles further he caught up with a caravan and noticed the bulging shapes of wheels and other car parts tied to the camels' sides. The few men in long blue robes who accompanied the animals were walking, but one of the camels was carrying a passenger, a woman. She started to wave frantically when she saw the Land-Rover but Anton didn't stop. He remembered the encounter with the desert man the day before – the long curved dagger the man had been wearing, and his own inability to communicate – and gave the caravan a wide berth without slowing down.

He continued on his way over the sandy track, winding slowly through a landscape of low bushes and scattered thorn trees. Far to the west under an azure, cloudless sky, he could make out the vague outline of some mountains but otherwise the land was featureless. At one time he passed between two huge baobab trees, towering over the Land-Rover. They stood alone in the pink sandy surroundings like fat gnomes that appeared to have been planted by some mischievous god who'd played a prank and had put the trees upside down, their roots up in the air and their branches beneath the ground.

Then he saw a group of women walking barefoot through the sand, precariously balancing baskets and round gourds on their heads. Soon there were more people on the road, and every now and then he overtook a donkey cart, which was conveying bulky goods towards the town; as he passed it the young men leading the animals invariably waved, smiling at him, their white teeth flashing in the sun. It was obvious that he was approaching Bobodiou and its varied human activities and that modern life was only just around the corner. And suddenly there it was: a roadblock manned by gun-toting soldiers. This was civilisation at last, so much more dangerous than the Sahara!

Anton felt instinctively that he had to be very careful, and stopped at a respectful two yards from the barricade while the soldiers came forward.

'Where you going?' shouted the commander, a sergeant.

'Isn't this the road to Bobodiou?' asked Anton meekly.

The sergeant seemed to be taken aback. 'Yes, yes . . . Bobodiou.' Then he regained his aplomb and barked: 'Who are you? And where you come from?'

'I'm Anton . . . I'm Dr Felsen and I've come from Europe . . .'

'From Europe?' The sergeant's mouth fell open. 'That's a long way from here, man!' Then he exclaimed: 'Ah!' while a look of understanding came into his eyes. 'I understand. You coming for the conference, yes?'

Anton didn't have the slightest idea that there was a conference in Bobodiou but suddenly he had a brainwave and replied: 'How did you guess that?'

'That's simple,' said the sergeant proudly. 'The whole world is coming to the conference. But, man . . .' he began to shake his head, 'man . . . why you not come by plane? You should have come by plane.' He held up a reproving finger as if he were speaking to a dumb child.

'Why is that?'

'Because you're late. You'll sure miss the conference.'

'But I still have time, no?' bluffed Anton.

'No you haven't! It's starting this afternoon.'

'Goodness me! I didn't realise.' Anton's face looked crestfallen. 'What am I to do?'

'All right!' shouted the commander, shooting into action. 'We got orders to search all vehicles, but we won't have no time for that if you going to the conference. You'll have to hurry, man.' He turned at once to his soldiers, barking: 'Open that barrier and let the car pass!'

'Thank you so much, Commander,' said Anton with a straight face, but he breathed a sigh of relief once he had passed the obstruction.

Within less than a mile he began to approach the outskirts of Bobodiou, a muddle of shacks and small adobe houses surrounded by vegetable patches. Then he entered real streets and came upon the first policemen.

Bobodiou's police force was renowned for its great efficiency in extracting fines from drivers, or even from pedestrians if no other victims could be found. They usually lurked behind street corners to pounce upon unsuspecting motorists as these swerved to avoid the many potholes or the rubbish which lay everywhere in heaps bang in the middle of the streets. The police would then accuse them of driving recklessly, or on the wrong side of the street, or both when the victim was a stray tourist and they saw an opportunity to extract a double fine.

But as Anton drove into Bobodiou he saw none of this. Gwemboka had given strict orders, and the piles of rubbish, some of which had been accumulating for years, had been cleared and the worst potholes had been filled. Gaily coloured banners spanned the streets and there was a general feeling of festivity in the air. The world was coming to Bobodiou; this was a very special time and all 'normal' activities were to be suspended for the duration of the celebrations. And so the police, one of the most corrupt forces in the country and a thorough nuisance wholeheartedly loathed by the population, were well behaved.

Anton soon understood that the word 'conference' seemed to be a kind of password. He merely had to pronounce it and the police at once became extremely helpful. They even smiled and told him that the conference was taking place in the Riverside Hotel.

If this is the way to get through town easily, thought Anton, why not? He was beginning to enjoy himself. I might as well go and see what that famous conference is all about.

A quarter of an hour later he stopped in front of the hotel, squeezed his old Land-Rover with great difficulty into a narrow parking space, assisted by two obliging policemen, and entered the impressive lounge where he noticed a poster: International Geological Conference.

Holy cow! thought Anton. An international geological conference here in the middle of nowhere? Who'd have believed this? And he hurried to the reception desk.

12

'The conference, Sir?' The receptionist seemed surprised. 'But it's started . . . You say you've come from Europe to participate? Wait . . .' The man beckoned to a female attendant who came forward. 'Is the auditorium still accessible?' he asked, 'or have they locked it?'

'I don't know. I'll go and have a look.' She went into a corridor with Anton following close upon her heels, opened a side door and peered into a dimly lit auditorium where the applause indicated that a speaker had just finished his presentation. Without further ado Anton pushed past her, went in, found an empty seat and sat down.

The conference had been somewhat of a disappointment so far. There had been talks about improvements in extraction techniques; about progress in open-pit mining; the expected shortage of certain metals and possible substitutes; coltan production and the consequences of the unstable political situation in the Congo on supplies; and so on. There had been nothing really exciting and so it was with anticipation that the participants awaited the last speaker, an unknown scientist who was going to talk about 'A new method of detecting deposits of rare metals'.

'Who's that fellow who's going to speak?' whispered the organiser of the conference, leaning over towards the director of the French Geological Institute who was sitting next to him in the first row.

'He represents the Belgian Geological Institute,' replied the latter. 'To tell you the truth, I don't really know him. In fact, I've never heard of him. I invited my esteemed colleague Professor Briart instead of this man. I expect there must be a good reason for his presence. He's probably got something really interesting to say. At any rate . . . the title of his talk sounds interesting.'

In the first row Jack Smally sat eagerly waiting. He had spent most of the morning balancing precariously on top of a lorry full of goats. And up there he'd had plenty of time to think about Pauline whom he had abandoned in that car in the dunes, lifeless. But he didn't doubt for a second that he'd done the right thing. If she had to be sacrificed for his glory, so be it. He had a mission to fulfil and he would carry it out to the end. He wasn't going to be put off by such a minor upset.

When he had reached the hotel he had rushed into his room, washed perfunctorily, changed quickly and grabbed Anton's papers. He'd run to the auditorium, getting in just as the lights were dimmed and had plonked himself in a free space on the first row reserved for the VIPs, as if this were his natural place. The organiser of the conference had no idea who the man was who had belatedly occupied the seat next to him without so much as a 'by your leave', but he didn't want to interrupt the first speaker who had just started his presentation. Then a smell as of mature cheese hit his nostrils. He tried to shift as far away as possible in his seat, but the revolting smell kept wafting across to him throughout the different presentations, and it was with a sense of relief that the organiser got up and invited the last speaker, a Mr Jack Smally, to present a new method of detecting deposits of rare metals.

Anton, who had just sat down, couldn't believe his ears when he heard this. 'But . . . but . . .' he stammered, and became extremely agitated as a diminutive man rose from the first row and marched on to the stage.

Smally was prey to a jumble of emotions. This is my moment, he thought. A small step up to the stage, but a giant step towards fame . . . He looked a bit dishevelled, but when he stepped into the limelight, smelling more strongly of goat cheese than ever, his whole demeanour conveyed the message: Here I am. I've come to conquer. He turned towards the audience, put his papers on the lectern, cleared his throat and said: 'I'm going to present my new method of detecting deposits of rare metals.'

Anton felt his blood rush to his head. This went beyond the limits of decency. This was unheard of! He wasn't going to let this pass and as Smally opened his mouth and began to read, he jumped up and shouted across the audience: 'I protest!'

At once everyone turned round and all eyes were fixed on Anton.

'That man has no right to present this as his own!' he shouted. 'Those are my papers and my ideas!'

Mayhem ensued, and everyone started talking excitedly while the organiser of the conference kept calling: 'Silence! Silence!'

Smally was not having any of this and began to scream at the top of his voice: 'I've been invited to speak and I'm going to speak!'

'Impostor!' yelled Anton.

'Don't listen to that man!' shouted Smally, his face red. 'He's merely an insignificant subordinate. He has no right to be here. I fired him!' And, turning towards Anton: 'How dare you! I'll deal with you when I get back to Brussels.' And then again to the organiser: 'If I'm not allowed to speak, I'll file a complaint. You will hear from me!'

'Silence, silence!' the organiser kept calling, and the auditorium finally quietened down. 'We must let this man . . . Mr Jack Smally, speak. His name is on the programme.'

'Ah!' exclaimed Smally, turning triumphantly towards Anton.

'All right!' shouted Anton. 'Let him begin! We'll see how far he gets.' Then he blurted out defiantly: 'He's sure to get stuck on the formula!'

When he heard the word 'formula' Smally felt sweat breaking out. That damned Anton fellow! Why hadn't he explained everything to him? Suddenly his nerves seemed to give way, he began to panic and had a blackout: he couldn't remember a word of the talk he had prepared so carefully the previous days. As he stood speechless, there was dead silence and everyone held their breaths. Then, as if awakening from a dream, Smally picked up the papers and started to read them in an unsure, shaky voice. When he got stuck on a difficult term and had to read it twice before being able to pronounce it, a few people in the audience began to jeer, but with a superhuman effort Smally managed to carry on, muttering incoherently. Then, finally, he came to the formula. As it was projected on the screen, a voice came from the audience: 'Could you please explain this formula? What does the factor α stand for?'

'Euh . . .' mumbled Smally evasively. For what seemed an endless moment he stood there, staring at the formula with a blank expression on his face. The only sound was his irregular breathing. Then someone in the audience exclaimed: 'He doesn't know!' A few people now began to boo, and within no time the whole conference room was in turmoil. There were catcalls, and a voice could be heard shouting: 'He's an impostor!' Then the whole audience joined in shouting: 'Out! Out!' and a wave of booing rose up from the floor to the stage.

Smally stood there, motionless. He opened his mouth trying to say something but no words came. This was the end. This was Waterloo! All of a sudden he had only one idea: to flee, to get out of here before they caught him and, like Napoleon, banished him to St Helena. And he turned and fled while the audience continued to boo and stamp their feet.

Total chaos now reigned; the lights went on while all the participants of the conference began to talk excitedly. Then Anton jumped up, came forward, leapt onto the stage and called out, his voice ringing clearly over everyone's heads: 'Shall I take over and explain the formula?'

Unexpectedly Merril B. Hanclaus, a famous mining tycoon and one of the guests of honour, stood up. 'I think we should let this man speak,' he said, turning to the organiser.

The organiser nodded agreement, saying: 'Could you please introduce yourself?'

'I'm Anton Felsen . . . Dr Felsen from the Belgian Geological Institute,' replied Anton, and he started the lecture all over again, going through the main points without any need for the pages which lay scattered around his feet. He talked enthusiastically about microwave lasers, about giving them frequencies so close that they interfered, and about fine-tuning them to adjust the frequency of the interference term until it coincided exactly with the ground frequency of a selected metal: the frequency that made the electrons orbiting the atoms jump to the first excited level.

'But that's impossible!' came a voice from the audience. 'If it did work, it would be the most revolutionary invention in geological exploration of the last decades!'

'I fully understand your scepticism,' agreed Anton. 'I thought for a long time myself that it was impossible. I worked on this for several years without finding a solution but then, last summer, I managed to solve the riddle. So I built a mobile detector functioning on these principles and I have just tested it in the Sahara. And I can tell you that it works. Only yesterday I was able to locate some extremely rich deposits of tantalum and . . .'

When he heard the word 'tantalum', a representative of a French mining company jumped up like a jack-in-the-box. He was so agitated that he nearly fell on the person sitting in front of him. 'Where are these deposits?' he shouted.

'Don't say a word,' warned a Canadian. 'I'll see you after the conference. We want that concession.'

'Can we buy your detector, please?' asked a smiling Chinese.

If the beginning of the conference had been somewhat disappointing, the end more than made up for it. It was first-class drama, and as the conference broke up, the air was electric. Excited discussions went on between small groups of participants while they streamed out of the auditorium. Several prominent mining directors began to converge on Anton, but Merril B. Hanclaus was the first to get hold of him. His time schedule was very tight – he had to catch a plane back to America within two hours – but he cornered Anton and took him by the elbow. 'Don't sell to anyone before contacting me personally,' he insisted, pressing his card into Anton's hand. 'I want your detector and I'm prepared to offer you your weight in gold for it. And I'd like you to come over to America and work for me,' he added before walking out precipitately.

As he went into the bar Anton was surrounded by prominent members of the mining community. They all wanted to buy him a drink while he began to tell them the story of how he had driven through the Sahara all on his own.

13

After Smally had fled the auditorium he rushed to his room, locked the door and sat on his bed while blood throbbed in his ears. How could this have happened? He simmered with the indignation of it all. When he had risked his life to get back in time! And that dreadful Anton! He had been quite certain that he was finished; that he'd got rid of him. How could he have turned up here at the very last minute, like Blücher appearing on the battlefield of Waterloo in the nick of time to defeat Napoleon. Defeat! Total defeat. And that appalling booing. He seethed with anger when he thought of the unfair treatment those scientists had given him. Puffed-up frogs they were, all of them. Thinking themselves better than anyone else. Better than him! If only he were their director, he would show them what he thought of them. They needed to be cut down to size.

And that awful Pauline! he thought. I should never have listened to her. I shouldn't have come here to give that lecture pretending it was my discovery. This could ruin my career. They will have me up for unethical behaviour. Damn, damn! I must get back to Brussels and give my version of events before the news spreads. I must get out of here and catch the next plane to Europe.

But that was easier said than done. The organisers of the conference would waste no time in alerting the police and then they would all be after him. He would be like a fox with the hounds hot on his heels. Better to get out of here right now before the whole police force started to look for him. But how could he leave the hotel unseen? Everyone would recognise an important, well-known figure like him the moment he set foot out of the door.

Then he saw a solution: he would disguise himself – there was no other option. But how? he wondered. Put on a false beard or a wig? A wig! Suddenly he thought of the wig Pauline had brought with her. It was a mop of bright-red hair, which she had stuck on once for a fun party. Then he noticed her clothes lying on the bed and had a brainwave. He was about the same size as Pauline, and she had brought a suitcase full of clothes. Yes, that was it: he would disguise himself as a woman!

He undressed in a hurry and began to dig frantically in the case but found nothing but miniskirts. 'Damn, damn!' he exclaimed. He had rather hairy legs and couldn't possibly wear a miniskirt. Why didn't that fool bring a proper long skirt which a decent man can wear, he reflected bitterly.

Then, as he threw out all the clothes in a frenzy and came to the bottom of the suitcase, he found what he was looking for – a long red flowery chiffon skirt – and without hesitation he put it on. It fitted perfectly.

The most difficult part was the top. He picked up one of Pauline's silken bras, slipped the straps over his shoulders and then tried to fasten the hooks behind his back, but just couldn't. How the hell do women do it? he wondered. They must have rubber arms and eyes in their backs. Finally he stood in front of the mirror, turned round and with the greatest of efforts managed to hook up the bra, twisting his neck and terribly straining his shoulders.

It was fortunate Pauline didn't have huge breasts like his wife but, still, there was a lot to fill inside that bra. Luckily, she had brought heaps of underwear and he quickly began to stuff Pauline's smalls into the bra until it bulged satisfactorily. Now, he reflected, what else? Yes! I've got to shave. He picked up his electric razor and began to shave till his chin felt as smooth as a baby's bottom. Then he applied some of Pauline's face cream, make-up, rouge and lipstick, sprayed himself with her perfume, stuck the wig on his head and put on one of her blouses. When he looked at the over-all effect in the mirror he was mightily pleased with himself. I make a really attractive woman, he thought. If I met myself like this in the street, I would find myself very seductive. I could easily fall for myself.

There only remained the shoes now, but these turned out to be a real problem. Pauline's feet were a size smaller than his, and it was with the greatest difficulty that he managed to squeeze his feet into a pair of her high-heeled shoes. He put on a headscarf, found his passport and plane ticket and stuffed them into one of Pauline's handbags. He was about to pick up his suitcase when suddenly he saw a big problem: to get out he had to pass through the lounge, and if he pulled his suitcase behind him he was sure to be stopped by the receptionist who would ask why he was leaving the hotel without checking out.

He made a quick decision. The main thing was to reach the airport where he could change into men's clothes in one of the toilets. If his suitcase had to be sacrificed, so be it. All he needed was a change of clothes, which he quickly stuffed into a carrier bag. He left the room, passed the reception desk with measured steps – he was not used to high-heeled shoes – slipped out of the lounge without being stopped, and walked towards one of the few taxis that were always waiting in front of the hotel. 'The airport,' he squeaked in a high-pitched voice as he sat down, making himself as inconspicuous as possible in the backseat.

He breathed a sigh of relief when they reached the airport without being stopped by one of the many police patrols on the road. He paid, stepped out and walked into the airport as if on stilts, swaying his hips exaggeratedly, but this only seemed to add to his attractiveness and a few Africans, who were doing some repairs, whistled as he passed by.

Inside there was a great to-do. The first foreign delegations for tomorrow's great African–European cultural event were beginning to trickle in, and security guards seemed to be everywhere. Smally was cautiously moving forward when a foreign delegation, which had just arrived, walked straight towards him. At once he recognised the man in front: he was the Belgian Minister of Education whose protégé Smally had been for years and who'd given him his present job. Smally recoiled instinctively, forgetting that he was a woman and that the Minister would not recognise him in his disguise, and hid behind a pillar, eyeing the Belgian delegation with apprehension while they passed by.

When the coast was clear he emerged from behind his pillar, looking furtively around, and began to move stealthily towards one of the toilets. He had nearly reached it when he felt a heavy hand fall on his shoulder. It startled him so much that he jumped up, screamed, dropped his bag and scurried away, but he was unable to run fast because of his high-heeled shoes. He hadn't covered more than ten yards when the guard caught up with him, held him in an iron grip and called for help. Soon he was surrounded by armed guards sticking their guns into his face while he stood there, shaking.

14

'One must learn to walk before one tries to run,' said Amadou Sékouré. He had a habit of speaking in oblique images, especially when the discussion became heated. 'What I mean is: we neither have the strength nor the experience to launch a frontal attack. So let's bide our time and see what turn things take.'

'I don't agree!' Juan Rodriguez sounded adamant. 'We must attack immediately! From the north, west and south smaller rebel forces are converging on the capital. I've just had news that they've made contact with each other and also with our outposts to the east of Bobodiou. We've shut off the last possible route of escape.' He rubbed his hands. 'The noose is complete. And in the centre of it sits the big spider. This time we're going to catch him. Only a miracle can save Gwemboka now. We're going to tighten the noose until it closes around his neck. Let's take the capital without any further delay!'

'I'm not sure,' replied Amadou hesitantly.

'But this is the best moment yet!' objected Juan Rodriguez. 'The security forces are busy protecting foreign dignitaries and the armed forces are dispersed around the country. Now is the time!'

'Yes, yes!' shouted another rebel brandishing his Kalashnikov. 'What are we waiting for, that's what I want to know? What's the point in getting so close to the capital and then just sit here and do nothing? Comrade Juan is right. This is the perfect time for an all-out attack. They're busy for the moment, but once the festivities are over the tyrant is sure to turn his attention on us and crush us!'

Amadou thought for a long while. Then he spoke: 'Your arguments sound reasonable and, believe me, I fully understand your impatience. We have worked for months to get this far; your support has been unfailing, and your devotion is worth more than all the weapons in the world. If we launch a surprise attack now as you suggest, maybe we will win. But maybe not. And even if we do, it will be at the cost of many lives – your lives, and those of many innocent citizens who have suffered too much already. I am responsible for the success of our revolution . . . but I'm also responsible for you. I want us to win, but I also want you to live. If we are to build a better world, I will need people to build that world – I will need you. All of you!'

He paused for a moment, letting his eyes wander over his

comrades-in-arms who were sitting around him in the yellow sand, their faces tense. Then he spoke again. 'The most difficult part is not the battle for Bobodiou. The most difficult part is what comes afterwards: the battle for the hearts and minds of the people. And I will need many arms and heads to win that battle. I will need your enthusiasm.

I don't feel it is right to sacrifice your lives,' he continued. 'It's not yet time to attack. Even if our enemies are busy, they are still strong. And there are also foreign troops in the country. We mustn't give foreign powers an excuse to intervene, as happened two years ago. And they would intervene if expatriates were killed. No, it's better to wait. I feel that time is running out for the tyrant. A few more days' patience is all I ask. Let's have faith.' He looked at his men. 'What do you think?' he asked simply.

Presently a seasoned revolutionary stood up. 'Commander,' he said, 'we have followed you for so long now that we would be lost without you. You are the soul of the revolution, and if you feel it is better to wait, we shall wait.'

15

'Where are you going?' inquired Amadou some time later when he saw a few rebels stealthily picking up their guns, and preparing to move off.

'Oh,' said one of them apprehensively. 'We were just going into the bush with Juan.'

'What are you going into the bush for? I'm sure you're trying to hide something.'

One of the men moved nervously from one leg to the other. 'It's about those women,' he finally admitted.

Amadou got up and addressed the man sharply. 'What is it about those women? I want to know!'

'Well . . .' confessed the man shuffling his feet. 'It seems that we no longer need them as you're in good health again. Juan said we should dispose of them.'

'And what exactly does he mean by that?' came Amadou's angry voice.

'He means . . . well . . . you know . . . to take them into the bush and shoot them.'

'What!' Amadou turned to the man and shouted in his face: 'Are you off your nut? Where's Juan?'

A few minutes later Juan Rodriguez appeared from behind a tent, apparently in no hurry to face the rebel leader.

'Is it true what I've heard?' hissed Amadou, his face tense.

'Is what true?'

'That you wanted to sneak away with these two women and have them shot behind my back?'

Juan's lips set into a tight expression and he blurted out: 'They've become a liability.'

'Man, have you taken leave of your senses? How can you even think of such a thing? When they saved my life!'

'But, Amadou . . . Don't you see? They know too much. Especially the older one. I don't trust her. She's . . . *muy lista* . . . how do you say that . . . yes, very cunning. She knows our position and our weakness. If we release these women, they might give us away. The success of the revolution must take precedence over all other considerations. And if a few lives have to be sacrificed for it, so be it.'

'Shut up!' yelled Amadou, trembling with rage. 'They never protested against being brought here by force. On the contrary, they've done everything they could to restore my health. They trusted us and we shall trust them. We shall treat them with all the respect they deserve while they're here. And if they want to leave, we'll escort them to the edge of the area we control and set them free.'

Juan Rodriguez was not pleased. He couldn't go against the rebel leader but he advanced one more argument: 'What you propose is dangerous. Even if you trust them, the tyrant's police are sure to be lying in wait in Kanibasso to capture them. And they will show none of your kindness. They have the means to make their victims talk, and they will make them talk. And where do we stand then?'

Amadou thought for a while. 'There's sense in what you say,' he agreed. 'They're probably safer in the capital. We'll have to smuggle them into their embassy in Bobodiou where the staff can arrange for them to be sent back home at once.'

He now turned to his men who had drawn nearer while the discussion had been going on. 'I warn you not to touch a hair on those women's heads. You will all answer personally for their safety. And I want to add that they deserve our admiration. Our country could do with a few more women like them. If our men were as brave and as dedicated as these two women, we would be living in paradise.'

The men had been listening in silence, heads bent low, but Juan Rodriguez was not yet silenced. 'That's all very well,' he objected, 'but how do you intend to smuggle them into Bobodiou? Every access road is blocked.'

A man now came forward. He was known as Rasta because of his appearance: long braided hair hanging down disorderly from his head, and a scraggly beard. 'I know a way into Bobodiou where there are no roadblocks,' he said. 'It's a rough, hardly used track through the bush but it leads straight to the capital. And there won't be any problems in town. Carnival groups are singing and dancing everywhere in the streets. Even if there are police controls, the tyrant's police are so corrupt that they will leave anyone alone for the right amount of money. Especially foreign women working on a medical project.'

'All right,' agreed Amadou. 'You'll be their guide then.' He reflected for a moment. 'But how are you going to get through the town without being noticed? You stick out a mile with that hairdo of yours.'

'We could disguise him as their nurse,' suggested one of the rebels with a wide grin. 'Women in medical aid projects always have local nurses with them.'

'You must be joking! How can we disguise Rasta as a nurse? Male nurses are clean-shaven without any of Rasta's hair and beard.'

The men who had been ready to sneak out in the bush suddenly saw an opportunity to redeem themselves. They had listened to the conversation with mounting interest, and now stepped forward, their eyes sparkling. 'No problem, Boss,' they said. 'We'll shave him if you like.'

His hairdo was Rasta's greatest pride and when he understood the men's intentions he turned, ready to flee, but the men jumped on him before he had time to move, pinned him to the ground and sat on his legs and arms while he struggled desperately. Within seconds a pair of scissors was produced and the man who in his free time doubled as the camp's unofficial hairdresser set to work, grabbing Rasta's hair. The helpless man kept screaming 'No!' while shaking his head and contorting his body, but to no avail.

A circle of rebels soon formed around the scene. They began clapping their hands, swinging their hips and singing, their deep voices drowning Rasta's screams, while little by little his braided locks fell into the sand around his head.

When all was over, Rasta was a different person. He had looked impressive before. Now, clean-shaven, he seemed no more than a lean man and the light in his eyes had faded. They washed him, dressed him up in a white nurse's jacket which had been found in Marie's Land-Rover and soon the poor man, very subdued by now, was ready to guide the two women on their perilous journey into Bobodiou.

16

'Boss,' said two armed guards, pushing a struggling Smally into Security Headquarters, 'we've caught a terrorist.' They looked very excited.

'I'm not a terrorist!' yelled Smally who seemed to have recovered his self-assurance. He continued in a high-pitched voice: 'I'm an important person and I shall complain to my government about the treatment meted out to visitors in this country!'

The commander seemed to be taken aback by the vehemence of the woman's retort and sternly addressed the two guards who had brought in Smally: 'Are you sure this woman is a terrorist?'

'But, Boss, that's obvious. First of all, the headscarf. Then the way she was hiding behind a pillar in the airport . . .'

'You caught her in the airport?'

'Yes!' The guard nodded triumphantly. 'She was lurking behind a pillar, as I said, spying on a foreign delegation that had just arrived. And when I saw her emerge I was at once struck by her strange, stealthy way of walking . . .'

'Yeah,' cut in the second guard, pointing a thumb at Smally. 'This here subject's suspicious behaviour stood out a mile.'

'But that doesn't make her a terrorist!' The commander still didn't seem convinced. He didn't want to make a mistake and arrest an important foreign woman on false charges. 'Is there anything tangible?'

'We know a terrorist when we see one, Boss,' declared the first guard. 'We can almost smell it, Boss.' He tapped his nose with his finger while sniffing noisily. 'It's the training, Boss.'

Smally, who had been listening with mounting irritation, suddenly burst out: 'This is going too far!' He banged his fist on the commander's desk. 'These subordinates are totally incompetent. You must fire them immediately!'

So far the commander had done his best to give the woman the benefit of the doubt, but this was more than he could stand: he was not used to being ordered about by women and didn't like it a bit. His blood rushed to his head, he got up, strode over to Smally, stood squarely in front of him and yelled: 'Shut up, you hussy! In case you hadn't noticed, I am the commander here!'

Smally's pride was stung. How dare a lowly civil servant tell him to shut up! He wasn't going to take this, and he drew himself up to his full height. Even so, and in spite of wearing high heels, he was a full head smaller than the African and much less impressive. Still, he shouted back for all he was worth: 'This is no way to treat an important visitor. You give me your name and position and put me in contact with your superior. Immediately!'

'Oh that's how it is?' retorted the commander. 'So we are important.' His voice was scathing. Suddenly he burst out: 'And who are you to come and shout here in my office, Missus Bigmouth? If you're so important, what's your name and position?'

At once Smally realised that he couldn't reveal his true identity, and began to stutter. 'I . . . I . . .'

'And what were you doing at the airport?' The commander jabbed a threatening finger at the little man.

'I . . . I just went there to catch a plane,' replied Smally in a thin voice, taken aback by the man's aggressive gesture.

'If you were going to catch a plane, where's your luggage then?'

While Smally was searching for a reasonable answer, one of the guards intervened: 'Boss, I think that she smuggled a suitcase full of explosives into the airport to blow up the French President.'

'What! Where's that suitcase?'

'Several guards are searching the airport this very moment, Boss, but the situation is difficult and needs careful handling. What with all the important delegations arriving, we didn't want to go on full alert and couldn't possibly close off the airport. It would put us in a bad light internationally, wouldn't it?'

The commander now began to make menacing gestures. 'Where did you leave your suitcase, woman?' he shouted in Smally's face.

'I . . . I . . . well, if you want to know, I only brought a small bag. I . . . I never travel with a suitcase. So there!'

'Is that so . . . now, is that so . . .' said the commander in a mocking voice. Suddenly he turned to his men. 'Has she been frisked?'

'Don't touch me!' yelled Smally.

'Maybe she's got a bomb concealed under her clothes,' proposed one of the guards.

'I've got nothing to hide,' protested Smally in a high-pitched voice.

'And you cannot search me. That would be indecent! It is not allowed by international law. I'm a woman.'

'Call Mama Makumba!' barked the commander.

After what seemed ages a voluminous African woman came in. 'Frisk her!' ordered the commander. 'Leave no corner unexplored.'

'You come with me, Madam,' said the African woman firmly, grabbing Smally by the arm. He struggled valiantly, but her strong hand was clamped around his wrist like a vice, and she pulled him into an adjacent room.

Within seconds the men heard a loud yell followed by a shriek, and then Mama Makumba came rushing in, all flustered. 'She's a he!' she exclaimed, panting.

'What do you mean, Mama?' shouted the commander.

Mama Makumba stood there shaking, pointing an accusing thumb at the door. 'That there woman in there is a man,' she declared.

'You don't say! Are you sure?' The commander seemed unwilling to believe that such a thing was possible.

Mama Makumba didn't appreciate that her authority in the question of men could be doubted. 'I am an experienced woman!' she protested. 'I will explain.' And she straightened her bulky back, looked around importantly, and began her story.

'My eyes were straight away drawn to a big bulge right in the middle of her skirt. A bomb, I thought. She's hiding a bomb! I was very frightened that it might detonate if I put my hands on it, I can tell you.' She rolled her eyes to show how frightened she had been. 'But I knew my duty. The woman resisted, but I slid my hand under her skirt. And yes, she was hiding something. I touched it, and when it didn't go off I began to finger it very carefully.' Mama Makumba seemed extremely excited recalling the act. 'The woman went very quiet and let me handle her device, but by now I had an idea of what it was that she was hiding in her panties. To make sure I suddenly squeezed it hard and when that woman screamed in agony, I squeezed again, to double-check . . . There was no doubt about it: what I held in my hand was men's equipment!'

The commander sat there, spellbound, listening with open mouth, unable to utter a word.

'Yes!' continued Mama Makumba triumphantly. 'That there woman comes equipped as a man!' And she pointed an accusing thumb at Smally who had just emerged from the neighbouring room, bent double, holding his crotch with both hands and walking as if in great pain. 'I know what men's equipment feels like!' she exclaimed, holding up her fleshy right hand and moving the thick fingers expertly. 'And she's a man!'

'Well, well . . . who would have believed that?' muttered the commander. 'She . . . I mean he . . . looked very feminine to me.'

'That woman is not to be trusted,' intervened the first guard. 'We told you so, Boss. She . . . I mean he is a terrorist passing for a woman to commit a heinous crime more easily.'

'Throw her . . . I mean him in jail!' exclaimed the commander, shooting a hostile glance at Smally.

The first guard seemed to hesitate. 'Boss,' he said, 'there's a problem. 'Do we put her in jail with the men or the women?'

'You asshole!' barked the commander. 'With the men, of course.'

'But if we put her with the men, they'll rape her.'

When Smally heard this, he visibly shuddered. 'No! No!' he yelled. 'Don't put me with the men! I want to be put with the women.'

'We can't do that,' objected the commander. 'That would be immoral. How do we know that you're going to leave our women alone, eh? A man dressed like a woman is not to be trusted.'

The second guard had been scratching his head during the last minute or two. Finally he asked, pointing at the two bulges underneath Smally's blouse: 'But what about this here woman's breasts? They look real to me. And very attractive, too,' he added.

'Yeah, nothing missing there,' agreed the first guard.

Mama Makumba now came forward, her two big hands stretched towards Smally's blouse. 'Shall I squeeze them, Commander?' she asked.

'No,' sneered the commander, advancing towards Smally. 'I'll squeeze them, haha. I want to see for myself what they are.'

'Don't you touch my breasts!' yelled Smally, holding his hands protectively in front of him. 'And I'll tell you what you are. You're a bloody idiot, that's what you are!'

'What!' The commander stuck his fist in Smally's face and shouted: 'Shut up, you transvestite!'

The two guards gazed at their commander in awe. The things he knows, they thought. Then the first guard ventured a question. 'Boss,' he asked hesitantly, 'what does it mean to be a trash-vest-tight? Is that bad?'

'It must be bad,' ventured the other guard. 'This woman looks very creepy to me.'

The commander flared up. 'You dim-witted asses!' Then he shook his head, calmed down and said, as if speaking to nitwits: 'In practical terms

'. . . in practical terms . . . it means that we cannot put him among the men dressed like a woman.'

'That's what I said,' insisted the first guard. 'I know them prisoners. Some haven't seen a skirt for years. They'd go wild if they saw this here woman.'

'But Mama Makumba says he's not really a woman,' objected the other guard.

'Yeah, but he'd get raped before they find out.'

'I know what to do,' concluded the brighter of the two guards. 'We'll undress him before putting him with the men. That'll avoid a lot of confusion.'

Smally, who had stood speechless throughout the conversation, suddenly screamed: 'Don't you dare touch me!' He began to kick wildly when the two men approached, but one of the guards jumped on him and held him firmly to the floor while the other one pulled down his skirt and ripped off his blouse.

As the guards saw him lying on the floor in Pauline's bra, panties and high-heeled shoes, kicking his hairy legs, they began to laugh hysterically. Smally quickly crawled along and got into a corner holding a protective hand in front of his panties and bra.

The commander stood there, rocking with mirth. 'We . . . we haven't seen, haha . . . we haven't seen her breasts yet, haha,' he managed to say, doubled up with laughter.

'I'll show you what's in there,' offered one of the guards, advancing upon Smally.

'That's my job!' protested Mama Makumba. 'You men are not to touch no breasts here!'

Mama Makumba and the guard now started fighting over the unfortunate Smally, pulling him back and forth when suddenly his bra gave way and a selection of Pauline's underwear was strewn over the floor.

Meanwhile the second guard, not wanting to be left out, had begun to attack the panties. Smally resisted valiantly, pulling them up as the man tried to pull them down, until the flimsy nylon suddenly ripped and all was revealed while Mama Makumba timidly averted her eyes.

'See!' exclaimed the guards triumphantly. 'Now we can put him in jail with the other men.'

17

After the excitement at the end of the International Geological Conference had died down, Anton felt extremely tired and decided to lie down for a while. He walked to where his Land-Rover was parked, started to climb in but shrank back: it had been standing in the full sun and it was stiflingly hot inside. There was a big tree further along and he went to sit in its shade, wondering what to do. He simply couldn't face spending another night in his Land-Rover and began to stare at the hotel. Some of the windows on the second floor were open and the curtains were floating in the breeze. It all looked very attractive, but also very expensive. Why not give myself a treat? he thought trying to convince himself. I deserve a bit of luxury after the desert. And he went hesitantly into the hotel to inquire about rooms. He was in luck: one more or less affordable room was free for the night, and he made up his mind on the spot and moved in.

When he woke up late next morning he felt greatly refreshed. Sleeping in a real bed after having had a proper meal had done him a world of good. He lazed about for another hour, had a hot bath and finally decided that it was time for brunch. As he approached the rear terrace of the Riverside he noticed a chubby man who was sitting at one of the tables with a drink in his hand.

'Michel! What a surprise!' exclaimed Anton, crossing over to his table. 'I wondered what had happened to you after you went away so suddenly with that diplomat and left me alone in the Sahara. Did you get here in time to meet your man from the mining company?'

'Yeah, yeah. I was in time.' Michel turned to stare at a pretty African woman who just passed by, and his eyes followed her as she moved away, swinging her hips in a gracious movement.

'You seem absent-minded. Did they hire you?'

'Oh . . . yes . . . yes.'

'You don't seem very enthusiastic. Maybe you don't like the new job?'

'The job's all right,' replied Michel with an expressionless face as he eyed another young African woman.

'I don't understand you,' sighed Anton. 'You were so keen on getting that job. You always told me that a good job is so important to a man. You even wanted to get away from Europe because you no longer liked working in the lab and . . .'

'Who would have with that narrow-minded meddler they sent us as a new director?' interrupted Michel. 'You didn't like him either.'

'Oh by the way, guess who was on the programme at the International Geological Conference here in Bobodiou? You'll never believe this.'

'Not our famous Mr Smally?'

'How did you guess that? You haven't got a sixth sense, have you?'

'No. But as we were just talking about him . . . in psychology they call this an association of ideas. It's what you'd expect.'

'You amaze me! How do you know anything about psychology?'

'It's the long relationship with my psychologist, I suppose.'

'Your psychologist?'

'Well . . . yes. You know I had certain problems in Brussels . . . let's call them frustrated expectations . . . so I had regular sessions trying to resolve them.'

Anton smiled as he remembered a certain story. 'Was it him who advised you to use a rubber doll?' he inquired sardonically.

'Let's not talk about the past!' Michel sounded offended. 'Let's talk about the present. And while we're on the subject: it wouldn't surprise me if, where we find Smally, we find his new secretary. You know who I mean. That hot chick, Pauline. You haven't seen her yet?'

'Michel, I think you're going too far!' Anton shook his head in disbelief. 'Your sixth sense must be leading you astray.'

'No, no dear friend. You mark my words. It's just common psychological sense: where you find the boss, you find the secretary.'

'Smally and Pauline? I don't believe for a moment that there's anything going on there. How can you possibly imagine such a thing?'

'I may look absent-minded, but my eyes do see what's going on – unlike some of us here who seem to live in a dream world. Or maybe you're jealous and your mind refuses to contemplate the idea that Pauline is having an affair with someone else? That would explain it.'

'Now, hang on! Don't start that story again. That woman is an obnoxious, horrible creature, and I'm glad that I shall never have to see her again. And let me tell you that my interests are elsewhere. As a matter of fact, I'm looking for a girl who must be somewhere around here. The one I love, you know. And *my* sixth sense tells me that she's probably very near and . . .'

'Man, man, I can make neither head nor tail out of your babble. What a muddle! Anyway, you seem to be happy, and that's the main thing. By the way, what kind of lecture is our dear Smally going to give? I really wonder. He doesn't know anything about geology.'

'You mean at the conference? But that was yesterday! I gave the lecture.'

'What! I was sure it was going to be today. My company sent me to attend the lectures . . . that's what I'm here for . . . oh, oh . . .' He shook his right hand vigorously. 'Isn't there a programme of the conference with some information about the contents?' He looked at his companion with a glimmer of hope in his eyes. 'Or an abstract or something I can get hold of?'

'Don't worry,' said Anton in a honeyed voice. 'Your common psychological sense is sure to find a way out of this. But I wonder how you managed to get the date wrong. Don't they use the same calendars in the mining areas as they do in town?

'No, that's not it. It's just that I've been so busy I've lost track of time.'

'You've been busy?'

'Yeah, day and night.'

'Hey, that's not healthy! You can't keep working like that. You must give yourself a break.'

'Ahem . . . I'm not talking about work. What I'm talking about are the hours in between: at midday when I rush home. The late afternoon. And the nights. I'm talking about my . . . well . . . my love life.'

'Your love life?' Anton's mouth fell open.

'Yes.' Michel's face suddenly took on an ecstatic expression. 'You simply wouldn't believe it! It is a tale out of a thousand and one nights: man's wildest fantasies fulfilled. Sometimes I have to pinch myself to believe that it's really true.' He trembled with excitement. 'Nights like these are what I came into this world for.'

'But how come this has happened now?'

'Because I'm in Africa! This could never have happened in Europe. Just think of European women. They're difficult. They're choosy. They don't want this and they don't want that. Nothing is ever good enough for them. You have to court them, lay it all at their feet, and then they say "No, thank you," stick up their noses and walk out on you.'

'*I* never experienced anything like that.'

'That's because *you* have been very lucky. At birth you were dealt a hand full of aces. You were given the face of a god and a body women desire. While I, who am far better than most men, stand no chance whatsoever because those silly women prefer good looks to contents. The wrapping is what makes things sell nowadays.'

'Aren't you exaggerating? I'm sure that, with some effort, you might have found yourself a nice homely girl.'

'Don't be daft! I don't want a nice homely girl! I want hot stuff. Really hot! Like the ones you find on the Internet or in magazines. And boy, oh boy!' His hands began to move uncontrollably and his tongue almost hung out of his mouth. 'Who would ever have believed that this would happen to me in Africa?'

'So that's what's happened! You found yourself a nice hot African chick?'

'You've got it all wrong, Sir.' Michel drew himself up. 'Here you can have four women. And I have got myself four of the most gorgeous, sexy young things you've ever seen! And they're all over me and do whatever I fancy! If this isn't Paradise, then I don't know what Paradise is like. Boy, oh boy!' His whole face lit up. 'I'm the happiest man in the world.'

'You don't mean to say you have them all four together?' Anton looked shocked. 'Don't men over here who have several wives have to set up a separate home for each wife and visit them on different days, or something of the kind.'

'I don't know what they do or don't do over here, or what the customs are, and I don't care. What I do know is that I'm living my dream. That's what my psychologist said: "You've got to live your dream." And my dream is having them all four together!'

'But you can't do that!'

'Of course I can!' Suddenly Michel bent over to Anton and whispered: 'Listen to how I do it. Let me give you a few hints . . .'

'I'd rather not know about it,' replied Anton decidedly. 'There are things that ought to remain between husband and wife – or in your case, wives – and that, I believe, is one of them.' And he got up, for once causing Michel to stare at a man's back as Anton removed himself from the scene.

18

Raymond d'Elbreux was pacing up and down the lounge of the Riverside Hotel in Bobodiou, getting more nervous with every passing minute. I shouldn't have accepted this invitation, he thought, I really shouldn't!

It was always the same. People lured him into doing things that seemed such a good idea at the time, and then the wonderful ideas turned out to be big mistakes. Look at my marriage – if that's what you can call it, he reflected with bitterness. Pauline! When she'd told him the story of her youth he'd felt scandalised that such things could have happened to an innocent helpless girl. What she'd had to put up with! How could life have treated her like that? It seemed so unjust. And a chivalrous impulse had impelled him to offer her marriage. His parents had been very upset but he had stuck to his word and married her.

And what a disaster it had been! Very soon she'd made it clear that she wasn't interested in sex. Maybe she'd had bad experiences as a child? Or maybe she was too young? Anyway, after a while he had stopped bothering her, or expecting anything at all. Then he found they had very little in common, and he'd left her to do as she liked. She was extremely sensitive and got easily upset, probably as a result of her unstable youth, and he had to be constantly on the alert not to worry her or impose things on her she didn't like.

Little by little he had withdrawn into his shell and had pursued his own interests – his love of opera – outside the home. Opera! His one great solace! With every passing year he had retreated more into the world of opera, lived for opera. He had a good voice, but that seemed to be about as much as life had given him.

Then, out of the blue, came this invitation: they wanted him to go and sing in Bobodiou! The French President would be there, and other foreign dignitaries, and television crews from all over the world. Not even in his wildest dreams had he ever believed that such a thing would happen to him, a shy man who had always lived in the shadows! But there it was, and he'd accepted. Naturally he had accepted. They wanted him to do it. How could he have let them down? But now that he was about to step into the limelight, his courage totally deserted him. He wanted to hide, to be somewhere else. He was certain that he would fail abysmally. He would step onto the stage in front of the public and have a blackout! He would be unable to remember the lyrics . . . or his voice would be hoarse. He just couldn't face it.

Again he began to pace up and down nervously. One hour to go, only one more hour. And he wouldn't be up to it! All this because I don't dare say no, he reflected shaking his head. That's the story of my life. My whole existence has been a sequence of disastrous choices because other people have always manipulated me. And I've let them. I've always been scared stiff of upsetting them. For the umpteenth time he stopped in front of the huge festival display board. There he was, announced as 'A tenor who will present a selection of arias of his own choice'. Less than an hour to go . . .

He looked absent-mindedly at the other announcements. Yesterday there had been a world conference on mining and geology featuring many renowned specialists. They'd had to face the public, too, but at least, if they had a memory lapse, they would have been able to read their texts. As his eyes wandered over the list of participants, a name suddenly came into focus: Jack Smally from the Belgian Geological Institute was on the list. But that's the institute where Pauline works, he thought. And that's her new director. How small the world is!

Just then, behind him, he heard the man at the reception desk exclaim: 'Missus Smally!' The receptionist was a tall, handsome African, and Pauline had always smiled at him as she passed by his desk, singling him out for her attention. He'd been off duty for two days and was surprised to see her coming into the hotel in such a dishevelled state.

'Missus Smally!' he repeated, pronouncing it 'Somalee' and putting the stress on the last syllable. 'What's happened to you? And where is Mr Somalee? Is he with you?'

When he heard the name Smally, Raymond looked up thinking, oh, that's the director's wife. The woman was talking in a low voice to the receptionist and had her back towards Raymond, yet her shape seemed strangely familiar. I must have seen her somewhere before, he reflected. Finally the woman was handed the keys and turned, ready to go to her room. As she did so Raymond had a shock. But . . . but that's Pauline, he thought. No, it can't be. I must be hallucinating.

He was intrigued and followed her at a distance as she disappeared into one of the long corridors on the ground floor. She had just unlocked the door of her room and was about to go in when she realised that someone was coming up behind her and looked round. When she recognised the man her mouth fell open. She stared at him with panic in her eyes and mumbled: 'Raymond! What . . . what are you doing here?'

When Raymond reflected on his life much later, he would say that this had been the single defining moment when his past life had toppled over and come down with a crash. Suddenly all the indistinct feelings that something had been wrong, the vague impression of unease, scattered images of Pauline seeming to run circles around him, became clear in his mind like a picture that comes into focus. In a flash he understood. He saw how for years he had been led up the garden path, how he had been cheated upon and lied to, not once but systematically.

It was as if a dam had broken and, once it had given way, the flood ran out with such wild fury that nothing could have held it back. He rushed forward, clasped his hand round her wrist so strongly that she screamed with pain, and pulled her inside, slamming the door behind them. He hurled her onto the bed, slapped her face with the palm of his hand, ripped off her clothes and threw himself upon her. All the frustration, the suppressed anger of years welled up as he penetrated her and shook above her like a savage beast, until the moment of explosion, of liberation. Then he got up, straightened his clothes and went out, turning his steps resolutely towards the auditorium where the opera performance was to take place.

'You're late,' whispered the assistants nervously when he arrived backstage to dress for his performance. 'The Presidents are waiting.'

'So what!' Raymond spoke with a defiant intonation in his voice. A few minutes later he stepped onto the stage and stood erect, facing the dimly lit auditorium. He looked at the indistinct shapes below him with the eyes of someone towering above them, stretched out an arm and made a sign with his hand to impose silence. Finally, when all was quiet, he began to sing. Slowly, majestically, his voice rose above the gathered mass of dark shadows, gaining strength, increasing in volume until it filled the whole space, until there was nothing else left in the hearts and minds of the audience but the voice of this powerful man.

19

A thunderous ovation greeted the end of his fifteen minutes' performance, and it continued while the two Presidents stepped on to the podium to shake hands with Raymond. And then, suddenly, the incredible happened. Before anyone could do anything, Raymond stepped forward as if pushed by an invisible force and burst out singing 'La Marseillaise' in front of an audience that for a moment seemed unwilling to believe what their ears heard:

> Allons enfants de la Patrie
> Le jour de gloire est arrivé,
> Contre nous de la tyrannie . . .

For seconds, as his majestic voice flung out the cadenced, rousing words, the public remained spellbound. Then the audience rose as one man and joined in with the powerful lyrics. It was incredibly moving. Everyone sang the anthem, even President Gwemboka. He seemed prey to deep emotion. He hadn't felt like this for years, in fact since he had served as a young sergeant with the French foreign legion. In a flash the glorious words brought back the good old days of camaraderie, the nights around the campfire, the adventurous life . . . tears welled up in his eyes and he felt a strong pain in his chest as his heart started beating rapidly and irregularly. Then he grasped the French President's hand.

The French President too was trembling with emotion. Who would ever have dreamed of this? He had always thought that the deep link between Africa and Europe was dead. But it wasn't. It had been resurrected. This was a day of glory. This was indeed a day to remember.

All cameras turned towards the podium to fix this fabulous moment forever . . . they moved from Gwemboka and the French President to this unknown tenor whose extraordinary act had started it all. There he stood, this formidable man, his face lit up, his defiant voice enflaming the audience as he thrust out the final couplet of 'La Marseillaise':

> Aux armes citoyens,
> Formez vos bataillons . . .

When the last note had died down there was deep silence. Then all the people in the theatre, Africans and Europeans, fell into each other's arms. And on the stage Gwemboka and the French President both turned to Raymond and embraced him.

Everyone was happy; everyone was smiling and speaking to each other. This was something that had never happened before. No one would have believed it ever could have happened. But it had, and for one instant, there in that theatre in Bobodiou, there was peace in the world.

20

It wasn't quite correct to say that everyone was happy. There may have been peace and harmony in the hearts of most of those who witnessed that historic moment, but among them was one man who was shocked to the core: Mamboulou. The Minister of Home Affairs and Internal Security may have had a chameleon's ability to change colour as the wishes of his boss dictated, and he was a master at contorting his body into impossible shapes when it came to sheer survival, but there was one issue over which he refused to budge: he was a true nationalist. Nothing could have deflected him from the principle that had guided his earliest actions; that had made him stand up against the colonial occupier and risk his life for it.

When he heard that national anthem which every sinew in his body had always hated, and saw his own president singing it with emotion plainly written on his face while grasping the hand of the French President, he felt deeply betrayed. There was no peace in his heart, only sheer outrage.

For twenty-five years Gwemboka had led everyone to believe he was a nationalist, and Mamboulou had admired him for it. If there had been one thing that had tied him to his president, this had been it: the conviction that they were both sincere patriots; that they had fought together to liberate their country from a government that had fully collaborated with the old colonial power. But today the scales had fallen from Mamboulou's eyes. Today the tyrant had shown his true colours. This man, whom he had believed in, was a traitor, a puppet in the hands of those hated foreigners.

For twenty-five years he had served a traitor! Mamboulou could understand greed, corruption, terror, and much more of what the dictator inflicted on others. But to sing that hated anthem? To betray the very foundation of his beliefs – of the revolution of twenty-five years ago . . . that was more than he could bear!

All at once Mamboulou's cowardice gave way to an overpowering desire for revenge. The fear which had ruled his feelings for so many years was suddenly swept aside by moral outrage and nothing could stop him now. He would act whatever the risk involved. He would expose that despicable man. He would ridicule the fat ugly pig . . .

21

After Raymond had left slamming the door, Pauline lay on her bed in a state of shock, unable to move. How could her husband have suddenly turned up here? What had come over him? She didn't understand.

After a long time she raked up enough courage to get up, stumbled into the bathroom, lowered herself into the king-size bathtub and turned on the tap. She felt as if she'd been profoundly soiled and a great need to cleanse herself took hold of her. She began to spray water over her skin and scrubbed herself vigorously. Then she rinsed off the soap, lay down and little by little let the hot water envelop her sore body. As the soothing heat relaxed her, images of the last few days went through her mind.

When she had regained consciousness in that big car, she found herself lying in a most awkward position, and her body hurt terribly. She tried to sit up and looked around. Where was Jack? Then she realised how thirsty she was and began to search for the water bottles: they had gone! Suddenly it dawned on her that Smally must have taken them and that he had abandoned her to her fate. The pig! And in her rage she began to hit the windscreen, screaming: 'Pig! Monstrous, monstrous pig!'

After a while she calmed down. She must get out of here! She tried to move the levers to open the driver's window but nothing happened. Something had gone wrong with the electric circuit. Then she stood up and attempted to push open the driver's door above her head, but couldn't manage. It was too heavy and she was much too weak. Finally she climbed up to the side of her seat, steadying herself by holding on to the steering wheel, put her back against the door and pushed hard. Just as she felt it move, her foot slipped off the seat, her head hit the windscreen and she was violently sick, vomiting all over the place.

For the next few hours she gave herself up to deep despair. How the hell could Jack have done this? She was sure she was going to die in here, and she lay huddled in her corner, extremely thirsty.

After what seemed ages she heard sounds. She began to scream and finally a dark-brown face appeared above her. A few men opened the door, one let himself down and hauled her out, and then they gave her some water. Next they began to take off the two accessible wheels and dismantle any part that could be taken away. They did so quickly and efficiently as if they were used to that sort of thing, producing the necessary tools seemingly out of nowhere. Then they tied everything onto their camels, tied her on top of a camel, too, and set off.

The rocking movement of the camel made her feel seasick and she vomited several times more. She feared that there was worse to come: she was certain that they were going to rape her and then kill her. She had never felt so frightened in her life but nothing happened, and reaching the capital a few days later was like an anti-climax. The caravan stopped at the outskirts of Bobodiou late one morning and the men, who were surprisingly courteous, helped her to get off her camel.

As she began to walk into town on very stiff legs, the hot sun bore down upon her and she started to sweat profusely. The nearer she got to the centre, the more difficult progress became. Throngs of people, dressed in colourful outfits, were filling the streets, singing and dancing and blocking the way while small bands produced deafening music. She had to push her way through the crowds, but she smelt so strongly of camels and vomit that the dancers recoiled at her approach and made way for her. By the time she reached the hotel her clothes were drenched with sweat, she stank up to high heaven and felt like a piece of garbage.

And then her husband had caught her! How he had got here was a mystery. He had always been so on tenterhooks not to upset her. And suddenly that puppet, the spineless man whom she had dominated and played about with, had become an enraged tiger. He had beaten her, thrown her on the bed, ripped off her clothes like a madman and literally raped her, filthy as she was. Even now the lower part of her belly still hurt terribly and her cheek, where he had slapped her, kept throbbing with pain.

What was to become of her after this? Whom could she turn to now? Where could she go? All the security she had cultivated so carefully over many years had vanished. It was as if the ground had collapsed under her feet and she felt giddy. How could this have happened to her? It was unjust, really unjust. Suddenly rage surged up in her. It was all Anton's fault! He had made her do this. And look where it had landed her!

After an hour of miserable thoughts and brooding over the black future that awaited her, she climbed out of the bathtub and began to rub herself with a soft bath-towel. She blow-dried her hair and took a long time to make up. Her cheek was slightly swollen but through the careful application of face cream, make-up and powder she managed to mask most of it. Only then did she notice her open suitcase and her clothes strewn all over the floor. And most of her underwear had gone! This was another mystery. What had happened?

She dressed, was not pleased with what she saw in the mirror and tried on one thing after another until after half hour or so she was satisfied with the result. She wanted to appear her very best. She needed it after the awful experiences she had gone through, and in the end she did succeed in looking extremely attractive. She suddenly realised that she'd hardly eaten for three whole days. The thought alone made her ravenous but, more than food, she needed a drink to give her a boost. She went to the bar, plonked herself on a stool, ordered a stiff drink and a bowl of snacks, telling the barkeeper to put it all on the room account, downed her drink, ordered another one and then started to munch her snacks. She sat there listlessly, her elbow on the bar, her chin in her hand while dark thoughts kept invading her.

It was getting towards dusk when, one after the other, small groups of people came streaming into the bar and began to occupy the places around her. Pauline was not in the mood for any form of socialising but couldn't bring herself to leave. The newcomers were talking animatedly and from where she was sitting she overheard scraps of conversation. There was an excitement in the air that even she, in her downcast state, noticed.

'Incredible,' said a man near her. 'What nerve!'

'I would never have believed it had I not been there myself,' said another. 'And what a voice!'

'Yes, absolutely out of this world.'

'Did you notice how the cameras moved in on him?'

'Yeah! I've been told that there were several TV crews. By tonight he'll be over all the world's TV screens.'

'I understand that he's totally unknown.'

'Yes, that's what makes this such a special occasion. A most memorable event. Today we saw a star being born.'

'What's his name?'

'Raymond something. I didn't catch the rest. He must be French.'

Pauline, who had been pricking up her ears, suddenly understood it all. Raymond had come here to sing! She now sat up and said, looking important: 'His name is Raymond d'Elbreux. And he's Belgian, not French.'

The men turned towards her in surprise. 'How do you know that?' asked one of them in a snooty voice.

'Because he's my husband,' she replied proudly.

At once the men around her fell silent and stared at her in awe. 'Oh, I'm so honoured,' said one of them, coming forward and shaking her hand. 'How exciting to meet the wife of a celebrity.' He looked at her with deference.

Another one pressed forward: 'Is what I heard true?'

'Could you express yourself more clearly?' requested Pauline who was beginning to enjoy the situation. 'I may be the wife of a famous singer but that doesn't make me clairvoyant.' She bestowed a seductive smile on the man who reddened visibly and stammered: 'I . . . I've just heard that your husband has been asked to sing in La Scala in Milan.'

'And in the Met in New York,' added another man.

'Who knows?' replied Pauline mysteriously.

'May I . . . would it be too much to ask you for an autograph,' inquired the man who had first come forward to shake her hand and was still holding on to it.

'That'll be a pleasure,' said Pauline, turning towards him with beguiling eyes.

'May we offer you a drink?' two or three men proposed eagerly.

Wild thoughts full of glitter and light whirled through Pauline's head while she sat there on her bar stool, blouse tight over her proud breasts, and a miniskirt advantageously showing off her long legs, folded over each other. Raymond a famous opera singer! That changed everything. This was the opportunity of a lifetime. She would give what it took and get him back. Yes, she could do it. She would be able to handle him. Suddenly she was certain of it. And what a man he really was. How he had taken her on the bed a few hours ago. Like a furious animal he had been. What hidden talents he'd got! It was new, all so new to her. But she would take it in her stride. Milan. New York. Travel. Luxury. Interviews. Her photo on the front page of magazines . . . Her head spun.

And like royalty bestowing attention on lesser humans she sat there, the centre of a group of men who looked at her in admiration, waiting for her to speak. She had fallen effortlessly into a new role, one that really befitted her: she was a celebrity now!

22

After they had left the rebel camp, Marie and Gael started their perilous journey towards Bobodiou along an almost non-existent track. As Rasta had promised, they didn't encounter any roadblocks but the track was so sandy and bumpy that progress was extremely slow, and it took them hours to reach the shantytown that surrounded the capital. Marie was ready to continue through the narrow alleyways but Rasta had second thoughts and directed her towards a small compound on the outskirts.

As they drove into the enclosure, a few men who had been sitting in the shade got up and tried to make them reverse out, but Rasta jumped down shouting: 'It's me, Rasta!' He quickly took off his white nurse's jacket and began to make gestures as if he still had his long braided hair. When the men recognised him they began to touch his close-shaven head in surprise.

'It's a disguise,' explained Rasta. 'Secret mission.'

Suddenly the men burst into loud guffaws, slapped their thighs and laughed so much that tears rolled down their cheeks and they had to sit down on the ground. 'Secret mission,' they mocked while rubbing their hands over their heads. 'No hair, secret mission, haha!'

It took Rasta minutes to impose silence and set the men to work, but in the end they began to hide the Land-Rover under cloth and branches. When it had finally disappeared from view Rasta suggested that the women cover their heads and walk a few yards behind him. Finally he and a couple of the men set off on foot for the rest of the journey, followed by the women. They progressed with great circumspection, first through the filth of the shantytown and then through the throngs of singing and dancing people who filled the streets of Bobodiou. When they reached the Belgian Embassy Rasta instructed the two men to stay around. 'They'll be watching,' he told the women. 'If you need them, just make a sign.' And then he vanished among the crowds.

The ambassador wasn't in. They told Marie that he was attending a special concert in town, like all other foreign dignitaries, and wouldn't return that day. But Marie was a personal friend of the ambassador and she also knew the first secretary. When she explained their predicament and the need to get out of the country, the man promised that the ambassador would see them first thing in the morning and arranged for the two women to be put up for the night in a small hotel a few streets away.

When they were finally alone, Gael turned to Marie and said abruptly: 'I don't want to go back to Brussels.'

'Don't be silly! Why?'

'I don't want to run the risk of bumping into Anton.'

'I see.' Marie's voice was full of irony. 'You prefer to run the risk of falling into the hands of the police maybe? Or of that dreadful Juan Rodriguez who wanted to shoot us?'

'I don't mind leaving the country, but I don't want to go back to Brussels.'

'Well, let's have a meal first,' suggested Marie. 'We can think about it while we're eating. Let's go to the Riverside before it's completely dark.'

The Riverside's restaurant had an extension alongside the garden. Tables and chairs had been placed on a narrow terrace to allow people who so wished to have their supper outside. These tables were arranged for intimacy, for couples wanting a romantic evening. They were separated from each other by bamboo screens, which prevented diners from viewing couples at neighbouring tables who held hands or kissed. Flanked by the hotel and the screens, they resembled small alcoves opening up to a wide lawn of coarse grass.

People who weren't staying in the hotel were usually not allowed to eat on the outside terrace but Marie, who knew the management, had no difficulty in arranging for the rules to be bent and soon a helpful waiter led them over the lawn to one of the remaining free tables. As they sat down waiting to be served and began to sip a welcome drink, the little lanterns hanging over the tables lit up, lending an air of enchantment to the scene. Nothing seemed to be able to disturb this picture of harmony when suddenly a woman appeared and stared at them brazenly.

23

The woman, who had been walking along the grass bordering the terrace, seemed to have no inhibitions of any sort and stopped in turn at each table, peering at the occupants, oblivious of their desire for intimacy. After glancing with indifference at the two women she moved around the bamboo screen to inspect the next table. The man who was sitting there had just finished his meal and was now vacantly gazing over the lawn. In a flash she recognised him.

'Anton!' she shouted. 'Fancy you being here!'

'I don't believe this!' exclaimed Anton, remembering the conversation he'd had with Michel no more than a few hours ago. 'Pauline! Somehow you always manage to turn up where you're not wanted, even on the other side of the Sahara.'

Pauline didn't like the tone of Anton's reply. 'I have a good reason to be here,' she said in an offhand voice. 'But you? I never thought I would have the displeasure of seeing you again after you disappeared so suddenly from the lab without so much as offering an explanation. You know what they call that sort of behaviour? They call it a breach of contract.'

'Breach of contract, my foot!' retorted Anton. 'I've just learned that

Smally fired me. But tell me, is what I heard true? Rumours have it that your secretarial role included some very special services. This would explain why you're here when our Smally was going to give a talk at the International Geological Conference. You remember the report I handed over to you? He was going to present it pretending those were his ideas! You know what they call that?'

Pauline seemed to be taken aback and pressed her lips tightly together in an unpleasant pout. Then she burst out: 'I don't care about Smally. The swine! He left me for dead in a car up on a dune in the desert and I was saved in the nick of time by a camel caravan.'

'You don't say! That must have been the car I saw. I wondered how it could possibly have got up that dune. So it was our Smally who did it . . . Well, well . . . what a nitwit! And I passed a camel caravan yesterday morning and saw a woman waving. Was that you?'

'Yes! I didn't recognise the man behind the wheel but let me tell you that I wanted to shoot the selfish bastard. Not coming to the rescue of a woman in distress! But now I know you were the driver, it doesn't surprise me one bit.'

'As sweet as ever, I see. Well, you don't seem to be any the worse for your misadventure in the desert. Matter of fact, you look positively elated. What's happened? Has Smally repented and proposed to you?'

'How stupid you can be if you try! I am married and I intend to stay so. My husband, Raymond, has just given a gala concert . . .'

'In Brussels?'

'No, here in Bobodiou . . . It's here he gave his performance.'

'Do you mean to say you actually went to listen to your husband singing?'

'No,' she admitted. 'I . . . I just missed the concert. In fact, I'm looking for him right now. You haven't seen him around, have you?'

'Who would have believed it? Raymond singing here.'

Suddenly Pauline bubbled over with excitement. 'Yes. And what a performance he gave! He sang divinely! It seems he's made a terrific smash. He's become a star. Everyone is talking about him. Contracts have been flooding in from famous places: from the Scala in Milan, from the Met in New York. Think of that! I'm going to travel all over the world. Stay in five-star hotels. Live in luxury. I'm going to be rich!'

'You surprise me.' Anton shook his head. 'You really surprise me. You run off with Smally, he leaves you for dead in the desert and then you turn up here cooing over your husband like a turtledove. Telling me he's got a divine voice. When you've never given a damn about your husband.

Always laughed at him, cuckolded him, told him to shut up, denigrated his talents, never allowed him to sing when you were around.'

'Oh, did I?' replied Pauline coldly. 'I can't remember.'

'You can't remember eh! You don't want to remember, that's more like it. You'd do well to have your memory tested.'

'As rude as ever! So I need to have my memory tested, eh? I'll show you that my memory's good enough. Do you know who managed to convince Smally to steal your ideas and told him to give the talk? I did. And I schemed to have you thrown out of the lab. So there!' She stood mockingly in front of him.

'And well it served him!' Anton laughed triumphantly. 'Luckily, I arrived just in time for his presentation. And I wouldn't have wanted to miss the show for anything in the world. Would you believe it? The little nincompoop wasn't capable of explaining anything, even with my papers in front of his nose. He fled after being booed by the whole audience! He ran away, the coward, and I gave the talk.'

'So you think you've won again, eh? Then just wait for this one. I never told you, but this time you've really asked for it!'

'My dear woman,' replied Anton coldly, 'let me remind you that I haven't asked for anything. That I've never wanted anything from you. Not in the past. Not now.'

'I know!' Her face was contorted. 'I was certain I knew what men wanted; that I'd always get my way with them. And I did, till I met you. I thought you were such easy game! I fell upon you, pushed you into corners. And what did I get in return? Nothing.' Pauline stared at him with fury in her eyes. 'I might as well have tried to seduce a pile of bricks for all the reaction I got! Monsieur just refused my advances. It was humbling to have to try out all the tricks a woman has up her sleeve, only to draw a blank. You humbled me . . . Yes, you did!' She drew a deep breath. 'For a while I even thought I was in love with you. I was determined to get you, and once I had you in my net . . . how I would have made you suffer! I wanted to see you crawling at my feet, begging me to love you.'

'You foolish woman! What delusions you had!' Anton shook his head. 'How can you have been so blind?'

But Pauline was not to be deflected. 'And when I offered myself on a silver platter you refused me! You pushed me away. A simpleton like you! Finally I realised what it was. You were the faithful type, think of that! Faithful to a stupid shit of a girl who can't have known a quarter of what I know about making love! But she beguiled you with her big childish eyes, didn't she?'

Anton stared in disgust at the hated face. 'Careful! That's enough!'

'Don't you look at me threateningly! How you could prefer a silly girl to a woman like me is beyond me. But I made you pay for it. More than you realise.' Suddenly her laughter rang out defiantly.

'Oh shut up! I don't want to listen to any more filth coming out of your mouth.'

'But you're going to listen, my clever one.' Pauline's voice was full of contempt now. 'And you won't like what you're going to hear. Some three months ago I found out where you lived and thought I'd go there one morning, ring the bell and try to seduce you . . . Yes, I was going to throw myself at your feet. I was just about to press the bell when a man came out of the front door and let me in – men are taken in when I smile at them. I found the door of your room and knocked, but there was no answer. And then I discovered that it was unlocked and let myself in . . . and you weren't even there!'

'What! You went into my room!'

'Shut up and listen, you fool! And then I saw those photographs of a silly girl with big eyes. I was so furious that I wanted to tear them up and throw them out of the window . . .'

On the next terrace someone drew in a deep breath, while Anton hissed: 'Go away! Leave me alone! I don't want to talk to you.'

But Pauline continued, sneeringly. 'But *I* do want to talk, my dear man. And for once you're going to be interested in what I've got to say, because I can tell you that my words will make you sit up. When I stood there in that ugly little room of yours and saw those stupid photographs on the wall, I nearly gave up and then . . . I happened to look in the street and saw that the silly girl of the photographs was coming. I knew at once what to do. It was sheer luck, but I played it for all I was worth. And I pulled it off, haha!'

She emitted a shrill laugh, while Anton's skin was tight over his face and his fists were clenched.

'I can still see it as if it happened yesterday. I quickly undressed, left the door slightly ajar and began to speak as if I were talking to you, and there she was, peeping through the crack. As I looked round I saw her horror-struck eyes. You should have seen her face! She stood there gaping, as if she'd seen a ghost. And, quick-witted girl that I am, I said, pretending you were in the room: "What a good lover you are, Anton . . . Shall we do it once more?" And then I heard a cry and the girl turned and ran. You can't imagine how pleased I was with myself. I had eliminated her! She'd swallowed it all. That was her, wasn't it, the love of your life? Fair hair and light eyes. How insipid she looked!'

Anton lifted himself up from his chair, shaking with rage, his breath coming in quick gasps. His hand brushed a glass from the table, scattering it into a thousand pieces. 'So it was you!' he exploded. 'It was you who ruined my love . . . I'll kill you for this!'

His fist shot forward but Pauline was too quick. She had been ready for his reaction and jumped back. It was pitch dark by now, and as Anton plunged forward he tripped over a chair and fell flat on his face, while Pauline shouted triumphantly: 'I ruined your silly love affair, yes, and I would do it again!' Then she ran away over the grass, emitting a high victorious laugh while Anton was scrambling to get back on his feet. He lunged forward to catch her but she had already disappeared into the African night.

24

When Gael heard the brazen woman shout 'Anton!' she shrank in her chair, unable to react. Then, with an almost superhuman effort, she shook herself free and began to get up, but before she could move she felt Marie's hand pushing her back.

'You stay here,' Marie whispered. 'Don't run away again. This time you must face the music.' And she held Gael firmly pinned to her chair.

And she sat there, trembling, while the words from the table next to theirs floated through the bamboo screen. While the voice of that women penetrated her ears, resonated in her mind and opened the doors of remembrance. It stabbed at the wound, the deep wound, until it lay open again, bleeding freely. Gael wanted to block her ears but she sat there paralysed, forced to listen to the words of that vile woman. And then, as the ghastly voice carried on, she understood that she had fallen into a conjurer's trap. She had been tricked into seeing what hadn't been there. And in her horror and haste she had fatally wounded the man who loved her . . .

She had not questioned what she was convinced she had seen. She had thought only of her own pain, never of the torture she'd inflicted on him. Gael's body began to shake uncontrollably as she realised how faithless she had been. She had not believed in Anton. Whatever the odds against him, she should have gone to him and asked him what had happened. She should have trusted him, always. But she had run away without giving him a chance. Red-hot flames of shame shot through her, and she hid her face in her hands.

Then she felt Marie's arm around her shoulders, Marie lifting her out of the chair, pushing her towards the bamboo screen and the table behind. And she heard Marie's voice urging: 'Go to him. Go to him now!'

By the time she stumbled forward and looked at the table and overturned chairs on the next terrace, there was nobody there . . .

Part Six

1

As he lay on the camp bed in his Land-Rover, tossing and turning, Anton was thinking of his unexpected encounter with Pauline. What an absolute nightmare that woman was! He had been beside himself with rage when she had thrown the story of her foul deed triumphantly in his face. How could she have done such a thing to Gael? It was fortunate that he hadn't been able to lay his hands on her. He might have murdered her!

But at last I know what happened, he reflected, calming down a little. No wonder Gael no longer wanted to have anything to do with me after having been tricked into believing I betrayed her with that horrible Pauline.

Everything was clear to him now: why Gael had run away to Africa; why she never wanted to see him again; and he also understood the reaction of her mother when he'd gone to her house a few months ago. I must find Gael, he thought. Explain everything to her. But will she believe me?

The previous afternoon he had checked that there was a place called Kanibasso some hundred miles east of the capital; at the hotel reception they had even told him they knew the Belgian woman who ran the dispensary. He was determined to get there as soon as possible, and had intended to set off after breakfast, but as he was lying awake at four in the morning he decided to leave town immediately.

The din of music and the dancing had gone on till late into the night but now the streets of Bobodiou were empty. There wasn't a single policeman in sight, and even the soldiers manning the roadblock on the eastern road out of town were fast asleep. They didn't wake up as he approached them slowly, and Anton didn't stop.

He had been following the dirt road to Kanibasso for about two hours when day broke and the sun rose in front of him. The rays shone straight into his eyes nearly blinding him, and he had slowed down to a crawl, driving very carefully to avoid the many potholes, when suddenly the bush to left and right came alive. Armed men seemed to rise up from the earth as if by magic and started shooting. Anton stopped at once and sat dead still, stunned, waiting for what was to come.

2

That same morning Gael and Marie were sitting in a small restaurant near the Belgian Embassy in Bobodiou. Gael seemed impatient and her face was drawn. 'Do we really have to waste our time here?' she kept pressing. 'I want to go and look for Anton immediately.'

'Well, *I* don't,' replied Marie resolutely. 'I need my breakfast first.'

'But if we don't hurry, he may be gone,' pleaded Gael.

'We'll have to wait anyway,' said Marie firmly, 'because we're going to see the ambassador. The embassy put us up last night and the ambassador has given us priority over all his other appointments. It would be very bad manners if we didn't show up when he expects us. There are some minimum levels of politeness one has to observe, in Africa as anywhere else. So we might as well have a hearty breakfast while we're waiting.'

'But I don't want to see the ambassador! He'll only tell us to go back to Brussels, and I don't want to go back there!' Gael's voice sounded shrill. 'I want to stay here and find Anton.'

Suddenly Marie became very annoyed. 'Yesterday afternoon you told me that you didn't want to go back to Brussels because you didn't want to run into Anton. And now you're telling me that you don't want to go back to Brussels because you want to find Anton. Try to make up your mind, *ma fille*.' She gave Gael a disapproving look. 'And please do realise that, whatever you want to do, you'll have to wait for me. And my order of priorities is different from yours. I am going to have my breakfast first. And afterwards we'll go and see the ambassador.' Then she added: 'And let me tell you that you'll have some explaining to do when he offers to evacuate us and put us on the first plane to Europe.'

While Marie was tucking into her breakfast, Gael sat nervously folding her paper serviette into tight squares and then began to crumble up her toast.

'You'd better eat,' observed Marie cool-headedly. 'It's not proper to waste food in Africa.'

'I can't. I can't get a bite down my throat. I . . . I just can't.'

'Please yourself,' said Marie.

Ten minutes later they walked to the embassy and within a short time they were ushered into the ambassador's office.

He and Marie were old friends, and as she entered he came forward and affectionately clasped her hands. They began to talk about mutual acquaintances and things of the past while Gael became increasingly restless.

'Well,' said the ambassador after a while, looking at his watch, 'I'm afraid we haven't much time for a chat, however pleasant it is to see you again. But I'm glad to tell you that my secretary has been able to book two places for you on the early-afternoon flight to Paris. You ought to be getting ready. You'll soon be out of here and out of danger.' He looked at the two women, beaming as if he had personally saved their lives.

Gael stood up at once. 'I'm not going to leave the country,' she blurted out. 'I'm going to stay here.' She stuck up her chin defiantly. 'I never asked to be evacuated.'

The ambassador couldn't believe his ears. This wasn't what he had expected. In the whole of his career he had never met a case like this, and he looked shocked. He immediately took Marie by the arm and led her into an inner office. 'What's all this?' His voice sounded upset. 'And who's that girl?'

'I'm sorry, André,' replied Marie. 'She's my assistant in the dispensary in Kanibasso. We were caught by the rebels, as you must have been told, and escaped yesterday.'

'Is that why she's unbalanced?'

'That's not it, I'm afraid. She fled Brussels and chose to work here because of an unhappy love affair. It's all a bit complicated and too long to explain, but she discovered last night that her young man was here and that he wasn't to blame for what had happened. So she's now filled with remorse and wants to find him whatever the dangers.'

'My goodness!' exclaimed the ambassador shaking his grey head. 'A love story in the middle of a revolution! What are we going to have next, I wonder? And who's the young man?'

'A certain Anton Felsen. He's a geologist.'

'A geologist? Maybe he came here for that conference? Wait a minute.'

The ambassador disappeared into the corridor while Marie went back to see what Gael was doing. She found her in an extreme state of agitation. 'Can we go now?' Gael insisted. 'What are we waiting for?'

'My dear girl,' said Marie with a stern face, 'you must learn to be patient. They're checking up on Anton. Don't cause more trouble than you have already!'

When the ambassador finally returned he had some very exciting news. 'A most extraordinary story,' he kept saying. 'Well, well . . . Really surprising.' He stood there for a while, nodding, while Gael was nearly frantic.

'What's happened?' she asked, unable to contain herself any longer.

'All in due time,' replied the ambassador soothingly. 'All in due time, dear girl. It seems there was a lot of confusion two days ago at the International Geological Conference, but that in the end Anton Felsen was allowed to speak. And when he delivered his talk it turned out to be the success story of the conference. The fellow – who's one of our compatriots, I'm proud to say – has apparently produced the most revolutionary invention in geological exploration of the last decades. All the mining companies are after his invention, but he may have already sold to the Americans: at the end of the conference an American mining tycoon took him aside, insisting he absolutely wanted to buy Dr Felsen's invention, whatever the price. And it's rumoured that he offered Dr Felsen his weight in gold, would you believe it? His weight in gold! Well, I suppose that tycoon can afford it, considering that he's one of the richest men in the world. And he also told Dr Felsen to drop everything and come and work for him in America.'

'Has he gone off to America then?' Gael nearly screamed.

'How am I to know, my dear girl?' replied the ambassador calmly. 'Well, I've done what I could.' He shrugged his shoulders. 'I can't do much more.' He turned to Marie. 'If you need my help, just tell the secretary.' He looked at her apologetically. 'I'm afraid I have to let you go now. I've got a busy schedule this morning but if you need anything, a car maybe, the secretary will provide it.'

As they left the embassy, emptiness enveloped Gael's mind. She felt so faint that she had to sit down on the steps.

'What is it?' inquired Marie, worried.

'He's gone,' wailed Gael. 'He's gone off to America. I'll never see him again.'

She sat there for maybe five minutes, her head on her arms, a picture of desolation, while Marie just waited. Then something seemed to stir in Gael. She suddenly jumped up yelling: 'Let's rush to the airport. Maybe his flight hasn't left.' When Marie hesitated, she insisted: 'Come on!' and caught her by the hand. 'Where's the car they promised us?'

Marie went to get the keys and they began to work their way to the airport through throngs of dancing people. Gael sat in the passenger's seat, a bundle of nerves. 'I hope we're still in time,' she kept repeating. 'Hurry! Please hurry.' And when they got stuck amid the mass of dancing people she exclaimed: 'Hoot! Do drive on! Push them out of the way! We'll never make it. If his plane has left I'll go crazy!'

'Look here, Gael,' said Marie. 'I'm not going to kill anyone to allow you to get to the airport a bit quicker.' Her patience was wearing very thin by now. 'There's no point in hurrying when you've wasted three months already. A few minutes more won't make a great difference. If you'd really wanted to keep him, you shouldn't have run off so impetuously, convinced you'd been wronged.'

Gael bit her lip and shut up. Then a resolute expression came over her face. 'If he has left,' she said with stubborn determination, 'I'll catch the next plane to America. Wherever he has gone, I will find him.'

3

'Tell me,' asked Marie when they'd finally got out of town and were speeding towards the airport. 'Is Anton a fat man?'

'Not at all.' Gael looked offended. 'He's lean and very handsome.'

'In that case I hope he's put on weight since you left him,' she commented dryly. 'Maybe he has. Men who have been abandoned often compensate for it by eating lots of sweets.'

Gael cut her short at once. 'Anton doesn't eat sweets! He follows a very healthy diet!'

'How much does he weigh then?'

'Marie, please! Stop pestering me with irrelevant questions.'

'But this is a very relevant question.'

'Why?'

'I'm trying to work out how rich he's going to be.'

'I don't follow you.'

'Well,' explained Marie, 'wasn't that American mining tycoon going to pay him his weight in gold? That's why every pound he has put on is important.'

'And may I ask what that's got to do with me?'

'Oh, but the fact that he's going to be rich may be essential for your relationship.'

'I don't care whether he's rich or poor. It's him I want, not his money.'

'Yes, I can see that, but the question is not what *you* want. In my experience, the richer men are, the more demanding they become. I wonder whether he'll still be willing to put up with an impossible girl like you once he's rich? The question is therefore: will *he* still want you?'

'Do you think he still loves me?' Gael suddenly seemed apprehensive.

'I'm not certain what'll happen the moment he stands on that scale and sees the gold pile up on the other side but I'm sure that, last night at least, he still loved you.'

'How can he still love me after what I've done to him? Do you think he'll ever forgive me?'

'Didn't you hear what he shouted to that woman? He shouted: "You've ruined my love. I'll kill you for this!" Only a man in love would react like that.'

Just then they drove into Bobodiou Airport and Marie said with barely hidden sarcasm: 'So let's catch him before he gets all that gold.'

She immediately began to work the connections she had, at the airport as anywhere else in the country, and for the next hours Marie and Gael did the round of all the airlines, pestering the staff. It turned out that no one had any information about Anton. There were no flights to America that day anyway, and the name Felsen didn't figure on the passenger lists of any of the planes that had taken off or were going to take off for Europe. After several hours they had to accept the obvious: Anton hadn't left by plane.

4

In the meantime, Anton wasn't very happy. It turned out that he'd driven straight into the main rebel camp east of Bobodiou. It was fortunate that the rebels had realised that Anton's Land-Rover was not a military vehicle, and had just fired warning shots. But he had been arrested and they'd locked him up in a small, improvised jail while a few armed men stood guard around the entrance.

After sitting there for a couple of hours, hungry and thirsty, he was starting to feel desperate when a guard appeared and made a sign to follow him. He was taken to Amadou Sékouré to be interrogated.

'Why are you driving a vehicle loaded with equipment and jerrycans?' asked the leader with undisguised suspicion.

'Because I drove here from Europe,' replied Anton gruffly.

'What? Are you saying you crossed the Sahara?' Amadou sounded sarcastic.

'Yes . . .'

'Then where are the others?'

'Which others? Oh! There are no others. I crossed the Sahara on my own.'

The rebel leader shook his head. This man was plainly lying. 'Would it be too much to ask you why you should have wanted to do such a thing?' he inquired without even attempting to hide the irony in his voice.

'I did it because I wanted to find my girlfriend.'

'Oh is that so? You crossed the Sahara and then drove straight into our camp looking for your girlfriend!' Amadou Sékouré found it difficult to remain civil after such overt lies and came straight to the point: 'How did you know about our position?'

'I didn't know about your position!' countered Anton defensively. 'If I had, I wouldn't have driven straight in here, would I?'

'Hmm . . . that's true of course. Why did you drive into our camp then?'

'Because I was on my way to the dispensary in Kanibasso. That's where my girlfriend works. She's a volunteer in a medical project. Doesn't this track lead to Kanibasso?'

All of a sudden Amadou Sékouré seemed very embarrassed. 'Your girlfriend's name isn't Gael by any chance?' he asked.

'Yes, that's her name.' Suddenly panic rose in Anton's eyes. 'Nothing's happened to her, has it?'

'No, no. Rest assured. But I didn't know that someone was looking for her,' admitted Amadou. 'She never told me.'

'Was she here then?'

'Yes . . . I had the privilege of meeting her. If you want to know . . .' he hesitated, '. . . she saved my life.' His eyes softened. 'She's a very brave girl.'

At once Anton dropped his defensive attitude. 'Yes, she's brave,' he agreed and stepped forward, holding out his hand. 'I'm Dr Felsen from Brussels. Pleased to meet you.'

'Pleased to meet you, too,' said Amadou, shaking hands. 'So you did cross the Sahara?'

'Why don't you believe me? I would go to the other side of the world for Gael. I lost her through no fault of mine, and I'm trying to find her. Please tell me where she is? Is she still here?' There was a sharp ring of urgency in his voice.

'No. I'm afraid she's gone. Our men smuggled her and the woman who's her boss into their embassy in Bobodiou yesterday. They will have taken a plane out of the country by now.'

'Oh no!' Anton's hand flew up in front of his face. 'To have got so close, and then to have missed her!' He sat down, looking very dispirited, shaking his head.

'You see . . .' explained Amadou apologetically, 'the situation over here may turn ugly at any moment and I thought that they would be safer in Europe.'

'Well, thanks anyway,' said Anton, trying to put on a brave face. 'At least, she's safe.'

'What do you plan to do now?' asked Amadou after a while, staring at him with compassion.

Anton shrugged his shoulders. 'What can I do?'

'Why don't you stay with us?' offered Amadou. 'There's no longer any point in driving to Kanibasso, and I don't think you can return to Bobodiou at present. It's better to bide your time.' And when Anton nodded agreement Amadou ordered his guards to watch over his well-being and give him something to eat and drink.

5

Half an hour later a European who seemed to occupy a high rank in the rebel army strode over to where Anton was sitting in the shade.

'You seem to have interesting equipment in your vehicle,' he commented.

'Yes, I've got some geological equipment.'

'You're not connected to any of the mining companies over here, are you?' inquired the man sharply.

'No.'

'Why then are you driving a vehicle loaded with equipment and jerrycans?'

'Because I drove here from Europe.'

'Through the Sahara?'

'Yes . . .'

'On your own?'

'Yes . . .'

'But, man, you must be mad! Why do such a thing when you can take a plane?' The European looked sternly at Anton.

'I thought it would be more of an adventure.'

'I see now what you are. You're a dreamer.' The man dug a packet of cigarettes out of his pocket and offered it to Anton. 'No? Well, never mind,' he said, lighting a cigarette.

He sat there for a while smoking, engrossed in his own thoughts. Amadou seemed to have befriended this man, so, he thought, I'd better be friendly, too. He held out his hand. 'I'm Juan Rodriguez,' he said finally. 'Ex-Sorbonne student,' he added with a proud expression on his face.

'And I'm Anton Felsen. I'm a geologist.'

'So you're a geologist but you're not connected to any of the mining companies. Hmm . . . strange.' He looked squarely at Anton. 'Tell me . . . what do you think about the impact of mining on the development of a country?' And, without leaving time for an answer, he suggested: 'Wouldn't it be altogether better to nationalise a country's natural wealth so that its profits go to the people instead of to a few rich shareholders?'

'But . . . but that's politics! I don't know much about politics.'

'Man!' exclaimed Juan Rodriguez. 'Politics is the stuff of life – the beginning and end of everything. The questions I'm asking are fundamental! Look, you're quite young. It's not too late to learn the fundamental revolutionary principles.' He stared hard at Anton. 'Have you heard about our revolution here?'

'In town there were lots of rumours about rebels wanting to get rid of the President. What's his name? Gwembalo or something?'

'Gwemboka,' corrected Rodriguez as he began to explain his worldview. 'But it's not just him we want to get rid of. It's the whole system of colonial servitude. The relationship between master and dog.'

'Didn't all that end half a century ago? The colonial powers no longer rule Africa.'

'You don't seem to understand. The Europeans are *still* here. They're here for the gold, the oil and the timber. And the Americans have also moved in.'

'But don't Europe and America give aid? And the colonial era can't have been all bad. Didn't the Europeans develop Africa? Build a lot of infrastructure, for example?'

'They built roads and railways, yes, but to call that development! Those roads and railways went straight from the mines to the coast to allow the primary commodities to be shipped out. All the wealth was systematically carried off to Europe. As for the Africans . . . they were just good enough to do the dangerous work in the mines, or gather the rubber and palm oil on plantations, but no more.'

'That seems to me a very one-sided reading of colonial history,' protested Anton.

'It's the true history which is never taught in Europe!' Rodriguez pointed a warning finger at Anton. 'And this history is repeating itself! Today the Chinese have come. They, too, are talking about development and the African leaders are smiling and falling over themselves to welcome them. When they should be up in arms! Because the Chinese want to do exactly what the Europeans did a century ago. They want to extract the continent's mineral riches so that their own economy can grow. Africa is a continent of commodities for the taking. And the interest of the Chinese ends there.'

'You're surely exaggerating!'

'Not at all! Just take a close look at what's happening. What kind of development aid do the Chinese offer? Roads and railways! And where do these go? Surprise, surprise. From the mines and forests straight to the next harbour. And they don't even want to employ African workers as the Europeans did in their time. They're bringing in their own workers to build the infrastructure!' He sighed. 'No! No one really wants to develop Africa.'

'But can't the proceeds from mining, for instance, be used to stimulate the local economy? To create good jobs that make use of the Africans' education and motivate them to study and have fewer children.'

Rodriguez shook his head. 'Dream on! That's not the aim of mining companies.'

'What about the royalties they pay?'

'Royalties!' Rodriguez spat out the word in contempt. 'They go to corrupt fat cliques who eat up all the money that's supposed to go into development. And where does that leave the remaining 99 per cent of the population?'

'But aren't things beginning to change in Africa? It seems to me that there's hope.'

'Hope? You use the word "hope"? Then look at the Niger Delta. People there are sitting on top of one of the world's richest oil deposits. But they're not swimming in wealth! Oh no! They are up to their necks in stinking, filthy pollution. That's all they're left with. None of the proceeds of the oil bonanza trickles down to them. All they get are empty promises, a lot of dirt and a kick in the pants.' He took a deep drag from his cigarette and shook his head in disgust. 'Before 1960 the fat cliques were living in Europe. Now they're living here. That's just about the only major change that's occurred in the last half-century. And, if anything, it's made things worse. While the rest of the people are starving, the big men are eating up everything in collusion with foreign companies and with the support of foreign governments.'

That man would make an excellent politician, thought Anton as he looked at Juan Rodriguez who had paused to clear his throat. One of the demagogic type.

'Today we are once again witnessing a scramble for Africa,' carried on Rodriguez. 'This time it's not occupation by colonial troops. The partition is much more insidious: foreign companies are now carving out overlapping zones of influence. A European company takes the timber, a Chinese one the copper, an American one the oil, and so on. And the wonderful thing about it is that the armies of the local strongmen now assure the protection of those foreign exploiters. Foreign governments no longer have to bear the heavy cost of colonial administration and armed protection!'

Juan Rodriguez shook his finger. 'So don't have any illusions! The second partition is much worse than the first. It's a free-for-all. Companies from all over the world are now elbowing in to lay their hands on Africa's natural resources. But the day the continent is exhausted, they will just drop it like an orange from which all the juice has been pressed and leave the Africans behind to soak in the filth, which is all that will remain.'

6

The festivities were drawing to an end in Bobodiou. A few more days and quiet would descend once again upon the town after the frenetic activities of the last week. The police, the security forces, the hotels and restaurants, and especially the power supply, had almost cracked under the strain. But most foreign dignitaries had already flown home and soon everything would turn back to the calmer pace of African life as usual.

President Gwemboka smiled. The previous week had been exhilarating. The celebrations had been an enormous success; they had surpassed even his wildest expectations. Yes, his twenty-five years in power had become world news. And the emotions he had gone through! Tears came to his eyes when he thought of his meeting with de Lattignie. Years had fallen off him when they had talked of the good old days.

And the French President! In the colonial era, when he'd been no more than a simple sergeant, the President of France – de Gaulle at the time – seemed far above him, almost a demigod. And now he, Gwemboka, had been personally honoured by the successor of that illustrious statesman. He had clasped hands with the French President on stage while that opera singer had sung 'La Marseillaise'. The emotion had been so strong that his heart hadn't recovered from it. For two days now he'd felt a sharp pain in his chest but he had tried to ignore it. The festivities weren't over yet; there was one more special event he had to attend to: the unveiling of his new portrait in the Riverside Hotel.

Then his thoughts went to the rebels who were rumoured to be everywhere around the capital, and resentment welled up in him. They would, of course, choose the moment of his celebration to try to spoil the fun. Who did this rebel leader, a certain Amadou Sékouré, think he was, to do that to him? Just wait, he thought. You just wait. One more event to attend to and then I'll get you! And I'll make you pay for all the nuisance you have caused.

Another day of patience and he would be free to turn his attention to the rebels. And he would crush them under his heel like dirt. Revenge would be his. No, no one was going to topple him. He was going to be President as long as he lived.

Rebels had tried to overthrow him before and had been defeated. This time, too, they would be pushed back and disappear as dew before the sun. The French would help him out again as they had done before. They had too many interests in his country to let rebels upset the apple cart. No, he needn't worry, especially since the French President himself had come to Bobodiou. Yes, the special bond with *la France* was still alive. Maybe I'll give the new mining concession to the French after all, he mused. And to hell with the Chinese.

Suddenly there was that pain again and he rubbed his chest. Maybe it was the stress of the last week. He would see a doctor – a French doctor – once the festivities were over.

7

In the main rebel camp east of Bobodiou Juan Rodriguez walked up to Amadou, looking extremely pleased. 'I've had news from some of our men who are operating in Bobodiou,' he announced. 'They say the capital is one vast carnival scene. We could easily infiltrate the town, mix with the crowds and seize Gwemboka. And once we've got him we should execute him in public to set an example to all the world's tyrants. And there's more. It seems that the French President is there too, and with luck we could capture him and take him hostage. That would create headlines the world over. We could extract large concessions in exchange for his release. Nationalise the mines for example . . .'

'We're not going to nationalise anything,' interrupted Amadou firmly. 'Two years ago a rebel force wanted to do just that: nationalise the mines. And what did it bring them? The intervention of French paratroopers. No, we can't afford to take that risk. We must learn from the mistakes of others.'

'But the soil belongs to the people! We must throw out those capitalist exploiters!'

'We will do what's within the limits of feasibility,' retorted Amadou. 'Don't you understand that we need the expertise of foreign mining companies? You don't honestly believe our people will get the minerals out of the ground with spades, do you? Without the collaboration of foreign companies our mineral wealth will just stay where it is: deep in the ground, and that wouldn't be of any use to anyone. But we can press for a revision of the mining contracts and claim a more equitable share of the profits. That is realistic. We're going to work with those foreign companies that are willing to subscribe to real development, not throw out the lot indiscriminately. And as to the French President, let's leave him well alone. It'll be difficult enough to bring the revolution to a good end as it is. We shouldn't be creating problems where they don't exist and then start looking for answers to those problems.'

Juan Rodriguez was, however, not so easily put off. 'But we need a new start!' he objected. 'We've been discussing this for years. I've told you a thousand times that, if we're to build a new society, we must first destroy the old one. The dictator, his ways of acting, the mining companies he colluded with, his henchmen, his police, the lot! It's a matter of justice! We have to set an example. We have to listen to the people's voice. They want revenge. They want to see blood, the blood of the tyrant.'

'That's not justice! That's continuing the old ways of tit for tat. If we catch the tyrant alive I don't intend to execute him in front of the people; we'll hand him over to the International Court of Justice! And we're going to reincorporate most of the police, the army and all those who served under the tyrant. Very few of them are real criminals. We want reconciliation. Start in harmony, not in a bloodbath.' And to make sure that he was understood, Amadou stood squarely in front of Juan and spoke straight in his face: 'I'm the leader here. And we shall organise everything as I see fit.'

8

'Mr President,' said the military adviser, 'it's lucky that you're back from Bobodiou. There are some very serious developments. A well-organised rebel force has surrounded the capital and there are rumours that Gwemboka's troops are beginning to desert him. If nothing is done to push back the rebels, the capital could easily fall into their hands. We must act urgently. A few thousand well-equipped men would do the trick. Shall I order the paratroopers to get ready?'

'Do I understand that you suggest we save Gwemboka?' asked the French President, barely able to hide his revulsion. 'When you know very well that he's a tyrant. One of the worst sort!'

'Allow me to remind you, Mr President, that we never had to complain about him. He's always protected our strategic interests and allowed French companies to exploit the mines. Of course, we had to pay him well for the favour.' He smiled. 'But I dare say that it worked out to our mutual advantage. It was stability of a kind.' Suddenly his face clouded over. 'Unfortunately that era may be about to end. Mr President, I have it from well-informed sources that the rebels do not intend to respect our mining interests. We must intervene to stop them,' insisted the military adviser.

'But what about the people over there who have been oppressed for so long? Who desperately want to get rid of Gwemboka? Think of what he's done to his country for twenty-five years! Such a promising country, and look at the mess he's made: the economy has collapsed; the country has become a police state; and anyone who can get out is fleeing – to France if possible. Can we let this continue much longer?'

'Mr President!' The adviser's voice sounded severe. 'May I remind you that you've been elected to serve the interests of your own country, of *la France*. Whatever the situation, foreign policy dictates must be subordinated to our national interests. If these coincide with what foreign populations aspire to, so much the better. But, if not, our national interests must prevail. First and foremost, we have to defend the needs of our companies, of our own citizens. Think of our people in Bobodiou who count on us. Think of our mining companies who contributed generously to your election campaign.'

'So you suggest business as usual? You seem to have forgotten that we saved him once before. He promised to become more tolerant then. And as soon as he was safe again he forgot all about his promises; he became even worse than before. He's a double-dealing, cheating, unreliable tyrant and I would not shed a tear if he were toppled. He's a leftover from a past era, the sort of ruler that stops any hope of development. Don't you understand? There's no hope for Africa as long as people like him continue in power!'

The military adviser stared at the President with mounting panic. 'There's something here I don't understand,' he said. 'We've always seen eye to eye in matters like these, and now . . . I can't think what's come over you.'

The President sat there for a while in silence. Then he spoke. 'Yes, you're right. Something has changed in me.' He focused a searching pair of eyes upon the adviser. 'Have you ever listened to "La Marseillaise"?'

The adviser was completely taken by surprise. 'Of course,' he stammered, 'I've heard it hundreds of times. Our national anthem. How could I not have listened to it?'

'You've heard it, yes. You've sung it. But have you ever thought about the words? About their meaning?'

The adviser was taken aback. 'Naturally, I know the words. I . . . I really don't understand what you're driving at.'

'I, too, thought I knew them. I've listened to these words so often, at so many official ceremonies. But it was only recently that they struck me in all their force. That I understood. Listen to what I have to say.' He held out a hand to stop the adviser from interrupting. 'Listen.

'It all happened in Bobodiou. Until the moment that tenor came, nothing special had occurred. We had been served a selection of traditional African music and dances, all charming and innocent, and the afternoon was just passing by slowly. But when that opera singer stepped onto the stage the atmosphere changed. Have you ever been somewhere and been aware that something out of the ordinary was about to happen? I sensed it at once. He started singing . . . and it was moving, no . . . it was divine. You could almost feel, no . . . see the notes emerge from his lips and fill the hearts of the people. The audience was electrified. Spellbound!

When he ended his last aria there was deep silence. It lasted seconds . . . became almost palpable. And then the public rose as one man and there was a thunderous ovation such as I've never heard before. But that was not what I wanted to tell you. It was when Gwemboka and I stepped onto the stage to congratulate him that the incredible happened. It was so unexpected, so sudden, that it took us all by surprise, but once it had started, no one could stop it.'

The President paused for a few moments. Then he carried on.

'It was as if an unseen power suddenly caught hold of the singer and propelled him forward. And then "La Marseillaise" burst forth from his lips. When he defiantly threw out those powerful words, it was as if all the oppression of a lifetime fell off him . . . as if a wind of liberation blew through the theatre. I've never experienced anything like it. It was majestic. It was like a cry for freedom!'

The President looked at his adviser. 'I see that you think I've become an idealistic dreamer. That I have taken leave of my senses. But it's not like that. I'm just trying to tell you how it felt. How it affected me and, I believe, the others. Trust me, I haven't lost all sense of proportion. It may seem so to you because you weren't there. But to those who were there everything was crystal clear. This was an historic moment. A moment of revelation! And I had the privilege – yes, the privilege – to be present. To witness it!'

The adviser kept quiet now, awed by the President's words, by the tone of his voice. 'It was that singer,' said the President. 'An immense strength seemed to radiate from him as he stood there and sung our national anthem. We have listened so often to it without ever really thinking about the words. But there, in that theatre in Bobodiou, I realised what those words meant. There, suddenly, their message was thrust upon me as that tenor sang: "Against us tyranny . . ."'

The President's eyes seemed illuminated by an inner light as he gazed at his adviser. 'Our national anthem was a plea to liberate us from oppression. Two centuries ago we started a revolution. We were surrounded by tyranny and our situation seemed hopeless, but we fought back, fought to free ourselves from the chains of bondage. We sang "La Marseillaise" to gather courage, and we did free ourselves.

But what did we do to others? We kept them subjugated!' The President lifted an angry finger. 'How can we pay lip service to the great principles of freedom, equality and brotherhood when we help to keep others oppressed? That's what I asked myself. Yes,' he nodded, 'something changed in me there and then. When that tenor flung the words of "La Marseillaise" into our faces – defiantly, victoriously – it was as if he broke the spell . . . the spell that has kept Africa in bondage for so long. He set in motion a wave that may end by engulfing a continent. It felt like the dawn of a new era.'

The adviser sighed. 'So, you don't want to send in the paratroopers?'

'No! Don't you understand? We have tried the old ways for forty years now, and look at the misery it has brought. Look at what Africa has become. They all pretend that the liberation from colonialism happened forty years ago. That's a fallacy! The people merely swapped a foreign tyranny for a local one. No, the real liberation has still to take place. And it has to happen soon. It can't wait much longer.' The President stared straight at his adviser. 'We need a new start,' he said. 'We need to be true to our principles. Forty years is more than enough. It's time we made a clean breast of it – time to allow a new era to begin. And this tenor . . . he lent words to it. He carried the hope of a continent, the longing to be liberated. I understood. And the audience understood.'

'I don't understand what you're proposing,' muttered the adviser shaking his head. 'How can we abandon our people over there? Our interests? If you don't want to send in fresh troops, maybe we could use the paratroopers that are already there. If we move them swiftly, they may yet stop the rebels.'

'No!' The President shook his head with great conviction. 'We're not going to do that. On the contrary, I'm going to order our troops to withdraw from strategic positions and not to intervene in any military action. They will assemble at certain points around the French nationals, and behave like UN troops, only intervening to protect their lives. I told you that we can no longer carry on as usual. We would be betraying the hope Africans have invested in us. We would be betraying our own revolution. No, tyrants have to be swept away, of whatever stripes and colours. Let's wipe away the past. We must think of the future now. The people believe in us. We cannot disappoint them again. Africa deserves better than what it's got so far. Much better!

'And I believe, *mon ami*,' added the President, turning towards his adviser, 'that by living up to our principles we are serving the long-term interests of our own country much more than you are willing to admit. If we can save Africa, we'll be saving the world . . . and ourselves.'

9

It was late afternoon by the time Marie and Gael returned empty-handed from the airport. Gael was beside herself with anxiety and bombarding Marie with questions: 'How can we ever find him now? What if he's left by car? Where do you think he's gone?'

'Please, please,' Marie said, 'one question at a time. How do you expect me to know whether he's left, and, if so, where he's gone? I haven't got my crystal ball with me right now. But I do know that it's no use running about with our noses to the ground trying to follow the spoor, as we've done so far. It's much more convenient to let other people do the running for us. I do have a few connections, and they may be able to get us the information we need. You stay here while I see what I can do.'

When Marie returned an hour or two later, Gael was nearly frantic. She jumped up asking: 'Have you found anything out?'

'Have some patience, my girl. They're searching.'

'Who's they?'

'The informal network. I'm not going to explain. And I've also contacted Rasta and his men. In the meantime, let's have something to eat.'

By the time night fell they'd learned that Anton had reached Bobodiou after crossing the Sahara. His Land-Rover, which carried a lot of jerrycans and equipment, had been parked near the Riverside for two days, but it was no longer there. Nobody knew whether Anton had parked it somewhere else or left town altogether.

'Let's go into town and search every corner,' implored Gael.

'No,' replied Marie with determination. 'We shall wait until tomorrow. When daylight comes, the network will continue to search. What we need now is a good night's rest.' She handed Gael a cup of tea and as she watched the girl sipping it she thought: and this time I've made sure that you'll sleep well.

10

A large crowd had gathered in the lounge of the Riverside Hotel the next morning, waiting for Gwemboka to arrive. All the local people of any importance in the capital were there, and they were getting more nervous with every passing minute. Had something happened? Everyone knew that the rebels were closing in. It was whispered that shots had been heard that morning barely fifteen miles away. French aid workers had been seen leaving in droves. Where were the French troops? The people assembled in the hotel lounge were shifting anxiously from one foot to the other. They would have fled, too, had it not been for fear. They knew the price they would have to pay if they upset Gwemboka. Fear held them in its grip. Nothing else could have made them foregather in this hour of danger.

Then a gleaming stretch limo drew up in front of the hotel, the door was opened and guards saluted as the President began to climb out of the car with great difficulty. He was very late, as befits a president. The presidential guard surrounded Gwemboka as he advanced slowly into the hotel lounge towards the wall where for the moment only the photographs of General de Gaulle and Mao were visible. Gwemboka's new portrait was concealed under a length of crimson cloth.

A man in military uniform now marched forward with measured steps, lifting his legs high. When he reached the wall on which the portrait to be unveiled was hung, he turned round, saluted the President, grabbed the rope that held the piece of cloth, and pulled. As the cover came down and the new portrait was revealed there was a sharp intake of breath from all those present.

It was Gwemboka's portrait, and his huge chest was covered in medals, but where his face was supposed to be somebody had stuck the head of a black pig. The pig's ears were hanging down limply on either side of the head, the end of the snout was bright pink, and the two vicious small eyes glinted maliciously. And underneath the portrait was written: 'Down with the fat ugly pig!'

There was dead silence while Gwemboka's eyes almost popped out of their sockets. His blood rushed to his head, his breathing came fast and irregular, and his hand went to his heart. Suddenly someone in the crowd began to laugh, unable to contain himself any longer; then another joined in, and after that the whole room burst out into uncontrollable laughter.

It was more than just normal laughter. It was an outburst of hysteria, the eruption of a volcano that had been held back for too many years and now blew its top off. Wave upon wave of roaring laughter rolled through the lounge, shaking the Riverside to its very foundations, carrying all before it, sweeping away twenty-five years of oppression.

Gwemboka stood there while the hurricane of mocking laughter whirled around him. His ears throbbed, his arteries stood out on his temples and he felt his heart beating as if it were about to burst. Then he began to tremble on his feet, he gasped for breath, a sharp pain shot through his chest and suddenly he collapsed in a heap on the floor in front of his portrait with the pig's head. And still the people were laughing, tears rolling down their faces, tears of liberation.

11

After some time a few officers of the presidential guard seemed to come to their senses and started to yell contradictory orders. All was confusion now. The people rushed forward, shouting excitedly as they caught a glimpse of the great bulk lying there motionless, while several guards tried to push the people back and others ran about calling for help.

'We must telephone! Call an ambulance!' yelled one of them.

An officer elbowed his way to the reception desk and ordered the receptionist at gunpoint to ring the hospital. The frightened woman took ages to find the hospital's number, and when she dialled it, it was engaged. The excited officer wrenched the phone from her hands and pointed his gun threateningly towards the receiver, shouting: 'Quick! An ambulance or I'll shoot.' Finally he realised that there was no one at the other end of the line, only an engaged tone, and slammed the receiver down while the receptionist tried to push the gun away with a trembling hand.

'We'll take the President to the hospital in his own car!' shouted another officer.

They attempted to lift up his inert body but he was so heavy that it took four men to move him, dragging him by the legs and arms. Progress was difficult. The public had closed in and the guards found it almost impossible to make headway through the dense mass of people. Pushing against the crowd and pulling the massive body of the President along, they finally reached the presidential car, but when they attempted to heave the body inside they were unable to, however much they tried.'

'A truck, a truck! We need a truck!' yelled a guard.

Just then a small pickup truck passed by and the guardsmen sprung forward and stopped it at gunpoint. When the driver emerged, his eyes wide with fear, his arms stuck up in the air, he was rudely pushed aside by the barrel of a rifle while an officer of the guards shouted in his face: 'Your vehicle has been confiscated!'

The officer got behind the steering wheel, the guards undid the flap at the back, and with a combined effort they lifted up the President and shoved him inside. The small truck was already moving off when a few guards jumped in next to the President's body while another one ran alongside, only just managing to pull open the passenger's door and dive into the empty seat. The driver turned the pickup truck round with screeching tyres and set off along the riverbank, heading for the hospital at full speed.

They had covered no more than fifty yards when the road underneath the truck was ripped open by an explosion. The vehicle seemed to be catapulted up in the air and then turned over towards the riverbank, shedding its load of guards together with the President's body. As they rolled down the steep bank, several guardsmen managed to cling to the edge, but nothing could stop the President's heavy bulk. It kept rolling down, gathering speed, and disappeared with a loud splash into the muddy-brown river.

When they heard the loud bang, everyone streamed out of the hotel. They all began to run towards the spot where the explosion had taken place, but when they got there the President had well and truly vanished. Later it was claimed that those who had arrived first had seen something looking like a big body bob up for a fraction of a second. Then the jaws of a huge crocodile appeared, snatched the body and pulled it under water. But, then, no crocodiles had been seen in the river for a long time, and there had been such great confusion that it was probable that these were no more than false rumours.

12

While these dramatic events were taking place in Bobodiou, Anton sat facing Amadou in the shade of a big baobab tree some sixty miles towards the east, talking animatedly. He was telling the rebel leader about his encounter with a man from the desert and his inability to communicate.

'So you've noticed that Western ways don't get you very far over here?' commented Amadou.

'Indeed. And that has set me thinking. Maybe all peoples in the world have values best adapted to themselves, and have created societies in their own image?'

'Quite right. No one would argue that the Italians and the Japanese have identical societies and think, act and live the same way, would they?'

'No, obviously not!' Anton thought of the *dolce far niente* of Rome, of the total lack of discipline of the Sicilians, and smiled. He wondered what Tokyo would look like if it were peopled by Italians. Probably a lot less regulated. And Naples would certainly not be what it was if it were a Japanese city.

'Even the French and the English pretend to have separate cultures,' continued Amadou. 'Yet they differ less from each other than many neighbouring African tribes whom you in the West all lump together under the heading "African". In fact, there is more cultural and racial variety in Africa than in all the rest of the world combined. And come to think of it, we Africans may be fundamentally different from all the others.'

'I don't see why. Don't all humans have genes that are basically the same, whether they're born in Africa or anywhere else?'

'Haven't you read about the origin of human races? Don't you know the story of humankind?'

'Yes, but tell me . . .'

'Let me summarise the main facts. It's well established that modern humans originated in Africa, maybe two hundred thousand years ago. So I suppose that originally all humans were black.' Amadou looked at Anton and chuckled as he suddenly imagined him turning into a jet-black man.

'But then, possibly sixty thousand years ago, one small group of humans crossed the Red Sea and migrated out of Africa. And they multiplied and gradually began to spread through Asia, finally ending up in Australia,

Europe and America. And, as they moved, their physical appearance, their cultures, their ways of thinking were fashioned by the climates of their new homelands and by the incredible challenges they encountered.'

'That's right . . .'

'Today's Europeans, Asians, Americans and North Africans are all descendants of those wanderers who moved out of Africa. But not the black Africans. We were the ones who stayed in the tropical environment we knew. Our cultural trajectory and that of the rest of humankind parted ways sixty thousand years ago. We were not fashioned by the challenges of radically new environments. And as a result African values could well be fundamentally different from those of other peoples.'

'I must admit I've never thought of it that way.'

'But it's essential to recognise this and accept it. That's why systems that are successful in Europe, America or Asia will not necessarily function well in sub-Saharan Africa. We may have to come up with a whole new approach before we can solve the problem of African development: a system adapted to us, Africans, and our way of being.'

'But we already have capitalism, socialism and communism . . . and Asian values . . . and now we also have Islamic values. Isn't that enough?'

'No, because my theory is that all those systems are based on the cultural environments in which they were developed. A system specific to Africa was never developed because all modern philosophical systems of thinking originated in Europe and America. And, of course, all the old philosophies, that may or may not have any relevance to modern society, originated in Asia. Think of Islam, Confucianism, Buddhism, Christianity and so many other religious or philosophical systems.' Amadou paused for a while. Then he carried on: 'You see, there exists no all-encompassing blueprint for development created by Africans, or even one devised by outsiders, but specifically adapted to us.'

'You mean it will be impossible to develop Africa otherwise?'

'Yes. And we need such a system urgently because Africans have begun to move out of their continent of their own free will in the last few decades. And when that trickle turns into a massive flood, it will be too late to solve any problem, African or other.'

13

Minutes after Gwemboka's huge frame had sunk into the river with a big splash, the presidential guard went berserk. Those impressive thugs who had terrorised the population without restraint for many years, and whose appearance on the streets had been sufficient to instil fear in the people, went all over the town on a wild rampage, driving about in their small open jeeps, wielding their automatic guns and shooting at anything that moved. At once life in Bobodiou came to a standstill. People went into hiding behind doors and walls, trying to make themselves as inconspicuous as possible, trembling like frightened rabbits in their holes, hoping not to be seen.

As the shooting began, Marie desperately tried to wake Gael, shaking her vigorously.

'What, what . . .' Gael finally mumbled.

'Quick! Quick! We must reach the embassy before it's too late.'

'What's happened? What time is it?'

'Nearly midday! Oh, it's all my fault,' moaned Marie. 'I gave you a sedative that was much too strong.'

'A sedative?'

'Yes, in your tea last night. But this is no time for pointless talking. Come on, quick!' she repeated. 'Rasta and his men are waiting outside. Get dressed. We must be out of here. They say that Gwemboka has died and his guards have gone crazy.'

Gael dressed as fast as she could, took a sip from the cup of tea Marie offered and was ready to go. They ran out of their hotel with Rasta and two of his men in the lead, and Gael following. Marie, who was the slowest, trailed behind.

As they turned a corner and came within sight of the embassy, Rasta and his men spotted a military jeep in front of the entrance. The moment the guards saw them they began to shoot wildly. The men withdrew like lightning back round the corner but Gael, who was still slightly dazed, carried on. Rasta tried to hold her back but it was too late: they heard a cry and Gael fell to the ground.

14

Barely half an hour had passed since Gwemboka's death, and the news already had begun to spread around the country. The Africans no longer used their tom-toms to do this. They now had a modern version of the tom-tom: the mobile phone.

Within two hours even the remotest police outposts and army barracks had heard the shocking news, and everywhere officers began to discuss what to do. And most of them hit upon the same solution. In the power vacuum left behind by Gwemboka's death, fighting was certain to break out in Bobodiou. They decided to wait for the outcome and, in the meantime, do nothing. And once the fighting was over they would pledge allegiance to whoever came out on top and appointed himself the next president. That was by far the most sensible attitude.

The news had also reached the rebel camp. A messenger had come running into the camp and told Amadou the story, which he'd just got from one of his contacts in town via his mobile.

When Amadou heard the circumstances of Gwemboka's death he began to swear: 'Damn! He has vanished after all. Damn, damn!'

'But no, Boss. He's died!' protested the messenger.

'Maybe,' grumbled the rebel leader, 'but we haven't got his body. He may be dead, yes, but people will say that he's still alive. Or that his ghost is still alive, which is the same to all intents and purposes. And even that this ghost now lives inside a giant crocodile. Don't you see what this means?'

The men around him stared at their leader with expressionless faces.

'It means that he'll become the crocodile god, enter folklore and live on in the tales grandparents will tell their little grandchildren. And they'll tremble with fright before going to sleep, and be afraid that the giant crocodile will sneak up at night to devour them. Damn! Now he'll go on living forever.'

While Amadou was giving his views on African beliefs, Juan Rodriguez was becoming very impatient. 'You're just sitting there babbling about fairy tales while they're shooting in Bobodiou!' he exclaimed. 'Look here, you must order our boys to move forward. This is the moment. Let's launch an all-out attack!'

Amadou cut him short at once. 'I don't think that's the right thing to do. Now that the tyrant has disappeared, the different factions are certain to start fighting among themselves. And the balance of power is changing rapidly. I'm sure that the government's troops will begin to desert in droves. Let's wait a little more. I feel that the town may yet fall into our hands without having to fire a single shot, like a ripe apple falling off a tree.'

Juan Rodriguez suddenly flared up, unable to control his temper any longer. 'I don't know what's come over you,' he hissed. 'Yesterday you told me you didn't want to nationalise the mines but wanted to work with foreigners. And now you just sit there and refuse to go into battle. That's not what I call a revolution! That's not what I've fought for! You're betraying all our ideals.' He stared at Amadou, his eyes flashing with anger. 'If we can't even agree on such elementary matters as nationalising mines and fighting, I don't want to stay with you another day! I'm going to South America. There, at least, there's still room for a man with real revolutionary ideals like me.' And he turned on his heel and left, shaking with rage.

15

After Gael had fallen, Rasta shot forward while the bullets whizzed past his ears, and within a second he had dragged her round the corner. At once the three men picked her up and ran off as fast as possible, carrying the unfortunate girl on their shoulders while diving in and out of side streets to escape the guards who were coming after them in their small jeep.

'Is she badly hurt?' came Marie's frantic voice.

'Don't know!' yelled Rasta. 'Can't stop to check.'

By the time they got into the shantytown, Gael was no longer conscious and her breathing had become very faint. They entered a small shack whose occupants Rasta appeared to know, and stretched Gael out on the ground.

'Quick!' shouted Marie. 'Run to the Land-Rover and bring the boxes with medical equipment. Hurry! For God's sake!'

Gael's left shoulder was soaked in blood and Marie set about cutting open her blouse and trying to stop the bleeding. A quarter of an hour later the men reappeared, panting, carrying the boxes, and Marie immediately began to clean the wound with trembling hands while Rasta, who remembered that he was now an assistant nurse, handed her the materials. Marie disinfected the wound, managed to stem the flow of blood, bandaged the shoulder and then gave her an injection of antibiotics.

Gael had been extremely lucky. The bullet had hit neither an essential organ, nor even any of the bones, but had gone straight through the fleshy part of the muscle and come out the other side. Still, she had lost a lot of blood. An hour without help and she might not have survived.

By now the shooting had got much closer and Rasta was becoming very nervous. 'We must go,' he insisted.

'But she can't move,' protested Marie. 'She isn't well enough.'

'Then we carry her,' said Rasta firmly. 'If we don't get out of here, we'll all be killed.'

They wrapped a long piece of dark-blue African cloth around Gael, picked her up and began to walk quickly, slipping through the dark alleyways like shadows avoiding the light, remaining under cover of the shacks as much as possible.

After some time they reached the compound on the outskirts of the shantytown where the Land-Rover had been hidden. The men who'd been guarding it removed the branches and cover and helped to lay Gael down on the backseat. When Marie climbed behind the wheel, Rasta seemed to hesitate. He felt that it was his duty to guide the women back to the rebel camp, but he wanted to stay in town where they needed all the help they could get to locate and protect the isolated rebels. Marie took the decision for him.

'You stay,' she said. 'I know the way back perfectly well.'

'All right,' he agreed, 'but we'll come with you till you reach the track.'

As Marie set off, they kept looking around anxiously for Gwemboka's men until they joined the narrow dusty track. Here Rasta and his men jumped out and as the Land-Rover began to wind its way through the bush, following the path they'd taken only two days ago, Marie breathed a sigh of relief. Now she wouldn't have to return to the rebel camp and run the risk of falling into Juan Rodriguez's hands. Instead, she was going to drive straight to the dispensary in Kanibasso where she had the medicine to take proper care of Gael.

16

Two hours after Gwemboka had disappeared, Mamboulou's special brigades moved in to impose order in Bobodiou. This was the moment the Minister of Home Affairs and Internal Security had been dreaming of for twenty-five long years, fearing he would die before it came. He felt elated, especially since he himself had been the architect of the tyrant's downfall. When his men had found those caricatures of Gwemboka in the crates brought by the Russians, he'd been obliged to have them burned. Nevertheless, he thought them so funny that he'd kept back some of them for his own enjoyment, hiding them in his house in spite of the high risk this involved.

For twenty-five years he hadn't dared oppose Gwemboka, but something fundamental had changed the day his president had sung that hated French national anthem. The mouse finally stood up, ready to bite the lion. The evening before Gwemboka's new portrait was to be unveiled Mamboulou had a brainwave. This was a unique chance to ridicule the tyrant in front of everyone. One of his most trusted security agents worked in the Riverside Hotel and the man had sneaked into the lobby in the early hours of the morning and pinned one of the caricatures, a pig's head, on the tyrant's portrait. And it had paid off beyond all expectations.

At last! thought Mamboulou. The power was his for the taking and he was going to give what it took to grab it. He was going to be the next president.

17

In the Belgian Ministry of Education in Brussels a civil servant was standing nervously next to the Minister. The latter was a corpulent man with a ruddy complexion, but this time he was almost crimson.

'What's this?' he barked, pointing at the animated cartoon that was running on his screen.

'It's an email, Minister. It arrived a few days ago while you were in Africa.'

'Who sent it?'

'I don't know. It's anonymous. It was sent from an Internet café.'

'Can't we catch the scoundrel who sent it?'

'I've tried to collect as much information as possible, Minister,' replied the civil servant in an ingratiating voice, 'but I'm afraid that it will be impossible to identify the sender. The Internet café the mail was sent from is usually very busy at night, and the owner doesn't remember everyone who was there several evenings ago. And he made it clear that he's not legally responsible for the messages sent out from his café.'

'What! But look at this! It's simply scandalous!' The arteries stood out on the Minister's temples and it seemed as if they were going to explode at any moment.

'I've seen it, Minister,' nodded the civil servant, 'I've seen it.'

It was a very unusual email indeed. It carried the title: 'The Occupations of a Civil Servant' and was made up of moving cartoon images accompanied by a song. The song, completely innocent in its usual version, is well known in several languages. Originally French and called 'Frère Jacques', it runs as follows in English:

> Are you sleeping, are you sleeping?
> Brother John? Brother John?
> Morning bells are ringing, morning bells are ringing.
> Ding, dang, dong. Ding, dang, dong.

However, significant modifications had been made to the text in the email, and the song ran:

> Are you horny, are you horny?
> Mr Smally? Mr Smally?
> How your balls are ringing, how your balls are ringing,
> Ding, dang, dong. Ding, dang, dong.

The accompanying cartoon showed a man hanging with outstretched arms from the inside of a bell, as if he were the clapper. The man was naked except for a small T-shirt which sported the name Smally, while a woman called Pauline had grabbed his private parts and was swinging Smally back and forth by means of these, making the bell ring to the accompaniment of the song.

Underneath was a subtitle: 'The Adventures of Jack Smally in Africa'.

The Minister looked at it again and yelled: 'Find out what happened!

Ring the Belgian Geological Institute immediately. Leave no stone unturned. We must get to the bottom of this!' And then he hissed: 'We must suppress this! If it leaks out, there will be a dreadful scandal.'

But it was too late. The email had been sent to a number of newspapers and to several members of the Opposition, and was already doing the rounds of the country.

18

The week after Gwemboka's disappearance from the scene of African politics was not a particularly good time to be in Bobodiou. Minutes after his death the presidential guard had begun shooting. Then, in the afternoon, Mamboulou's special security brigades closed in. As they attempted to chase the presidential guard out of town, gunfire could be heard everywhere. But the men of the presidential guard were not so easily dislodged; they were fighting for their survival. Now that their protector had gone, they knew what fate awaited them if they lost. They were also the best-trained and best-armed troops in town, and by the evening of the second day they had regrouped and counterattacked, and the shooting intensified around the barracks of the special security brigade.

By the morning of the third day the police shot into action. They suddenly attacked the presidential palace, which had been left virtually undefended by the presidential guard, and to their delight found a stash of weapons and cash. But they soon fled the palace in fright when they discovered it was crammed full of malevolent charms.

By the middle of the week General Babadoulé, Chief of Staff of the Armed Forces, finally managed to assemble most of his troops and began moving them from the outlying barracks towards Bobodiou, confiscating any vehicle he came across to transport his badly armed and badly dressed men to the capital. The general was relieved that his troops hadn't run into rebel forces, not realising that the rebels deliberately kept moving out of the way to let his battalions pass and do the fighting for them.

The shooting now intensified as the four different factions fought it out among themselves during moments when they were not breaking down doors and looting whatever remained in the houses. By the end of the week most of the civil population had disappeared from town.

The presidential guards who had recaptured the palace dug themselves in and kept on shooting randomly, but they were running out of ammunition and beginning to look like a spent force. The police, too, had dwindled in numbers. Some of the policemen had donned civilian clothes and slipped out with the rest of the population, their pockets filled with the cash they had found in the presidential palace.

Mamboulou's special security brigades had fought valiantly for the last few days and had managed to reoccupy the area around their barracks. They then began to press towards the centre of the town and, as they advanced, took several shops by storm and discovered large stocks of beer and other alcoholic drinks. After having spent a week shooting with little time to sleep, nothing could stop them. The bout of drinking that ensued had a devastating effect, knocking out most of the men and putting paid to Mamboulou's aspiration to become the next president.

By now the armed forces had managed to bring in their artillery. Three of their big guns still functioned properly, and they had pulled them into the capital behind confiscated trucks. After a lot of towing and pushing the guns were finally in position opposite the gates of the presidential palace and the cannonade started. General Babadoulé had also brought in the two planes of the air force that were still operational, and instructed the pilots to bomb the barracks of the special security brigades. Unfortunately, the pilots had targeted the large covered market instead, and by the time they discovered their mistake there were no bombs left; all they could do was return to the international airport before the planes ran out of fuel.

And while all this was going on, the rebels were sitting a few miles from Bobodiou, biding their time, waiting patiently for their adversaries to finish each other off. With each passing day more soldiers, policemen and even members of the special security brigades deserted to join the rebels. Two entire army brigades, which had been marching slowly towards the town from the outlying districts, didn't even bother to go into battle. Instead, their commanders offered their services directly to Amadou Sékouré, the rebel leader.

19

After Amadou had explained that Gael had returned to Europe, Anton endeavoured to make the best of the situation into which fate had put him. The rebel camp wasn't such a bad place to be in while the fighting was raging in Bobodiou. Anton had taken a liking to Amadou and enjoyed the interchange of ideas with him, even if conversation tended to be somewhat lopsided, with Amadou doing most of the talking and Anton trying to take it all in. But as the days went by the rebels became increasingly absorbed in what was going on. They had to adjust their positions as the armed forces passed by on their way to the capital, and were also occupied mopping up the old regime's renegades.

Left to himself, Anton gradually fell into a state of lethargy. Thinking of what had happened to him became positively painful. For a while everything had gone so well. Abandoned in the Sahara, he had nevertheless managed to cross it against all odds. He had become the star of the International Geological Conference after the participants had booed Smally out of the auditorium. And he had found out why Gael had run away from him.

Then luck had run out. He had nearly got to where Gael lived, only to learn that he had just missed her! She had returned to Europe, and now he was the one stuck in Africa!

He would have to start all over again; there was nothing to do about it. He would drive back to Bobodiou when the fighting was over, wait for the airport to be opened, fly to Belgium and search for Gael. He felt utterly desperate.

20

Meanwhile, in Belgium, the weather had been awful for weeks on end. Day after day millions of people dragged themselves to their jobs in the morning, ground their way through their work like depressed ants and long before they were released from their chores it was already dark. By the time they had struggled home through the pouring rain they felt totally dispirited and just collapsed in front of their TVs like zombies, only to find that there was no local news of any interest and that the TV programmes were even duller than usual.

The 'Frère Jacques' email had therefore been a godsend, and the newspapers and TV and radio stations milked it for what it was worth. They had sent their best reporters to ferret around and soon discovered that here was one of the juiciest scandals of the last few years.

As Smally was not yet back from Africa, a daily had sent a reporter to the Belgian Geological Institute to see what could be found out in his absence. He had interviewed several members of the staff – who did not wish to be named – and the paper now published a summary of their views. It was clear that the scientists and technicians at the institute had the lowest of opinions of their new director. Comments ranged from total incompetence, to sabotaging scientific work, to being run by a KGB man. Smally had clearly made a complete mess of the institute in the few months he'd been at the helm.

Why had he been promoted over the heads of well-qualified scientists, the daily asked, when he had neither the qualifications, nor the administrative or human capacity to run an institute which had such an outstanding international reputation?

At once accusing fingers began to point at Dufour, Minister of Education. It was whispered that Smally was his protégé, and that this had been the only reason for his promotion.

Soon more was dug up. Smally had not gone alone to Africa. His secretary, the Pauline of the email, had accompanied him. And when her files were gone through it turned out that she had left without official permission!

Then came worse: the institute's credit card company received a claim for the bill of a luxurious hotel suite in Bobodiou! This was too good to be true, and the tabloids jumped on it.

One title ran:

SMALLY SCANDAL!

> After cutting scientists' travel budgets, director pays for week's holiday in exotic resort with the lab's credit card!
>
> Is it really necessary for a director to take a week off to attend a two-hour conference? Have his secretary accompany him to keep him occupied as suggested in the email? Book the most luxurious hotel suite in the most expensive hotel in

Bobodiou? And pay for all his and his mistress's personal expenses with the lab's credit card? With taxpayers' money!

The newspaper's editor-in-chief seemed shocked. He suggested in no uncertain terms that there was only one option for the government if it had any sense of responsibility towards its taxpayers and its voters: to refuse to honour the credit card and let Smally pay for everything out of his own pocket. And next refer him to the Ministry of Justice, which should judge him for his total disregard of all standards of decency.

Then, the following day, a broadsheet carried the title:

SMALLY STORY: Worse and worse!

We have just learned from the French Geological Institute that Smally went to the International Geological Conference in Bobodiou under false pretences. The invitation had not been addressed to him but to the previous director, Professor Briart. Unable to attend, the latter had intended to send one of his brightest scientists, a Dr Felsen, who had developed a revolutionary method to detect rare metal deposits. Instead of fulfilling the wishes of Professor Briart, it seems that Smally stole Dr Felsen's papers, fired him and went to the conference pretending he had invented the method himself. By a fortuitous coincidence Dr Felsen who, it should be stressed, had travelled at his own expense, turned up at the conference just as Smally began his presentation. When Smally was unable to explain any of the formulae and was booed out of the auditorium by the international participants, Dr Felsen was allowed to take over, and managed to save the reputation of the Belgian Geological Institute.

It goes without saying that this is shameful, irresponsible behaviour of the worst sort. We should not allow an impostor to ruin our country's reputation and turn us into an international laughing stock. We cannot tolerate that our government supports such people, promoting them to jobs well above their competence solely for political reasons. We shall not rest until we get to the bottom of this case, and until the government cleans up its stinking Augean stables.

21

Anton had been a week with the rebels when Rasta arrived in the camp, back from Bobodiou. Within minutes Amadou called Anton over.
　'I've got bad news,' he said. 'Your girlfriend didn't leave for Europe.'
　Anton's face brightened. 'Oh, but that's good news!'
　'I'm not sure. She was shot down in Bobodiou a week ago . . .'
　'What!' Anton sunk down. 'She's dead?'
　'No. Apparently she was saved. She had no more than a flesh wound.'
　'Thank God!'
　'Yes, but there's a mystery. Her companion drove her out of town towards our camp, but they never got here.'
　'Where is she then?' Anton's voice rose in panic.
　'I have no idea. I'm really sorry.'
　'Do something! Let's search the area immediately!'
　'Wait. First let me see what I can find out.' And Amadou immediately ordered those of his men who had a mobile phone to search around for news, while Anton paced up and down like a tiger in a cage.
　An hour later he called out to Anton. 'They're safe! They've gone to Kanibasso.'
　Minutes later Anton was on his way, determined that this time nothing would stop him.

22

He had been driving for an hour or two, advancing slowly along a rutted, sandy track, when he saw some dunes, palm trees and a few scattered dwellings ahead. This must be Kanibasso, he thought. Soon my quest will be over.
　As he reached the first dunes he caught up with a few swaying figures, a man and three women, walking along the track. The man was leading the way, strolling along lightly, a twisted stick in his hand, but the women, probably his wives, were carrying huge loads on their heads. They stopped when they heard the sound of an engine and turned round wherever

they were standing, literally blocking the track. As he caught up with them, Anton asked: 'Kanibasso?' The man nodded and pointed his stick forward, a big smile across his face, while the women stepped out of the way to let the Land-Rover pass.

A minute later Anton entered the settlement of adobe houses. The dispensary appeared to be somewhat out of town along a dusty track, and he carried on. Finally he noticed several people sitting in the sand, among them a one-legged man; others had bandages around their arms or heads. This is it, thought Anton, and he slowly turned into the opening in the low wall that surrounded the dispensary.

Somehow he was full of apprehension. His heart began to beat wildly and his mouth went dry as he climbed out of the Land-Rover. Would Gael be all right? And how was she going to react when she saw him? Would she believe him when he told her the truth of what had happened?

As he stood there, an older white woman detached herself from a group of Africans and came forward. Her eyes went from the fully equipped Land-Rover to the Belgian licence plates, and as Anton advanced hesitantly towards her she stared at him with undisguised relief. He was about to open his mouth when she clasped his hand in hers and said: 'At last! You have arrived.'

Anton failed to grasp what was going on. 'Isn't this the dispensary?' he stammered. As the woman nodded affirmation, he continued: 'Isn't . . . isn't this where Gael works?'

'You're Anton, aren't you?'

'Yes . . . but where's . . .'

'How wonderful. How absolutely wonderful!' exclaimed the woman, ignoring his question. She stood there, holding his hand affectionately while looking at him as if he were the prodigal son who'd just returned home. 'I nearly despaired.'

'But Gael?'

'Oh, Gael, yes . . .' She nodded as if Anton's questions had only just penetrated. 'Yes . . . She's been such a worry lately.' She looked up. 'You wouldn't believe how obstinate young women can be. So unreasonable! First they don't want to listen to you when you tell them they've made a big mistake and had better make up for it. And then, when they finally realise they've made a big mistake, it's almost impossible to stop them rushing off to make up for it.' She shook her head. 'Girls! I was much more sensible when I was her age . . .' She suddenly tilted her head, thought for a while, and then corrected: 'At least, I hope I was.'

'I'm . . . I'm afraid I don't understand what you're talking about.'

'It's Gael I'm talking about, of course. She's sweet, yes, but I think she needs a firm hand to guide her.' The woman looked at Anton's hand, which she was still holding in hers, as if she were wondering whether it was firm enough.

'Oh!' she exclaimed suddenly. 'I haven't even told you who I am. I'm Marie. And please, don't just stand there. Come and sit down.' She pulled him by the hand and made him sit at a low table in the shade of a tree. 'Make yourself comfortable,' she said. 'You must be tired after your journey. I'll go and prepare some tea.' She was about to be off when she turned round, sounding cross: 'May I ask you why you disappeared that evening? I'd like to know why. Everything would have been so much easier had you stayed at your table. It would have saved a lot of unpleasantness. And where have you been the whole of last week?' She stopped for a second or two, eyeing him inquisitively. 'Still, the main thing is that you got here . . .' She added one last question: 'Come to think of it, I really wonder how you knew we were here? You must tell me all about it later.' Then she turned and disappeared into the kitchen, leaving Anton behind, flabbergasted.

23

A quarter of an hour later she returned with two cups of steaming tea, put one in front of Anton and sat down in her own place, adjusting the cushions to make herself really comfortable.

Anton was about to open his mouth but before he had time to say anything she spoke: 'You wonder where Gael is, don't you?'

'Yes. And is she all right?' He looked very worried.

'Now, why do you ask that?'

'Well . . . in the rebel camp they told me that she'd been shot.'

'So that's where you've been. Did you meet a man called Juan Rodriguez over there?' And without waiting for the answer she warned: 'He's not to be trusted!'

'He's gone.'

'What do you mean by that?'

'He had a quarrel with Amadou and said he was going off to South America. I think he wants to stir up a revolution there.'

'I can see him doing just that!' Marie smiled. 'So you've met Amadou?'

'Yes. Nice man. We got on very well. But is Gael all right? And where is she? You still haven't told me.'

'Oh, Gael. I've sent her to an oasis up north this very morning. She'll be back in two days. She was becoming impossible.'

'But isn't she wounded?'

'Yes. I thought that the wound would keep her quiet for a while, but no. She's a tough girl. Up and about within three days; you wouldn't believe it. Said she wasn't going to waste her time here. She was determined to return to Bobodiou to search for you. Just imagine! As if having been shot once wasn't enough. That's why I sent her up north. I've already had more problems than I bargained for.'

'But how did she know I was in Bobodiou? And why does she suddenly want to find me when she ran away from me in the first place? I don't understand.'

'I see . . . I'd better start at the beginning, otherwise you're not going to understand anything . . .' Marie looked at him as if he were a somewhat backward boy. Then she thought for a while. 'I'm not really sure what the beginning is.' She sighed, an apologetic expression on her face. 'All right. Let's start about a week ago . . . That's much better, I think. Yes, let's start on the day of that concert in Bobodiou.' She nodded a couple of times, as if to show that she was agreeing with herself, and then spoke: 'Night was falling and Gael and I just sat down on a terrace in the gardens of the Riverside Hotel waiting to place our order, when a young woman passed by. And when she moved on to the following terrace we heard her exclaim "Anton!"'

'What! You . . . Gael was sitting on the next terrace!'

'Yes. And she heard every word that was spoken.'

'My God! Oh my God . . . so then she knows?'

'Yes, she knows everything. We heard that wicked woman boast how she had got herself into your room, and had enacted a scene designed to make Gael believe you were having an affair . . .'

'But then . . . why didn't she come to me?'

'She couldn't. She just sat there, trembling, while that dreadful voice carried on in the growing darkness, not ten feet away. You could have knocked her over with a feather. Finally, when that horrible woman ran away laughing triumphantly, Gael seemed to wake from a deep lethargy. She drew herself together and I pushed her on to your terrace, but you were no longer there. You had disappeared.'

'If only I had known . . . if only . . .'

'Maybe it was better like that. I don't know what she would have done had you still been there. She might have gone down on her knees begging you to forgive her . . . it wouldn't surprise me.' Marie lifted up a finger. 'Now, that's something a woman should never do.' She shook her head firmly. 'Anyway, when she couldn't find you that evening, she nearly went off the deep end, accusing herself of not having had faith in you; of having made you suffer, and I don't know what else. Personally, I don't think that having made you suffer matters so very much.' She looked at Anton weighing him up. 'You can cope with a bit of suffering. You're the strong type. And, anyway, it does men a lot of good to suffer for the woman they love.'

'But how could Gael have come across Pauline that morning in Brussels? I still don't see how that could have happened. I didn't leave my room the day she was supposed to have returned from London.'

'She returned a day earlier from her course and went to your room in the morning to surprise you. And then she had the shock of her life.'

'Oh no! How unjust!'

'Indeed. She kept crying her eyes out after that. For weeks on end. All for nothing.' Marie shook her head in disgust. 'She couldn't cope with it. She just wanted to be far away from it all. That's why she came to Africa: to forget, and help people whose miseries were greater than hers. I realised that she was very unhappy, but being what she is, she was unwilling to open her heart to me. She preferred to suffer in silence!'

'How she must have suffered . . .'

'But in the end I managed to worm the story out of her. And when I told her that the facts didn't correspond with the feelings and that she'd made a big mistake, she got quite upset. She wouldn't admit of any other possibility, the stubborn girl. Until that evening in Bobodiou. There she learned how that woman had tricked her into believing you were having an affair. She just couldn't forgive herself after the truth had been revealed. She's been devoured by remorse ever since. Only wants to do one thing: find you and lay her love at your feet.'

'If only I'd known she was there!'

'Well yes . . . You just can't imagine how impossible she's been ever since. She insisted we stay in Bobodiou to find you, when the embassy had arranged for us to leave the country. Finally we learned that you'd given a talk at that International Geological Conference. And there were rumours that you'd been approached to go to America. When she heard that, she nearly went crazy. Suddenly it was impossible to keep her in Bobodiou. She wanted to jump on the first plane to America. She was determined to find you, wherever you were.'

'But I hadn't come for that conference! It was sheer coincidence that I got in there. I crossed the Sahara with only one idea in mind: to find her.'

'Well, the silly girl didn't know that, did she? Then the shooting started, and as we fled to the embassy she was shot through the shoulder. She might have been killed.'

'Don't say such a thing!'

'But that's not what's bothered her since we've been back. No, she got it into her head that you might have been wounded or killed. She's been worrying herself to death about what might have happened to you. She kept imploring me to let her go back to Bobodiou. I told her that she should have faith, that everything would turn out all right, but no, she just kept repeating: "How could I have done this to Anton?" As if it were her fault! And she's determined to return to Bobodiou the moment the roads are open, whatever my objections. All I've been able to do to delay her is send her up north to an oasis for an inoculation round. What luck that you've come at last. I was really at my wits' end.'

Suddenly Anton got up. 'I must go and find her,' he said determinedly. 'She cannot carry on like this, living in uncertainty.'

'Don't be daft,' replied Marie holding him back. 'You're not Gael. *You* at least are going to be reasonable. It's no good setting off now. Night is nearly falling; you'd just get lost and that would only make things worse. No, you wait till tomorrow morning and look for her then. It's better to spend the night here. You can sleep in her room if you like.'

'All right,' agreed Anton reluctantly. 'Where does she sleep?'

'In the little room with the curtain further along the corridor. Listen, you look so tired. Why don't you go and lie down and have a rest. I'll prepare supper.'

'Thank you,' said Anton and turned into the corridor while Marie got busy in the kitchen.

24

Anton's heart began to pound as he stood in front of the curtain that closed off Gael's room. This was where she had lived, slept, suffered all these months. He felt as if he were nearing the end of his long pilgrimage. He slowly pulled the curtain aside and stepped inside. It was like crossing the threshold of a sacred shrine and he was overcome with emotion as he looked at the bed she had left only hours before. He touched the little pile of clothes that lay on one of the shelves, ran his fingers over the small objects that lined the walls. Gael! She was present in every corner of this room.

As he sat down on her bed he saw her small notebook next to her pillow, picked it up with a trembling hand and began to read. Darkness was creeping in but he didn't notice; he just read. And as he read what she had written, her joy, her dreams, her sadness and sorrow penetrated his heart.

When he'd finished, waves of strong feeling ran through his body. He lay down and buried his face in her pillow, the little book clasped against his chest. Within seconds he was fast asleep.

Half an hour later, when Marie had prepared supper and came to fetch him, she found him slumped on the bed, breathing deeply and regularly. A smile played around her lips as she looked at him, and she quietly pulled the curtain and let him sleep.

25

Anton had slept for at least ten hours when he woke up shivering. He felt stiff from having lain in an uncomfortable position, and his brain seemed as numb as the arm which had been squashed under his body for the best part of the night.

It was dark and eerily quiet. Where am I? he wondered, trying to piece his thoughts together. Where are the rebels? As he sat up he banged his head on a low shelf. It made such a din that he was certain he'd woken up everyone. The guards would storm in within seconds and point their guns at him. He waited tensely while rubbing his head, but no one seemed to move.

His eyes were getting used to the darkness by now and he found himself staring out through the mosquito netting of an oblong window. Where am I? he wondered again. The stars were there, most definitely, flickering faintly. He touched the hard bed on which he'd slept and felt a blanket underneath his body. That's why I'm cold, he reflected. I've fallen asleep in my shirt on top of a blanket.

Then, in a flash, it all came back to him. This was Gael's room. He had slept on her bed! When he realised where he was he lay very still for a long time. How close she was to him here. Gradually he let her presence enter his mind. As he did so he became aware of the strong undercurrent of sorrow left by the many nights she had spent in this room, tossing and turning, unable to forget her pain. And now he felt the same deep pain.

There was a glimmer of light outside, and he got up and crept quietly out of the house. Towards the west the stars were so bright that the whole expanse of the sky seemed to be twinkling. Then he turned to face the other way where the darkness seemed less dense. He stood there, inhaling the cool air of dawn, when suddenly the eastern sky became infused with streaks of red and orange. An early bird began to sing as Anton walked out of the compound towards the dunes, and by the time he reached the palm trees a chorus of birds was greeting the new day and doves were cooing overhead among the leaves. He sat down against the rugged stem of a tall palm tree and stared out over the oasis from where the smoke of many small fires was rising.

Anton felt elated. What a beautiful morning, he thought. And what a beautiful day! This is the day we're going to be reunited. Only a few hours separate us now. Just a few more hours, Gael, and I will hold you in my arms. And then I will never let you go . . .

26

When he returned to the dispensary he found more than fifty Africans waiting to be taken care of later in the day. My God, he thought, is this the kind of work Gael is doing? How can she cope with it?

'Oh, there you are!' exclaimed Marie who was sitting at the table, cutting up a steaming pancake while sipping a cup of tea. 'I wondered where you'd gone.'

'Just a stroll to stretch my legs,' Anton excused himself. Then he pointed at the waiting Africans: 'Do you have that many people every day?'

'It's not unusual, though we've had a bigger workload lately. There are large numbers of wounded who've escaped from Bobodiou. You wouldn't believe the horrible wounds bullets can make. Nasty business, war.'

'Does Gael have to take care of the sick and wounded, too?'

'Of course. She didn't like it much at the beginning, though. I could tell that she'd never done that sort of work, but she's not easily put off. You wouldn't think it, considering how delicate she looks . . . She's about my height and *I* can't be called tall by any stretch of the imagination.' Marie gave a deep chuckle. 'But she's a tough girl . . . a real treasure . . .' She looked at Anton and suddenly said: 'You don't know how lucky you are, young man.'

Anton blushed. 'I do know,' he replied softly. 'I wouldn't give her up for anything in the world.'

'Well . . .' Marie pondered for a while. 'Let's not exaggerate. She can be very stubborn if she puts her mind to it . . . Yes . . . she's a wilful young woman. But I see that it's no good telling you . . . Love is blind. And if you've crossed the Sahara to find her, you're surely not going to listen to anything like that.'

Marie took a sip from her cup and motioned Anton to follow her example. 'You'd better start your breakfast before it gets cold,' she said as if reproaching him. 'You didn't have your supper last night. If you continue like that, you'll find yourself too weak to stand up to Gael.' And she laughed heartily at her own wittiness.

They ate for a while in silence, listening to the quiet chatter of the Africans outside the compound. This is how Gael spent her mornings during all those months of separation, thought Anton. Sitting at this table with Marie. Drinking from the very cup I am putting to my lips. This is her world now. And then he became infused with a sudden awareness: I would gladly spend the rest of my life with Gael here if she wanted me to.

'You know . . .' Anton spoke hesitantly. 'I think I like Africa. It's so different from anything I've ever seen before.' He looked shyly at Marie. 'What . . . how does Gael feel about this?'

'I would say that she loves Africa . . . but I mustn't speak for her. She's quite capable of expressing her own opinions. I think you ought to ask Gael all this.'

'That's what I'm going to do,' said Anton, getting up. 'Would you please tell me how to get to that oasis up north where she's staying?'

27

Gael had been inoculating babies almost since dawn, and by mid-morning she needed a break. She yearned for some solitude, wanted to be away from it all, from the whining children and the incessant babble of the excited mothers. And more than anything else, she wanted to be alone to think of Anton.

Bamboko, her driver and medical help, was not pleased when she told him she was going to eat her sandwiches in the dunes. He had been very worried about Gael lately. He took great pride in his work and felt it was a let-down that Missie no longer appeared interested. She had become absent-minded and looked very unhappy since her return from Bobodiou. Her wound seemed to be healing quickly, but maybe that was just an appearance? Maybe she'd been hit by a bullet charged with malevolent power? Maybe it had damaged much more than her shoulder?

Bamboko felt personally responsible for her well-being and wanted to help her, but he just didn't know how to set about it. He had finally consulted his mother who'd given him some herbs which, she claimed, had magic powers. He was to mix them with the food Missie ate, or put them in her tea, and her condition would improve at once, but so far Bamboko had not been able to slip into the kitchen to try out his mother's remedy.

And now Missie wanted to go alone into the dunes! It was well known that malevolent spirits were haunting such places. If she ran into a bad jinni, he would bewitch her and her condition would surely get worse. How could he tell her? Reluctantly, he let her go and his worried eyes followed her until she disappeared among the dunes.

After some plodding through the loose sand Gael reached the top of a high dune, panting with the effort. She still felt quite weak, although she was unwilling to admit it. She sat down on the crest and began to eat her sandwiches, staring around with disinterested eyes. The track that led to Kanibasso passed below the dune and from there on ran southwards to lose itself in the heat haze. From her high vantage point she gazed out over the endless emptiness of the desert, which extended far beyond the horizon. Was Anton somewhere out there? What had happened to him? A hundred times in the last days, these questions had tortured her. Every sinew of her body longed for him and her soul cried out for him. If Anton disappeared, she would have no reason to live on.

Today the Earth itself appeared to have joined in her mourning. The sky, which at this time of the year was invariably blue and clear, had turned a dirty grey. A thick, colourless blanket seemed to have slid over the land, weighing down upon all that lived and oppressing the mind. The wind was playing in the loose sand, lifting up the thin top layer, and grains of fine dust were streaming off the ridge of the dune. Otherwise, nothing moved; there was nothing but desolation.

'Please, please,' she suddenly burst out, 'wherever you are, return to me. I need you! Come back or I shall die!' But the desert around her remained as empty as ever. No one answered her cry and she sat there, forlorn, lost amid the vast expanse that stretched below her feet.

I must do something, she thought, or I'll go mad. I must find Anton. I won't return to Kanibasso. I'll tell Bamboko to drive me straight to Bobodiou when the inoculation is over, whatever Marie says. That's what I'm going to do.

She felt relieved that she'd finally made up her mind and was about to return to the field hospital when all of a sudden a ray of sunshine pierced the cloud cover. As her eyes followed the shaft of light, she saw that it illuminated an object a few miles away, coming straight towards her: a car! Little by little, while Gael stared at it, strangely fascinated, it came closer, leaving a trail of dust behind.

She held her breath, unable to avert her gaze while the car drew nearer. She could now make out that it was a Land-Rover, carrying jerrycans and equipment on a roof-rack as if it had come from very far.

Gael's heart began to race madly. Anton, she implored. Please let it be Anton. And she suddenly jumped up as if urged by an uncontrollable impulse, and began to wave her healthy arm wildly.

The driver seemed to have seen her. He swerved away from the track and went straight for the foot of the dune . . . the Land-Rover came to a halt in a cloud of dust . . . the door was flung open . . . Anton!

A cry escaped from Gael's lips and she started to skid down the dune while Anton rushed up towards her calling out: 'Gael!'

Her feet ran like lightning, and Anton had only managed to climb the first few yards when she leapt into his arms and they tumbled down the dune, laughing and crying, clinging to each other as if they would never let go.

Part Seven

1

By the time the week of fighting was over in Bobodiou, Smally was a different person. A man of regular habits and order, he had been forced to share a small, dark, stinking prison cell with several huge Africans. He, the born administrator who had always taken the boss–subordinate relationship for granted – with him in the position of boss, naturally – had been catapulted into a primeval world of brutal physical power relationships. He was barefoot and dressed in a striped prison outfit two sizes too large, but even so he had still tried to impress his importance upon his fellow inmates until one of the enormous Africans had shouted, 'Shut up you wimp!' and slapped him full in the face with his ham of a hand, sending him reeling into a corner where he lay for a while, dazed.

After that, no more Napoleon for him! He realised that, if he wanted to survive, he would have to make himself subservient and crawl in the dust. And soon he did crawl.

The little food that was brought in was systematically grabbed by the strongest men. After two days Smally was so hungry that he went down on his knees begging for a few crumbs. Then the shooting started, and the bombing, and he had retreated into a corner of his jail, cowering, fearful he would die. This was a totally new experience for him. Nothing in his life had prepared him for it. As he sat there, shaking every time he heard an explosion, he would have given anything to be back in a secure environment where law and order reigned. Even life with his wife now seemed paradise in comparison. He had reached the point where he no longer cared for anything, not even for his career. If only he could survive this ordeal and be back in Belgium, have a stable job – any nine to five job would do – a room just for himself, and enough to eat.

2

Back in Belgium the 'Smally Affair' had developed into a full-blown national scandal. The weather hadn't improved, but the newspaper circulation had picked up significantly and the public had woken from its wintry lethargy, eagerly discussing the latest developments on trains and buses, in offices and at home. Then, an unexpected twist in the tale had them all sitting up, their eyes bright with excitement. In its morning edition one of the tabloids carried the title:

LATEST REVELATION IN SMALLY AFFAIR: he's a sex-devil!

The story ran as follows:

> Yesterday one of our reporters managed to interview Pauline D., the infamous secretary who set the balls rolling, or, rather, the bells ringing. He questioned her about her role in the unsavoury affair as she arrived at Brussels airport en route to Milan where, according to her own statement, she was going to join her husband, the opera singer Raymond d'Elbreux who is giving a performance at the Scala after his great success in the Met in New York.
>
> She vehemently protested, claiming she was an innocent victim. It had all started soon after Smally became director of the Belgian Geological Institute. He had called her into his office, locked the door and raped her there and then. She had tried to resist but he was not a man you could oppose. 'Once lust had taken possession of him, his forces increased tenfold,' she said, 'and he became an enraged beast – a devil.'
>
> – *Why didn't you report him after that?*
>
> 'He warned me not to, saying that nobody would believe the wild accusations of a mere subordinate. He threatened to fire me on the spot if I revealed anything and added that he would make sure I would never find a job again. I innocently believed that my misfortune would end there, but that was not the end of the nightmare. It was the beginning! Time and again he called me in and abused me. I lived in constant fear but what was I to do?'

– *Some members of the institute's staff nevertheless claim that you were the one who started the affair.*

'I categorically deny this. And please, don't call this an affair! He wasn't interested in a normal relationship where the woman consented. What gave him a kick was to possess women against their will. He was completely warped.'

– *Did he abuse other female members of the staff?*

'I wouldn't be surprised, but if so, they're unlikely to divulge what happened to them. Anyway, I'm sure I was the chosen victim. He made me his secretary so that he would have me near him all the time. I was desperate but I was so ashamed of what my family would think of me if this leaked out that there was only one option: keep it secret and try not to think.'

– *Did he have a great sexual appetite?*

'He raped me three, sometimes four times a day. He forced me to do things I shudder to admit.'

– *How could you accept this?*

'I was scared stiff. He was dangerous and lost all self-control when opposed. And he was a man of great power. When he stared at me with those hypnotic eyes, I became putty in his hands. It was as if he'd drugged me; I just obeyed him blindly. In the end I lost all my will-power. I became his plaything, his slave.'

– *Why did you accompany him to Africa?*

'He couldn't get through the day without having sex several times. He forced me to go with him because he wasn't certain he'd be able to find enough local women to satisfy his lust.'

As Pauline D. left for Milan where she will attempt to reconcile herself with her husband, we wish her good luck.

It is clear we haven't yet come to the bottom of this stinking cesspit, but we promise our readership that we will keep digging.

3

The next day the same tabloid managed to interview Smally's wife:

> Pressed into saying what she thought of the secretary's story she declared frankly: 'I'm not in the least surprised. Yes, he was obsessed. He had only one thing on his mind in his free time: sex. But I wasn't one to be under him,' she stated haughtily. 'At home I was the boss.'
> Asked how she felt now that the news was out, she admitted: 'I'm ashamed that my daughter should have such a father.' And she added that she was going to file for a divorce and demand financial compensation.

Two days later another tabloid, *The Daily Chitchat*, carried an article on its front page:

SMALLY SCANDAL: Exclusive interview with Pauline D.'s solicitor.

> Back from Milan, Pauline D., the victim of Smally's sexual abuses, was spotted coming out of a solicitor's office in Brussels. She refused to comment but her lawyer was more willing. He said that he was going to claim huge damages for all the agony and fear his client had suffered. He also stated that he would be asking for a life sentence if Smally returned to Belgium. 'That sex maniac is not to be trusted with women,' the lawyer said. 'Men like him shouldn't be allowed to roam the streets freely and stalk innocent victims.'
> Asked about Smally's whereabouts, the lawyer surmised that he was probably still in Africa, biding his time. 'And I'm of the opinion,' he added with a stern face, 'that the local population ought to be warned of the danger. It would be best for husbands over there to keep their women inside their homes in order not to stir up the man's uncontrollable sexual instincts. No woman will be safe until that beast is locked up behind bars.'

4

Back in Bobodiou, the presidential guards, the special security brigades, the police and armed forces were all exhausted at the end of the week's fighting, and the rebels took the town without firing a single shot as Amadou had predicted. Some of Gwemboka's henchmen had managed to escape, but Minister Mamboulou and General Babadoulé were caught, and together with a number of high-ranking officials, had been pensioned off. Most of those in the lower ranks, however, were due to be reintegrated in the new administration.

Restoring the town even to its previous miserable state was a far more daunting task. The presidential palace was in such an appalling state that a complete overhaul was needed before it could be occupied by the new President and his staff. It was also whispered that it was so stuffed with objects charged with malignant witchcraft which the tyrant had hidden in every nook and cranny, that it had to be thoroughly cleansed, just in case. In the meantime Amadou set up office in one of the ministerial buildings that had survived more or less intact.

He was about to start his first day in office when he heard shouting in the corridor: a man from the Solar Bear Company was demanding to see the President immediately. Amadou already had a full schedule, but the man from the mining company insisted, claiming that his impromptu visit was of the highest importance, and he was finally given priority over all other appointments and ushered in.

'Congratulations,' he said with a thick Russian accent. 'We are very pleased you are new president. We have done much to get you here, remember?' And he gave Amadou a wink loaded with significance. Then, without further ado, he came to the point of his visit. 'Now you pay back, *da*.'

'Pay back?'

'Not in money,' the Russian hastened to clarify. 'We don't want money.'

'What do you want then?' Amadou seemed baffled and not too pleased.

'We want exclusive rights to mining of rich platinum deposits up north.' And almost as an afterthought, the Russian added: 'And five-year tax break.'

When he saw the President's face contract, he added: 'That is minimum we expect for help we provided to make you President. We supplied arms, remember?'

Amadou was shocked to the core. This was not what he'd envisioned when he had started the rebellion. He had always thought that removing Gwemboka would constitute a clean break with the past but now, on his very first day in office, the past was presenting itself already, making claims for the continuation of old practices.

'I shall have to think about this,' he replied in an offhand tone.

'But this is minimum we expect,' insisted the Russian. And he repeated 'Minimum,' as if this lent greater weight to his words.

Amadou controlled himself with great difficulty. 'I will soon call a meeting with all the mining companies,' he said sternly. 'You'll hear from me in due time. Goodbye.'

'But . . . but . . .'

'Can you please show the gentleman out,' said the President to the guards who stood in attendance. They caught the Russian by his elbows, pushed the loudly protesting man into the corridor and escorted him out of the building without further ado.

5

For two weeks now Boris and Igor had been languishing in a prison cell and it had been no fun. The prison warders had found a devilish pleasure in insulting them and sometimes kicking them with their heavy boots. But at least there was fetid water to drink and they had been given some maize and a few crusts of stale bread. The second week, however, had been particularly unpleasant. One morning the warders vanished. For a day the Russians enjoyed the peace but then they heard intermittent, muffled sounds of shooting in town and, later, the vibrations of explosions as if bombs were being dropped. They realised that something very serious was going on, and also that they had been abandoned to their fate.

It was dark, damp and stiflingly hot in their underground cell. There wasn't a breath of air and at times the two men thought they were going to suffocate.

'I wish I were in Siberia,' sighed Boris. 'Think of the wide open spaces, the cool air . . . Life is so much healthier in Siberia . . .'

'What's our embassy doing?' wondered Igor. 'Why don't they come and rescue us? We're going to rot here.'

At night there was the scuffling of rats and once or twice, when they had dozed off, they woke with a sharp pain when a hungry rat suddenly bit a finger or a toe trying to eat it. Soon the men fell into a deep depression, certain that they'd been forgotten and were going to die here, and end up being devoured by the rats.

Then, one morning, they heard voices in the corridor. They were extremely weak by now but with a superhuman effort they managed to thump on the locked door of their cell and finally attracted attention. Before long came the sound of a heavy hammer banging against the door, the lock gave way and a few surprised Africans peered in.

The two Russians were taken above ground, given water and food, and allowed to wash. The next morning they were shoved into a car and a guard drove them into town.

'As sure as not, we're going to be executed,' whispered Boris, trembling with fear.

6

They were taken to some kind of official building and told to wait.

'This must be the local KGB building,' surmised Boris.

'*Da*,' nodded Igor. 'This is very bad.'

After some time they were led into an office where a lean African was sitting behind a desk, facing them. As the two Russians stood there, not knowing where to look, shuffling their bare feet, they heard the man address them: 'I hear that the henchmen of the previous government abandoned you in prison. This is just one more example of what the tyrant did to those he considered his enemies, and I apologise for the way you have been treated. You are free to return home and I hope that you will tell your people that we intend to be fair and open-minded and repair the damage done to the good name of this country by the unjustifiable actions of the tyrant.' The African made a sign to one of the guards, while saying: 'You can go now.'

The two men had listened to the speech with mounting surprise, and then relief. Boris was all too glad to be able to return home, but Igor thought of Viktor Ippolitovich and hesitated. Somehow, he felt that their boss wasn't going to be pleased to have them back. In his mind's eye he also saw the interminable winter which had already started in Moscow, and he didn't like what he saw. So he stared at his bare feet, looking very embarrassed and ventured hesitantly: 'Couldn't we stay here, please?'

The African looked at the dishevelled man, visibly annoyed. He had agreed to receive these foreigners to create international goodwill and thought they would have been happy to go home.

'I don't see what useful work you would be able to do in this country,' he said bluntly.

'Oh, but we can do useful things,' replied Igor. He drew himself up. 'In fact, we do nothing but that. You see . . .' he lowered his voice to a confidential level, 'we came here with important mission . . .' Suddenly he hesitated. Should he reveal everything? But then he thought that this man ought to know how important they were, and he blurted out: 'We brought over lots of weapons and ammunition! For rebels, you see! And dollars, too.' He looked around rather proudly while Boris tried to make himself as inconspicuous as possible, thinking: The ass! The brainless *mujik*!

'So it was you!' exclaimed the African, getting up abruptly. Boris recoiled when he saw the man come over to them. This is the end, he thought. This man knows now and will have us executed.

Then, to his surprise, the African opened his arms and embraced first Igor and then him. 'This is a great relief,' he blurted out. 'I was told that the arms were smuggled into the country by a Russian mining company.'

'No, no. *We* brought them in.' Igor nodded importantly. 'Nothing to do with mining company. It was only concurrence of circumstances that mining equipment came at same time.'

'Now I understand why the tyrant had you thrown into prison. He would surely have killed you had he lived. So it was you who saved us!' Amadou spoke warmly. 'You risked your lives for the revolution. You are heroes! Ask for anything and it shall be given to you.'

The two men stood there, gaping. Then Boris, who was the cleverer of the two, spoke. 'If you permit . . . we don't know how to address you . . .'

'I'm the new President, but for the friends of the revolution I am Amadou Sékouré.'

'Well, with your permission Amadou Sékouréovich, we like what you propose . . . yes, we like it very much. But we are tired and hungry and this needs serious reflection . . . Would you permit us to stay for one week while we think about your generous proposition?'

'No need to ask,' replied Amadou as he walked out of his office between the two men, an arm around each shoulder. 'You need peace and restoration. Go and spend a week in the Riverside Hotel, courtesy of the government, and come to see me afterwards to tell me what you have decided.'

7

'I have called you, directors and representatives of the different mining companies operating in my country, to discuss how we are going to build a future together.'

Before Amadou had time to carry on, the representative of the Solar Bear Company jumped up. 'I want to know where this government stands with respect to exclusive exploitation rights I talked about,' he said loudly.

This set off a volley of murmurs and comments.

'What is this about exclusive mining rights?'

'This is outrageous!'

'Who's that man? Is he a Russian?'

'We will not accept deals done behind our backs! Business should be conducted out in the open. We all have equal rights. We all pay our royalties.'

The President now stood up: 'Quiet, gentlemen, quiet!' he urged. 'There are no exclusive mining rights.'

'What!' shouted the Russian. 'But we expect special treatment!'

'Whether you expect it or not, you will not get it!' retorted Amadou.

The Russian looked really vexed. 'I'm not going to accept this!' he yelled. 'You will hear from us!' And he left in a huff.

A Chinese now stood up. 'But we have been promised exclusive rights to a particular mining area,' he protested. 'And we're going to stick to the agreement! We paid for it!'

'Gentlemen,' called out Amadou, 'I have not asked you to come here to squabble over past arrangements. The promises you are talking about were made by the tyrant. He is dead and whatever he arranged died with him. Those agreements are null and void.'

'Mr President,' said a ponderous voice, 'you cannot go back on previous contracts! It's simply not done.'

'Gentlemen, please, hear me out first. I have called you here today to discuss plans for a new long-term future. We want to start on a fresh basis and I am asking for your collaboration. Let me explain. As you all know, this country is dirt poor because the previous government was corrupt through and through. Any money that came in was squandered by the ruling cliques. We will now need a sustained effort for many years to lift our people out of abject poverty, but we haven't got any money – the government's coffers are empty. And we cannot even tax our people – they have nothing.'

'Maybe he wants to tax us instead?' a man from one of the mining companies could be heard saying.

Amadou continued unperturbed. 'How can we begin anything when there's no start-up capital? We need revenue to build up this country, but the only riches we have lie in our soil. I therefore want to ask you for your understanding. All we need is a bit more justice . . .'

A thickset man suddenly stood up, red in the face. 'With all my respect, Mr President,' he said, 'let me remind you that our shareholders have put up the money we're spending in this country and that we are beholden to them. Are you proposing to rob them? Is that what you call justice?'

A great uproar now ensued. 'Maybe he intends worse!' exclaimed someone. 'He wants to nationalise! Maybe that's what he calls justice?'

'Nationalise!' snorted an American. 'But communism is dead and buried! There's only capitalism now!'

'Yeah!' said someone else. 'And capitalism says that what's good for the shareholders is good for the economy. And therefore it's good for the world.'

Amadou held up a hand. 'Gentlemen, gentlemen, rest assured that we do not intend to nationalise. Africa needs all the help it can get. We need foreign expertise. We couldn't do without your assistance.'

'Hear, hear!' came a voice from the audience.

'We don't want to rob foreign companies. But, equally, we don't want them to rob us. We want a fair deal. Our people need money more than your shareholders. Our needs are so much greater, so much more urgent. You are rich, and still you want more. You call that justice? We are poor and want a better deal and you would begrudge us that?'

'How do you suggest we explain that to our shareholders?' asked someone.

'There is absolutely no need for your shareholders to suck the last little penny out of poor people. It's simply immoral. Tell them to lavish a bit less on themselves; to reduce their wasteful lifestyles. They will not even notice the difference. But the people over here will.'

'Mr President, if you don't want to play ball, we'll go somewhere else!' said one of the managers, pretending to get up.

'Gentlemen, you are free to go. If you don't like our conditions, we shall turn to other companies willing to go along with us. You can no longer dictate your terms. The world is changing.'

'You won't be able to do anything without us,' warned the representative of one of the mining companies. 'Without mining there will be no development. Without us you will remain poor forever.'

'As far as I can see,' replied Amadou calmly, 'mining by itself has never brought real development to this country. It will only bring development if the revenue is shared and invested in projects that lay the base for long-term growth. I know, and you know, that we have been robbed for decades. By you, the mining companies, and by the tyrant. You were hand in glove. You got out all the commodities and paid off the ruling cliques while our people starved. We can't let this continue. We must do something about the appalling conditions over here. But we won't be able to if all our wealth is carried off and the people over here are left with nothing but a few crumbs.'

'So we're the ones to blame, is that it?' said a voice rather sharply.

'Not at all! African governments have created a terrible mess since independence. They have systematically shielded violent or corrupt regimes in the name of African solidarity and continue to do so. It's high time that we made a clean breast of it; that we, Africans, recognised our mistakes and admitted our guilt. But you, too, bear a heavy responsibility. You have been willing to shut your eyes and collaborate with the most brutal dictators, as long as you could get the oil and minerals out. And even if a few European nations now claim to be guided by moral considerations and refuse to collaborate with tyrants, unscrupulous nations are just waiting to take their place and buy out ruling cliques by pouring money into their pockets.'

'We're paying the correct price!' protested a Chinese representative. 'And we provide aid and give cheap loans in exchange for natural resources. We contribute generously to your development.'

'Don't call this development,' retorted Amadou. 'What you're doing is the same short-term economic exploitation we've had since the beginning of colonial times. Africa has just been a provider of the commodities manufacturers on other continents demand as input for their economies. Do you want this to continue for another half-century? Until the disaster is obvious to everyone? Until chaos reigns, precluding any economic activity, even mining? No, we need a new approach to development right now.'

'Mr President,' objected someone in the audience, 'what's your development got to do with us? It doesn't affect us. It's your problem.'

'That's what you think,' retorted Amadou, 'but you're sorely mistaken. If you carry on as usual, the African revenge will be terrible. Already today Africans are willing to cross the Sahara on foot in order to escape. That's nothing compared to what you're going to see in the future. By the time our wealth is exhausted there will be so many Africans that the continent will be bursting at the seams. The world's rich nations will try to keep the Africans inside their continent by blocking all the exits, treat the continent as if it were a concentration camp and surround it with barriers. But they won't be able to keep them inside!'

He drew a deep breath while looking at the assembled heads. 'No,' he said, 'they'll break out and flood Europe . . . and Asia . . . and America. That will be the price the world will have to pay for today's short-sighted exploitive attitude. The Africans will flee, just as rats flee a sinking ship. And Africa will be sinking by then. It will be a huge shantytown, a wasteland. No trees will remain, no wild animals, nothing of the unspoiled beauty people come to Africa for. Nothing will remain but small plots of eroded soil worked to exhaustion, and these plots will no longer be able to feed the people trying to subsist on them. There will be wars and untold atrocities in such overcrowded conditions. There will be genocide and millions upon millions of refugees . . . homeless people who will be wandering about aimlessly, trying to get out.

'It will be the worst epoch the world has ever known. Africans will be moving out in their tens of millions. And they will not integrate into the societies where they happen to end up, because there will be no jobs for them; because they will be as uneducated as ever and be unable to function properly in the high-tech societies of the late twenty-first century. They'll be poor outcasts, rejected by the rich around them, and they will react by taking from those rich. They will be treated as criminals, but they'll keep coming all the same, year after year, flooding foreign countries. Is that what you want?'

'This is too depressing!' exclaimed one of the mining representatives. 'I don't want to know about it.'

'But surely, market mechanisms will solve that problem in good time?' objected another participant.

'I don't think capitalism will be able to solve this conundrum,' countered the President. 'We've had a century of it already and look at the results! Where there's been progress, it has been so slow that Africa will still be nowhere in another century. We're stuck in a deep hole and will be unable to work ourselves out of it if we count on market forces alone.'

'Are you suggesting that socialism is the answer then? Or maybe more aid?'

'We've had too much socialism already, and too much well-meant aid. If the rich world keeps giving, Africa will never develop and the population will just continue to grow. No, that's unsustainable.'

'What system are you referring to then?' asked someone.

'If I knew the answer, I can assure you that I wouldn't be asking you to help me find it. But I do know that we need something that goes much further than economic growth driven by a desire for material enrichment. We need to devise a system based on African values, or at least incorporating concepts Africans can live with; a new vision for a sustainable future.'

Amadou looked around at the assembled body of men. All eyes were fixed on him now. He was young and seemed unimposing, but his words had made an indelible impression.

'When I look at Africa,' he concluded, 'I should despair. But I don't. I believe in the future. I believe in a new world. We must collaborate. We must try out things that have never been practiced before. And we shall find a solution.'

The assembly room was very quiet as Amadou spoke his last words. 'You can no longer pretend that Africa is not your responsibility. All countries on Earth are interconnected. We are all in the same boat now. Our future is also yours. And it is extremely urgent to change the way we are doing things if we are to leave a world behind us that will still be worth living in.'

8

A well-known Russian newspaper whose name would seem to indicate that it was speaking the truth but which, according to some, should more correctly be called *The Daily Pack of Lies*, published the following article in the editorial column of its morning edition:

LATEST DEVELOPMENTS IN BOBODIOU

Yesterday the new rebel government informed our embassy that it would not honour the promises made to the Solar Bear

Company, a mining company active in promoting development in the country. The new President is reported to have claimed that any contracts previously agreed were null and void. Needless to say, we oppose such shocking behaviour. Governments should respect all international agreements, and the rights of foreign companies and their agents. How can international relations function without the rule of law, that's what we'd like to know?

We are now free to tell our readers that, despite what its name might lead them to believe, the Solar Bear Company is a Russian company. Before starting operations in Africa a slight but clever alteration was made. By changing one letter in its original name, the company was able to hide its origin and thereby avoid the hostile attitude Russian activities have to put up with abroad.

We also want to inform our readers that, although the Russian government owns some of its shares, the Solar Bear Company is a private company and, like all Russian companies, it strictly respects the rights of its shareholders and the international engagements it has subscribed to.

In the same way we expect international contracts to be honoured by all countries, irrespective of a change of government. How, we ask, can companies operate abroad if governments don't abide by internationally agreed rules? We are especially pained by the revisionist attitude of the new rulers. We want to stress that the rebels who form the new government managed to get where they are solely due to the enlightened policies and staunch aid of the Solar Bear Company. Indeed, we are now at liberty to inform our readers that the weapons that allowed the rebels to overthrow the previous government were smuggled into the country cleverly concealed between mining materials destined for the Solar Bear Company.

The rebels should consequently be extremely grateful and give favourable treatment to this company. It is therefore all the more grating that the new government seems to have singled out this particular Russian company for punitive treatment. This is yet another example of the hostility towards Russia, which is fostered by Western nations that claim to be our friends but in reality do their utmost to criticise us and sabotage our foreign interests.

We cannot tolerate the irresponsible attitude of the new

leaders in Bobodiou. There is no other alternative but to put pressure on the rebel government, and we have the means to do so. We shall keep our readership informed about any further development in this most outrageous case.

9

Boris and Igor had been on government-sponsored holidays before. Twice they had spent a week with their wives in a small studio in a huge apartment block on the outskirts of St Petersburg, and last summer they had even been to the Black Sea, but never in all their lives had they seen anything like this: the luxury, the food and drinks, the tropical nights and . . . they hesitated to admit it . . . the ladies. Pretty young women with swaying hips, shiny eyes and a mischievous expression on their brown faces. And the things they did!

Within a week the two men had added more words to their French vocabulary than in the last five or ten years in the secret service in Russia. Not that they would really be able to use most of those new words in the secret service or even in public, but still . . . they had lived the dream of a lifetime. How could they bear to return to the Russian winter after this? To grey days in grey offices? To borscht and cheap vodka?

In one of the rare moments when they managed to surface from the sea of blurring drinks, hot sun and women, they had gone to the Russian Embassy. They wanted to find out what exactly had happened to those four crates they had brought from Moscow in case the President wanted more details. They found the embassy buzzing with the latest developments in the relationship between the new rebel government and Russia; no one seemed to be interested in their story. Finally they learned from one of the employees that the crates had not contained weapons, and that Viktor Ippolitovich had set up a trap for them. When they realised what had happened they were shocked to the core. They had served their government loyally for more than twenty years, only to be betrayed by their boss – to be delivered into the hands of a tyrant to be killed! But they had survived, and in the few days that remained before they were to see the President, they'd begun to think hard. If they were to get their own back, they would have to take personal initiatives; they weren't used to that, but they were determined. Twice they went back to their embassy for specific information, and gradually a clever plan began to materialise out of the alcoholic vapours that so far had dimmed the proper functioning of their brains.

No one would have recognised these two men as they strode into the presidential palace after their week in the Riverside Hotel. There was a bounce in their step, a self-assurance that had never been there before. And as they stood in front of the President, Boris spoke, his voice firm this time.

'Amadou Sékouréovich,' he said, 'we have given your generous proposal serious reflection it deserved and we have come to conclusion. We can be very useful to you and your government. We have heard about your new ideas for future and fully agree. We believe that government should be there for people, to serve people. And we want to help. With your permission, we think we can be useful in contacts between your government and Russia. We understand that there is point of friction – large debt towards Russia . . .'

'Yes!' interrupted Amadou. 'That's something I don't understand. The Russian Embassy just notified us that we owe them half a billion dollars. Half a billion! I've never heard anything more outrageous! Do you know what this is all about?'

'Amadou Sékouréovich.' Boris spoke with all the gravity he could muster. 'We have made enquiries about this and are in position to tell you that origin of this debt goes back long time. Debt was in fact contracted twenty-five years ago.'

'But that's when Gwemboka engineered his coup d'état! How can Russia have lent him half a billion dollars at that time?'

'With your permission, Amadou Sékouréovich,' said Boris, 'Soviet Union, as it was called at time, didn't lend him half billion dollars. We have found out that disputed sum at time was ten million dollars.'

'What! Why do they want half a billion then?'

'Cumulative interests over twenty-five years, Amadou Sékouréovich.'

'But that's scandalous! They must be applying at least 10-per-cent interest rates. That's usury!'

'More than 15 per cent, Amadou Sékouréovich. We were given to understand that those rates were usual for untrustworthy borrowers in those days.'

Amadou seemed extremely upset. 'And what did Gwemboka need those ten million dollars for?'

'Amadou Sékouréovich, it appears that Gwemboka didn't ask for any money. The Soviet Union gave it as part of aid package. It was intended to advance cause of communism. But when Gwemboka refused to accept Soviet base in his country, Soviet Union claimed money back. And apparently tyrant was unable to return money, saying he had already spent it.'

'But this whole story is ludicrous!'

'We fully agree, Amadou Sékouréovich, and we propose that debt should be cancelled. We are ready to offer all our experience in matter. We know person responsible for Africa in Moscow who concocted all this twenty-five years ago.' Boris spoke firmly, while Igor nodded vigorously. 'And if you would allow us to invite him, we are certain we can make him see reason once he is here.' The two men looked expectantly at Amadou.

'By all means!' affirmed the President. 'That sounds good. I give you carte blanche. Invite that man, or whoever you think necessary.'

When the two men left the presidential palace and stepped into the gleaming Mercedes that was waiting to drive them back to their hotel, they rubbed their hands in satisfaction. They, or rather the government, would invite Viktor Ippolitovich to come to Bobodiou, and once he was here . . .

10

Meanwhile the Smally Affair kept capturing the public's attention in Belgium. When the staff of the Belgian Geological Institute tried to enter the inconspicuous building where they were attempting to carry on their work in spite of everything, they invariably had to push their way through a throng of reporters who kept sticking microphones in their faces. Some members of the institute were getting so fed up that they wanted to take their Christmas leave well before time, just to be away from it all. The problem was that Smally, who was still the official director, had disappeared and Pauline, the secretary, had resigned, so the staff didn't know whom to apply to for a holiday. And Stephen, whom Smally had appointed as unofficial vice-director during his absence, had no real authority. Everyone just ignored him.

The only one who was not averse to being interviewed was Emile. From early morning on he stood outside the entrance, giving his opinion. He had already appeared several times on local TV channels and was well on the way to becoming a mini-celebrity in the town where he lived.

As the days went by, the stories he told became ever more dramatic. Yes, he had foreseen it all the day Smally walked into his kitchen and began to monitor the amount of coffee he used for the ten o'clock break. Yes, Smally had been spying on everyone. Yes, he was a mini-dictator who didn't tolerate any opposition; he just laid down rule after rule, as if these were military barracks and he the commander-in-chief. No, he didn't have any real scientific qualifications, and the scientists weren't pleased; how could you expect them to be so? Several of the best had already left to work elsewhere.

While the newspapers were chewing over this information, there was a bombshell. After being pressed for several days, the infamous secretary had consented to another interview. The tabloid which managed to secure an interview with her – in exchange for a fair amount of money, it was whispered – now carried this sensational title on its front page:

SMALLY, THE TRUE STORY:
a reincarnation of Napoleon!

Exclusive interview with Pauline D.

When asked whether it was true that Smally had dictatorial tendencies, Pauline D., the woman who had the unfortunate privilege of having been the sex maniac's secretary, admitted hesitantly that this had been the case.

'While he had me in his power in Brussels I was too scared and distressed to take such things in,' she declared. 'It was fortunate that I didn't have to share my free time with him. Being in his hands during working hours was already more than I could cope with. It was only when he forced me to go to Africa and I had to spend twenty-four hours a day with him that I discovered even scarier aspects of his personality.'

– *What did you discover then?*

'He had a small statue of Napoleon in his luggage, which he put on his bedside table. When I asked him about it, he said it wasn't Napoleon but him. I didn't grasp what he meant until a day or two later, when I unexpectedly entered the hotel suite and found him standing in front of the mirror, fully dressed, looking at himself. He stood there, one hand on his chest, his fingers stuck between the buttons of his jacket, and on his head was a hat he had flattened out sideways.'

– *What impression did that make on you?*

'It was then that I understood the full extent of his megalomania. I realised that he saw himself as a reincarnation of Napoleon. I was extremely frightened after that because I knew he was a dangerous madman and I had to be very careful. Had I opposed him in any way, my life would have been in great danger.'

When our reporter asked her whether she believed him to be a killer, she suddenly fell silent and refused to make any further comment. It is clear to us that there is another very painful episode which the unfortunate Pauline D. is not yet ready to reveal for reasons of her own. However, we will leave no stone unturned in our search for the truth, and will keep our readership informed about any new development in this most scandalous affair of the last few years.

11

The well-known Russian newspaper which, according to some, deserved to be called *The Daily Pack of Lies*, published the following short press communiqué:

> New developments in the conflict between
> Bobodiou and Moscow

> The untrustworthy rebel force which now rules in Bobodiou has so far made a hash of governing the country. It has shown total disdain for any past agreement and, in particular, appears to be set on bullying a Russian mining company when it is in no position to do so. The fact is that the local government still has outstanding debts with Russia to the amount of half a

billion dollars, no less. This gives us the leverage we need to put pressure on the rebels, and our embassy has notified the new President of our intention to reclaim this debt. He seems to have understood the weakness of his position and has asked for a special Russian envoy to be sent to Africa.

A last-minute release from our Ministry of Foreign Affairs informs us that Viktor Ippolitovich Boronov, our great Africa specialist, is ready to fly to Bobodiou tomorrow to sort out the mess the new government has created. He will need all the courage he can muster to deal with the ungrateful people over there and to overcome the unforeseen obstacles that some, no doubt, will try to put in his way. It is brave of him to leave the safety of Russia for such an insecure country, but apparently a select reception committee will take care of him the moment he steps off the plane. We sincerely hope that he will get the special treatment he fully deserves.

12

In Belgium, meanwhile, the Smally Affair refused to die down. Dufour, the Minister of Education, was unwilling to admit guilt but his position was becoming increasingly precarious. Exchanges of accusations between the Opposition and Dufour's party became more acrimonious with every passing day. The government had already acceded to the demand not to honour the institute's credit card, but the Opposition and most of the nation's newspapers scented blood and now wanted Dufour's scalp.

Members of the Opposition kept pestering the government. They returned constantly to the Smally Affair, thereby disrupting the normal functioning of Parliament, and even with the Christmas holidays in view they didn't relent. 'This is the greatest corruption scandal of the last decade,' they claimed, 'caused by a minister who promoted an inept civil servant to a job far beyond his capacity. Dufour and his party promised to clean up public finances when they came to power. Is this how they intend to do it? By letting one of their party members waste taxpayers' money on scandalous expenses?'

'What is the Minister of Education waiting for?' they asked. 'Is he going to turn a blind eye to the list of abuses which is growing more numerous by the day? Will he keep shielding his protégé, even if he is a sex monster of the worst sort? An impostor and a megalomaniac who believes himself to be a reincarnation of Napoleon? The man should have been locked up in a mental institution years ago. When Dufour promoted that madman to the post of director of our prestigious Geological Institute three months ago, he personally vowed for the man's integrity and competence. And yet everyone in the institute declares that they never had a more incompetent director. Worse than that, Smally has made a mockery of the term "integrity". Maybe Dufour knew all about it? He and Smally were close friends for many years. If that's the kind of person Dufour is promoting, he shouldn't be Minister of Education! Why doesn't he admit his guilt and step down?'

Then, suddenly, a new twist in the Smally Affair electrified the nation. It appeared that Happy Bobo Cars, a car hire company based in Bobodiou, had charged the price of a new four-wheel-drive vehicle to the institute's credit card company. Within days, the full story became known as reporters began to dig into the unsavoury details of the affair.

The *Daily Gossip* reported:

> SMALLY: why a Bobodiou car hire company is requesting the complete refund of their biggest four-wheel-drive vehicle!
>
> Smally rented it for a day to drive to an animal park with his secretary and, needless to say, he once again paid with the institute's credit card. But then something mysterious happened: he never returned the vehicle. It was discovered days later lying on a dune seventy miles north of Bobodiou, a total wreck. Since Smally has inexplicably disappeared, the firm has filed claims against the Belgian Geological Institute's credit card company for a new vehicle. And so our government is being sued for full damages!

TV and radio commentators now urged Pauline D. to come forward, declaring that she had been in that vehicle with Smally and therefore knew what had happened. Finally the secretary agreed to speak, saying that she was going to reveal the whole truth, but what was not disclosed was the amount of money that had changed hands to make her talk.

The next day the tabloid which had managed to extract her confessions published the interview under the shocking title:

SMALLY: sex maniac, madman and killer!

Pauline D., the ex-secretary of the Belgian Geological Institute who was forced to accompany her boss on his trip to Africa so that he could satisfy his basest bestial instincts, told us that up till now she had been hesitant to reveal the worst. But when pressed to tell the truth about the abandoned four-wheel-drive vehicle, she finally gave in. 'Yes,' she admitted. 'Smally rented that car pretending he wanted to take me to an animal reserve, but instead of driving south to the reserve he drove north into the desert in spite of all my pleas to turn back.'

'The moment he was behind the wheel,' declared Pauline D., 'he seemed possessed. He said he was participating in the Paris–Dakar Rally and was in the lead. He was racing along at eighty miles per hour over a rough track when he spotted a tall dune. He screamed that driving up that dune was part of the rally and shot straight up it, but he'd only got halfway up the slope when the car toppled over and landed on its side. He fell on top of me and I was knocked out.

'When I regained consciousness he'd gone. He had abandoned me, leaving me for dead! And he had taken all the water bottles with him! I would have died of thirst had I not been rescued in the nick of time by a caravan, and carried back to Bobodiou tied on top of a camel.'

– *What do you think of him now, after your miraculous escape from death?*

'That he was not just a megalomaniac and a sexual monster. He was also a madman and a killer!' said Pauline D., prey to strong emotions. It is clear that talking about this most painful of episodes revived all the anguish she must have felt at the time.

'It was only after he'd left me for dead in that car in the desert that I was able to break the hold he had over me,' she said. 'I realised that, unless I got out of his claws, he would strike again. I still have nightmares about it and live in constant fear that he will return to abuse me and then kill me.'

After these revelations there was no stopping the Opposition. 'This is more than a clear case of non-assistance to a person in danger!' they yelled in Parliament. 'It's attempted murder! How can Dufour remain Minister after this? And how can his party remain in government when one of its members is a criminal of the worst sort and Dufour shields him?'

Dufour refused to step down, the Opposition introduced a motion of no confidence on the spot, Parliament voted, and the government fell.

13

A month or so later Lottie was sitting at a table in 'Les Menus du Roi', one of the more exclusive restaurants in Brussels, gazing around, trying to take it all in. Opposite her, Eddy, her husband, was smiling. 'I hope you're pleased with my choice.' He looked at her eagerly. 'What do you think of this place?'

'I'm impressed.' She put her hand on his and gave him her most bewitching smile. 'You've chosen the right place. This is really classy. The very top!'

'Well,' said Eddy, visibly enjoying the praise, 'I couldn't possibly have taken you to one of those rowdy café-bars we've been to before. Anything might happen there. But not here! This is just right for our anniversary.'

As Lottie surveyed the place with sparkling eyes, she saw a couple sitting at the bar some twenty feet away. The man was thickset with a heavy chin and seemed quite old but the woman, who had her back towards them, seemed much younger. 'Turn around slowly and have a look at those two people behind you,' whispered Lottie. 'He's old and ugly whereas she's quite young and nice. What a badly assorted couple they are. Some women just aren't lucky. But I am,' she said, looking at her husband with eyes full of admiration.

'Champagne!' her husband motioned to the waiter who was hovering near their table. When the waiter had gone the husband got up. 'I'm just going to wash my hands.' He smiled at Lottie. 'Make sure nothing happens to you while I'm gone.'

Lottie giggled. 'What could possibly happen to me here?'

'You look so pretty, anyone would want to run away with you. So don't you get into trouble! I won't be a minute.'

At the bar drinks had already been ordered, and after some vigorous shaking the barman poured the foamy liquid into two glasses, added slices of lemon and pushed the glasses along the counter. The woman picked them up, handed one to her companion and said with an alluring smile: 'Cheers.' As she did so she turned sideways and Lottie recognised her. 'But . . . but that's Pauline!' she exclaimed and started waving frantically, calling out 'Pauline!'

Pauline had already noticed Lottie when she walked in with her husband, but had turned away. Stupid fool, she thought, seeing Lottie calling her. I suppose there's nothing to do now but to go and say 'hello'.

She bent over towards her companion, saying: 'Excuse me a minute,' and advanced slowly to Lottie's table.

Lottie didn't seem to notice Pauline's reticence. 'How extraordinary to meet you here!' she burst out. Suddenly she lowered her voice. 'You know what we're doing here?' And without leaving Pauline time to guess, she supplied the answer: 'We're celebrating our fifth wedding anniversary!' She beamed. 'Yes, our fifth wedding anniversary, imagine that!' She began to nudge Pauline, not seeing the hostile stare in her eyes. 'And that's why my husband has taken me to this expensive place. I'm so happy.'

Just then the waiter came along with a bottle of champagne in an ice bucket. After the man had left, she blurted out: 'We're going to have champagne. Only the very best will do tonight.'

At last she realised that Pauline hadn't said anything. 'And how about you?' she asked. 'You must tell me what's happened to you. When you suddenly disappeared from the lab we were all very intrigued. Some of us were really worried, but after they heard that you'd sneaked off to Africa with Smally . . . well . . . then everything was clear to everybody, even to the dumbest chick in the lab. But I'd expected something of the sort all along.' She giggled. 'I know the tricks you've got up your sleeve!' She now put a hand on Pauline's arm and looked up at her with big questioning eyes: 'Tell me, is it true that Smally is a sex maniac?'

Pauline pressed her lips together and gave her a cold stare.

'But I read it in the papers,' protested Lottie. 'So it must be true. And you said it yourself. You were interviewed!' She stared admiringly at Pauline. 'Fancy that! Reading about you in the papers. It was so exciting.'

Pauline cut her short at once: 'I don't want to talk about it!'

But now that Lottie had the privilege of speaking to a celebrity she was not to be stopped. 'Oh, and I've read about your husband. I've seen his photographs in several magazines. He's a famous tenor now! Who would have believed it? And, of course, I realised immediately why you weren't coming back to the lab. We're no longer good enough for you now that you're going with him to all those famous opera places. The magazine said that he was singing in the Gala in Milan after performing in the Wet in New York. I really envy you. What a life you must be leading . . .' She sighed and gazed at Pauline with undisguised admiration. 'But why haven't I seen pictures of you? I was so looking forward to seeing you in the magazines, but it's always your husband surrounded by other women.' She added: 'Pretty women! You'd better keep an eye on him or he'll run off with one of those beauties.'

Suddenly Lottie's attention was drawn to the man at the bar who kept staring at them, and she remarked: 'You never stop, do you?'

'I . . . what do I never stop?' muttered Pauline.

'No need to pretend. You're at it again.' Lottie gave Pauline a wink full of significance, while pointing a thumb towards Pauline's partner. 'I suppose that's your latest . . . ahem . . . conquest? But he's not very attractive. And much too old for you if you ask me; probably even older than your husband.' She was unable to hide her disappointment. 'If you want a lover on the side, you should at least find yourself a young attractive one.'

Suddenly Pauline burst out: 'Don't talk about my husband! The swine! He no longer wants to have anything to do with me. Told me I ridiculed him and cuckolded him. Would you believe that?'

'Well, ahem . . .' replied Lottie taken aback.

'And don't call that man over there my latest conquest! I'm just . . . well . . . going out with him. If you really want to know, I'm working for . . .' she lowered her voice, 'for an escort agency. A decent woman has to do something to make a living.'

Lottie snorted. 'A decent woman! And you're working for a sorting agency! And as it happens, it's that one over there whose number has come out of the machine.' She pointed at the thickset man at the bar. 'Just your luck! Heeheehee . . .' And she began to laugh so much that she had to clutch her sides.

So far Pauline had tried to remain calm but she was unable to control herself any longer. 'Stop it, you fool!' she shouted. 'You've done enough harm as it is. There's no need to ridicule me on top of all the rest!'

'What . . . what do you mean by "all the rest"? I haven't done anything.'

'You haven't done anything? *You?*' Pauline pointed an accusing finger at Lottie. 'When everything is your fault! Yes, everything! And don't look at me with those big, vacuous eyes of yours. It's you who kept egging me on! You made me try to seduce that pig of an Anton. And he refused me, the simpleton.'

'I told you that you wouldn't succeed.' Lottie laughed – a high-pitched victorious whinnying. 'Serves you right!'

Her laughter so upset Pauline that she burst out: 'I did succeed!' She stamped her foot. 'I ruined his silly love affair. So there! And I was determined to ruin him, too. I convinced Smally to fire him and give a talk in his place and . . . and naturally Smally insisted on taking me to Africa . . . And then the idiot got lost in the desert and left me for dead in a car. And when I was finally carried back on a camel, my husband was there and . . . and he raped me!'

She took a deep breath while Lottie sat staring at her with open mouth, imagining all the scenes Pauline's words conjured up. Such things would never happen to her, not in a lifetime. What an adventurous life Pauline had led. Fancy her being on a camel in the desert!

Unaware of Lottie's reveries, Pauline continued, a vindictive stare in her eyes: 'And to think that you started it all with that stupid bet idea! Why I listened to a brainless chicken like you is beyond me. I should just have ignored you. But for you I would still have a secure job in the lab. I wouldn't have gone to Africa . . .'

'I didn't make you go to Africa!' interrupted Lottie, but Pauline carried on: '. . . And if I'd stayed at home, my husband wouldn't have gone away to sing; and I might still be happily married, and God knows what else wouldn't have happened. Yes, it's all your fault!'

'I haven't done anything!' protested Lottie again.

'But you started it all! It's like that butterfly effect. You're the butterfly that beat its wings and . . .'

'I'm not a butterfly!' interrupted Lottie, quite upset now. 'It's you whore . . . I mean . . . you who're a butterfly. *I* am a faithful wife. I stay with the one flower I've got: my handsome Eddy. I'm not fluttering all the time from flower to flower like you.' She again pointed her thumb at the heavy man at the bar. 'And now you've landed on top of a big fat flower. Or, in this case, he'll probably land on top of you heeheehee . . .'

'You stupid fool!' Pauline was shaking with rage now. 'You never understand anything, do you?' She advanced threateningly towards Lottie.

'Pauline, what's happening to you?' stammered Lottie, recoiling in her chair. 'You're not your cheery old self today.'

'You're not your cheery old self today . . .' Pauline imitated Lottie's high-pitched voice. 'How do you expect me to be my cheery old self when you've destroyed my life? And now you're just sitting there, babbling about your fifth wedding anniversary. How dare you fling your stupid happiness in my face? It's insulting! This is just too much!'

Suddenly she grabbed the bottle of champagne from the ice bucket and, with one swift gesture, poured the contents over Lottie's head. 'Here's my anniversary present to you!' she yelled. Then she hurried back to the bar, picked up her coat shouting to her companion: 'Come on, we're going somewhere else!' and she rushed out.

When Lottie's husband returned seconds later, he found his pretty wife in a dishevelled state, her hair dripping with sticky cold champagne and her mouth gaping. And as the waiter and a few other guests came to her rescue, they could clearly tell from the look in her eyes that she had not understood.

Part Eight

1

It was early May when Anton was ushered into the office of Merril B. Hanclaus on the fortieth floor of the imposing skyscraper in New York that bore the famous man's name. He found him sitting behind an immense desk, phoning. The tycoon stared at Anton from under thick bushy eyebrows, made a sign to take a seat and continued his conversation. As Anton looked at him, he was impressed by his forceful personality. He could see that this was a man used to getting what he wanted, a man who made short shrift of anyone who opposed him.

So this was the great Merril B. Hanclaus, the archetype of the American capitalist – a self-made man who'd worked his way up from poverty to riches through hard toil, entrepreneurial spirit and an unfailing sense for financial deals. He had started at sixteen selling hotdogs from a stall in a street in New York, and now he was one of the richest and most powerful men in the world – a man who could make or break the lives of thousands.

And he certainly had broken the lives of thousands. He'd made much of his money through buying up companies, pulling them apart and selling off the most valuable bits and pieces while closing down the rest. This was what the logic of capitalism demanded. It brought dynamism to the economy and was therefore in everyone's long-term interest. But what about the people who happened to be working in those less valuable parts? thought Anton. How to explain to those thousands of employees, thrown out like discarded leftovers ready for the rubbish heap, that this was all for the best?

Five years ago the tycoon had turned his attention to mining. Mining companies were in debt up to their necks because metal prices had been falling for years, but his unfailing flair had told him that they would soon be due for a spectacular rise. It was the right moment to enter the market! Within a short time he had acquired some of the top companies at knockdown prices, and now he was trying to consolidate his position by staking out claims to the most valuable African deposits.

Merril B. Hanclaus's voice rudely interrupted Anton's reveries. 'Why did you wait so long to come and see me?' he asked abruptly. 'I haven't got an eternity, you know.'

'Oh, well . . .' stammered Anton, taken by surprise. 'I . . . I had other things to do.'

'For five months? Other things? More important than seeing me?'

'Oh, but they were important,' replied Anton softly. He smiled dreamily – these had been the happiest months in his life. He had spent them with Gael in the dispensary, and everything had been so simple, had felt so right that until recently he hadn't given the morrow a single thought.

'Maybe you've been doing the round of other mining companies to see how much they're willing to pay for your detector, is that it?' suggested the tycoon with undisguised suspicion.

As Anton didn't answer, the man went straight to the heart of the matter: 'So where do we stand?' he barked. 'Have you made up your mind? Are you going to sell to me?'

Anton had been debating that question for some time now. His money was running out faster than he'd expected and he knew he would soon have to do something about his life. After a few weeks of hesitation he had opted for what seemed to be the easiest way out. He had taken a plane to New York to sell his detector, but now that the moment had arrived he simply couldn't bring himself to do it. There were so many secondary issues to take into consideration and he wasn't certain that selling to Merril B. Hanclaus was the right thing. He sat there for a while, undecided, and then said quietly: 'I don't really know.'

When he heard this, the tycoon exploded. 'What! First you make me wait five months and then, when you finally get here, it's to tell me you don't know!' Then, all at once, he calmed down. He'd understood Anton. The young man was just trying to buy time to get the most for his detector. Yes, that's what he was doing. Merril approved of that. That's exactly what he would have done in Anton's position. All right, he thought, I'd better offer a good price. People who know tell me that it's the most revolutionary invention in geological exploration in recent decades.

He now turned an engaging smile on Anton. 'OK,' he said. 'I'll give you your weight in gold as I promised you in Bobodiou.'

Anton was astounded. He had expected to be thrown out, not this, and just sat there for a few seconds thinking everything over in his mind.

'Young man,' insisted Merril, seeing that Anton still hesitated, 'I want to buy your detector. You *must* sell it to me.' He stared at Anton with piercing eyes. 'Right!' he exclaimed when Anton still didn't react. 'You can come and work in my company. But you'll have to work hard to justify your wages.'

This was certainly not what Anton had in mind. How could he tell the man without upsetting him? Suddenly he had an idea: 'I don't really feel American enough to do that,' he replied.

'But you might be an American!' protested Merril. 'You've got the "can do" mentality. Look at what you've achieved! You invent a revolutionary method to discover deposits; you build a detector on these principles and finance it with your own money because you believe in it; you cross the Sahara by yourself against all odds and test your detector; and you chase your boss out of the conference room in Bobodiou when he's trying to present your invention as his own. Young man, you're a pioneer and a daredevil. You're the type America needs. You're the kind of man I want in my company!'

A year ago Anton would have jumped at such an opportunity but he was no longer the man he'd been a year ago. I crossed the Sahara, he thought, and that's exactly what's made all the difference.

It had been like crossing an invisible line that separated one world from another. Like going into the full fire of battle for the first time and coming out alive on the other side. It had been the turning point in his life. His views of the world, his beliefs, his priorities, had changed beyond recognition. Yes, crossing the Sahara was what had done it. And on the other side he had found Africa and Gael.

'Look here, young man,' continued Merril who was visibly becoming impatient. 'You sell your detector to me. Just name your price. And I'll up it with a top job in my company. Well paid. Extremely well paid! You're young and, if you work hard, you'll make it like I did. How do you think I became a billionaire?'

Anton reflected for a while. He fully understood what this was all about. From here two pathways led to his future. One built in gold, with 'billionaire' flashing in bright letters on the far horizon. But he might never get to that horizon. And it would be a very lonely road.

Then there was a second road, much narrower, winding and rather dusty. He would have to walk it slowly, not rush along it in a stretch limo. But he would not walk it alone. He would walk it with Gael, and all along that road would be written: 'happiness'.

Either I will have money, but no time or happiness, he reflected. Or else I will have little money but time and happiness. It's up to me to choose.

Anton eyed Merril B. Hanclaus with interest. There he was, still going strong at seventy-six! What motivates men like that, he wondered, to rush about at their age, trying to add to the money they already have? He was said to be worth billions of dollars. He could spend a billion dollars every year as long as he lived without noticing the difference. Anton tried to imagine how to spend a billion dollars every year – three million every day! On what? On luxury cars or private jets? But you could only be in one car or private jet at a time. On expensive clothes? On food? That wasn't possible. One could eat up maybe a few thousand dollars a day, picking the most luxurious foods prepared by the best chefs, and accompanied by the world's most expensive wines. Would Merril B. Hanclaus be able to spend the money on personal health care then? On having his private medical doctor and a couple of nurses accompany him wherever he went? That might be expensive, but wouldn't cost millions of dollars a day. On holidays? But this man was said to be such a workaholic that he had never taken a holiday in his life! He was so much against the idea that he highly disliked having to concede paid holidays to his employees. On women then? Bedecking them with gold and diamonds? A woman costing three million a day would have to be worth it! But no, pondered Anton. He couldn't imagine Merril B. Hanclaus cavorting with women at his advanced age. So how could he spend his money on anything that gave meaning to life? And yet he wanted to make more money. Would he carry on till he dropped dead? Why did he do it?

This is the time to find out, thought Anton. He suddenly looked at Merril B. Hanclaus and asked abruptly: 'Why do you do this?'

The great man seemed dumbfounded. This was not the answer he had expected. 'I'm not sure I know what you're talking about!' he barked.

'Oh, I just wondered why you keep working and trying to make more money at your age.'

'Are you trying to be funny or what?' thundered Merril B. Hanclaus, staring at Anton in utter bewilderment, as if the question had never occurred to him.

'No, no. Don't take offence. It's just natural curiosity. Considering that you are one of the richest men in the world I just wondered why you carry on working.'

'Are you daft? How can you ask such a stupid question?' The tycoon shook his head in disbelief. 'That's the way things are in life. Either you win or you lose. Either you make money or you go under.'

'But don't you want to stop? Isn't there anything else in life?'

'What?' The man's eyebrows shot up, and his face plainly showed that he thought Anton a dangerous anarchist, or at least a very deranged type. Then it cleared up. 'Ah. I understand what you're driving at: religion and all that. If you want to know, I do go to church since that is what's expected of any respectable person. And like any citizen with decent moral standards I give to charity. But all in the right proportion, young man. Work comes first.'

Anton sat there, stunned. Have we come down from the trees for this, he thought. Is this then the bright endpoint of human evolution? Is this what life is all about?

And thinking of Africa where this evolution had started a few million years ago, what was going to happen if men like Merril B. Hanclaus were let loose on it? Was this the way forward? Work, mining activities, frenetic digging leading to maximum gain for some, and maximum disruption of the environment, pollution and a pittance for the local population. What a mess humans are making of their planet, reflected Anton. Do I really want to add to it by selling my detector?

'What about Africa?' he suddenly asked.

The tycoon looked up in utter astonishment. 'What about it?' he retorted.

'Well, don't you ever think of the impact mining has on it? Haven't you ever thought of directing part of the profits mining brings towards African development? What I mean is, can we really stand aside while Africans are screaming for help, and let them drown in their misery?'

Merril B. Hanclaus shook his grey head over such muddle-headedness. 'Young man . . .' He spoke gravely. 'You're a dreamer. If you come to work for me, you'll have to learn to keep business and charity apart. So are you going to sell your detector?'

'I'll have to think about it,' said Anton calmly. And he got up quietly, turned and softly shut the door, leaving behind him a totally astounded man who swallowed hard a couple of times.

2

At six next morning Anton was woken up by the loud ringing of the phone in his hotel room. He was requested to go and see Merril B. Hanclaus at once. Entering the office half an hour later, he found the tycoon staring at him with a tired face.

'I don't know what you've done to me,' he said when Anton sat down, 'but I've been awake for hours. I hardly slept last night. And that's not very good at my age.'

'I'm sorry to have caused you trouble,' mumbled Anton, not quite awake yet at such an early hour.

'I'm not blaming you,' retorted Merril B. Hanclaus. 'It goes much deeper than that . . .' He hesitated as if he found it difficult to carry on. 'You see . . . sometimes, when I look at the world I've helped to create, I don't feel satisfied. And that feeling has been growing stronger these last years. I suppose that, when you get to my age, you start thinking about your life . . . whether you did the right thing . . . and you wonder if you'll ever be able to straighten everything out before you die. And then you came yesterday and . . . well . . . you were the catalyst.' He pointed a finger at Anton, almost as if he were accusing him.

'I'm not certain I knew what I was doing yesterday,' apologised Anton. 'I just wanted time to think, I suppose.'

'Oh, but you knew very well what you were doing! You didn't speak idle words. All during the night I kept seeing your face and hearing your honest plea. You know . . . people are not often honest with me. They just say what they think I want to hear. But you were honest.'

He paused for a while, and then continued: 'Look here, I'm not a dreamer like you. Your priorities are not mine, and I don't understand all of what you stand for, but that doesn't necessarily mean that I disapprove of you.' He looked Anton straight in the eye. 'I can see that you would do things differently, and maybe you're right. You mentioned Africa and I think I can see your point. What you're worried about is that your detector will spark off a frenzy of mining activities that will lead to large-scale destruction without creating long-term development, is that it?'

Anton nodded in surprise. The tycoon had put exactly into words the unease that had been torturing him these last weeks.

'I shall buy your invention,' carried on Merril B. Hanclaus. 'That is . . . if you're willing to sell to me . . .'

When Anton nodded agreement Merril B. Hanclaus immediately picked up the phone and began shouting instructions into the receiver.

'You can go to my financial manager,' he said after he had finished the conversation. 'He'll arrange the details with you.'

Anton was about to get up when the tycoon held him back.

'Wait,' he said, 'I haven't finished yet . . . Don't get me wrong. I accept your reservations about Africa. I do want to contribute to leaving a better world to those coming after me. I have no children of my own to bequeath my fortune to . . .' He turned away, as if speaking these words had caused him great pain. 'And this morning I suddenly knew what to do: I'm going to leave a legacy – a fund for the development of Africa. I myself won't have time to look after it, and anyway, I wouldn't know where to start. I haven't got your mind, and especially not the many years you've still got ahead of you. So . . . would you like to run it?' He looked eagerly at Anton.

Anton sat there for a while, speechless. Then he managed to stammer: 'But . . . but I have no qualifications whatsoever to run a fund.'

'Young man,' countered Merril B. Hanclaus, 'you're too modest.'

'But I've never done anything like that!'

'Son,' said the great man, 'someone like you doesn't need diplomas or experience for that sort of thing. I know you. If you put your mind and enthusiasm to it, you are capable of doing anything. Look here . . .' He stared at Anton with piercing eyes. 'You won't have to bother about the financial side. I've got enough men who can do that. What I need is someone with a vision, an open mind and time on his hands. Someone who's willing to put up with all the discomforts and find out what works in Africa. And you are that person. You've got the idealism. And the guts. Go out there, son,' he ordered, 'drive around, talk to as many people as you can, take stock of the situation and come up with ideas. I understand that you find it difficult to accept a fixed work schedule but I know there's no need to impose anything upon someone like you. I trust you. I give you a free hand.'

Anton seemed unable to react. Finally he stammered: 'But why? Why me?'

For ten, maybe twenty seconds Merril B. Hanclaus didn't answer. Then he seemed to have made up his mind. 'OK, I'm going to tell you why I'm doing this,' he said as if trying to justify his action – more to himself than to Anton. 'I've got to come to terms with my past. Yes, the time has come.'

He looked away, his gaze turned inside towards the dark secret that lay hidden there. 'We've all got something in our lives we're trying to run away from,' he confided. 'It's no good. However much we push it down, it keeps coming back to haunt us. You see . . . I once had a son . . .'

He sighed deeply, a very old man now. Then he carried on, speaking slowly. 'The time has come to lay the ghosts of the past to rest. Yesterday, when you left this office, it was as if history repeated itself . . . I . . . I must speak about it . . .

'It all happened many years ago . . . Yes, I had a son. He was like you . . . he had the same dreamy look in his eyes . . . I wanted him to be a businessman, an empire builder like myself, but it was no good. One evening I called him into my office to discuss his future. I told him that I was fed up with his dilly-dallying, said that he would have to make up his mind, work for the firm or else . . . And then he asked me the same question as you: "Why?" he asked. After that I exploded and threw him out. That same evening he was killed in a road accident . . . and my wife left me and died of a broken heart a few months later . . .' Merril B. Hanclaus buried his face in his hands to hide the tears that rolled from his eyes. 'I've never got over it,' he murmured after a long silence. 'I've been a workaholic ever since, trying to forget.'

He looked at Anton who sat there very still, his heart filled with compassion. After a while Merril continued: 'But I do want to make amends. What's the point in leaving an immense fortune when I die? My distant relatives will just fight over it like bloodhounds and the lawyers will get most of it. And what's the good of that? It's not too late to make amends,' he repeated. 'I'm going to create this fund and put a large part of my fortune into it. And I want you to run that fund in memory of my son. I want to call it the Jerry Hanclaus Africa Fund. Will you accept?'

Anton nodded agreement, prey to great emotion.

'I'm not a dreamer,' said the great tycoon, 'but the world needs dreamers. Dreamers like my son and like you. I've nearly finished my role down here. I cannot do much more. I can't do what my son would have wanted to do. But you, young man, you can. I want you to go out and try to create a brighter future for all of us. You were right yesterday when you said that we cannot stand aside while our neighbours are screaming for help.'

Suddenly Merril B. Hanclaus got up, came over to Anton who had risen from his chair and gave him a long, affectionate hug. 'Had my son lived,' he said, 'he might have been like you. I would have been so proud of him.'

The great man kept his arm around Anton's shoulders as he led him to the door. 'I wish you all the luck,' he said. 'And come back in a year or so to see me . . . if I'm still around,' he added jokingly. 'Now go to my financial manager. He's waiting in his office.'

3

The manager didn't at all seem pleased when Anton entered his office. 'Are you Anton Felsen?' he asked. And when Anton nodded affirmatively the man said in a cold voice: 'It seems that Merril Hanclaus wants to buy a detector from you.' He stared at Anton. 'Have you got it with you?'

'I'm afraid not,' replied Anton, trying to remain serious.

'But you ought to have brought it with you if you want to sell it! Where is it?'

'It's in my Land-Rover . . .'

'Your Land-Rover? That's a car, isn't it? Is it parked far away from here?' When he saw Anton hesitate, he insisted: 'Could you go and get that detector?'

'That would be difficult.' Anton looked at the man with an amused face. 'It's sitting in a compound . . . in a dispensary.'

'In a dispensary? I don't understand. Where's this dispensary?'

'In Africa . . .'

'What!' It was now clear to the manager that he had made a fool of himself, and he didn't like it a bit. 'I should've known!' he yelled. 'I should've been wary when Merril Hanclaus told me to pay you in gold! Pay him his weight in gold, he said! I think the old boy is going gaga, or else he must have been joking.'

'I think he's very serious about it,' objected Anton calmly.

'Serious? You know what he told me? That if I hadn't got the gold, I was to pay you any price you asked! Just imagine: any price you ask for a detector that's not even here! If I write you a cheque, you may just run away with it for all I know. How can we be sure that this so-called detector exists in the first place? And what is it for?'

'I don't think it's very useful to try to explain that to you.' Anton had a sardonic smile on his lips. 'But I happen to know a well-qualified geologist who's working in Merril Hanclaus's company, a certain Didier Verenikov. He knows all about it. I shall contact him immediately. So, let's get on with everything. I weigh a hundred and seventy pounds. How much would one hundred and seventy pounds of gold be worth at current prices?'

The manager pressed his lips together. Disapproval was written all over his face but he refrained from making any more comments. He picked up a financial paper, checked the price of gold, got out a pocket calculator, punched in the numbers and sighed. 'Well, it's Mr Hanclaus's business,' he muttered. 'Too bad if he wants to do this.'

Suddenly Anton reflected that he was no longer alone in life now. There was also Gael to take care of. He nodded politely to the manager and suggested: 'Could you make it twice that amount?'

This time the manager turned his head away and stared out of the window in total disgust. Finally he focused a couple of hard eyes on Anton, reluctantly dug a cheque out of his drawer, wrote it out and pushed a document in front of Anton's nose, saying: 'Sign here.'

When the transaction was over and Anton had pocketed the cheque, the phone rang. Anton heard the manager confirm: 'Yes, it's done . . . What? Yes, twice his weight in gold . . .' Then the man's face contracted as he continued to listen. 'But . . . but . . .' he eventually managed to protest, 'I . . . I don't agree. Are you sure?' Suddenly Anton heard Merril's voice shout through the phone. It was so loud that the manager had to hold the receiver away from his ear. 'Right,' the manager mumbled at last. 'As you say . . .'

He put down the phone, looking dazed. Then he seemed to wake up from his stupor and stared at Anton with undisguised antipathy.

'Anything wrong,' inquired Anton. 'Has Merril Hanclaus changed his mind? He no longer wants the detector? Shall I give the cheque back?'

'No, that's not it.' The manager shook his head. 'I just can't understand what's come over him. I would never have believed it if I hadn't heard it with my own ears. He wants to put a lot of money into a not-for-profit fund. Five hundred million dollars, imagine! It's unheard of! I'll have to sell some valuable assets to rake up that amount of money. And there's worse. That's only the beginning. He wants to add more after a year, and every year after that, depending on the results. And you know what he calls results? Giving the money away to develop Africa!'

'I know,' admitted Anton. 'We talked about this just before I came down to see you.'

'He must have gone off his rocker!' The manager spoke with vehemence. 'That's no way to conduct a business. That's throwing money down the drain! But what can I do about it?' he continued with clenched fists. 'It's his money and he's never listened to anyone.'

Then, abruptly, he burst out: 'And guess who he wants to run that fund?' The manager pointed an accusing finger at Anton. 'You!' He looked at Anton as if he were a poisonous snake. 'I wonder what your role has been in this whole unsavoury business? Who are you anyway?

No one has ever heard of you.' He shot a cold, hostile glance at Anton. 'And how do you plan to run such a fund? I'm curious to know.'

'Oh, well . . .' Anton was taken aback. 'I haven't yet had time to think about it . . . I suppose that those countries that have honest governments will receive large sums to go into education and the building up of small-scale local industries and infrastructure. I don't really know . . . I'll have to find out.'

'What! Is that how you plan to run a fund? You haven't got any experience and you're going to throw good money away?'

Suddenly Anton felt his blood rush to his head. Once again he had been about to cower before a rude bully who was yelling at him, exactly as he had done his whole life. But no, he wasn't going to take any more of this.

He got up, put his hands on the desk and leaned over towards the surprised manager, his eyes shooting fire. 'How I plan to run that fund is none of your business!' he shouted in the man's face. 'You're just there to put the money in the kitty!' He banged his fist on the desk. 'That's your role. The rest is not your concern and you can keep your nose well out of it! And you'd better obey the orders and make sure the money is in the kitty, or Merril Hanclaus will have you by the scruff of the neck in no time.' And he turned on his heel and walked out slamming the door, leaving a speechless manager behind.

4

Life had been good to Gael. These last months had been like heaven. All the dreams she had ever had as a young girl had come true. In the morning she would wake up in Anton's arms in the small bed in her room. They would breakfast with Marie who always fussed over them like a mother hen, and then Gael would start her daily chores with a light heart. And when the day was over they often strolled into the dunes, arms around each other, to sit down in the sand and look at the sunset. Some evenings, while she sat there with her head against his shoulder gazing at the glorious colours in the western sky, the Tuaregs would begin to sing, and as the faint sounds of their voices floated up from the oasis below and enveloped her soul, the feeling of happiness was so strong that it brought tears to her eyes.

Then, with great reluctance, Anton had gone to America to sell his detector, and within a week she'd found out she was pregnant! They had just been living for the day and never taken any precautions, but there it was. And, of course, she had to discover it during his absence. When she realised how much this was going to change their lives, she panicked. They'd never even talked about having babies. What if Anton didn't want her to be pregnant?

As Gael looked at the first stars twinkling overhead, anxiety invaded her. Ten days he'd been gone already and there still was no news. Maybe they'd offered him a job in America? Her heart contracted at the thought that they might have to leave Africa. She had refused to think about it so far, but she was well aware that they couldn't carry on forever like two carefree birds without a thought for the morrow. Yet she hoped with all her heart that he wouldn't accept a job in America. Or in Europe for that matter.

There was nothing in Europe that interested her now. Yesterday she'd received a letter from her mother, and reading it she realised how far their worlds had grown apart:

Dear Gael,
You haven't written to us since you left for Africa! Do I need to remind you that it's your duty to inform your parents of all that's happened to you, or at least to let us know that you're well?

As we hadn't heard from you for such a long time, I'm sure you understand that we were very worried, especially after we learned about the upheavals in Bobodiou. I pestered your father for weeks, and finally he went to that medical organisation you work for and met the director, a Dr Wilbert. Such a decent man! Your father was very impressed. Anyway, the doctor said that you were still at the dispensary, that as far as he knew you were all right, and that nothing had happened to you during the fighting over there. So that's a great relief to us. But you must write.

There is some important news which I have to tell you, because it concerns you directly. It's about Trevor. He wasn't likely to remain single for long after you jilted him. Dozens of young women must have had their eyes on a man like him and . . . well . . . he's going to get married! It seems that Trevor met his future bride at the local riding club a few months ago. Naturally, Trevor's mother is very pleased, especially as the bride's mother plays bridge with her. The local press is full of the wedding, which is due to take place this coming August. So, even if you repent and hope to reunite yourself with Trevor when you return to Belgium at the end of your year's contract, it will be too late.

My heart bleeds when I reflect how stupid you have been. To think that without your idiocy you would now have been that superlative man's wife. I still haven't got over it, and I think I never will. How could you have thrown away your happiness and let yourself be seduced by a worthless womaniser? But let's not talk about that and open old wounds again.

I must insist, though, that you send your congratulations to Trevor. I don't expect you to apologise for your unspeakably bad behaviour to him. That's not in your nature. But you should at least send him good wishes for his future marriage. It's important to do the right things in life, and that's one of them.

A good piece of news is that the horrible man who seduced you has not turned up again. I think he's gone off somewhere else, and good riddance. So it's safe for you to return home when your year is over. Oh, and I want to let you know that your previous job is no longer available. I've heard that Mr Vangroenten has gone bankrupt. He seems to have been unable to keep his clientele in spite of having expanded his shop. So you'll have to look for another job when you return to Brussels in September.

Don't hesitate to come back to live with us. You know that we're your parents, and we will always be so in spite of your inexcusable behaviour of last year. I hope that your stay in Africa has put some sense into your head, and that you will be a more reasonable girl when you come back. Do write soon.

Your loving mother.

5

On his last day in America Anton went to see his ex-colleague Didier Verenikov to discuss how to forward his detector to Merril B. Hanclaus's mining company. Didier had changed a lot in the half-year he'd been working in America. He had become an extremely efficient person, and not five minutes after Anton had entered his office he had already moved on to the business aspect of their meeting. He judged that it would be useless to take the prototype out of Anton's Land-Rover and have it sent to New York. Instead, he decided that it made more sense for Anton to email the plans and description of his detector and send all the computer programs.

'No problem,' agreed Anton. 'I'll return to my parents and dig up the lot.' He sounded confident, but wasn't. The thought kept nagging him that his parents might have cleared out his room during his absence and thrown away all his papers. That would be a real disaster.

When the business transactions were over it was nearly twelve and Anton suggested having lunch together. 'OK,' agreed Didier, 'but not more than half an hour. There's a restaurant nearby where they serve quick lunches.'

Over the meal they talked about the Bobodiou conference. Didier had heard the story of Smally's rout and thoroughly enjoyed it. 'What happened afterwards?' he asked with great interest. Anton had no idea. Smally seemed to have disappeared from the face of the Earth and as far as he was concerned that was fine.

Then Didier told him that the Belgian Geological Institute had ceased to exist.

'How can that be?' exclaimed Anton. 'How could they have fired the people working there? Most of them were on permanent government contracts.'

'They haven't fired anyone. The institute has simply been divided between different Belgian universities.'

'But that's terrible!'

'What else did you expect? Give power to one idiot and he'll ruin the best-functioning institution.'

Anton nodded: '. . .Or country for that matter.'

Didier shrugged his shoulders. 'Anyway, it's turned out well for us. I've been able to convince the brightest scientists and technicians to come and work here.' And he concluded: 'That's the way it is in life. One man's loss is another's gain.'

Anton disagreed. 'It's a real shame the laboratory has disappeared,' he said. 'I don't think there'll ever be another one like it.'

6

Back at his parents in Belgium Anton fortunately found all his papers untouched, but even so it took him several days to produce a document Didier would be able to understand, and email the information.

He felt tired and relieved when he was finally on the plane to Bobodiou. He tried to read but just couldn't concentrate. Scenes of his life in Kanibasso kept sliding into his mind. These last five months in Africa had been so unlike anything he'd ever known before. He had been totally carefree and had liked his simple existence. He loved life in the African bush: the mornings when the sun rose in all its glory and a chorus of birds greeted the new day; the smiles of the people, the laughter and human warmth . . . and Gael . . .

Did he really want to leave all this behind and start this new project? He sighed. Why had Merril Hanclaus chosen him? But, of course, he knew why. Something had passed between them, a current of empathy that transcended age and culture, and he felt warmth in his heart when he thought of the old man. I believe that he looks upon me as his son, he reflected.

And how extraordinary that Merril had understood why I hesitated to sell my detector! How had he managed to put into words what I myself felt only vaguely? He was again struck by the insight of the great man.

But how can he possibly imagine that I can run this fund? thought Anton. I feel so inadequate. Yet Merril must have known what he was doing. He has a reputation for always making the right decision and seemed absolutely certain of himself. Anyway, I'll have to do it now. I promised the old man I would . . . but how on earth do I start a project like this one?

He sat there for a while, looking out through the window at the endless barren plains of the Sahara, which were sliding away underneath the plane and seemed totally unreal from that height.

Knowing so little, at least I don't have any prejudices or preconceived ideas, he pondered. Maybe I could ask Amadou and other leaders like him what they think about everything. Yes, that would be a good starting point. And I shall certainly have to tour Africa as Merril suggested . . . maybe in my Land-Rover . . . that way I could go to remote places and find out what the problems are and what might work in Africa . . .

Suddenly he was again assailed by doubts. What a huge responsibility this fund was – too much for one person alone! Then, in a flash, he realised that he wasn't alone: Gael would be at his side. And he knew that he would never find a more ideal partner for this kind of project. Gael's soul seems to reach out effortlessly towards the African people, he thought. Women and children spontaneously hold hands with her. They just open up when they see her, and entrust their problems to her. And women and children are three-quarters of Africa!

Yes, he reflected feeling more confident now. Together we'll be able to do it. How lucky I am to have Gael! I just can't wait to get home to tell her about this! And suddenly it dawned on him that he looked upon the dispensary and Africa as home.

7

A lot had changed in Bobodiou in the few months since Gwemboka's death. There was a feeling of optimism in the air, of rebirth. One could see it in the way people talked openly about everything, about their country and its future. Anyone who had been here before would have been struck by the difference.

Driving from the airport to the town they would hardly have believed their eyes. Anton was no longer bumping along a potholed road with progress halted by checkpoints manned by gun-toting policemen out to get your money. Instead, there was a wide new tarmac road all the way to town, and the few policemen he encountered were busy regulating the traffic at those points where work was still under way. This is more like Europe than the old Africa, he thought while his taxi sped towards the capital. But with a large dose of extra sunshine. And there's a different feeling here. This is undoubtedly Africa.

The Riverside Hotel was still there but it had been thoroughly refurbished and was gleaming under a new coat of paint. When Anton entered the lounge and looked round there was something missing. For a while he was unable to pin it down; then, suddenly, he realised what it was: Gwemboka's portrait had gone together with de Gaulle's and Mao's. Village scenes painted in bright colours now covered the walls, and the lounge was decorated with a medley of masks, musical instruments and tropical flowers. All the warmth of Africa seemed to radiate from it. A new era has begun, Anton reflected. Most definitely.

At the reception desk an efficient clerk completed all the formalities in a short time, and Anton was led to his room by a young woman dressed in an elegant traditional garment. What a pleasure, he thought. It all looks so effortlessly normal, yet who would ever have believed this possible only half a year ago?

He took a bath, changed and went out to the terrace to have lunch at one of the tables alongside the big pool and palm gardens. As he sat down in the shade of a huge sun umbrella and looked round he noticed a man who was attacking his meal with great gusto. Then he recognised him, got up and went over to his table exclaiming: 'Michel! What are you doing here?'

Michel Legros was busy forking a load of steaming rice and meat into his mouth and his cheeks were bulging with the food he was chewing, but he managed to mumble: 'Aen whot oar yo doin hear?' without taking the fork out of his mouth.

'I've just come back from America. And you?'

Michel didn't answer straight away but took his time to finish the last mouthful. Then he swilled down a glass of wine, sighed contentedly and said: 'I'm just here for a few days . . .' He paused to wipe his mouth with his napkin, and then continued: '. . . to arrange things for the mining company.'

'Will you stay with me while I have my meal?' asked Anton. 'You must tell me what's happened to you since we last met in December.'

'You really want to know?'

'I'm dying to. But let me order first . . .'

8

Smally had just emerged from a loud telling-off by his African boss and was about to go on duty with a long face.

'You're an inefficient, dumb, lazy bum,' his boss, a huge man, had shouted towering over him. 'You're here to serve the customers, not to criticise them! I heard nothing but complaints from our clientele yesterday. One more complaint and I'll kick your arse!'

'How unjust fate has been to me,' grumbled Smally as he set off fuming, dragging his feet. 'Why should a man like me have to put up with this?'

When they had released him from jail he'd been told that he wasn't allowed to leave the country. The Belgian government had apparently refused to honour the expenses he'd run up on the lab's credit card. Happy Bobo Cars hadn't been paid, and the car rental company furthermore claimed it was his fault the car had been wrecked. When it was supposed to have been fully insured! A local African judge had sentenced him to remain in the country and work until he paid off the car hire company. But first he'd have to pay back the debts he'd incurred at the Riverside by working there. He had applied for the post of director but they'd made him a waiter instead!

He'd written to his friend the Minister of Education in the Belgian government to protest strongly, but had received no reply. Then he'd gone to the Belgian Embassy to see whether they could bail him out or maybe contact his wife who, he was sure, would immediately send the funds to liberate him. But, instead of doing what they could for a man like him, they'd told him that the Belgian government was unwilling to advance a penny and that his wife was divorcing him. So there he was, stranded in a primitive country where they refused to treat him as befitted his rank.

And that deceitful Pauline! Apparently, she'd survived the accident and been allowed to leave the country. Why hadn't they forced her to pay at least half the costs? Worse, he'd heard that she had started a court case against him, claiming huge damages for non-assistance to a person in distress – that person being herself, naturally.

It was clear that everything was her fault, come to think of it. She had lured him into doing all this. How could he ever have believed in her? And now that court case! Was that all the thanks he got for having been nice to her, for indulging her whim to go and see an animal park? He should have driven straight to that park and fed her to the lions, that's what he should have done. Would have served her right!

As he went out into the gardens towards the open-air restaurant, muttering and grumbling while looking around to see if there were any of those awful customers to be served, he noticed a man sitting at a table trying to catch his attention. He began to move reluctantly towards him, when suddenly he jumped aside and hid behind a palm tree.

'Did you see that?' asked Anton.

'What?'

'How strangely that waiter behaved.'

Michel turned around. 'Which waiter? There's no one.'

'He's hiding behind that palm tree,' said Anton, pointing at the tree in question. 'I don't believe this. And I had the impression he's white.'

'Man,' commented Michel, 'you must be hallucinating. You ought to eat, that's what it is! It's common knowledge that an empty stomach can give you hallucinations.'

'I'll show you that I'm not hallucinating,' retorted Anton, and he called out: 'Waiter, waiter!'

When there was no reply Anton got up and strode briskly towards the palm tree. He went round it and unexpectedly found himself face to face with Smally.

'Well, I never!' exclaimed Anton. 'What are you doing here?'

'I'm just standing here,' mumbled Smally, turning bright red and trying to make himself as inconspicuous as possible.

'Why are you dressed as a waiter?'

'Because . . . because that's what I'm doing for the moment . . .'

'If you're a waiter, you are supposed to come forward and serve people when they call you,' said Anton sternly.

'Right! Get back to your table,' hissed Smally. 'I was just coming.'

'Well, hurry up then!' shouted Anton, looking down upon him. 'If you're doing a job, you must do it properly, or I'll complain to the management and then you'll be in for a good thrashing!'

Suddenly a huge African popped up behind Smally and grabbed him by the collar. He turned the little man towards him, lifted him up and yelled in his face: 'I've seen what's going on! I heard it all! What do you think you're here for, man?' As Smally didn't reply because his feet were hanging ten inches above the ground and he was nearly choking, the boss supplied the answer himself: 'You're here to work until you've paid off your debts. And if you're not going to be more productive, that'll take at least ten years. And I don't want to be looking at an asshole like you for ten years, got it?'

He dragged Smally off to an inside office where a page printed in big letters was pinned on the wall. It carried the title 'Rules and Regulations of the House'.

'Read!' commanded the chief of staff, pressing Smally's nose into the text. And as not a sound was forthcoming, he shook him bellowing: 'I can't hear you! Read aloud!'

Smally began to read with difficulty, his voice muffled, and when he had finished, the boss shouted: 'Now, make sure you memorise what you read. Rules and regulations are there to be obeyed, man! If I ever catch you shying away from your work again, I'll personally give you a thrashing you'll remember for the rest of your life!'

After this he catapulted Smally out of the hotel towards the tables, yelling: 'Go and do your duty now. And be quick about it!'

Smally ran towards the table where Anton and Michel were sitting and stopped in front of them, panting, his notepad and pencil at the ready.

'Well, well, what a surprise!' exclaimed Michel, eyeing the little man whose face was still bright red. 'Our Smally has been reduced to the status of waiter. How the mighty have fallen! There is some justice in the world after all.'

Anton picked up the menu. 'Let me see . . .' he said. 'What am I going to have?' Then he turned to Michel asking: 'Do you think he's capable of taking an order?' pointing a thumb at Smally.

'I'm not sure. I think he's lost without a secretary.'

But they had underestimated the effect of the threats from Smally's boss, and the new waiter noted down the order faultlessly. He was about to go to the kitchen when Anton warned him. 'You'd better be quick or you won't get a tip.'

'Yeah,' added Michel, 'and we'll complain to the management about the lousy service.'

After Smally had disappeared at a run, Michel said, 'This really makes my day,' and he leaned back with an expression of extreme satisfaction on his round face.

9

'There's something that puzzles me,' remarked Anton after a while. 'I thought you looked positively unhappy before Smally turned up. Didn't you tell me when I saw you last time – when was that . . . six months ago? – that you were the happiest man in the world? What's going on?' He stared attentively at Michel. 'And you've put on weight!'

The smile vanished from Michel's face. 'Maybe I have,' he retorted defensively.

'But how's that possible? You were so active a few months ago . . . well . . . you know what I mean . . . women . . . that you had no time to eat.'

'Women!' snorted Michel. 'Don't talk to me about women! If I have to choose between a good meal and a woman, the meal wins hands down. Meals are the ideal partners. You don't have to court them or treat them with care. You can count on them any time. You just sit down and have them whenever you feel like it. You can vary them every day without any fuss. No, man! A meal. That's it for me!'

'I don't understand,' said Anton, shaking his head in disbelief. 'What's happened to your wives? Have you lost them?'

'No . . . I've still got them,' replied Michel with a sour face.

'Why then this expression of disappointment?'

'Would you believe it? They're pregnant! All four of them! With thick extended bellies.' He looked totally disgusted.

'But that's wonderful!'

'Yeah! You think so? Then listen to what they told me: "No more hanky panky," they said. "We have to be careful." That's what they told me! And where does that leave me? It's all an excuse, that's what I think.'

'But you were so happy to have four women.'

'You tell me! Four bothers instead of one, yes!'

'But you must realise that pregnant women are affected by their condition! Try to understand them and be patient. They'll be different after they've had their babies. They'll be willing again.'

'Don't you believe it! Things have changed fundamentally, and for the worse. Before, I played them off against each other and managed to get everything I wanted. But now! They seem to have ganged up against me. I'm in the minority. Totally neglected!'

'But just think! You're going to be a father. Think of the happiness of it. Quadruple happiness in your case!'

Michel snorted. 'Don't talk to me about babies. They're nothing but nuisances! I can already see their mothers going gaga over them, their attention riveted on the screaming brats who will be the centres of their worlds. Real spoilsports they are, babies. Why they suddenly had to come is beyond me.'

'Well, dear chap,' laughed Anton, 'I thought that you were at least aware of that possibility before you started your active love life. They usually tend to come as the result of it, you know – unless you take precautions, of course.' He nodded his head as one who knew.

'To tell you the truth,' admitted Michel, 'I never gave it a thought. Real flesh-and-blood girls were so new for me when I started that I thought of nothing but the fun. And see where it's landed me!'

'Don't be so negative. I bet you'll be delighted once the babies are there. You'll be elated when you hold them in your arms – that is, of course, if your wives let you,' added Anton with an ironic smile.

Michel looked sullen. 'That's maybe what I dread most. Those babies!'
'But you'll be so proud to be a father.'
'No I won't!' He got up brusquely and stood back. 'Take a good look at me,' he said with grave concern in his voice. 'Just look at me!'
'What's wrong with you? Men change a lot when they become fathers. Don't be so pessimistic. I'm sure you'll make a good father.'
'That's not it!' Michel seemed really distressed. 'With the luck I have, the babies might just look like me. Think of that! Not one ugly baby but four in one go! Four babies looking like me! I couldn't bear it!'

He stood there for a while as if he were staring into a dark future. Then he shook his head and sighed: 'I'm the unhappiest man in the world.' And he left with sagging shoulders.

10

As Gael's father returned home one day he found his wife collapsed on the divan, speechless and with a white face.

'What's the matter?' he asked, worried. 'Aren't you feeling well?'

Gael's mother just pointed at a paper that had fallen out of her hand and was lying on the carpet. Her husband picked it up and noticed that it was a telegram addressed to 'Mr and Mrs Fernley, 84 avenue des Hirondelles, Brussels.'

As he read it, his eyes brightened:

> Gael Fernley and Dr Anton Felsen have the pleasure of inviting you to their wedding, which will take place at the Belgian Embassy in Bobodiou on the 1st of July at 11 a.m. A reception will be held afterwards in the gardens of the presidential palace in the presence of His Excellency President Amadou Sékouré.

There was a note at the back:

> Belgian participants are requested to notify Mr Dublaigny, secretary at the Ministry of Foreign Affairs, at least ten days

beforehand in order to allow him to book plane tickets. The trip and all other expenses will be taken care of by the organising committee.

'Well, well . . .' he said after he had read it. 'This is a great surprise. What do you think, Meg?'

'But haven't you seen?' protested Gael's mother, who seemed to be recovering from her state of shock.

'What?'

'She's going to marry that man, that womaniser!'

'Oh, well,' remarked her husband, 'she's over twenty-one, isn't she? So . . . whomever she wants to marry, there's nothing we can do about it. And I think we should trust Gael's judgement.'

'But . . . but how can she throw herself at such a worthless man when she should have married Trevor?'

'How can you say he's worthless? Have you looked at the invitation? This man is a doctor! And how can he be worthless when the President himself is going to have the reception in the gardens of his palace? There is something here that's way beyond our understanding. We'd better go and find out.'

'But I can't go! I couldn't face that man!'

For once her husband stood his ground. 'Whatever you do,' he said, 'I shall go. I'll be proud to be received by a president. And I'm curious to meet my future son-in-law. And as to you, I strongly advise you to come with me. I think you should let bygones be bygones.' With that he withdrew and went up to his study.

11

The wedding ceremony was over and guests were slowly trickling into the garden of the presidential palace in Bobodiou. Among them were several ministers and ambassadors, first and foremost the Belgian Ambassador; also present were representatives of African governments who wanted to take advantage of the occasion to meet Anton in connection with the Jerry Hanclaus Africa Fund; and, of course, Anton's parents and his sister, and some of his and Gael's friends. Almost the last to arrive were Gael's parents, and finally the young couple.

Gael's mother seemed ill at ease but her father was clearly enjoying everything. He leaned towards his wife, whispering: 'Listen to what the Belgian Ambassador just told me. It's a most extraordinary story.' He was so excited that he had to struggle to keep his voice down. 'Gael's husband is famous! He's apparently produced the most outstanding invention in geological exploration in decades and has sold it in America. And they've paid him his weight in gold! In gold,' he repeated, staring sideways at Anton as if he had suddenly changed into a golden statue. 'And that's not all! One of the richest men in the world has created a development fund worth hundreds of millions of dollars. And you know who's going to run that fund? Gael's husband! The Ambassador rightly said that our country should be proud to have a citizen like him. And to think that he's our son-in-law!'

Just then the President came walking across the lawn and when he noticed the newly-wed couple he went straight towards them. 'Anton and Gael,' he said, 'let me congratulate you both. It's a real pleasure to welcome you here.' At once the photographers moved in and began to shoot pictures of the young people with Amadou standing between them, his arms around their shoulders.

After the photographers had finished, Anton introduced his family and then began to look around for Gael's parents. When he saw them standing apart from everyone else he touched Amadou's elbow asking: 'Would you allow me to present my wife's parents to you?'

The President immediately walked over towards them and shook hands. 'So nice of you to have come,' he said. 'You may have lost a daughter, but you have gained a son. How pleased you must be!'

'I'm not so sure,' joked Anton. 'My mother-in-law doesn't know me very well. She's a woman of strict principles and it wouldn't surprise me if she didn't think highly of me. We've met only once, and very briefly at that, and I don't think I made a great impression on her on that occasion.'

Gael's mother blushed visibly and made to move away, but the President held her back. 'So, you are Gael's mother,' he said, looking at her with genuine affection. 'It's an honour for me to meet you. Do you realise', he continued with a twinkle in his eyes, 'that without you I wouldn't be President.'

'How . . . how can that be?' stammered Gael's mother, certain that he was pulling her leg but not knowing how to respond.

'Because, you see, your daughter wouldn't have been born without you.' He paused a second. 'And so she wouldn't have been able to save my life!' The President now began to tell the story of how Gael had been brought to the rebel camp when he was delirious with fever, and had given him injections and cared for him until he was better.

Gael's mother stood there very still, looking deferentially at the President. When Amadou finished his tale, she just kept staring at him as if she were unable to take it all in. Then she blurted out: 'Did she really do that? Oh I'm so proud of her!'

'And well you should be,' assented the President. 'You're lucky to have such a daughter. I shall remain indebted to her forever. And let me add that as her parents, you will always be welcome in my country.'

'We're extremely honoured,' replied the father, noticing that his wife seemed dumbstruck.

'I would also like to say a word on behalf of Anton,' continued Amadou. 'I'm sure that, if he failed to impress you, it's because of his modesty. You must believe me when I tell you that he is one of the most outstanding men I've ever had the pleasure of meeting . . . No, let me continue,' he said as Anton tried to stop him. 'If I hadn't known your daughter, I would never have understood why a young man like Anton would have crossed the Sahara on his own to find her. And he found her, against all odds. The life story of these two young people is absolutely extraordinary. I know that they are Europeans, but I am proud to offer them the honorary citizenship of this country. Yes,' he nodded, 'the world would be a better place if there were more people like these two.'

He was about to carry on when he noticed that some of the other guests who had been patiently waiting were trying to attract his attention, and he turned towards them. Just then Marie came strolling into the gardens, late as always, and Gael at once tugged her mother along to greet her.

'I've been wanting to meet you,' said Marie after they'd been introduced. 'Let me tell you that your daughter is a very brave girl. So uncomplaining, you've no idea! And happy at last.' Marie sighed. 'It's always a blessing when two young people find each other. Real love is what makes life worth living.'

Gael's mother didn't reply but just stood there, rigid.

'So different from when she first came to the dispensary,' continued Marie. 'I felt that something was wrong but she didn't want to talk to me about it. For months she kept it inside her. You can't imagine how stubborn she can be.' Marie suddenly looked hard at Gael's mother. 'Now, I wonder where she got that trait from?'

'And then, when I finally squeezed the story out of her, it didn't make sense. She was convinced that the man she loved was having an affair behind her back. That's why she'd run away, the silly girl. When she had absolutely no reason at all to do so.'

'But she had,' protested Gael's mother. 'What would you have done if a man seduced you and then turned out to be a womaniser?'

Marie flared up at once: 'Anton never seduced your daughter. It was pure love that was being born between them. And he never had an affair behind Gael's back. He loves Gael and no other. But there was a woman who engineered a make-belief scene out of spite because Anton didn't react to her advances. And Gael, silly girl that she is, fell into the trap! Anton's a truly honest man.'

'But . . . but you don't understand. She had promised to marry someone else!'

'I see . . . you dearly wanted her to marry another man. And when Gael and Anton fell in love with each other, it upset your schemes – is that it?' Marie looked sternly at Gael's mother who shrank under her look. 'Let me tell you that if life doesn't turn out as you want, that's no reason to set yourself against it. I think it's high time to forget about yourself and make peace with Anton and your daughter. Are you going to let misplaced pride stand in the way of these young people's happiness? Do you really think that's right?'

Seeing the Belgian Ambassador making signs to her, she was about to join him when she turned back: 'And let me add one more thing. Gael at least made amends when she discovered that she'd made a big mistake. She was willing to risk her life to find Anton and beg him for forgiveness.'

'She . . . she risked her life?' mumbled the mother, but Marie had already gone.

'Yeah, that's what she did,' answered an African who had been standing next to Marie and had listened to the conversation.'

'Who are you?'

'I'm Rasta,' he said. 'So you're Missie's mother.' He twisted his finger around one of the braids that were beginning to grow again on his head. 'I'm her medical assistant. I didn't know what to do when the revolution was over but then I thought: I'm going to work for Missie and Madame. I liked it immediately. I knew I would, when Madame and I bandaged Missie that time she was shot down by one of those mad guards last December.'

'What's this? She was shot down!'

'Yeah, and I saved her life,' affirmed Rasta as if this had been the most ordinary thing in the world. 'Bullets flew past my ears, but I ran towards where she was lying on the ground, bleeding, and pulled her to safety. Afterwards we carried her on our shoulders, running as fast as we could, while the guards came after us, shooting.'

When she heard this, Gael's mother was overcome with emotion. She, who was usually such a stiff old stick, now took Rasta in her arms and held him tight. 'You saved my child,' she kept saying, 'you saved her! Oh bless you, bless you.'

It took Rasta some time to extract himself, but once he was free he remarked casually, 'Oh, it was nothing. I would do it again any time,' before hastily removing himself to a safe distance.

'Oh, bless you,' Gael's mother kept mumbling, 'bless you all.' Suddenly, as she looked at Gael and Anton, tears rolled down her cheeks. She went to where they were standing, took their hands into hers, and said humbly: 'Will you both forgive me, please.'

12

The news spread like wildfire in Kanibasso. It was whispered that these were Missie's last days here; that she was going on an important expedition around Africa, and that the President had given her his personal support. Rasta immediately offered his services. He had heard that there were many dangerous places in Africa where they shot at people, and assured Missie that with him she would be safe. He was disappointed when she declined his kind offer, saying that Anton planned to visit only those countries where conditions were stable and governments followed responsible policies.

Someone who was not disappointed was Bamboko. Gael's popularity had shot up to such heights that the number of patients in the dispensary had tripled. Being Missie's personal assistant and driver, he was so swollen with his new importance that he was strutting about the whole day, organising the patients and lining them up.

Marie was less happy. 'The work you're giving us,' she sighed. 'And after that you'll be off and leave me with everything.'

'No, I won't!' protested Gael. 'I shall return after my honeymoon.'

'A honeymoon! Lucky girl. Anton is sure to take you to a very exclusive place. He's got the money to pay for a luxury trip now.'

'Well . . . that's not quite what we're thinking of. We . . . we're thinking of going back to England for a few weeks . . . to Deal where we spent such wonderful days last year.' Gael looked very excited.

'Oh . . . I see . . . You're a true romantic. And are you really coming back to the dispensary afterwards?'

'Of course. I have to finish my contract, haven't I?'

Suddenly Marie suggested: 'Why don't you stay on? That way the medical experience you've acquired won't be lost. And it would be so much better for you and the baby. I don't know how you think you're going to travel with a baby in Africa?'

'That's exactly what Anton said when I told him I was pregnant. He wanted to call off the whole project, but I made it quite clear that I'd never accept such a thing. I don't want to stand in the way of a unique project like this one.'

'And quite right you are! If a woman makes her man abandon what he wants to do, he will bear a grudge his whole life, even if he's sincere at the time he renounces.' Suddenly Marie looked up. 'Why don't you tell him to go off alone?' There was a glimmer of hope in her eyes.

'No way! I'm not going to let him travel on his own. I couldn't bear the thought of him being out in the bush alone. Think of the dangers he might run into without me. He might get lost, or heaven knows what.'

Marie looked at the slender young woman standing in front of her, exuding confidence. 'So you are going to protect him?'

'Naturally. Anton is so vulnerable. He needs to be protected. And *I* know how to take care of him.'

'But didn't he cross the Sahara on his own?' remarked Marie with an ironic smile.

'Yes, but that was different. That was to find me. But now we must stick together to remain lucky, don't you see?'

'I see very well what you mean . . . Don't get it into that head of yours that you're irreplaceable.'

'I'm not getting anything into my head. I just don't want to lose him again!'

'All right, all right. Don't get upset. So you think he'll be safer with you?'

Gael nodded vigorously. 'I know what to do if he falls ill out there in the bush. I'll take medicine with me. And two are always stronger than one. I'll be able to help him out with lots of things.'

'But the baby?'

'Well, I told Anton that he should look upon the baby as an asset for his project, not a liability. I convinced him that it would make contacts so much easier in Africa.'

'But it'll be months before the baby arrives. And you're not going to have it in the bush, are you? Maybe you should at least stay in the dispensary till after you've given birth?' insisted Marie.

'Why couldn't I give birth in the bush?' objected Gael. 'African women do it all the time.'

'You haven't got their strength!'

'That's what Anton said. So we'll go to a hospital when the time comes, and have the baby delivered there.'

'And you really believe that's enough?'

'That's already a lot in Africa. Look what African women have to put up with. And no one fusses over them. They just have to go on with their work, don't they?'

Marie shook her head. 'I would strongly recommend that you take a few weeks off. Anyway, you'll find out in due time. And afterwards?'

'I'll carry my baby on my back when we go into the villages. Like that the women will recognise me immediately as one of their own.'

Marie looked at Gael's fair hair, her white skin and blue eyes. One of their own? she thought, amused. But then . . . maybe Gael is right. Most of what a person is lies in the heart.

'So you really want to go?'

'Of course I want to go! I couldn't think of a better cause than this project; or of a more interesting life. You know . . .' her eyes shone with an intense light, 'Amadou told me he was proud of me. He said I would be the African women's ambassador; that I would have to learn about their needs and stand up for their cause. And I will.'

Marie sighed. 'I wish I had your youth and enthusiasm. I'd go with you immediately. But I've had my time, I suppose. One can't start life all over again . . . a pity really.'

13

Two days later the time had come for Gael to drive to Bobodiou where she was going to join Anton before setting off on their honeymoon.

When they were standing around the Land-Rover that was going to take her away, Marie suddenly turned her head.

'What is it, Marie?' asked Gael, worried.

'Oh . . . nothing. Don't bother.' But as Gael took her hands Marie blurted out: 'I can't bear the thought of the emptiness here without you.'

'Don't worry, Marie.' Gael spoke with all the warmth she felt in her heart. 'We'll always come back here. This is our home.'

Suddenly Rasta stepped forward. '*I* will stay with you, Madame,' he said, trying to sound cheerful. 'Missie doesn't want me anyway. She didn't want me when I offered to accompany her through Africa, and she doesn't want me for this trip either. She doesn't think that there will be any shooting where she's going. So I shall stay here instead and protect you!' And to show that he was willing to make the best of an unsatisfactory situation, he flashed a smile at Marie that made his teeth sparkle in the sun.

As Gael was about to climb into the Land-Rover, Marie held her back and hugged her for a long time. Then she put her hand on top of Gael's head, closed her eyes and whispered: 'All the luck and happiness to you, dear one.' She embraced her once more, saying, 'I'll miss you,' and Gael got inside and closed the door.

'I'll be back after my honeymoon!' Gael called out, her voice ringing through the open window as the vehicle began to move. Then the Land-Rover gathered speed and disappeared in a cloud of dust, leaving Marie behind with tears in her eyes.